P9-DBL-622

WILL'S
WAR

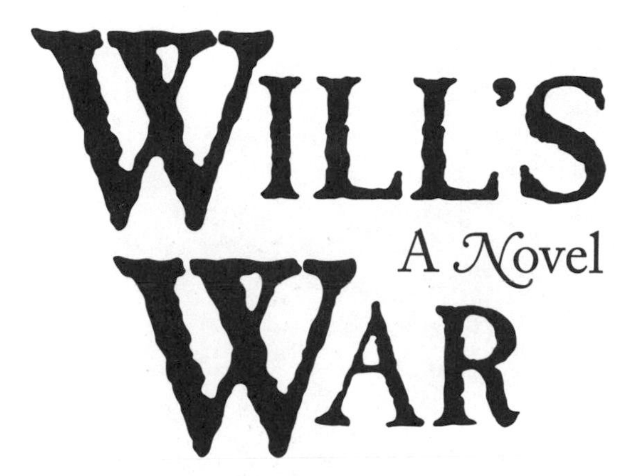

JANICE WOODS WINDLE

LONGSTREET PRESS
Atlanta

Published by
LONGSTREET PRESS, INC.
2140 Newmarket Parkway
Suite 122
Marietta, GA 30067

Printed in the United States of America

1st printing 2001

Library of Congress Catalog Card Number: 2001091086

ISBN: 1-56352-639-5

Jacket and book design by Burtch Bennett Hunter

In memory of our son

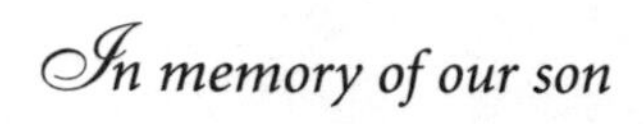

Charles Kendrick Windle
April 11, 1966–April 1, 2000

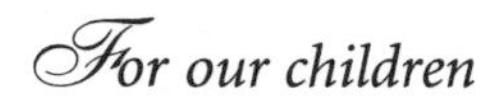

For our children

WAYNE AND MARY JANE WINDLE

VIRGINIA AND RANDY SHAPIRO

And for our grandsons

WILLIAM WAYNE WINDLE
JOHN WILTON WINDLE
BENJAMIN EMMETT WINDLE

WILL'S
WAR

PROLOGUE

Seguin, Texas, America.

The train carried the body of the young woman from Karnes City to Seguin, Texas. It stopped at San Antonio and Cibolo, Marion and McQueeney, and at each station the passengers inside drew away from the windows, comforting each other on their dreadful, untimely loss. Outside, along the tracks, crowds of strangers became more and more vocal and abusive. Only the harsh breath of steam and the screams and thunder of the great iron wheels drowned out the sound of stones and insults hurled by those they passed. Within the car, they whispered praise of this woman who had been so loved, had lived so boldly and had died so young. A dark-suited band played the music of Handel, Mozart and Krug in counterpoise to the insistent drumming of the wheels on the tracks. Beyond the windows, cold, hard faces cursed the people on the train, believing they were in league with those who had so recently blackened civilization with their barbarous acts.

When the train left the San Antonio station, a brick carried away a window and shards of shattered glass clattered on the coffin. A cold December wind howled into the coach and whipped the dark coattails and veils of the mourners. Two men moved between the ruined window and the coffin as if to draw the hatred away, like enemy rifle fire, from the body of the woman they had loved. The darker man was one of her brothers. The other, a slender man of elegant bearing, wearing several diamond studs that had belonged to his grandfather in Germany, was her husband.

Because of the Great War in Europe, the German-Americans on the private railroad car symbolized to many Texans the evil that had nearly brought the world to its knees. The native sons of little Texas towns like Karnes City, McQueeney and Cibolo were suffering and dying at the hands of the faraway Huns while the Germans at home sang their alien operas and attended their masked balls and whispered opposition to the war, just as they had opposed slavery and secession from the Union two generations before. Now the newspapers pleaded for all good Americans to root out Germanism in all its forms.

As the train pulled into the depot in Seguin, both men breathed a sigh of relief. The hundreds of people meeting the train had names like Stautzenberger, Baenziger, Starcke, Koehler or Krezdorn, Schultz, Wuest, Koch, Kluth, Muelder, Saegert and Halm—names that could have populated a town by the Rhine. In Seguin, Texas, Germans and people of German descent had been at the heart of the community for nearly a hundred years. Although they had retained their Old World language and culture, Germans were respected by most people in the community and tensions between Southerners and Germans—"Raggedies" and "Squareheads"—were not as severe as they were in other towns. The sorrow of the mourners was eased somewhat by the knowledge that they were bringing the young woman home to a place and to people she had loved.

After the train reached the depot, people spilled from houses and from brick-front buildings along the streets and a procession formed behind the great black hearse. The body passed through lines of children waiting along the road. It moved south beneath the great green archway of hackberry trees along Austin Street, passed the fine houses and mansions of Senator F. C. Weinert, the Blumbergs, the home of Dr. Knolle, the pharmacist Madeline Gerlich, and the huge brick palace of Emil Mosheim. From wide porches the families watched the somber parade. Within the houses, Christmas lights lay upon mantels and cast colors from green tinseled trees.

On the procession moved, past the red brick German Methodist Church, the Koepsel home, and into the heart of town to the courthouse square and the Mendlovitz Dry Goods Store where upstairs in the Klein Opera House the woman had performed so beautifully. Turning east on Market Street, the procession passed the Nolte Bank and the St. Andrews Episcopal Church where the bells tolled their terrible tale, and passed the Plaza Hotel where the woman had recently danced on the rooftop until dawn. Then it was north again, along Crockett Street past her father's drugstore and to his home on Milam Street.

The pallbearers carried the casket into the parlor. The yard and the porches filled with neighbors and strangers. So many people came to pay their respects that it took most of the afternoon for the line of mourners to pass the open casket. When only family and close friends remained, the dark man raised his violin to his cheek and played a lullaby of Brahms.

At the Riverside Cemetery, next to the jade-green Guadalupe River, the woman was lowered into her grave. Next to her were the graves of her mother and grandmother. Here in the earth were three generations of a family that had escaped intolerable conditions in Germany to find a better life in Texas. The women had died violently, two before the age of thirty. Now, as night descended, the dark man wondered if he should stand guard over the graves. He feared that rabble from San Antonio or Leesville would try to destroy the headstones as they had done in several other cemeteries where Germans were buried.

As the moon rose into the black December sky, the dark man pulled his collar close and looked out at the gravestones gleaming like skulls in the night. He thought about the many German families who had struggled all their lives to escape the injustice and prejudice of their times. *All they had wanted was to be American*, he thought, as he uncoiled his whip and prepared to defend their graves.

I.

Weinert, Texas.
May 1917

It was hot. The parched earth smelled like burning tar, the sun seared the air with a yellow haze, air so dry it seemed brittle as crystal and was filled with an incessant ringing sound that consumed the mind and made it difficult to think or even pray for rain. A small wind walked from the west through failed fields and dry stubble, pausing now and then to whirl about in the dust, raising dervishes, incongruous dancers on the thirsting prairie. There were no trees to cast shade or bring relief to a flat, featureless horizon and there were no birds nor singing of birds anywhere near.

The house was in the heart of town along a railroad track reaching straight as God's spine from Weinert to Abilene and then to Fort Worth and then on to the unknowable East. Shifting veils of heat rose from the burning rails. Above the haze and dust devils, above the brown grasses and the bitter, colorless town, the cloudless sky was an intense blue.

On the porch of the house, Virginia King Bergfeld looked for evidence of Heaven in the great lonely dome of the sky, looked for where angels might make rain by weeping for the dying earth, but all she saw were vultures circling, waiting.

As the long day wore on, Virginia could not shake the feeling that something terrible was about to happen. The haze, the heat, the vultures were signs, but there was more. There were the strangers. Hard men watching, asking questions of their neighbors who later refused to meet their eyes. It was a feeling of overwhelming anxiety, a tightness in her chest, an unusual awareness of the beating of her heart, an intense and unpleasant sensitivity to touch, as if her nerve ends had crawled too close to the outer layer of her skin. "This is not like me," she said aloud to the fading day. "It's just this place. The heat. This awful town."

More than one hundred miles away in Fort Worth, the man called Grimes boarded the westbound train. He was tall and lean, his face bronzed and creased, his eyes the color of pewter, dull from looking too long at horizons. He settled into the seat, tipped his wide-brimmed hat over his eyes and thought about what he must do. Tom Grimes listened to the rattle of the rails and wondered if this was the day he would die.

In the Bergfeld home, the evening meal passed in near silence. Virginia looked at Will and tried to see into his mind. Did he feel what she felt? The coming of something sinister? If he did, he would not say. He would hide what he felt in silence, as he did now except to ask for the peas she had coaxed from her garden or the cornbread she had baked at first light before the heat came down. He felt her eyes, looked up and smiled, and as always, when she met the eyes of the man she had married, she was nearly overwhelmed by the miracle of their love. Will had come into her life like a whirlwind, a darkly handsome adventurer who was as genuine and open as a child, yet deep as an unexplained sonnet. She had touched every fissure and contour of his body, had breathed his breath, whispered intimacies into his lips, was in touch with his every sorrow, his every desire and passion, but there were hidden corners of his soul she could not reach. Not that he held back, but it seemed those corners were lost to himself, as well. It was where his anger dwelled, she knew. An anger that made him sometimes a stranger; that made him say and do things that were totally unexpected and out of character—things that seemed the words and deeds of a far less gentle man. The only predictable thing about Will Bergfeld was his love for her and their daughters, a love absolute and eternal. He was a mystery, this man she adored, this wild, daring, unpredictable, loving, often infuriating father of her children. He was a strong man. A good man. A man who merely held the world to an impossibly high standard, a standard no mortal could achieve. And when the world fell short, his anger came and tried to make things right again no matter what. She looked at her children, Little Virginia, her cloud of hair white as a dove's wing and Mary, dark as Will, with those same penetrating eyes that gazed at you a bit too long, a bit too deep, as if trying to see the secrets within your mind. There was love in this house. Love enough to compensate for life in a land as barren as a Biblical wilderness. *Surely this good, strong man will allow no harm to come to our little home. What harm could possibly penetrate the shield of love my man has forged around us?*

Tom Grimes stared out at the dark sliding by. He knew they crossed the Brazos by the shifting sound of the wheels on the track. Again, the shifting octave of the clattering iron wheels signaled they had crossed the trestle over Big Smokey Creek, at Cisco.

Grimes turned and saw the other men were sleeping, rocking, eyes empty or closed, their bolt-action 1903 Springfield rifles standing between their knees. *How ironic,* he thought, *that the Springfield was an almost exact copy of the German Mauser, so similar that the American government paid royalties to the German Mauserwerke. Now there would be war and the Kaiser would be paid royalties for the rifles that paid death to his soldiers.* Killing had become very confusing since the battleship *Maine* went down and Grimes had sailed for Cuba to fight a foreign enemy.

Nothing was simple anymore. Most of the Rangers on the train he had known for years. But the Federal agents were strangers known only by their reputations, reputations he did not respect. Grimes did not like these men with their secretive ways and strange loyalties. And as they passed the trestle over Hubbard Creek he wished he were somewhere else, someplace where he was better able to tell what was right from what was not.

When the meal was finished, the dishes done, the little girls bathed and dressed for bed, Will opened the chest in the hall. It contained bedding, two Colt revolvers, an unfinished painting of his sister Louise, his paints and brushes, and a violin his mother Elisabethe had brought from Germany. The violin was a Guarneri, had been in the family for three generations, was one of the few objects he treasured, certainly the most valuable thing he owned. As he tuned the instrument, the violin seemed almost miniature, dwarfed by the breadth of his shoulders and his large hands. As the children played on a pallet on the floor, Virginia moved to the old upright piano on which she had learned to play as a child, and Virginia and Will began to play now in the little house in the heart of town.

Rarely did they discuss what they would play, one just started and the other almost immediately followed. Usually the choice was Virginia's. She would shuffle through the sheet music purchased from Will's father's drugstore until she came to a tune she fancied, then she would begin. Will never used sheet music. He held all the music he had ever heard in his mind, a marvelous gift that never failed to astound and mystify his wife. They played Brahms, then the old spiritual *Down by the Riverside*, a favorite of Will's because of the line, "I ain't gonna study war no more," then a piece by Schubert from the operetta *Lilac Time* that had been written and performed the year before in Vienna.

The house filled with harmony. The oven of the day cooled. The little girls were suspended half awake, half dreaming. Virginia's fears fled, carried away by melody. She watched Will as he played, the music seeming to flow through his fingers from some wellspring inside his tall, slightly swaying body. *He could have been a concert violinist like his mother,* Virginia often thought. But Will did not have the capacity to build a life on just one foundation. He was too curious, too impatient, too filled with the need for action, a verb of a man, her Will. There was too much in the world to see and do and experience. Music was merely one of his loves, no greater or lesser than his love of racing his motorcycle or his love of a good fight or of justice. As she watched the graceful ballet of his fingers, the subtle play of expression that animated his strong, almost noble features, Virginia wondered if music came from the mind or from the heart or from the hands or from some mystical alliance among all three. The house was filled with the gliding gifts of Schubert.

Outside, the moon rose full and yellow, the air now so clear the lunar edge was sharp as a blade. A breeze lifted the lace curtains in the windows and played in Mary's long, dark hair. The wind touched Virginia. Suddenly she was unexplainably cold. She paused in her playing, her fingers resting on the keys. Her nameless anxiety had returned. She shivered and Will lowered his violin and asked what was wrong.

"Listen," she said.

"What?" he asked, his head tilted, his brow furled.

"The prairie dogs. They hear a train." The breeze carried the plural conversation from the prairie dog towns along the tracks. The little animals always heard the train long before the sound reached human ears. If you were meeting someone on the train, their barking was a signal to leave the house and it would be followed exactly four minutes later by the wail of the arriving train's whistle. But there was no train scheduled for this time of night.

"Something's coming," Virginia said.

"Yes," Will said. He looked at her with those eyes that see inside, then he closed them, raised his violin and began to play again. It was not a song Virginia knew, but something different and haunting, fragments of melody summoned from some dark mythic Teutonic forest. The house was filled with music. The house was filled with fear. Outside, there was silence. Virginia knew a train had arrived and that there must be a reason why they had heard no whistle.

Grimes stepped from the train. There were eighteen men in all, heavily armed Texas Rangers, federal marshals and Secret Service men. They formed into groups and spread out into the town, guns at the ready, their steps stirring clouds of dust in the dry roads. They moved quickly, steadily, as if they had planned exactly where they were going. A hound howled. Other dogs barked in response. In soft contralto complaint, cows near death from thirst lowed at the intruding strangers. Grimes thought there was nothing more sorrowful than the sound of a slow-dying cow, a sound too often heard these days when there was no rain and few farmers had access to water. A screen door slammed. Shadows passed lamp-lit doorways. From the Bergfeld house came the lament of Will's mother's violin.

They came like something in a dream. Slowly, but suddenly there, filling the house with the scraping of their boots and the smell of sweat and iron. Grimes crashed through the front door, others battered down the back. They followed the barrels of their guns into the room. Virginia screamed, then rushed for the girls, scooping them up as they, too, began shrieking in terror. Virginia's greatest fear was that Will would fight the intruders. She could see the vein in his neck rise blue and knotted with outrage. *Please God,* she prayed, *let Will go easy.* Will set the violin carefully down, then stood tall and turned to face the man called Grimes. There was violence in his eyes.

"Don't, Will!" Virginia screamed, half to God and half to her husband. Grimes took Will by the shoulder and spun him around and manacled his arms behind his back.

"Well, boys," Will said, his voice on the edge of control, "if you don't have enough guns, I've got two I'll let you borrow."

One of the federal marshals grasped Virginia and pushed her against the wall. "Can't you shut them brats up?" he growled.

"Leave them be," Grimes called to the man. "We only want the man."

"What for?" Bergfeld asked.

"You know damn well what for," Grimes said.

Will knew.

As Grimes led him out the front door, Will looked back at Virginia. "Telephone your father," he said, and then he was gone and Virginia was left alone in the house with the night, her children and her dread.

So this is the bad time. The day one prays never comes or that comes only to others, leaving a legacy of both guilt and thanksgiving. It is that dark time, the prophesied season of suffering we must all endure. It is the trial God sends us to give life meaning, like he sent Job. The family has been assaulted, our home violated, my husband taken away in chains by strangers. But it is not death. It is not facing the lions or the gallows or that moment when you realize your last breath has been taken and there is no more.

How fortunate I have been in my life to have experienced nothing truly terrible. It is a blessing that left me unprepared for what I must do. I am an actor without a rehearsal. I don't know my lines. My inclination is to leave it at God's door. He knows best and all will come out fine in the end. But that is the myth of life. In my heart, I am absolutely certain that Will has done no wrong and is innocent of whatever he is charged with doing. But Will often gives the impression of wrongdoing. My father warned me. He called Will a loose cannon, a man who would one day bring me grief. But he has brought me more happiness than I ever dreamed would come my way. Now he is gone and the prophesied trouble has come and I am unprepared for the task ahead.

II.

Seguin, Texas.
May 1917

n the day of the night Will was taken, before she found the terrible thing on the road to Monthalia, Virginia's mother, Bettie King, heard the call of Peachtree's pet owl. It was the signal that the hermit from the Guadalupe River bottoms had come to see if there might be some chore he could do in return for buttermilk or leftover pie.

Bettie watched him approach with his wary, sideways gait, and she wondered how a man could allow himself to become so wretchedly disreputable. Although it was relatively warm, he was wearing several layers of clothing, each layer the most tattered and bedraggled of any garment worn in all of Christendom. Beneath his battered derby hat there was little to see of his face. A wild wreath of unkempt hair and beard hid everything but his bright, violent eyes; the eyes of a beast, some said. And that was why most everyone in town was afraid of Peachtree and avoided him whenever possible, which was not difficult because he preferred the silences and solitudes of the river bottoms to human company. Peachtree lived in a cave in the riverbank. His home was surrounded by a rampart of old automobile parts, cast-off refrigerators, scraps of old wagon wheels, and a marvelous miscellany of rummage and junk he had rescued from the trash cans of Seguin. He was known to come out of his cave each night to prowl the town and do all manner of minor mischief. Although Bettie was uneasy in his presence, she was the one of the few in Seguin, besides Will Bergfeld, to befriend the strange recluse.

Peachtree appeared to be ancient, but he was actually Will's age. The story of how he came to Seguin was obscure and it had many versions. One tale told that he had been the youngest child of the Petries, a family of German bluebonnet painters who had come through the area years before. He had been a terribly difficult boy, wildly unpredictable, antisocial and disobedient, often running away to live for days like a wild creature in the woods. Another story was that he had been raised by a family of possums, like Rudyard Kipling's Mowgli who lived among the wolves. Whether he was their son or not, he had briefly lived with the Petries, but his trips back to them had become less and less frequent, until finally, he left for good and settled into his cave on the Guadalupe. The Petries were apparently relieved to be shut of him, because they had never come back to take their wild child home.

Today Peachtree tied his owl to the boot scrape and Bettie made him wash his hands with strong lye soap before letting him through the screen door into the kitchen. He sat down at the table and watched her pour a glass of buttermilk. Will, who had been a childhood companion of Peachtree, claimed that the hermit was intelligent and that they sometimes had long conversations about life. But in Bettie's presence, he spoke more with his strange expressive eyes than with his lips. And he was now staring at the knife she was using to cut him a slice of pie.

"Let me sharpen this," he said, reaching, taking the knife from her hand.

"It's just for cutting pie," Bettie said. "How sharp does it need to be?" A chill slipped down her spine as she watched Peachtree test the blade on his thumb.

"You'll see," Peachtree said, his voice rattling in his throat, his eyes ablaze with something Bettie could not read. Then he took the knife, unchained his owl and left for the barn.

Later that morning, Bettie's father, who everyone called Papa Leonard, picked Bettie up in his wagon. They traveled out along the Capote Road from Seguin toward the little community of

Monthalia, close to Gonzales. Papa Leonard was telling her the old stories of the German migration into Central Texas and how those who fled to America were among the liberals opposed to Bismarck. Many were musicians, writers, artists and free spirits. Those who made the long ocean passage to America and the arduous overland trek to Central Texas were the best, most talented, most adventurous of their generation.

Once again Papa Leonard told how the German immigrants had suffered and died from hurricanes and fever and Indians and outlaws along the trail north from Indianola. Of his family of six, only Papa Leonard and a brother had survived; the rest were buried in shallow graves along the way. He told how they had come to the sweet hills around Seguin and the woods and meadows along the Guadalupe River, and how they stopped to put down roots in the American wilderness.

Bettie listened patiently to the often-told stories. The wagon moved through ragged pastures of gaillardias, Engelmania, daisies and Wild Verbenas flowers, all struggling against the tyranny of the sun. The horses seemed to hurry from shade to shade, then slowed beneath spreading oaks before moving out into patches of sun again.

Bettie touched Papa Leonard's sleeve. "Don't you know I've heard all this a thousand times?"

"It's always good to remember who you are," Papa Leonard said. "Especially in these troubled times."

Bettie resolved to pass the stories on in the family from generation to generation. But she was not sure she could bear to tell of the great storm that killed their neighbors, and destroyed their home, filling her forever with a fear of thunder. These were stories she herself had lived. Now, as they approached the old Moss homeplace, the hard horror of that experience came back in a rush. She remembered how the storm's rising water had driven rattlesnakes from beneath the earth in huge roils of poisonous flesh, how as a young girl she had spent a night alone in the storm protecting the bodies of dead neighbors from ravaging wolves. It had been a long night that night, a night that lasted for more than forty years. For still, when the wind rises and the sky grows dark and the rumble of thunder drums on the air, Bettie always hears the howling of the wolves and, to her shame, cowers in terror behind her bedroom door until the storm passes. She thought about all she had suffered, all the hardships of life on the frontier. *How far we've come since those desperate days. How civil our world is now.* It was then they saw the man in the road.

He lay in a wagon rut, his back to the sun, his arms spread, his clawed hands filled with earth. At first Bettie thought he was wearing a white wool coat and had passed out from the heat. Then she knew. The man had been lashed with a cat-o'-nine-tails, tarred and feathered and left for dead. She had always heard such things were done to people, but never really believed it could be. Papa Leonard pulled on the reins to stop the wagon and Bettie leaped down and moved to the man's side. He was still. Flies and ants had already gathered on his terrible wounds. He had been stripped, thrashed with a whip of leather tied with barbs of iron, his skin laid open like dozens of small red mouths. Hot tar had been poured into the wounds, then feathers scattered on the tar. There was very little blood, for the tar had cauterized the wounds. Bettie felt for a pulse. It was there, but strangely irregular. She ran to the wagon and removed a canvas tarpaulin, placed it on the ground by the wagon rut, then carefully rolled the man over onto the tarp.

"I know this man," Papa Leonard said. "His name is Nagle. He lives on a farm up there. Looks like he tried to crawl home."

"Why this?" Bettie asked. She was numbed by the incomprehensible reality before her.

"Because he's German," Papa Leonard said. He glanced quickly back down the road, then ahead.

"How far is his place?" she asked.

"Not too far, about five miles south of Polecat Creek."

"Let's take him there." Together, gripping the canvas tarp, Bettie and her father dragged the man to the wagon, then wrestled him up onto the bed. He groaned once, then was silent. Bettie shooed away the flies, folded the tarp over his nakedness. She tried to wipe the tar and feathers from her hands, but the glutinous mess simply transferred to her skirt.

They drove on. Bettie tried not to think. *Thinking is to ponder the existence of evil, to admit that God had created beings capable of such cruelty. The God I know would not have been so remiss. The God I know created creatures with perfectible hearts, beings in His own image. To think makes me wonder why God allows such things as war and injustice and the purposeful torture of men such as the farmer who lies nearly lifeless in this wagon.* They drove on.

The hooded figures stepped out from the trees. They wore black robes. Bettie's first thought was that they must be terribly hot dressed in such ridiculous gowns. There were five men. One reached up and grasped the traces, another looked into the back of the wagon.

"Where you goin' with that heinie?" one man asked, and he started to drag the farmer out of the wagon.

"Don't!" Bettie said. The word was sharp as a pistol shot. Surprised at the force in that single syllable, the man stepped back, then walked forward to where Papa Leonard was gripping the reins in white fists. The man paced back and forth, looking at Papa Leonard. Bettie could see his eyes moving beneath the hood.

"What's your name, old man? Ain't your name Moss? Ain't you German too? Boys, we done got another heinie." The man grabbed Papa Leonard's arm. "Git down!"

Bettie reached across Papa Leonard and pulled the man's hand away. "Now you listen to me, young man!" The words were spoken softly, yet they were filled with controlled fury. "If you touch a hair on my father's head, if you even look at me crosswise, my husband Henry King will hunt you cowards down to the ends of the Earth, and you will die like a dog—real slow!" They backed away. It was obvious the name Henry King was known to the hooded men. She drew back the whip and then touched it to the mules and they bolted away in a jangle of harness and drumming hoofbeats. "Don't look back, Papa," Bettie said. "They aren't worth our spit."

Soon they arrived at the Nagle place. Frau Nagle must have had a premonition for she was standing in the doorway with a rifle and with two German shepherds by her side. When she saw the wagon she came running. She gasped once when she saw her husband, averted her eyes, her lips moving in prayer. Then she took a deep breath and began to tend to her man. Bettie and Papa Leonard helped her carry him into the house. After they pushed aside the turnips, potatoes and dried sausage being prepared for dinner, they laid him on the kitchen table.

"He needs a doctor," Papa Leonard said.

"We'll get Dr. Meyer in Seguin," Bettie said.

Frau Nagle was looking at her husband's injuries, her hands hanging at her side. "I don't know where to begin," she said. Bettie knew the woman was strong and willing. If it had been a broken bone she would have set it. If it had been a snake bite she would have sucked out the poison. But how do you tend to this, the lacerations, the burns, the awful feathers?

"Get a folded blanket and raise his feet," Bettie said. "Don't worry about the cuts. They look worse than they are. It's the burns that might be trouble. Flush out with cool water. Then cover with a clean dry cloth until the doctor comes. And you might get a cold compress for the head bruises. It's possible the burns have damaged the nerves and there won't be that much pain when he wakes."

"What about the feathers?"

"Clean them off best you can. But leave the ones stuck in the cuts. Don't try to remove them. I'd wait for the doctor."

Although still unconscious, Nagle was not having trouble breathing and his pulse was more regular than before. "We'll go for the doctor now." Bettie looked out at the fading light. "With a little luck he can be here first thing in the morning."

"What about the men who did this?" Papa Leonard asked.

"I don't think they'll come here," Bettie said.

"I wish they would," Frau Nagle said as she looked over to where her rifle stood by the door.

"He'll be all right, Mrs. Nagle," Bettie said, and she and Papa Leonard mounted the wagon and turned the mules back toward

Seguin. They stopped at the first farmhouse that had a telephone and called Dr. Meyer. After Bettie explained the need for his help and gave him directions to the Nagle farmhouse, she asked him to get word to Henry as to why they would be late.

It had been long dark when they drove down Court Street in Seguin and turned toward the barn at the King place. Henry and Bettie's son George were standing there waiting anxiously. When Henry saw her coming through the gate, he appeared more distraught than Bettie expected. Then he took her in his arms. "I worried so," he whispered into her hair. Bettie wept as she told him what had happened.

They were getting in bed later that night when the telephone rang. At first Bettie wanted to let it ring. She just wanted to lie safe in the arms of her husband, to let his love help her forget what had happened on the road to Monthalia. After what she had seen, she wanted her husband's love to make her feel alive and whole and comforted. But then she realized a call this late at night could only be bad news. Bettie threw back the covers, rose and rushed to the telephone on the hallway wall.

When she returned, Henry was sitting up in bed. Her eyes told him that something was wrong. Before he could ask, Bettie told him what it was. But even as she said the words she could not believe what she was saying.

"That was Virginia," she said. "Will's been arrested for treason. They say he threatened to kill President Wilson. They took him to jail in Fort Worth." Bettie did not hear what Henry said then. Instead she thought she heard the howling of wolves.

III.

Fort Worth, Texas.
May 1917

The gray stone courthouse towered over Weatherford Street and the bluff road leading down to the sweltering pens of the Fort Worth stockyards. In the central tower, a clock big as a barn door announced the fact of noon to all points of the compass. It was the largest clock Louise Bergfeld Tewes had ever seen. She imagined the time could be told by cowboys miles away on the Chisholm Trail as they brought their herds to slaughter or to the railhead that she could see below on the wide soiled skirts of the Trinity River. She parked her bright red touring car against a hitching post next to a handsome little sorrel pony. There were only three other cars on the courthouse square, all of them black. As usual, Louise attracted the attention of everyone within eyesight. The men tried to disguise their staring from their wives as they watched the raven-haired beauty climb from the cardinal-colored automobile. She moved boldly and alone through the crowd of lawyers, clerks, tax collectors and deputies disgorged by the courts for the noonday meal, and then she passed into the cool immensity of the Tarrant County Courthouse.

The hollow hallways and chambers were filled with the chinking of spurs, the rumbling of voices and the amplified echo of the business of law being done. Groups of men stood in clouds of tobacco smoke, arms folded across their chests, hats hiding their eyes. Even though most of the departments and courts were recessed for lunch, the corridors were packed. Many had come to escape the heat and the stench of the stockyards outside. But most had come to maybe catch a glimpse of the many prisoners who had been recently rounded up, to see the traitors, the German spies and Wobblies who had sold their souls to the Kaiser. Louise had come to see her brother Will who was once again in trouble, *wouldn't you know.*

The authorities had denied access to the prisoners for much of the day. Louise waited with Bettie King and Will's wife, Virginia, and the two little girls in a boarding house on Throckmorton Street while Henry King negotiated with federal agents. Now, at last, largely because of Mr. King's contacts among the Texas Rangers, permission had been given. One by one, the prisoners were allowed to visit with their families and talk to their attorneys.

Louise met Henry King at the head of the stairs leading below. Together they walked down into the inner sanctum where the prisoners were packed into their cells and in large rooms with iron bars. Louise was astounded to see the farmers and working men who had been arrested with Will and were now herded below in the courthouse. Their families crowded around, reaching through the bars, everyone talking and crying at once in voices amplified by hard walls and high ceilings. Children wailed and clutched their mothers' skirts. Men called out for their wives or water or for justice or cursed the jailers. With some relief, Louise realized she and Mr. King were continuing past the cells and the angry, frightened men they held.

Henry King paused at a door guarded by a deputy. At a nod, the lawman fumbled through a ring of keys, then unlocked the door.

Louise entered a room so small there was hardly space for one visitor, much less a family reunion. Bettie King and Virginia Bergfeld and her two daughters had arrived before her. There were no benches or chairs and the women stood, looking terribly uncomfortable, watching Will perform magic tricks for the two little girls, who erupted with laughter when the mysterious coin appeared from a hand empty only moments before. Will leaned against a table, the only piece of furniture in the room, grinning from ear to ear, his deep laughter occasionally eclipsing the bell-like giggles of the girls. He stood as Louise rushed into his arms, held him tight and said, "Now what have you done?"

Will roared with laughter. "Here I have been waylaid by desperadoes, chained to a locomotive, torn away from home and family, cast ignobly in the hoosegow and you ask what *I* have done! More properly, my dear little sister, you should ask what *they* have done. I'm as innocent as a newborn babe. *They* are the guilty ones."

Louise pulled back to arms length, shook her head and smiled up at Will. "Then why, my dear big brother, are you inside the jail and they're out there with the keys?"

"I thought this might be a time for comfort, not recriminations," Will said. "Or maybe apologies from those criminals who put me here."

He turned to his father-in-law. "They didn't even have a warrant! Have you found out what's going on?"

"There's a lot of confusion. It was a statewide sweep. Probably hundreds of arrests. Most are members of your Farmers' and Laborers' Protective Association."

"Arrests by whose order?" Will asked.

"Someone at the highest levels of government in Washington. They say your arrest order was signed by the Attorney General himself, approved by the President."

The door opened and a slender, rather elegant man entered. He wore a beautifully tailored dark suit, a shirt so white it seemed to glow and a precisely knotted black silk bow tie. His hair was combed back from a high patrician brow. His eyes were dark, intelligent, slightly hooded and set wide apart beneath heavy brows darker than his prematurely graying hair. Even though there was no one feature that was particularly memorable, he seemed to possess enormous presence. As he moved forward to shake Henry King's hand, Louise thought he should be wearing a rose in his lapel.

"William Hawley Atwell, Will's defense attorney," Henry King announced, then introduced his family to the dapper little man. Atwell bowed over the hands of the ladies, then turned to Will. As they shook hands, it seemed to Louise their eyes locked for a very long time, each taking the measure of the other.

"I know your work," Will said. "You defended the labor organizers in Denver from trumped-up charges. Got them off."

"Trumped-up charges are the best kind of charges to defend against."

"Like mine?"

"We'll have to see, won't we?" Atwell said, his eyes never leaving Will's face. It suddenly occurred to Louise that the lawyer had no idea if the charges against Will were trumped up or not.

"I know your work, as well," Atwell said. "Ludlow, Colorado. You worked with Mother Jones organizing the coal miners."

"Sometimes I wish to God I hadn't," Will said, his voice low, his eyes finally breaking contact with his attorney's gaze. "Nineteen men, women and children massacred by Rockefeller's company gunmen. Maybe I should have let them be. They'd be alive now."

"We can only do what we know is right."

"I'm pleased with Mr. King's choice," Will said, a grin returning to his face. "You are famous and I thank you for accepting my case."

William Hawley Atwell had been brought from Dallas to counsel Will in the days ahead, negotiate his bond if required and defend him if he should be brought to trial. He had been retained by Henry King because Atwell was considered one of the best trial lawyers in America, a man who had successfully defended others wrongly accused of serious crimes, including several who had been railroaded by the enemies of organized labor.

"There's another reason I'm pleased with Mr. King's choice," Will said, pulling another coin out from behind Mary's ear.

"Why so?"

"When I was a boy I watched you defeat James Hogg in a debate. You put it on him good. Hoodwinked him to a fair-thee-well. May have been the first debate that old governor ever lost. Believe it or not, I can recall that debate almost word-for-word." Will paused and seemed to think back to that day. "And I figure any man who can outdebate James Hogg can win this case."

Again, his deep, musical laughter filled the room. As always, Will's laughter was infectious and the others, even Bill Atwell, could not resist a smile.

"If this case goes to trial, it will take more than debate skills," Atwell said.

"What then?" Will asked, as he reached over to Little Virginia and pulled a silver coin from behind her ear.

"Truth," Atwell said. He took the coin from Will's hand, passed it back to Virginia. "In a debate you can argue either side equally well, whatever side of the issue you're assigned. In a trial you must side with truth."

"What truth?" Will asked. "What is truth?"

"I didn't come here to debate, Mr. Bergfeld," Atwell said.

"Truth is God," Will said, serious now. "Truth is that Jesus lived. Truth is that love endures. And for the life of me, Mr. Atwell, I cannot think of a single other thing that is absolutely true."

Except for the chattering of the children and the sounds of voices and clattering iron filtering through the door, the room was still. Virginia thought Will seemed suddenly exhausted. Some kind of fire had gone out. And she knew he was afraid because he was acting like he was not.

"Mr. King, help him understand the gravity of this," Bill Atwell said with a sigh.

Virginia Bergfeld's father studied Will for a long moment. Then he spoke, his voice firm, yet not unkind. "Will. You have been accused of treason, of conspiring to overthrow the government of the United States, of threatening to kill the President. Your enemies are out to get you. If you are found guilty you could be put to death. I suggest you listen to your attorney. Not just to save yourself, but because you owe it to your wife and your daughters. I'm sorry I had to say these hard things in the presence of the ladies, but I suggest you treat this very seriously."

Virginia was crying softly, terrified now that the awful possibilities were out in the open. She moved into the shelter of Will's arm.

Bill Atwell unfolded a paper he had been carrying in his

pocket. "Listen to this, Mr. Bergfeld. It's from an editorial in a Tulsa newspaper." He read: "'The first step in whipping Germany is to strangle the Industrial Workers of the World. Kill them, just as you would kill any snake. It's no time to waste money on trials. All that is necessary is evidence and a firing squad.'" Atwell lowered the paper. "You've been a member of the Industrial Workers of the World, haven't you, Will?

"I have."

"Then for no other reason than this, I agree with Mr. King that we are in a very dangerous situation that could have extremely serious consequences."

"It's hard to take seriously what one can hardly believe," Will said. "And I can't believe this would be happening in America."

"Are the charges true?" Louise asked. "Any part of them? Will, you have to tell me!"

"How dare you ask?" Virginia cried. "Your own brother! Of course they're not true."

"Let him answer," Louise said, not backing down. "The government wouldn't go to all this trouble and expense without some cause. I know you, Will. I know how you carry on about the government selling out the people. I know how you rail about Rockefeller and other employers who abused their workers. I know how disgusted you are with President Wilson."

"I've spoken my mind," Will said. "But in this country that's no crime."

"Stop it. Leave him alone," Virginia said, angrily.

"I only want him to face reality!"

"Listen to us!" Bettie said, with some force. "We are family. This is no time to argue. Now is the time to love each other, support each other, to stand together as family. Will's life is at stake. We need to help him get through this."

"I'm sorry, Virginia," Louise said. "If I loved you and Will less, I wouldn't be speaking out." Louise *did* love Virginia, had always thought she was a wonderful life choice for her brother. But she knew Virginia did not understand Will's life-long pursuit of the edge. And Virginia did not truly understand the sharp blade of his convictions, his abhorrence of ignorance and greed in high places, convictions Louise shared. In a sense, Will was the spokesman for what Louise herself believed.

For a moment she studied this family her brother had married into. They were so different from her own family and most of the people she knew. They were so absolutely American. Bettie King, fair and freckled, her back straight as a gate, her graying hair swept back into a bun, her gray eyes almost silver, a country woman whose life was lived very close to the earth and to the absolute imperatives of the Bible. Henry King, large and imposing, a man of obvious substance and influence who a generation ago would have certainly commanded Confederate troops. He even limped, as if from a war wound, the result of a wagon accident years ago. And there was Virginia, pale as alabaster, lovely and fragile as a figurine. But Louise knew her brother. He would not have fallen in love with a woman who was as passive and vulnerable as Virginia appeared to be. Behind those light blue eyes there must be hidden passions, unexpected depths and heat that would have drawn her brother like a flower to the sun. Virginia was standing by Will's side and Louise smiled at the stark contrast between the two. It was a contrast that reflected the larger contrast between the Bergfelds and the Kings, and the even larger contrast between the Texans of Scotch-Irish descent and those whose families came from Germany.

"If this goes to trial," Atwell said, "I must have your solemn word, Will, that there will be no outbursts or grandstanding or magic tricks or incendiary speeches like the ones that got you into this situation in the first place. You must be on your best behavior and must trust me in all things and do exactly what I say."

Will nodded his agreement, saying, "I understand."

"Do you think it will go to trial?" Louise asked.

"I think probably so," Bill Atwell answered. "All the men who have been charged will have their cases presented to a Grand Jury in Dallas to determine if there is enough evidence to warrant a trial.

This is usually a rubber-stamp procedure for the prosecution, and the accused will be bound over for trial. In a few weeks, a trial date will be set before a Federal judge in Abilene. Then it's up to a jury."

"I have already arranged bond," Henry King said. "You'll be released in a few hours. Certainly by tomorrow. I suggest that you not mention this to any of the other fellows because most of them can't raise the bail and will have to remain in jail until the trial is over."

"I thank you for your help," Will said, reaching for and shaking Mr. King's hand.

"You may get out of jail," Bill Atwell said, "but you won't exactly be free. Everything you do, every word you utter, will be watched and analyzed. Every detail of your past will be studied and interpreted. So you must be vigilant. Above all, you must be careful."

"What can we do?" Louise asked.

"Right now I'll be putting together the defense team, developing strategies, organizing our case, preparing Will for the ordeal to come. So just be patient. But soon there will be a role for all of you. As Mrs. King said, this is a time to close ranks."

As their allowed visiting time with Will began to run out, Louise wondered why the real reason for his arrest had not even been mentioned. *They are all intelligent people, yet blind as bats, even the illustrious William Hawley Atwell. Will was arrested not because he is a socialist, not because he is a leader in the labor movement—he was arrested because he has a German name and America has declared war with Germany. That is the reason, pure and simple. And it makes me mad because Will is a better American than any of his accusers. And there is another reason. If Will were an ordinary man, living his life quietly out of the public eye, it would be different. But Will draws attention to himself like no one I know. Because of his remarkable good looks, he stands out in any crowd. He loves life and every aspect of his life seems to lift him high above his contemporaries. If he isn't making a speech in the square, he is racing his motorcycle through town or doing magic tricks for the children or playing his violin at the Klein Opera House or with the conjunto musicians from San Antonio. But his name is Bergfeld and they had to bring him down.*

Luke Kennemer, the Fee brothers, and the Jeter boys pushed on into the Swisher Canyon. They had been hiding out in the canyons ever since the night they had been drinking from Mr. Weinert's whiskey barrel behind Old Man Crouch's store and they had seen the trainload of government men round up Bergfeld and the others. The young men had slipped out of town, gone to the Fee place, gathered a cache of 30-30 rifles, sidearms and ammunition they had laid up just for such an emergency, and fled to the canyons.

Now they sat around a small fire, bragging about the girls who were chasing them, the wild game they had killed, and cursing the government men who might soon come to make them join the Army. As the night grew late and they were running out of stories, they swore allegiance to each other, come what may. After all, they had known each other all their lives, had shared the same experiences, had joined the Farmers' and Laborers' Protective Association at nearly the same time, had the same ideas about how a man should not be forced to do anything he did not want to do.

At about midnight, as Luke Kennemer was glorifying a few fights he had been in, they heard the sound of horses. Quickly they doused the fire, took up their rifles and moved up the sides of the canyon to position themselves behind boulders and brush.

The moon was high and nearly full. The government men came clattering down into the canyon, calling to each other, and even though there were only a dozen or so riders, Ross, the youngest Fee brother, thought they made more noise than an army. From behind a covering boulder, Kennemer whispered to Ross, "Like shooting fish in a barrel."

One of the riders came upon the ashes of their campfire. He called to the others and they dismounted. When they found the ashes were warm, their manner suddenly changed, they became quiet, crouching in the moonlight, looking cautiously into the shadows of the canyon.

Without breaking the silence, Kennemer raised his rifle and aimed it squarely at one of the officers.

The man called Grimes moved through the heavy woods toward

the place he knew Karl Hilmar Fulcher was hiding. The posse was large, far too large, and Grimes would have preferred to be alone. But he was accompanied by officers from the Palo Pinto and Hood County Sheriffs' offices, the usual Federal agents, and a crowd of local rowdies and ne'er-do-wells deputized by the sheriffs for the occasion. Like Will Bergfeld, Fulcher was a member of the Farmers' and Laborers' Protective Association and he was of German descent. Unlike Bergfeld, Fulcher had fled reportedly with a cache of weapons and a promise to kill any law officers who came after him.

As the posse closed in on a small canyon cut in wetter seasons by a creek, Fulcher stepped into view, only partially obscured by the thorny bushes. He was holding a double-barreled shotgun across his chest with both hands. It seemed to Grimes that the man looked right at him, more resignation in his eyes than fear. Grimes raised his gun, then lowered it as a hail of bullets cut down the underbrush where Karl Hilmar Fulcher stood. Then the bullets found the man himself and cut him down in a grotesque dance.

Grimes paused by the body. He counted twenty-three wounds.

"You didn't shoot," one of the officers remarked.

"He was dead enough," Grimes said, then walked back toward the horses.

IV.

Weinert, Texas.
June 1917

Virginia Bergfeld and her daughters stepped off the train into a world of sunlight, dust and disturbing disquietude. It was like walking onto a stage, the audience unseen but felt, hidden in dark corners of the theater, waiting for her to play a piano concerto she had forgotten or never learned. She was not exactly sure why she was here or what she would do. Behind them the locomotive engine wheezed and sighed like a winded giant, frightening the girls who looked back with alarm each time it hurled a heaving breath of steam. In the depot, the stationmaster watched them pass, not responding to Virginia's wave as he usually did, turning away with all but his eyes. Beyond the depot, the tiny town was motionless beneath the merciless sun. As they walked the familiar way, their footsteps awakened small clouds of dust, soft brown explosions that settled back down when they passed, obscuring their footprints, as if they had no substance or had not come home at all.

The houses along the street appeared abandoned, the porches empty, gardens surrendered to the tyranny of the drought. But Virginia knew the women watched from beyond the windows, wondering what the young wife of the German traitor would do, what she would say, how she would be, what would become of the children, what strange Teutonic rituals had been performed behind the closed Bergfeld doors. She could imagine them on the telephones now, a community of curiosity, seeking any new item of interest concerning the recent Grand Jury and the return of

Virginia Bergfeld and the unfortunate daughters of the man who would surely be hung if the truth be known. She could see the gossip moving along the line, like a snake, coiling in the wires, hissing in one ear after another. Sometimes Virginia could see shapes moving, watching, gray shadows within the rooms. Even the girls sensed that something was different, was wrong, and they clung to Virginia's skirts, looking around, wondering where the people were and why there were no children playing in the yards or along the streets. They walked on. Even with the girls by her side, Virginia had never felt so alone.

When they reached the house, they found the doors and windows boarded shut with slats of wood plundered from the garden fence. For a long while Virginia stood staring at her house, wondering how she would get in or who she might call for help. Their nearest neighbors, the Cockrells, had always been kind. But Dr. Cockrell would be seeing patients at his office, and his wife, the town postmistress, would also be at work. And Virginia could not bring herself to risk the censure she might find behind any other door. So she moved to the barn to look for a tool to tear away the boards across the front door, thinking all the while how ironic it was that she would have to break into her own house. The barn held the usual tools of a working farm, but most were either too heavy to lift or inappropriate for the task. Finally she found a crowbar. It was partially hidden by a wooden keg filled with what appeared to be sticks of explosives. Carefully, she removed the bar, told the girls to remain in the yard, and returned to the front porch. She amused herself by thinking if the crowbar did not work, she could always blast her way in with the dynamite.

As she pried out the nails, she felt an impotent rage building, gathering, like a summer storm. The nails screamed as they were pulled from the wood. Virginia felt like joining the nails in their screaming, and tears mingled with the sweat of her labors. After the front door, she attacked the windows, tearing away the boards nailed there, feeling an odd elation blending with her anger as she wounded the casements with the bar. It was as if she were punishing the house for not providing the sanctuary homes are obliged to provide.

Inside, the house felt strangely alien. Although filled with familiar things, it seemed like the home of a stranger. Even the piano, her china cabinet, Will's books and the family photograph album with its dark, tooled leather cover seemed stripped of any personal connection, as if the violation of the house had torn away any affection she had for this place that had been a container for their lives. The family had been gone only a few days, yet the house gave the impression that it had been empty for years.

As the little girls played quietly in their room, Virginia began to pack. It was difficult because she didn't know how long they would be gone or even if they would be back at all. She found herself hoping they would leave this house and never set foot in this terrible town again. *But what would that mean? If Will were found innocent, of course they would return. This was where their life was, where Will worked as a rural mail carrier, it was home. But if Will were to be found guilty?* She shuddered, then cast the thought away, squared her shoulders and began to gather the things Will would need. She wanted him to look his best for the trial. She opened the wardrobe where his good suit hung along with his ties and shirts and she began to remove his clothes garment by garment and lay them on the bed. Then she froze, her heart nearly stopping mid-beat and she struggled to tear her mind away from the vision that had come unbidden to her mind—the unthinkable thought that Will was dead and she was clearing away his clothes, assigning them to boxes in the attic or to charities for others to wear. The awful possibility that her thoughts might create a self-fulfilling prophesy struck her with a hammer of guilt. She sank to her knees, weak with dread, holding to the bedspread for balance. It was the first time she had seriously considered the worst, that Will would be taken away from this world forever. Virginia prayed that God clear the dreadful images from her mind. She forced herself to think of Will as he was, abundantly alive and exuberant and filled with a spirit so strong that it would surely prevail, come what may.

There on her knees Virginia began to listen to the sounds the house made. Boards expanding in the heat, the scratching of insects in the walls, Little Virginia singing a jump-rope song. She listened to her daughter, so sublimely unaware of the peril the family faced, and she felt a sudden and desperate need to be in the protective presence of her father. She longed to be a little girl again, safe in the family homeplace on Court Street in Seguin with its wide porches and gardens shaded by towering elms and pecan trees. She longed for the comfort of her mother's arms and the sound of her father's voice.

The last time she had telephoned her parents was the night Will was taken away. Although she had just been with them in Fort Worth, her need for them seemed greater now. She moved to the hall, settled into the little chair by the telephone, then lifted the receiver from its cradle on the wall. To her surprise, the first thing she heard was someone speaking her name. The Bergfeld telephone was on a party line with a number of other families and the neighbors were on the line now, obviously talking about her. Virginia quickly lowered the instrument from her ear. Surely it would be improper to listen in on the conversation. But someone had spoken her name. Didn't that give her a right to hear what they were saying? She could hear their voices, like the buzzing of swarming insects, and feeling no little shame, she raised the receiver again to her ear.

"I was proud to do my duty. There must have been more than a hundred witnesses. But I believe my testimony and Anna Bennett's testimony will be the heart of the case." Virginia recognized the voice as that of Mrs. Thurwanger, a woman of imposing stature who, as far as anyone knew, had no first name at all, and was known for intruding herself in everyone else's affairs. "I just told them the terrible things I heard Will say."

"About killing the President?" asked another voice Virginia didn't recognize.

"That and more."

A third voice asked, "Do you think Virginia knew about what Will was doing? I mean plotting revolution. Buying guns and dynamite. Maybe she didn't know. After all, she comes from a good family."

"How could she live with him all these years and not know?" Mrs. Thurwanger asked.

"Do you think she knew about Will and Anna?"

"That was before Will married Virginia."

"That's not what Anna told me," Mrs. Thurwanger said. "Anna lives on his mail route, you know. He delivers her mail. She told me he stopped by every day and they were intimate."

"How do you mean intimate? You mean they told secrets? Or do you mean they were, you know. . . ."

"He told her everything during those afternoon visits. That's why she was called to testify."

As Virginia continued to listen, the words began to be merely vocal sounds, devoid of meaning. In a strange sense, she was amused by the gossip because of its absurdity. If there was one thing she knew for certain it was Will's absolute fidelity. She lowered the receiver and the voices of the women became insects again. Virginia knew Will had courted Anna Bennett while she was away in college. Anna was an unusually attractive woman, rather flirtatious, Virginia had always thought, with long red hair the color of a West Texas sunset. Virginia had been surprised that Will had chosen her over that more exotic beauty who was his first love. Now Anna Bennett was a spinster who lived along Will's route. Virginia could not recall if she had ever seen them together in these last few years. She tried to remember if Will had even uttered her name. It seemed he had talked about everyone else on his route, but not Anna Bennett.

Virginia carefully placed the receiver back in its cradle. She leaned against the wall, surprised by the jealousy constricting her heart. But how could she be jealous when there was nothing to be jealous about? She knew in her heart that there were things she did not know, things Will had not told her. But not Anna Bennett. That would be something she would have instinctively known. She would have seen it in his eyes or felt it when they made love. And if Will had plotted to overthrow the government, she would know that, too, wouldn't she? It was impossible that she could not know so much. Yet she knew Anna Bennett had been Will's first love. And there was dynamite in the barn.

Night came down like a shade pulled quickly and thoroughly. It was too early for the moon and the only relief from absolute darkness was a rubescent glow from the Cockrell's windows. It was a light the color of Anna Bennett's hair. Virginia put the girls to bed and they immediately fell into the deep slumber of the innocent. *Their faces are untroubled and more beautiful,* Virginia thought, *than a painting or photograph could ever capture.*

For a while, Virginia paged through the family photograph album, a rough sketch of their lives together in this house, in this town. There were images of the house half-built, Will standing proudly before this gift to his new bride. Another page was of picnic scenes at a pond out from town. There were scenes of Will on his motorcycle, some with images streaked by motion the camera couldn't capture. There were pages of photographs of the little girls on the front porch in their Sunday best dresses, each page tracing their growth year by year. Oddly, it seemed they each wore the same dresses, frilly garments simply let out as the years went by. The last photograph mounted in the book had captured them all on the Indian motorcycle, Virginia behind Will, her arms clasped around his middle, the girls posed in the sidecar Will had built out of buggy parts. How happy they seemed, frozen there, in a high-hearted tableau. She imagined that one day far in the future someone would look at these faces and wonder who these people were and what their lives were like. They seemed so carefree. *Could this possibly be the family whose lives were soiled by tragedy? Was this the man accused of treason*? She turned the page and there was nothing there but an oblong of black. A space reserved for future images. There was nothing there but nothing. She closed the book and moved to the chest in the hall.

Beneath the bedding, next to Will's violin, were the two

revolvers. Virginia remembered when Will had brought the weapons home. She lifted the nearest Colt and imagined what it would be like to fire such a weapon. The thought itself made her wrist ache. *Were these the famous high-powered weapons Will was supposed to use to arm a revolution? The Bergfeld Armory. How absurd.* She placed the Colt back in the trunk, next to the violin, and thought what a curious juxtaposition of symbols the old trunk held.

The moon rose and rolled across the horizon, painting the edges of night silver. Virginia was not sure what time it was. The clocks in the house, unwound in their absence, had all stopped at different times. Even the ornate mantel clock that, according to family legend, was a gift to Will's grandmother from the Blind Prince of Hannover was silent. The night train from the east had come and gone. Virginia lay fully dressed on her bed aware that the locks on the doors had been broken. She wished now she had not unbarred the front door and windows. She listened to the sounds of the night, thinking she was too exhausted and confused to sleep. But she was wrong. Sleep came like a carriage caught and carried her away.

The sound was small and not unlike all sounds that walk through a house during nighttime hours, certainly nothing to cut through the veil of sleep and bring one back from dreaming. At first Virginia was lost, wandering that world halfway between dream and reality, part of her mind still on the porch of her mother's house, tasting the marvelous elixir of a honeysuckle blossom with her tongue, listening to the music of her mother's knitting needles. It was a kind of click like that, the sound, the small sound. Slowly the dream faded and Virginia opened her eyes wide and her heart began to drum against her ribs and she knew with absolute certainty that someone was in the house.

She lay still. There, again, the sound. In the parlor? In the hall? The slight creaking of the heart pine floor, boot leather, and there was the smell of tobacco and sweat. Outside her window, dogs were barking and she heard the yapping of a coyote. As she lay in the silver dark she prayed that she was wrong and that there was no one there. *Who would come into a house where they knew people were sleeping? But maybe they did not know we had returned. Maybe they thought the house was empty and they had come to find, find what? Things to steal? The guns? Evidence against Will? Maybe if I lie still they will leave and everything will be fine.* Then all her thoughts converged on the little girls. Her heart hammering, almost faint with the fear she felt, she willed herself to rise. *If I can only get to the guns,* she thought. She crept to the door of the bedroom, paused and listened so intently that she did not know if she heard anything or not. The silence itself was thunderous. Then, slowly, she pushed open the door and looked out into the dark hall. It was empty.

Crouching, almost crawling, Virginia moved to the chest. In the half light, she could see burned matches and a scattering of papers on the floor, the first absolute evidence of intruders. She swung around, sweeping the dark with her eyes. Nothing. But she knew someone was there, somewhere else in the house or in the dark, watching. By her knees was the old leather valise where Will kept important papers, records and mementoes. It had obviously been searched. She opened the chest and reached beneath the bedding for the guns, but the hard comforting steel of the Colts eluded her grasp. Both her heart and spirit plummeted as she realized the guns were gone.

Then came sounds from the barn. Voices. The rumble of something heavy being dragged. Virginia moved silent as a shadow through the house toward the back window. Three moving shapes were revealed by the moon, three men stood staring at the house. A chill walked down Virginia's spine as she realized the men had slithered into the house while she was asleep, apparently unconcerned that she and the children were there. The men now seemed to be arguing. As Virginia moved closer, straining to hear what they were saying, her sleeve caught a pot of mint on the window sill and it fell. With horrible clarity Virginia saw it begin to fall, turning, tumbling ever so slowly toward the floor. Instinctively, she reached for it, but only managed to knock another pot crashing to the floor. The sound was as loud as the collision of planets. The men turned and looked toward the house. One drew his handgun and, as the others watched, began walking back toward the house.

Virginia held her breath as he approached the back door. He came within a few feet of where she stood with her back to the wall by the open window. She could see his shadow on the floor, hear his breathing, smell the tobacco on his breath. He peered through the small window in the back door, his face against the glass. Then he turned and she watched him walk out of sight.

Remembering that the back door was still boarded shut, she thought the man was probably walking around the house to the front door. Virginia moved through the dark toward the front, pausing to look in on the children. For a moment, as she watched them sleeping, something strange, almost thrilling began to move and coil and build somewhere at her center. It was not that she was less afraid, but that her fear had been defined. What she feared had been given shape. No longer was she haunted by the unknown. These were merely men, flesh and blood, and she was determined they would not invade her home again.

The crowbar stood by the front door where she had left it. It felt warm in her hand as if still infused with the rage she had felt earlier in the day, a rage that now was no longer aimless, but ordered and directed toward strangers who would place her children in peril.

She stood by the door, crowbar raised, listening to boots on the porch. She could see a dark form through the glass pane in the front door. The man moved closer and as Virginia saw the doorknob begin to turn, she raised the crowbar and swung it against the glass with all her might. The door glass exploded with the crashing sound of a thousand crystal chandeliers falling. Virginia peered through the open space where the pane had been, and there, shocked and covered with broken glass, stood the intruder, his gun held loosely in his hand, his other hand brushing at the jewels of glass covering his hat and shoulders. Virginia noticed lights blinking on across the street and she could see the Cockrells in their nightclothes move out onto their porch.

Virginia stood in the door and shrieked: "Help me! Help me! They're trying to break into my house!"

Virginia looked down at the man's pistol, at his badge, then at his face. "How dare you! You know you have no right to be here," she said, her voice hard with anger. "I don't care if you do wear a badge. What are you going to do now? Kill us? Maybe arrest us and take us to jail? Look around you. You better think again."

The man looked over to where Dr. and Mrs. Cockrell were now moving toward the house. Then he turned, holstered his gun, and he walked quickly to where the other two officers of the law waited by their wagon.

V.

Abilene, Texas.
September 1917

The Taylor County Courthouse at 306 Oak Street in Abilene was not nearly as imposing as the courthouse in Fort Worth, perhaps because it was dwarfed by the magnificent old Grace Hotel where visitors from all over the Southwest were staying for the duration of the trial, a trial that an *Abilene Reporter* editorial claimed would become the most famous court case in history, certainly the biggest since the county seat had been moved from Buffalo Gap. On the few blocks surrounding the courthouse and the mission-style hotel, there was a carnival atmosphere. But it was not necessarily the relaxed and carefree gaiety of a county fair or a church social; there was just a touch of meanness in the mood of the milling crowds, of combative expectation, as if both collectively and individually they were spoiling for a fight.

Inside the courthouse there was a very real expectation of trouble. For one thing, there was an unprecedented number of defendants—a body of fifty-two labor activists, socialists, and suspected German traitors—a dangerous force in itself if it were to rebel against the authority of the court, or if its "armed and treasonous" confederates outside were to interfere with the due process of law. The chairs and tables had been chained to the floor, ostensibly so they could not be broken apart and used as weapons. As a further defense against disruption, a small army of armed Federal agents and Texas Rangers guarded the entrances and the windows, their presence adding to the sense that trouble was certainly possible, if not inevitable.

Even though they were only in the preliminary stages of the trial, every seat in the chamber had been filled and dozens of other spectators packed into the hallways, pressing forward for a view of the accused. Women especially noted that the darkly handsome Bergfeld bore a striking resemblance to Frances X. Bushman, the matinee idol who had starred with Theda Bara in *Romeo and Juliet* the year before.

Outside, on the courthouse lawn, a gaggle of entrepreneurs had set up stands selling lemonade, roasted peanuts, watermelons, paper fans, American flags and crafts of various sorts including tiny gallows, each bearing the name of one of the accused. A newsboy waved his papers and called out that the Dutch dancer Mata Hari had been executed in France after being convicted of spying for Germany. A smaller story on page two told of resolutions passed prohibiting people from speaking German in public or in the home and encouraging children to report any un-American activities of their parents.

Bill Atwell was not at all happy. In the months since Will's arrest, things had gone worse than he feared or even imagined. The Grand Jury in Dallas had been a travesty. It was a sideshow orchestrated by the prosecution and newspaper coverage that screamed for the blood of the defendants. The newspapers repeatedly carried statements from the prosecutors that were horrendously prejudicial to the accused. That the accused would be indicted and bound over for trial was never in question.

In a small room on the second floor of the Abilene courthouse, Bill Atwell instructed Will's family on the critical process of *voir dire*, or jury selection. Crowded around the conference table were Bettie and Henry King, Louise, Will, Virginia and the two little girls. Below, they could hear the banging and clanging of the hammers and chains being used by the workmen to secure the wooden benches and extra chairs.

"As you know," Atwell began, "during the past couple of days I have had several meetings with Will, with some of the other defense attorneys, and with a few of the other defendants. There have also been some hearings and conferences with Judge George Jack. All of our pretrial motions, based on the unlawfulness of the arrests, have been denied. This was no surprise because trial courts rarely dismiss a criminal case because of an unlawful arrest or illegal search."

Atwell explained that all fifty-two defendants would be tried at the same time, in the same trial, and that he was only one of twelve lawyers defending them. "I not only represent Will and six others, but I've been asked by the other defense attorneys to be the lead attorney for all defendants. You need to understand that I will not be required to spend much time and effort presenting the defense for my other six clients because they haven't been targeted by the prosecution. As you can tell from the newspapers, the prosecution has set its sights on Will, along with Powell, Risley and a couple of others. In fact, I believe that several of the defendants in this case were only indicted because the prosecutors hoped they would give damaging testimony against these target defendants in order to get themselves out of trouble. So far none of them have caved in to pressure from the prosecutors."

"Do we need to be here tomorrow when they pick the jury?" Virginia asked.

"Absolutely," Atwell replied. "It will be one of the most important days of the trial and I'll need your help." He explained how he, the prosecutor, Wilmot O'Dell, and the judge would question some sixty potential jurors. "The purpose of the *voir dire* process is to narrow down that panel to twelve jurors acceptable to both sides."

As Atwell paused and looked down at his notes, Louise could not help thinking that he seemed somehow different today. His demeanor reminded her of how she felt right before one of her performances at the Klein Opera House in Seguin. People would often ask her if she was nervous before a performance and she would respond, "No, but I'm calmly excited." She recalled how immediately before she stepped onto the stage she would take three deep breaths and say a short prayer. Louise believed in prayer before performance and she wondered if Atwell felt the same way.

After all, this was probably the biggest case of his career. She studied his calm, though intense, expression as he explained how the *voir dire* process works and she realized this case was as important to Bill Atwell as it was to her family. He was thinking so clearly, expressing himself so precisely. It was obvious to Louise that he was going to defend Will with all the skill and energy he possessed. For the first time since this entire ordeal began, she began to feel that Will just might have a chance.

"Here's what I need you to do tomorrow morning," Atwell continued. "I want all of you here at the courthouse at eight o'clock. The jury panel has been ordered here at nine o'clock, but it's important for all of you to be here ahead of them and ahead of the spectators. As soon as the doors open, I want you to come in and take seats on the benches that are along both side walls of the courtroom and as near to the front as you can. This will give you the best view of the jurors. And what I need you to do is to observe them closely. Both Prosecutor O'Dell and I will be allowed to eliminate, or strike, those we feel would not be able to render a fair verdict. I need you to help me determine which jurors might be sympathetic to our side and which ones might be intolerant or unforgiving or prejudiced. Maybe it's something in their manner. The expression on their faces. Maybe it's simply a hunch, something you feel. Make notes of what you observe. Sometimes a juror will subconsciously nod in agreement with one of the attorneys. On the other hand, sometimes you can see them shake their heads. Also, sometimes a juror will cross his arms in front of him, a sign that he is blocking out whatever is being said. Now, quite frankly, these are little things. But we don't have much to go by in selecting the jurors we want and those we don't want. Sometimes the little things are the most important things. Your participation is critical. Most people think that in a criminal trial the most important participant is the judge, or the attorneys. Not so. The jurors are the most important people in any criminal case and that's why I said that tomorrow will be one of the most significant days in the trial."

On the day the jury selection was to begin, Virginia sat next to

Louise on the side bench designated by Defense Attorney Atwell. As he had predicted, she had a clear view of the jurors who were now taking their seats. She looked out over the spectators—faces flushed, eyes gleaming with the promise of high drama, squirming in their seats, pressing forward on their benches, chattering and calling out like unruly children in an unsupervised schoolroom. For a moment, Virginia could not imagine how justice could be done in such an atmosphere. Then the bailiff stepped into the middle of the courtroom and shouted, "Everyone rise. Oh yea, oh yea, oh yea. The United States District Court for the Northern District of Texas is now in session. God save the United States and this Honorable Court."

Judge George Jack entered like a Roman Senator, his black robe billowing. After the judge took his seat, the bailiff announced, "Be seated, please," and he retreated to the corner of the room.

What a moment before had been a crowd of rowdy farmers and shopkeepers and rude thrill-seekers was suddenly a hushed and respectful, even reverent, gathering of neighbors. As the judge began the process of questioning the jurors, there was an aura of solemnity in the courtroom, almost of awe. Virginia was astounded at the transformation.

It was apparent to Virginia that things were preceding exactly as Atwell had described. The judge began questioning each juror. Virginia noticed that Louise, Bettie and Henry King were making notes as each juror responded to the judge's questions. Virginia placed a smiling cartoon face by the names of those jurors who looked friendly and a frowning face by the names of those who looked like they could be mean or hostile.

After Judge Jack asked his last question of the last juror, he turned to the prosecution and said, "Mr. O'Dell, do you have any questions of the jury panel?" The prosecutor rose slowly, smiled at the jurors and said, "I do, Your Honor."

Wilmot O'Dell, lead attorney for the prosecution, was a large man with a barrel chest, huge hands, a wide mouth, low forehead and almost no neck at all. His suit was rumpled and a bit too small for his enormous body, his tie askew, his boots scuffed beneath trousers hemmed for a shorter man. He could have been an athlete gone to seed, or a circus strongman past his prime. But his looks, Atwell knew, were deceiving. O'Dell had an excellent reputation as a prosecutor, and had an outstanding record with juries. He was a brilliant strategist with an encyclopedic mind and a passion for court warfare, especially a passion for winning. There were those in the legal profession who had always looked forward to a case when Atwell and O'Dell would confront each other before the bench. It would be an epic struggle. But strangely enough, the two had never met as opposing attorneys in the courtroom until this day. Now O'Dell moved to face the jury panel, introduced himself and his two assistants. He seemed completely at ease. He grinned boyishly at the panel and most of the jurors returned his smile.

"His Honor has already explained to you the general nature of this case. So in order not to waste your time, I will reserve my explanation of the charges against these defendants until my opening statement, when the twelve of you who will actually serve on the jury have been selected. However, I do want to ask one very important question. I think most of you realize that one of the crimes charged against some of these defendants could result in the death penalty. Is there anyone on this jury panel who feels that they could not serve on a jury in a criminal case where your decision could result in the death penalty for one or more of the defendants? If you have moral scruples or strong beliefs against the death penalty that would make it impossible for you to serve fairly on this jury, please raise your hands now."

Louise was praying that many hands would be raised, but none were.

O'Dell then thanked the men on the jury panel for their appearance. "I want you to know that even if you are not selected on this jury you have been helpful to the process." He bowed slightly to the panel, turned and took his seat.

The judge then called for the defense to question the panel. Louise wondered if Atwell was taking three deep breaths and saying a prayer. Then she realized that even if he was not, she was. Bill Atwell moved from his counsel table to the center of the courtroom and positioned himself as close to the jurors as possible. He introduced himself and explained that he had been selected by all the defendants to conduct this phase of the trial.

"Gentlemen of the jury," he continued, "each of these defendants has been indicted by a Grand Jury. The court will instruct you that a Grand Jury Indictment is not evidence of guilt. Do any of you think that because these gentlemen have been indicted by a Grand Jury that that means they are guilty of the charges? If so, please raise your hand."

For a moment, it appeared no hands would be raised. Several jurors exchanged glances, then a man in the second row held his hand high.

"Yes, I see you, sir. Would you please rise and state your name?

"Joe Bob Pierce," he said. He was obviously nervous, uncomfortable standing before a crowd.

"Mr. Pierce, you have indicated that you believe that since these fifty-two gentlemen have been indicted that would constitute some evidence in your mind that they are guilty, is that right?

"That's right," Pierce replied.

"Is this feeling so strong that even if the court instructed you that under the law you should not consider the Grand Jury Indictment as evidence of guilt, that you would still be influenced by the Indictment? Are you saying that you would not be able to follow that instruction and follow the law?"

"In all honesty, Mr. Atwell, I don't think I could follow it. I've served on grand juries and we tried not to indict anybody that we didn't think was guilty."

Atwell turned to the judge. "Your Honor, I believe Mr. Pierce is entitled to be excused."

Judge Jack nodded his head. "Mr. Pierce," he said, "I want you to remain seated until the recess at which time you will be excused. I want you to leave the courthouse and not have any further conversation with any of the members of this panel. Do you understand the instruction?"

"Yes sir, I do." As Pierce took his seat, both Judge Jack and Atwell thanked him for his service. Louise was delighted that Pierce had been dismissed. Next to his name she had drawn a frowning face. She looked over at Bettie and from her smile and nod she realized that Bettie had wanted Pierce off the jury, as well. *One down*, she thought to herself as she crossed Pierce off the list.

Atwell asked if anyone else shared Pierce's belief that a Grand Jury Indictment was evidence of guilt. The jurors looked around at each other but none raised their hands. Louise wondered how many of the others on the panel agreed with Pierce but were afraid to stand up and say so. That seemed to be the flaw in the process. They had to assume that the jurors were not only truthful but had the courage to express their convictions.

Atwell continued his questioning.

"Under the laws of this country all of us may own a gun or several guns. And we may keep them in our home. It is one of our constitutional rights, the right to bear arms. Does anyone here disagree with this law that allows us to own and keep weapons in our homes?"

No hands were raised and Atwell continued.

"Under the laws, these defendants, as they sit here today, all of them are innocent. Under our laws, they can never become guilty unless the twelve of you who are selected on the jury all agree that they are guilty of the charges against them beyond a reasonable doubt. Does anyone here disagree with this law which requires you to presume that every one of these defendants is innocent until proven guilty?"

No hands were raised and Atwell continued. "In this country, anyone can own dynamite and keep it in their house or in their barn or in a shed next to their house. Buying dynamite and keeping it on the premises does not violate any laws of the United States. Does anybody think it should be against the law to own dynamite and have it on the premises of your home?"

A juror immediately raised his hand. His name was Ted Davis. "Sure. I think it should be against the law if you're going to use it to blow up somebody's property."

"Yes, sir," Atwell responded. "I sure do agree with you there. But if you don't intend to use it to blow up somebody else's property, do you agree with me that it really is not against the law to have it on your premises?"

"No, in that case, no. In fact I've had dynamite on my property because I was using it to blast a pathway through a rocky hill behind my house."

"You don't believe you broke the law, do you?"

"No sir."

Defense Attorney Atwell thanked Mr. Davis and, after establishing that no one else believed owning dynamite was against the law, he continued. "Gentlemen, under the laws of this country, all of us have freedom of speech. It is guaranteed by the Constitution. During this trial you will hear a lot about conscription, or the drafting of soldiers into the Army. Under the laws of this country we can speak up for conscription or against conscription. In other words, it's perfectly lawful for you or any of your neighbors to say they like the draft or they don't like the draft. And they can even say they want to stop the draft. Does everyone here understand that under our laws it is perfectly proper to voice your opposition to the conscription of soldiers? If not, please raise your hand."

Once again, no hands showed and Atwell continued with his questions.

"I might also add that this freedom of speech includes any opinion we might have about political figures. It is perfectly lawful for citizens to say they don't like their Governor, even that they don't like the President of the United States. Does anyone disagree with our laws of free speech that allow our citizens to speak out against the President of the United States?"

No hands were raised and Atwell continued.

"Under the laws of this country, it is perfectly lawful and proper for any of our fellow citizens to join and become active in labor unions or farmers' organizations or any type of working men's unions. Now it will be pointed out during this trial that all of the defendants belong to a farmer's union called the Farmers' and Laborers' Protective Association, or the FLPA. Is there anyone here on the panel who has strong feelings against unions or members of unions that might make it impossible for you to be a fair and impartial juror?"

A man identified as Fred Baker raised his hand and was recognized.

"Before moving to Texas, I worked on the loading docks in New Orleans. I felt that we would've been a whole lot better off if we didn't have to fiddle with them unions. If these fellas are union men, I guess it would be heavy on my mind."

"So you're saying you don't think you could be fair to these defendants, is that right, Mr. Baker?"

"Not if they're union men. I think if you lived through what I lived through in New Orleans you'd hate the unions as much as I do."

Defense Attorney Atwell turned to the judge. "Your honor, I think Mr. Baker is entitled to be excused."

As the judge excused the juror, Louise and Bettie exchanged signals that Baker had been on their strike lists, and Atwell walked back to his position before the panel. He asked if anyone on the panel had any thoughts or feelings of any nature that might cause them to be unfair to the defendants. The panelists looked at their hands and at each other, shifted in their chairs. Louise hoped they were examining their consciences and that if they did harbor prejudice they would have the courage to admit it and not carry it on into the trial. After an uncomfortably long pause, a man raised his hand. Atwell acknowledged the juror who introduced himself as John Crane.

"My son has just been drafted and I'm pretty sure he's gonna be sent to Europe. From what I've read in the newspapers, these defendants have done things that would hurt the United States and help Germany. I'd like to see them go to prison, maybe even executed. If they risk my son's life, maybe we ought to take theirs. I'd like to see them punished for not backing our country, and my son, 100 percent against the Germans."

"Mr. Crane," Atwell said. "I know it took a lot of courage for you to share your thoughts with us and I want you to know how sincerely we appreciate it." Louise had liked Crane from the start. He had a kind face, appeared to be a good man. She realized now that reading jurors was not nearly so easy as she had thought. *Suppose Crane had remained silent and had not been stricken by either side. He could have been the voice that led to Will's conviction.* It was a sobering thought.

After Crane was excused from jury service, Atwell asked the panel if anyone else felt the same way as Mr. Crane. When several raised their hands, Judge Jack interrupted Atwell and took over the questioning. In response to his leading questions, the jurors said that even though they felt the same way as Mr. Crane, they had not made up their minds about the guilt or innocence of the defendants. After Judge Jack coaxed them into saying that they could keep an open mind and reach a verdict based on the evidence, they were not excused from the panel.

Judge Jack's interference was a clear sign to Atwell that the judge was unlikely to excuse any more men from the panel regardless of how they responded to the questions. Squarely facing the panel, Atwell said, "On behalf of all the defendants I would like to thank you for your attention and for your presence here today."

As Atwell returned to his seat, Judge Jack announced, "We will now take a thirty-minute recess. During this time both sides will exercise their strikes. When you return, the twelve of you selected as jurors will be called forward and sworn in."

As others exited the courtroom, Atwell immediately signaled Will's family to gather at the counsel table. "We have about ten minutes to discuss your observations," he said as they huddled around. "Then I'll confer with the other defense attorneys and make the final decisions on our strikes."

"Did anyone notice Abe Ellington?" Louise asked. "He was sitting right behind Mr. Crane. He nodded in agreement with everything Mr. Crane said. But he never raised his hand."

"I saw that, too," Bettie said.

"Good. I missed that," Atwell said. "I was looking at Crane. So we'll strike Ellington. Anyone else?"

After a moment of silence, Bettie King said, "Some of those men look like they could put their own mothers to death. But I can't really say for sure we should strike them."

After the lawyers submitted their strikes to the judge, twelve men who would together shape the fate of Will Bergfeld and the other defendants were sworn in and took their seats in the jury box.

Louise realized that Atwell had done more than select a jury. By his questions, he had actually conducted a trial. It was genius. He got the men on the jury to say they had not made up their minds that Will and the others had committed a crime. They had publicly declared that it was not unlawful to own a gun, or own dynamite, or speak out against conscription, or to speak out against the President, or to join a labor union. And these were all major factors in the charges against Will. In effect, what Atwell had done was take a giant step toward demonstrating Will's innocence even before the trial began.

When the session closed for the day, Bill Atwell was only slightly embarrassed when Louise hugged him hard and kissed him lightly on the cheek.

Now, at last, the trial itself was beginning. Atwell tried to shake the sense of foreboding he felt. He studied the jury and wondered who these people were and what they were thinking. In spite of his best efforts during *voir dire*, Atwell feared that most of the jurors leaned toward conviction. The newspaper stories, the backdrop of General Blackjack Pershing's boys marching off to the trenches, the hatred of anything German, the widespread belief that labor unions were sabotaging the war effort—all these things had to poison the minds of even the best and most fair-minded of men. It would be his job to draw the poison out, to clear all the irrelevant clutter from their consciences so they could focus on the facts and on the law. Bill Atwell had a deep respect for juries. And he looked at each juror in turn, seeking the goodness he knew was there. He wished a few were women, but, of course, jurors were selected from voting roles, and women could not vote, thus could not serve on juries. *Maybe soon*, he thought. *But not soon enough to help Will and the others.*

Atwell was concerned about the judge as well. His name was George Whitfield Jack, a former Shreveport city attorney and United States prosecutor with very little judicial experience. Judge Jack had been brought more than five hundred miles from Louisiana to try this case, an important and highly complex legal morass that normally would be tried by a judge with far more experience on the bench. Atwell feared Judge Jack had been assigned the case because, having been a U.S. prosecutor, he probably had a natural leaning toward the prosecution. The judge seemed comfortable on the bench and he looked out at the jury, the defendants and the crowd like an orchestra conductor about to raise his baton to cue an overture. He was going to be a problem, had already been one, and Atwell was not at all sure how to play him or if he could.

But Atwell's greatest worry at the moment was his client Will Bergfeld. For a sensitive, intelligent man, he seemed incapable of following directions. It was almost a kind of arrogance, a belief that he was right and the rest of the world was wrong—even his own defense attorney. Although Will was exasperating, Atwell found it impossible to dislike him. There was a sweetness to the man, a gentle, almost shy quality that seemed at war with his rough and tumble nature. Without doubt, he was a very complex individual. But after all the weeks they had been together, after all the hours of interviews, Atwell was still not absolutely sure Will was innocent of the charges against him. *The ironic thing about Will Bergfeld*, Atwell thought, *is that he is an innocent, whether he is guilty or not.*

Although it was mid-September and the summer drought had broken, the courtroom was hot, close and oppressive, as if all the good air had been breathed by the overflowing and perspiring crowd. Louise, Bettie King, Virginia and the children were squeezed together behind the defense lawyers. The girls were playing with paper dolls beneath the long benches. Virginia kept one eye on Little Virginia and Mary, the other watching for Atwell's signal. At certain moments during the trial, Virginia was to send the children to Will for hugs and kisses, demonstrating to the jury his loving manner and the beauty of his daughters.

As she waited for the trial to begin, Virginia could feel the hostility of the spectators who crowded in and around the courtroom. The activists in the street, on the courthouse lawn and in the hallways were absolute strangers and she wondered how they could dislike her so without knowing her. Louise had brought paper and pen for making notes. Bettie King had brought embroidery and the image of a bloody German-born farmer that she could not erase from her mind.

Although Atwell was the lead defense attorney, all of the defendants had their own lawyers. They were gathered at the long oak tables weighted down by mounds of papers and documents.

Now, Atwell caught O'Dell's eye. The prosecutor pointed his finger at Atwell, and nodded his head as if to say, "At last we meet and you better be ready because I'm going to lay you low." Atwell smiled and gave his adversary the thumbs-up gesture. And he knew from that moment on it would be a battle, no holds barred, no quarter given.

Wilmot O'Dell rose to make the opening statement for the prosecution. At first, he merely paced slowly before the jury, moving gracefully for a man so large. Then in a serious, yet surprisingly conversational, voice, as if talking to friends about a matter of mutual concern, he began to list the dreadful crimes of the accused and the specific charges that he intended to prove.

Of course, everyone in the courtroom knew what the charges were. They had been discussed endlessly in the street and in the bar at the Grace Hotel and in homes all the way to the Mexican border. But to hear them framed in legal language and spoken with understated eloquence by a gifted orator had a mesmerizing effect on the crowd and certainly on the jury.

"The government will prove," O'Dell said, his eyes passing

from juror to juror, "that the defendants did unlawfully, knowingly, wickedly and feloniously conspire and agree among themselves to incite rebellion and insurrection against the authority of the United States and to assault and kill its duly authorized officers and agents, including the President of the United States."

As Prosecutor O'Dell painted word pictures for the jury, images of rebellion, insurrection and conspiracy, as he told of purchasing high-powered rifles and dynamite, of blowing up bridges and capturing hostages, the crowd responded audibly with sighs and murmurs and even cries of outrage. Atwell thought Judge Jack hesitated a moment too long to bring his gavel down on these outbursts. He also thought that O'Dell's opening statement might have been a bit too long. For as he had progressed from point to point, covering the charges against each of the fifty-two defendants, the language growing repetitive, Atwell sensed that the crowd was getting restive and inattentive. These were things they knew. They were ready for action, for evidence, for punishment to be promised. They were eager to hear the ring and slap of hammers building gallows.

Finally Judge Jack asked for the defense to present its opening statement. Atwell rose and told the court he would reserve the defendant's right to make an opening statement until the close of the prosecution's case. As he explained to the other defense attorneys, all he could have done at this time was to deny the charges and further bore the jury. He would wait to refute the prosecutor's evidence until the jury was more alert and the spectators' hostility had hopefully cooled.

"Mr. O'Dell," Judge Jack said, "The prosecution may call its first witness."

"I call Ned Earl Calhoun," O'Dell said, his voice reaching to the last row of chairs and beyond.

All eyes followed Calhoun as he moved to the witness stand. He was an unusually gray man, Atwell thought. His suit, his hair, his pale complexion seemed painted from the same colorless palette with the same brush. He looked like a man who spent very little time out of doors, one of those anonymous kinds of people you would never recognize in a crowd, or who, once met, you would never remember. In spite of his pallor, he had a pleasant, round, unlined face and he smiled at the jury as he passed. The witness was sworn in. Atwell wondered, *What does this mild-looking man have to say and why has he been selected by O'Dell to lead off his case?*

O'Dell leaned on the witness stand, half facing Calhoun and half facing the jury. "Mr. Calhoun, where do you live?"

"I live in California." His voice was strong. He looked directly at the jury as he spoke.

"But until recently you lived in Texas, isn't that right?"

"Yes, sir. I grew up in Little New York, Texas. A little town down by Gonzales. My folks had a small farm there."

"And you worked there until you were married, isn't that right?"

"Yes."

"Tell us what you did then."

"I worked on my father-in-law's cattle ranch on Peach Creek near the Guadalupe River."

"The Applewhite Ranch?"

"Yes, sir. My wife is Rujean Applewhite."

"How long did you work on the ranch, Mr. Calhoun?"

"About two years."

"What did you do then?"

"I got a job with the First National Bank in San Antonio."

"How long did you work there?"

"Three years."

Prosecutor O'Dell walked from the witness stand to the jury box. He asked the next question directly to one of the jurors. "Mr. Calhoun, please tell the jury where you went after those three years at the First National Bank in San Antonio."

"I went to the penitentiary."

A plural exclamation filled the gallery. It had a sound like a thousand bees disturbed. Judge Jack pounded his gavel. Calhoun simply grinned sheepishly, as if pleased that he had offered the crowd this moment of surprise. Bill Atwell was totally unprepared for this strange admission and he wondered what O'Dell was trying to pull. He noticed that a few of the jurors were smiling, but all seemed confused by the revelation. Even the court reporter looked up, as if to confirm what he was putting in the transcript.

O'Dell continued. "Why were you in the penitentiary, Mr. Calhoun?"

"I was convicted of embezzling funds from the bank." Again the crowd buzzed, stirred, their boots scraping the wood floor.

"When and where was this?"

"November of 1915. Federal court in San Antonio."

Defense Attorney Atwell rose to his feet. "If the court please. Although I'm fascinated by the fact that the prosecution's witness is a convicted felon, I don't see the relevance to this case."

"Mr. O'Dell?" Judge Jack asked, obviously surprised by the witness's admission.

"A moment more and the relevance will be abundantly clear."

The judge seemed to turn his thoughts inward, as if making a difficult and weighty decision. "All right, Mr. O'Dell, you may continue."

Prosecutor O'Dell continued to stand by the jury, as if he were one of them, an objective, concerned citizen, the thirteenth juror. "But isn't it a fact, Mr. Calhoun, that you were falsely accused and falsely imprisoned?"

"Yes, sir, I was."

"Tell us what happened."

"I was convicted on circumstantial evidence. Notes and records concerning several embezzled accounts were found in my desk. It appeared that it was my handwriting on some of them. During the trial I denied that the handwriting was mine. But I had to admit that some of the signatures on the documents appeared to be mine. None of the officers in the bank stepped forward in my defense."

"So you went to prison."

"Yes, sir."

"But you did not serve your full term in prison, isn't that right?"

"No, I didn't. A fellow bank employee died suddenly. His name was Tommy Newsome. Among the papers found after his death was evidence that he had embezzled the accounts, not me."

"What happened then?"

"My family immediately took steps to contact the prosecutors. They urged them to obtain a pardon."

"And were you pardoned?"

"I was. In March of this year."

"Because you were innocent of any wrongdoing?"

"I had committed no crime. I was innocent."

"You were very thankful that the prosecutors were able to obtain the pardon, isn't that so?"

"I certainly was."

"And after your release did you have any conversations with the U. S. District Attorneys in San Antonio?

"Yes, sir."

"Tell us about those conversations, Mr. Calhoun." O'Dell returned to the prosecution table, folded down at his place like a great bear relaxing in its den. He was giving Calhoun the entire stage.

As the jury leaned forward, Calhoun told how he had returned to Gonzales after his release from prison and again worked for his father-in-law while trying to decide on his future.

When he was contacted by the San Antonio prosecutors he agreed to help them in their investigation of a labor organization. "They were especially interested in Will Bergfeld, one of its leaders," Calhoun said. "They told me about their suspicions that Bergfeld was working to overthrow the government through the Farmers' and Laborers' Protective Association. But they needed evidence. Since I'd been a farmer for a good part of my life, they thought I'd speak his language and could win his trust."

"Did you accept this assignment?"

"I did. Out of gratitude that they got me a pardon."

O'Dell was on his feet again, moving toward the jury box, a puzzled, attentive look on his face. "Now, Mr. Calhoun, where were you on May fifth of this year?"

"In Cisco, Texas. It was suggested by the prosecutors that I attend a meeting of the FLPA organization. I was to observe what went on and get to know Bergfeld if I could. Then report back."

"And did you meet Bergfeld?"

"Yes, I did."

Suddenly, Will sprang from his chair. "He's a liar! I never saw this man in my life!" The spectators jeered and the gavel pounded. Atwell remained composed, seeking to make sure the jury did not detect his unhappiness with his client's outburst.

"Mr. Atwell, if you can't control your client, I'll have him bound and gagged!" A few in the gallery murmured approval of the judge's threat.

Reluctantly, Will took his seat, grumbling under his breath. Order in the courtroom was restored. The witness smiled benignly, appearing to be an honest, reasonable, forgiving man who had just been maligned by a bully.

"Did you have a conversation with Will Bergfeld at the Cisco meeting?"

In a calm, clear voice, Ned Earl Calhoun told how he had borrowed his father-in-law's car and had driven from Gonzales to Cisco, how he had introduced himself to Bergfeld about an hour before the meeting started. "That's when he told me about his plan to kill President Wilson."

This time, it seemed the crowd was holding its breath. The jurors stirred expectantly; all twenty-four eyes swept to where Will Bergfeld once more jumped to his feet and quickly sat down again. Then all eyes swept back to the witness.

"He told you that he planned to kill the President?"

"He said he thought Wilson was an egghead who had become a capitalist puppet who wouldn't hesitate a minute to send working people to their deaths on foreign soil."

"In regard to killing the President, what were his exact words?"

"I'm not sure I can remember his exact words. But he started out by saying that one of the best things that could happen to this country was that President Wilson be assassinated. He said that he and two other members of the Farmers' union had discussed killing the President. Mr. Bergfeld told me that one of these men had actually been to Washington and reported back as to where and when they could pull off an assassination."

Will Bergfeld threw his head back and stared at the ceiling.

"Did he talk to you about conscription?" O'Dell asked.

"He said he was going to introduce a resolution at the meeting that the membership take up arms to fight against conscription. That they buy high-powered rifles to fight the conscription officers, even kill them if necessary. He said they also needed guns to rob banks to finance the rebellion."

"Now, Mr. Calhoun, you actually served time in prison for approximately nine months, and you know that if you came to this witness stand and perjured yourself you could go back to prison, don't you?"

There was no trace of a smile on Ned Earl Calhoun's face now. He was a picture of absolute candor and concern. "Yes, sir, I know that. I've been to prison once for something I didn't do and I'll guarantee you I'm not ever gonna do anything that would get me back there again."

"Thank you, Mr. Calhoun," O'Dell said. "Pass the witness." As the prosecutor moved back to his place at the table, he cast a brief look at Atwell—a glance that seemed to say *How do you like them apples, counselor*?

Defense Attorney Atwell stood, looked over at Will and found him looking back with confused and pleading eyes. "Please believe me," he seemed to be saying across the space. *Was Calhoun telling the truth or was he lying?* Atwell wondered. The thing about the capitalists sending the working men to their deaths on foreign soil sounded just like Will. Calhoun had been the perfect witness, absolutely believable, a sympathetic good ol' boy who had been wronged and then vindicated. And O'Dell was too smart and too principled to knowingly allow his lead witness to lie. But there was something wrong with the testimony. A flaw. And as Atwell approached the witness stand, he thought he knew what it was.

"Mr. Calhoun," Atwell began. "As I understand your testimony, the only reason you even went to Cisco last May was because the prosecutors in the U.S. District Attorney's office asked you to give them some help on their case. Is that correct?"

"Yes, sir."

"And it's my understanding that you agreed to this because they had helped you obtain a pardon."

"Yes, that's basically correct. I offered my help out of gratitude for what they had done for me."

"And what you want this jury to believe is that you drove from Gonzales to Cisco and had a conversation with Will Bergfeld that nobody else heard but you and he, isn't that correct?"

"That is correct."

"And you're asking this jury to believe that Will Bergfeld told you all these details, which if true, would clearly show that he and his organization were violating laws of the United States. Is that correct?"

"Yes, sir, that's exactly correct."

"And even though Will Bergfeld had never laid eyes on you before and had never spoken to you, you are here swearing under oath that for some reason he decided to open up to you and in effect make a long list of confessions to a long list of crimes. Is that your testimony?"

"Yes, basically that is my testimony."

"What you are saying is that Will Bergfeld confided all these confessions of guilt to you, a total stranger?"

"Well sir, Mr. Atwell, let me tell you exactly what happened because I think when you understand the entire conversation you'll see why he told me all those things. First of all, we just talked about this and that. He told me about his organization. Wanted me to join. I told him about my background. I told him I'd been a farmer down near Gonzales. I told him about my banking experience and I told him how I'd served time in prison for a crime I didn't commit. I told him I was innocent. But I didn't tell him I'd been pardoned. So it was clear to me at the time that he jumped to the conclusion that I must share his hatred of the U.S. government officials who put me in prison. He seemed to act like we were on the same side. He seemed to trust me. He just assumed I hated the government as much as he did. So that's why he told me those things."

Atwell realized his attempt to reveal a flaw in Calhoun's testimony was going nowhere. He was hitting a brick wall.

"How long did the conversation with Bergfeld last?"

"I'd say it was about, oh, twenty-five to thirty-five minutes."

"Is this the only conversation you had with him?"

"It is."

"And where did this conversation take place?"

"It was in the hall where they were going to have the meeting that night."

"And with all the people at that meeting, no one else heard the conversation?"

"Not so far as I know. We were down front and the meeting hall was empty except for people putting up tables and chairs back near the entrance."

"After this conversation took place, what did you do?"

"I left that hall, walked out the front door. I saw some people from central Texas and I was afraid they'd recognize me and question why I was there. I was afraid if they saw me they'd mention to Bergfeld about the pardon. Almost everybody down there where I'm from knew about my pardon. So I left and went back to Gonzales. Then later I reported what I'd heard to the prosecutors."

"So you didn't actually attend the meeting itself? You can't tell us one thing that happened there, or one thing that was said at that meeting, can you?"

"No, sir, I wasn't there."

"And you cannot tell us the name of one single witness who can confirm you were even in Cisco, can you?"

"No, sir, I can't."

"You're living in California now, is that right?"

"Yes, sir."

"So you came all the way from California for this trial. How did you get here?"

"Two United States marshals picked me up in California and escorted me by train to Tucson where we were met by more U.S. marshals who brought me here."

"Is the government paying all your expenses for this trip?"

"Yes, sir, they are."

"Are they paying you any other money for your testimony in this case?"

"No, sir, just my expenses."

"As I understand your testimony, you're involved in this case because you feel you need to pay back the government prosecutors for helping you get a pardon, isn't that correct?"

"That's certainly correct."

"And you expect this jury to believe that you drove all the way from Gonzales to Cisco to go to a meeting you never actually attended, and while at Cisco had a conversation nobody heard with a man you had never met before about crimes no sane man would ever admit. Is that what you're asking this jury to believe, Mr. Calhoun?"

"I'm not asking them to believe it. I'm just telling you that is what happened."

Atwell said, "No further questions."

"We have no further questions, Your Honor," O'Dell said, his pale blue eyes staring at Atwell.

Judge Jack asked if the witness could be excused.

Meeting O'Dell's eyes, Atwell shook his head. "Not at this time, Your Honor. I would like for this witness to remain available subject to recall."

As the witness was leaving the stand, Judge Jack called him back. "Mr. Calhoun," he said, "please notify the U.S. Attorney as to where you can be reached during the balance of the trial and make sure you're in the area in case you are recalled to testify."

For once Will was silent. The only sound in the room was the click and tap of Bettie's knitting needles as the judge ordered a recess and the spectators' hushed whispers became a torrent of voices as they moved to the courthouse lawn and the streets. Virginia stayed in the courtroom, kneading Will's shoulders, humming a tune softly to herself and hoping for Atwell to offer some reason why Calhoun's testimony was not as devastating as it seemed. Louise was reviewing the notes she made. She looked up at Atwell.

"Assume the man is lying. . . ."

"He is lying, Louise." Will said this tiredly, without emotion. "I swear I've never set eyes on that man! Never! What more can I say?"

"All right," Louise said. "Let's say he's lying. The question is why? What does he have to gain by lying? What's the motive?"

"Think, Will," Louise said. "Who's out to get you? Who wants you out of the way?"

"Mine owners," Will said. "Industrialists. Land grabbers. Strike-breakers. Anybody who gains from keeping the working man down. Middle men who steal money from the farmers' pockets. Bankers who charge exorbitant interest on loans for seed and machinery. Landowners who dam up streams so the farmer's land turns to desert. That's who, Louise. It could be any of them. I've publicly spoken out against all of them at one time or another."

After a moment of silence, Atwell suggested there might be more subtle motivations. "Think about Calhoun. Nobody would look twice at him on any street in Texas. He's a nobody, almost invisible. His life story has been pretty dreary reading. Scratching away on a small dirt farm. Being brow-beaten on his father-in-law's ranch. No place of his own. Drifting along. Then he had a chance for a moment of fame. The payoff doesn't have to be money. All his life nobody ever paid him any mind. Now he's the center of attention. A key witness in a big trial."

"He certainly isn't a nobody anymore," Bettie said. "By tomorrow everybody in Texas will know his name."

"Or maybe the motive was revenge," Louise said. "Payback for something Will did to him. Maybe years ago."

"Or something he thinks Will did to him but didn't," Virginia said.

"Will," Louise said. "Remember that man you whipped that time?"

"I remember doing it. I don't remember the man."

"Whipped?" Atwell asked.

Will nodded, remembering. "He was beating a boy. I told him to stop. He wouldn't. So I drove him off with a whip."

"Where was that?"

"Seguin. Not that far from Gonzales."

"Will, could there be any connection between Calhoun and that incident?"

"I doubt it. But there could be, I suppose."

"Well, obviously we can only guess why Calhoun lied," Atwell said. "But I don't mind telling you that the man's testimony has put us in a hard spot. He came across as a likeable, believable witness. But he was almost too good. It seemed like he had read the Indictment, then testified that you confessed to everything in it word for word. We know he's lying. But I don't know how we're going to prove it."

"I made some more notes," Louise said. "He just can't be that invisible. There were some one hundred men at the Cisco meeting. A number of the defendants in this case were there. Somebody must have seen him." She glanced back at her notes. "And he said he borrowed his father-in-law's automobile. That's something we can check. What kind of car? I doubt there were more than a half dozen cars in all of Cisco that day. It would have been noticed and talked about."

The sound of voices and footfalls grew louder outside as the bailiffs and Rangers brought back the defendants who were unable to get released on bail. A few shouting and shoving matches broke out among spectators who had lost their seats to others during the recess. "Back to the lions," Louise said, rising as the judge entered the courtroom. Will and his family returned to their assigned places. Then Judge Jack brought the court to order and Wilmot O'Dell called his next witness.

The man called Grimes moved to the stand. Without his hat, Virginia thought he looked like a different man than the Ranger who broke into her home. In fact, he looked like a man who rarely removed his hat and was quite uncomfortable without it, like other men might be uncomfortable without their pants. There were red lines on his forehead that his Stetson had rubbed. Above these lines his hair was fine, yellow and thinning, below his face was brown and rough as burlap. Virginia remembered seeing him come crashing through their door and she shuddered. Bettie reached for her daughter's hand.

W. T. Grimes would rather have been enduring the fires of Hell. He had been dreading his court appearance ever since the adjutant general had told him he had been listed as a witness. He had faced death as a soldier in Cuba and in a variety of gunfights over the years, he had seen his wife and his only child die, but the thought of testifying before a judge and jury made his blood run almost as cold as it ever had. Grimes was too tall for the chair and it was hard to know what to do with his feet. Sitting there, knees high, being led by the nose by lawyers was like being in a trap. He was not afraid of the truth, but he was not sure he knew what the truth was, especially in this campaign against the Farmers' and Laborers' Protective Association. He felt bad about Fulcher and he thought he might be asked about his death. And then there were the secrets he knew. Should he break his word and reveal these things? As he was sworn in, he wondered which oath had precedence. He had sworn to secrecy. And now he was swearing to reveal what he had promised to keep secret.

"What is your name?" O'Dell asked.

"W. T. Grimes."

"You are in the Ranger service?"

"Yes, sir."

"In what capacity?"

"Sergeant." Grimes tried to cross his legs, but found no room. He folded them back, feet trapped beneath his chair.

"Did you have some work to do in this section of the country in May of this year?"

"Yes, sir."

"Did you arrest William A. Bergfeld?"

"Yes, sir."

"Did you have a conversation with Mr. Bergfeld concerning this case when you arrested him?"

"Not a conversation. No, sir."

"Did he say anything to you about guns?"

"Yes. He said 'If you boys don't have enough guns, I have two good ones I'll loan you.'"

"What day was that?"

"I think it was the twenty-third. The night he was arrested."

"And he said he had two good guns he would loan you if you didn't have enough?"

"Yes, sir. That's about what he said."

"Did you find any guns on the place?"

"No, sir."

"Did you find any dynamite?"

"Yes, sir. Two kegs of dynamite were in the barn. About a hundred sticks."

O'Dell seemed to be making a calculation in his mind. "One hundred sticks of dynamite. Tell me, Sergeant Grimes, would a hundred sticks of dynamite be enough to blow up a bridge?"

Atwell rose. "Objection, Your Honor. Sergeant Grimes is not a demolition expert."

"Sustained," the judge said. "But I doubt it would take an expert to answer the question."

As O'Dell changed his line of questioning and began asking Grimes about his participation in the arrest of several other defendants, Atwell began to wonder why the prosecutor had brought the Ranger to the stand. Grimes continued to be a man of few words and what testimony he did offer did not seem very helpful to the prosecutor's case. Surely O'Dell had rehearsed what his testimony would be. Atwell decided that O'Dell must have expected more; that as an arresting officer Grimes would have been caught up in the passion building against the defendants. But it was clear that the Texas Ranger was his own man and O'Dell could not lead him around by the nose as he had hoped.

Finally, after O'Dell sensed that Grimes was not going to add much punch to the government's case, he said, "Pass the witness."

As O'Dell turned and walked back to the prosecutor's table, he passed Atwell who was opening a large envelope that someone had placed on the seat of his chair.

Virginia could not help contrasting the two lawyers: one a great grizzled bear of a man, the other so beautifully and precisely attired. She considered the impact each might have on the jury and wondered if the jurors might think Atwell was too fancified with his silk bow tie and the rose Louise had given him for his lapel. Each man seemed supremely self-confident. Yet, to her mind, O'Dell seemed like an actor playing the part of a trial lawyer rather than actually being a trial lawyer. Atwell seemed more genuine and she hoped the jury noticed the difference.

Atwell was astounded. The envelope appeared to contain copies of documents prepared by the United States Secret Service, reports on government investigations of its own witnesses and correspondence between witnesses and the government. Passages were heavily underlined, most pages contained hand-written remarks. At first Atwell was tempted to return the contents of the envelope. Surely these were things he should not see, information the defense should have been denied.

"Mr. Atwell," Judge Jack was impatient. "Are you going to question this witness or not?"

Atwell looked up from the document. "Your Honor, could we have a brief recess? Some information has come forward that might affect the questioning of this witness."

"How long will this take?"

"Five minutes, if the court please."

"All right," the judge said, not happily. "We will recess for five minutes. You may step down, Sergeant Grimes."

Atwell thumbed through the pages, scanning the contents. Here was a report on Mrs. Thurwanger with a hand-written note that read: "*A shameful gossip and known liar.*" A further note advised that Mrs. Thurwanger not be called as a witness. A number of letters from Old Man Crouch to an agent named Austin catalogued Will Bergfeld's alleged criminal activities over a long period of time. One letter stated that: "*Bergfeld is the most dangerous man in America.*" The file proved, as Atwell had suspected, that Will had been a target of secret government investigations for more than a year, a carefully coordinated campaign directed from the highest levels within the Justice Department. The file contained detailed logs of Will's activities, including the purchase of guns and dynamite. It also contained a hand-written application for membership in the FLPA. Filled with passionate and radical language, the prose was attributed to Will Bergfeld. A notation claimed that the application was provided by Anna Bennett who obtained the draft from Will Bergfeld himself. Heavily underlined on the application was the line: "*Would you be willing to follow a Moses?*" But the most extraordinary document in the file was entitled: "*Subjects of the Teutonic Order.*" It was a list of citizens of German origin who were being investigated as enemies of the United States. And high on the list was William A. Bergfeld.

Mystified, Bill Atwell looked toward the prosecution's table. Who could have delivered the envelope? Who could have access to this privileged information? Wilmot O'Dell was lecturing several of his team, his arms waving, his fingers pointing in the face of now one of his prosecutors, now another. Everyone's eyes were riveted on O'Dell—all except for one man. For a fleeting moment Atwell locked eyes with this man. Then Tom Grimes looked away.

After court resumed and Grimes was again on the stand, Atwell recognized that the Ranger was uncomfortable. Atwell waited to ask his first question for as long as he thought the judge would allow. He wondered how he might use this information, especially since nothing in the envelope had been offered into evidence.

Grimes was making every effort to hold his anxiety in check. He kept telling himself that the ordeal would soon be over and he could go home. *Go home to what?* He looked out at Bergfeld and his wife and the others he knew to be Bergfeld's large extended family. He looked at the children that had been in the home on the night of the arrest and he wished. . . .

"Sergeant Grimes," Atwell finally asked, "how many officers participated in the arrest of Will Bergfeld?"

Grimes was brought back from his wandering thoughts. "Uh, how many? There were eighteen of us."

"Did you knock on the door and tell them who you were before you went in?"

"No, sir."

"In fact, what happened is that all of you bashed in the doors and crashed through the windows with your guns drawn. Isn't that the way you did it?"

"Yes, sir."

"All of a sudden there were about twenty-five pistols and rifles and shotguns in Bergfeld's living room, isn't that right?"

"More or less. I'm sure that's right."

"That's why Will Bergfeld jokingly said, 'If you boys don't have enough guns I've got two I can loan you,' isn't it?"

"Probably so."

"He certainly never tried to hide from you the fact that he had two guns, did he?"

"No. That was the first thing he blurted out."

"Now will you agree with me that if Will Bergfeld intended to use those guns to commit crimes, he probably would have never told eighteen law officers that he had them in the house?"

"I agree. As I've already said, he wasn't trying to hide them."

"Sergeant Grimes, let's talk about the dynamite."

Louise noticed that Atwell was now talking in a conversational manner, as if to put Grimes at ease.

"Was the dynamite hidden?" he asked.

"No, sir."

"In fact it was in a keg with the word 'dynamite' written on it in big red letters, wasn't it?"

"Yes, I recall that. It was definitely not hidden."

"Can you agree with me that if Will Bergfeld intended to use this dynamite to commit crimes, he would not leave it where anyone walking by the barn could see it?"

"I agree that sounds reasonable."

Louise noticed that Prosecutor O'Dell appeared a bit displeased that his witness was being so helpful to the defense.

"While I'm thinking about it, Sergeant Grimes, would you please tell the jury who these officers were who crashed into Will Bergfeld's home?"

"There were Texas Rangers, U.S. Marshals and Secret Service Agents."

"When all of you exploded into Will's family home, did any of you have a warrant to search the home?"

"We weren't searching it."

"What were you doing in there then?"

"Arresting him."

"Did you have an arrest warrant?"

"I've never arrested a man in my life with an arrest warrant."

"Did you take Bergfeld's guns?"

"No, sir."

Virginia whispered to Louise. "That's not true. They took the guns when I got back. They also took the dynamite." Then she realized it must not have been Grimes who took the guns and explosives that night, so he had answered the question honestly.

"Isn't it true, Sergeant Grimes, that the Constitution of the United States guarantees a man the right to keep guns in his home?"

"It's true."

"And isn't it true that under the laws of the United States of America a man can keep dynamite in his barn?"

"Yes, sir, that's right."

Atwell paused, walked to the jury box, then faced Grimes again. "At the time all eighteen of you arrested Will, he was not committing a felony in your presence, was he?"

"No. I don't believe so."

"In fact, at the moment you men stormed into his home with guns drawn, he was playing the violin, wasn't he?"

"He was."

"Playing the violin for your wife and children in your own home is not a felony anywhere in the United States of America, is it?" In contrast to the accusation implicit in his question, Atwell's voice was calm and reasoned.

"No, sir."

It appeared to Louise that Grimes might wish to be anywhere in the world but where he was. He was so terribly uncomfortable that she almost felt sympathy for the man.

"Sergeant Grimes, do you now know that this arrest of Will Bergfeld was illegal?"

O'Dell rose. "Your Honor, he's been over this time and time again."

"What is the purpose of this line of questioning anyway?" Judge Jack asked.

Atwell's answer was directed to the jury as much as it was to the judge. "To show that from the very beginning of this case against Mr. Bergfeld, the government has acted recklessly, irresponsibly and unlawfully. And this includes the actions of the arresting officers, including Sergeant Grimes."

"Sergeant Grimes is not on trial here," O'Dell responded. "I object to questioning along these lines."

After Judge Jack pondered the point of law for a moment he said, "Mr. Atwell, you know that pretrial procedures resolved these questions about the arrests. I suggest that you either excuse the witness or pursue a different line of questioning."

Atwell turned back to the witness. "I do have one further question," he said, pacing before the jury. "Sergeant Grimes, was William Adolph Bergfeld's name on the German List?"

Again, O'Dell was on his feet. "Objection. Such a list is not in evidence."

"What list is this?" Judge Jack asked impulsively.

Atwell responded quickly because he could see that the jurors were leaning forward with interest. "There are lists, Your Honor, forwarded from Military Intelligence to the U.S. Attorney's office.

One is called *Subjects of the Teutonic Order*, a secret list of people the government wants investigated as possible German agents solely because they are of German descent. William Adolph Bergfeld was on that list."

O'Dell rose to object, but Judge Jack waved him back down.

Knowing the judge would soon cut him off, Atwell continued hurriedly. "Your Honor," Atwell said. "The German List is the most odious and flagrant abuse of a citizen's civil rights in the history of the Republic! And Mr. Bergfeld and these other defendants are victims of that abuse!"

Prosecutor O'Dell threw up his hands. He was furious. "It's not relevant! This list is not evidence!" A choral murmur rose from the crowd. This was the fireworks they had come to see.

"Hold it!" Judge Jack shouted at both lawyers. "We don't need any more theatrics from either one of you. Now just hold on a minute! In fact, I want both of you to take your seats."

It was obvious to Bill Atwell that Judge Jack now realized it was his own question that allowed Atwell to briefly explain the German List before the jury. Now the judge was deciding how he could gracefully regain control.

After a pause, Judge Jack said, "I will consider your objection in chambers, Mr. O'Dell." Then he turned to the jury. "Gentlemen of the jury, you are instructed to disregard any mention of this German List, whatever it is. I will study this issue and rule later on the admissibility of this evidence." He turned back to Defense Attorney Atwell. "At that time, Mr. Atwell, you may recall this witness and question him outside the presence of the jury. But not another word about this German List until I rule."

Atwell turned and looked at the angry prosecutor. Both of them knew that the inexperience of Judge Jack had allowed an ugly issue to be unwrapped. Whether or not the *Subjects of the Teutonic Order* list would find its way properly into evidence was uncertain at this time. But Atwell knew that the German List was squarely before the jury, whether properly presented or not. It was like throwing a skunk into the jury box and asking the jury not to smell it.

Now we're getting somewhere, Louise thought as the judge recessed until the next day. She had watched the jurors carefully as they had been told to disregard the German List. It was plain from the look on their faces that the list would be impossible to forget.

She caught Will's eye and knew they were both thinking the same thing. It was just such a list that had forced their grandmother to flee Germany in the first place. Now it had started all over again.

VI.

Stettin, Germany.
August 1867

Little Elisabethe Jurcza stood with her mother at her father's tomb in the Dorotheenstad Cemetery. She looked out at the architecture of death, the ornate stone structures that housed generations of her forebears. All had been carried to Heaven on the wings of angels like those carved on their monuments, abodes which she thought useless now since they had been abandoned in lieu of the Lord's mansions in the clouds. As she gazed at the tomb of Joseph Jurcza, she was aware of two smaller stone monuments, but she could not bring herself to actually touch them with her eyes. She could hardly think about who slumbered there, because it made her dizzy and sick and frightened to think of her little brother and sister who had been taken when she had been spared.

It had been two years since the unthinkable had happened. At the time she was only aware of hushed voices and closed windows and doors barred to friends and strangers alike. Something evil had come, she knew. Now she knew it was cholera and it was plundering the lives of their neighbors. But her house was strong, the walls thick, and her father was there, a rock, a good devout Catholic who had donated the kanterhaus, a music school, and who numbered priests among his best friends. He had been a large, handsome man, she remembered, with thick black eyebrows, a wide smile and a generous heart. She could still hear his laughter which was as natural a sound in their home as the voice of her mother's violin. She remembered the adoring look he lavished on her mother when she performed in the parlors of mansions and on the stage of the Berlin Opera House. And she remembered those huge hands applauding her mother's performance. She could almost feel those hands now, lifting her above his head and spinning her around and around while she held out her arms, like wings.

But the house grew silent and filled with the acrid smell of fear. The doctors in white came, then the priests in black. And one by one they died, first the children, then the father, the rock, were taken away and the great house was diminished by three souls, leaving disbelief and bitter sorrow.

After the funeral at the great cathedral, the priests who had often spent long hours talking philosophy and religion with Joseph Jurcza came to console his wife. Elisabethe heard her mother tell the priest that God should have taken her along with her husband, such was the depth of her grief. The priest had listened, then scolded her, telling her that her life had even more value now, and that she had been spared for a purpose.

Maria Theresa Jurcza had mourned her husband and her two children in tearless silence. For a long time, she avoided their many friends, the poets and musicians who had come to her home to discuss literature, opera and politics. Elisabethe had sometimes wondered if her mother was wandering in some shallow dimension of death, looking for the ghosts of her family. But little by little, Maria Theresa was able to climb back into the world of the living. Little by little she rediscovered the daughter who had been spared and she lavished all the love she had left on Elisabethe and it was abundant. They were two against the world. Two alone, but strong enough to bear their loss and face come what may.

In time, the poets and musicians returned to their home and in long evening soirees they railed at the deplorable erosion of freedoms in Germany and cursed the tyrant Bismarck and his persecution of first the Catholics and then the Jews. It was at one of these soirees that a priest and the burgomeister, Julius Schievelbein, came and told the intellectuals that their names were on a list targeted by Bismarck's secret police. He called Maria

Theresa aside and told her she must leave Germany. As a patron to the dissenters, she was a suspect and on the list of alleged traitors to the Reich. Since she was the Widow Jurcza now, she no longer had the considerable influence of her husband to protect her.

Then came the Texan. His name was Frederick Naumann, and according to what Elisabethe had heard whispered among the servants, he had once lived near and he and her mother had been in love. But their families had driven them apart because she was Catholic and he was Lutheran, an unacceptable faith, the awful spawn of Martin Luther—Godless in the eyes of many Catholics, including her mother's family. It was said by the servants that they would not be accepted in Heaven when they died. When it was forbidden for the two young lovers to be together, Frederick had taken his broken heart to America where he worked as a surveyor and lived the life of a cowboy in Texas and Mexico.

Now he was back. His old friend, Julius Schievelbein, had written to him of Maria Theresa's plight, "Your old girlfriend is a widow. She and her child are in peril."

After so many years Frederick Nauman had come to rescue the woman he loved. On the night of his arrival, Elisabethe listened as the priest, the burgomeister, Frederick and her mother discussed the plan of escape. "We can't just leave," her mother said. "So much has changed. Only two years since Joseph's death, and the country is at war, in chaos, my family, my friends are threatened. . . . We have no papers to get out. We'll be stopped at the border."

"There is a way, though," the burgomeister said.

"How?" Maria Theresa asked, her eyes wide.

"Tell her, Frederick." Their friend was hiding a smile behind his hand.

"Well," Frederick said. "You know I have always loved you, and I want you to be my wife. Come home with me to Seguin. In America we can be a family."

Maria Theresa collapsed into a chair. For several seconds she looked at Frederick, not quite meeting his eyes. Before she could speak, he said, "Maybe you'll learn to love me again. I'll be a good father to Elisabethe."

Maria Theresa looked at the priest for consent. "Father?"

"There are many roads to God," the priest said. "The important thing is not which road you take, but that you make the journey."

A few days later, the Texan and the Widow Jurcza were married in the new Catholic church in Bernau.

Elisabethe would remember the journey to the seaport of Bremen for the rest of her life. The roads were filled with refugees fleeing Bismarck's armies. They saw young men torn from their families and conscripted into the Army to fight the Austrians, leaving mothers pleading for the return of their sons. The terrified refugees moved on in a human flood toward Bremen and the ships that would take them to safety.

As they traveled, Elisabethe was torn between her two fathers: the one who had been at the center of her life for so long and this stranger she found she was beginning to love. Sometimes she felt guilty that her affections could move so easily from one to the other. But as time went by she could see that her mother, too, was growing more and more comfortable with Frederick Naumann. He was handsome, in a rough sort of way, lanky, with hair the color of wheat, and hazel eyes. In the months before their departure, he told stories of how life in Texas would be. Their home would be in Seguin, a town where there were many Germans, where German was spoken in the homes and schools, a place where they would be safe and free. "No young men will be taken from their families there, like those poor boys we saw back on the road."

Frederick told them how the Germans kept neat farms and had refused to get involved in the War Between the States. He said the Confederates came home in rags and lived in poverty in the war's aftermath. The Germans mocked them and called them Raggedies, he said.

"But now we live in peace. There are places along the Guadalupe River," he said, "where the stars are so bright you can read a book by their light. And they seem to come down close to the Earth. Sometimes I think you could almost climb them, hand over hand, like a ladder, all the way to Heaven."

Not only was Elisabethe falling in love with her new father, she was falling in love with Seguin.

When they arrived at the dock in Bremen, Elisabethe saw a remarkable thing. Through the crowd of refugees, a magnificent carriage came. It was pulled by four identical black horses and on its door was the crest of the Royal Hannoverian Court. As it drew near, the horses, frightened by the crowd, bolted, and the carriage careened into Frederick's wagon, breaking its axle.

A tall man in a dark suit stepped down from the carriage, seeking assurance that no one was hurt and ordering his footmen to help repair the wheel. He introduced himself as Emil Bergfeld and then introduced his wife, Antonie, and his son Arthur.

Elisabethe had never seen a boy as beautiful as Arthur Bergfeld. He was nearly as tall as his father, and when he had stepped from the carriage, she felt he was a prince stepping from a folk tale or a legend. As their parents talked, Elisabethe learned from Arthur that his father was The Royal Imperial Treasurer to the Blind Prince of Hannover.

"Where are you going?" Arthur asked, and Elisabethe was flattered that a beautiful story-book prince would show any interest in her. But his eyes were steady, his interest clear.

"Texas," she said.

"Wonderful!" he said, with obvious enthusiasm. "I envy you. What an adventure. I've always wanted to visit Texas."

"Actually, it's a town called Seguin. Lots of Germans live there. There are fields of flowers, much like Germany."

"Tell me more about Seguin, maybe I can go there someday."

Elisabethe repeated some of the stories Frederick had told on their journey. "There are places near Seguin, on the Guadalupe River, where the stars are so bright you can read by their light. And they hang so low in the sky that you'd think you could climb them like a ladder, hand over hand, all the way to Heaven."

Elisabethe and Arthur talked until the wheel was fixed, and the two families parted. As the carriage pulled away, someone in the crowd asked who young Bergfeld was.

"Der Jüde," came the reply. It was spoken like a curse.

VII.

Abilene, Texas.
September 1917

Once again the courtroom was packed. For several days now, a parade of prosecution witnesses had catalogued the many treasonous acts of Will Bergfeld and the other members of the Farmers' and Laborers' Protective Association, the secret organization that had allegedly schemed to overthrow the government of the United States. Louise Bergfeld Tewes listened to them with a sinking heart and rising anger. Even though Defense Attorney Atwell was able to diminish the veracity or the relevance of the testimony, the sheer weight of the accusations was more than damning. The witnesses seemed to be playing parts, reading lines provided them by the prosecution. Not that they were lying or encouraged to lie, but they were making an obvious effort to say what the public wanted to hear. After all, America was now at war with Germany, her sons were in harm's way, and all good Americans must do their part.

One of those good Americans was now swearing that he would tell the truth, the whole truth and nothing but the truth. His name was Spec Davis, a farmer and former member of the Farmers' and Laborers' Protective Association.

After a few preliminary questions, Prosecutor O'Dell asked him when he had joined the FLPA.

"About the middle of August 1916." He spoke slowly, directing his answers to the jury, as he had probably been instructed. But Louise thought his responses seemed unnatural, studied, not at all the personal contact with jurors that O'Dell had surely hoped.

"Was there an initiation?"

"Yes, sir, there was."

"I understand the first part of the initiation was to take an oath. Can you repeat that oath for the jury?

"Well, we were all called around, a half dozen or so at a time, and we placed our hands upon the Bible, then on a knife, a six-shooter and a whip. Then we placed both hands on the Bible again and repeated the oath. I can't recollect it exactly, but the substance of it was that we were to protect the life, limb and property of the members of the organization to the best of our ability, even to the loss of our own life."

"Was there anything concerning secrecy in the obligation?"

"Well, yes. We swore to keep secret all the business, the words and obligations of the Lodge. We should keep secret all books, papers, passwords, signs and so forth."

O'Dell walked away from the witness stand and asked the next question to the jury. "Tell, me, Mr. Davis, what was the penalty if you violated that sworn oath?"

"Death." The word was spoken, but it drew a soft collective murmur from the spectators.

"Do you recall the specific words regarding the penalty of death?"

Davis spoke almost apologetically. "A man that was a traitor to the organization or Lodge should have his goddamn head cut off and kicked at his dead ass. That was the words."

Again, a murmur from the crowd broken by a scattering of laughter.

The prosecutor asked, "Who spoke those words?"

"Mr. Bryant."

"The defendant G. T. Bryant?"

"Yes, sir."

"Would you rise and point out the man who spoke those words at your initiation?"

Spec Davis rose and indicated Bryant among the defendants. "He's right there. The man with the red tie."

Louise had met Bryant several times. He was one of the three national officers of the FLPA. He and the other two—Risley and Powell—had led the organization of the new lodges. Will had been taken with all three of them. He felt they were the kind of men who could save the country from Rockefeller. She remembered Bryant as a rather sophisticated man and doubted he would have used such language except to ingratiate himself with the tough-minded locals.

O'Dell said, "Let the record show that the witness has indicated the defendant G. T. Bryant." Then, following a pause, he asked, "After the oath, was there a lecture or talk?"

"Yes, sir. By Mr. Bryant."

"Tell us what it was."

"Mr. Bryant told us that we'd been run over, that is we had been stomped on by the government or by the capitalist class. And he went on to say that laboring men—I remember him naming places like Ludlow, Colorado and Arkansas—where helpless men, women and children had been shot down by United States soldiers. And he told us to arm ourselves. That we should arm ourselves with high-powered rifles."

"What else did Mr. Bryant say in his lecture?"

"He said we weren't going to fight in this war that was being forced on us, and if we were forced to fight, 'Shoot the goddamned son of a bitch that gave you the gun and return home as quickly as possible.'"

"Thank you, Mr. Davis," O'Dell said. "Your witness, Mr. Atwell."

When Atwell approached the witness he was smiling, as if he were amused at something the witness had said. "Mr. Davis, you said that a man who was a traitor should have his head cut off and kicked at his dead butt?" There was a tittering of laughter from the spectators. Several jurors smiled.

"Yes, that is absolutely what he said."

"Isn't it true that this Irishman Bryant was just making a joke when he said this?"

Davis squirmed in his chair. "I didn't take it that way."

Atwell grinned at the jury. "It seems to amuse some of us here. It is a bit tasteless, but actually quite funny. Did you hear any laughter when Mr. Bryant made that joking comment?"

"I didn't take it as a joke."

"You say it was part of the obligation? Those very words. That a traitor should have his head cut off and kicked at his dead butt?"

"Dead ass."

"I stand corrected. Kicked at his dead ass."

"I swear to that."

"But you also swore never to reveal those words. You know, Mr. Davis, your testimony today violates the sworn oath you took with your hand on the Bible at the initiation. Which is the true oath? The one you swore then or the one you swear now?"

O'Dell objected. "The question is argumentative. Counsel is badgering the witness."

Judge Jack sustained the objection, but he was still smiling at the alleged punishment for revealing Lodge secrets. Louise secretly applauded the clever way Atwell was handling this witness.

Defense Attorney Atwell stood next to the jury, his hand to his chin as if deep in thought.

"Now, Mr. Davis," he asked, "did you hold a position in the Lodge?"

"Yes, sir. I was secretary."

"Did you keep the minutes?"

"Yes, sir."

"As secretary, it was your duty to write down everything that happened at those meetings, isn't that right?"

"Yes, sir."

"Did you write down everything?"

"Yes, sir."

"Is there anything in those minutes that would indicate the Lodge was doing anything illegal?"

"I don't think so."

"Do they say you were conspiring against the United States?

"I was not."

"But you were a member and an officer in the organization?"

"I was."

"Did you agree to offer aid to the German Government? Is that in your notes?"

"No, sir."

"Did you agree to levy war against the United States?"

"I did not."

"Did you agree with anybody to blow up bridges or railroads?"

"No, sir."

"Or kill a conscription officer?"

"No, sir, I did not."

"But as secretary of the organization, if such things were planned, you would know about them and it would have been your duty to write them into the minutes, isn't that so?"

"I suppose."

"Then if we really want to know the truth about what happened at the meetings, all we need to do is read your minutes of what transpired, isn't that right?"

"Yes, sir."

"Where are the minutes?"

"I don't know."

"At your home?"

"They were, but I can't find them now."

"Do you think they have been destroyed?"

"I don't know."

"So all you know is that your minutes that would reflect everything that went on at the meetings are now missing and you don't have the faintest idea where they are, is that right?"

"Yes, sir."

"Did the prosecutors ever see your minutes or ask for them?"

"I think so. Two federal investigators came by my house and took them to the U.S. Attorney."

"Oh really," Atwell exclaimed, genuinely surprised. "Did they return the minutes to you?"

"I think so. But I can't find them."

"So the last time you can be sure you had these written records of these meetings was when you released them to be turned over to the prosecutors?"

"I think that's right."

"Were you afraid or worried about showing the minutes to the government prosecutors?

"No, sir."

"The reason you were so willing to turn all these papers over to the federal officers is that you knew there was nothing incriminating in them, isn't that right?"

"That's exactly right."

"About how many meetings did you attend where you took minutes as secretary?

"About fifteen or twenty."

"Tell me this, Mr. Davis. Would you go to meeting after meeting after meeting, and indeed serve as an officer of an organization that was engaged in criminal activity?"

"No, sir."

"Would you have continued to participate as a member and officer of the FLPA organization if you thought it was conspiring against the United States?

"No, sir."

"Or offering aid to Germany?

"No, sir."

"Or planning to kill conscription officers?"

"No, sir."

"Or planning to blow up bridges and railroads?"

"No, sir"

"Or advocating the assassination of President Wilson?"

"No, sir."

Atwell turned to the judge. "That's all I have for this witness, Your Honor."

It seemed to Louise that there was a subtle shift of mood within the courtroom. The hostility was still there, but she could tell that Atwell was gaining some emotional ground among the jurors and the spectators. In a way it was surprising, because with the rose in his lapel and his bow tie and dapper manner he was in such powerful contrast to the others. But what she sensed was that they were beginning to like him. He was like your favorite teacher in school, a person with superior knowledge, experience and understanding who was also approachable. He commanded your respect, but also offered respect in return. And she loved the way he had managed to get the jurors to smile. To maintain a sense of humor within the framework of such a deadly serious matter is a virtue Texans admire. She noticed O'Dell seemed a little less cocky as he called his next witness.

Oscar Lewis was a farmer who lived about six miles northwest of Weinert. He was a tall man with narrow shoulders and a thin face that held a half-smile, as if perpetually amused at the world and the human condition. He walked on the balls of his feet, loose-jointed, his long arms dangling. He reminded Louise of a praying mantis. As he settled into the witness chair, his smile widened and he looked around as if suddenly surprised and pleased that his audience was so large and attentive.

After determining that Mr. Lewis was a member of the Farmers' and Laborers' Protective Association, O'Dell pressed again for testimony about the secret initiation rites.

"When were you initiated into the FLPA, Mr. Lewis?"

"It was in May of this year. In Haskell."

"Was that before or after the Cisco meeting?"

"It was after."

"Who initiated you, Mr. Lewis?"

"Will Bergfeld."

"And were you pleased to become a member?"

"Not really."

"Could you explain to the jury what you mean?"

"I wasn't all that eager to join. Bergfeld had been after me for some time. He was after a lot of the boys around Haskell County."

"Did Mr. Bergfeld threaten you?"

"Yes, sir. He came to me and said I wouldn't be worth a hill of beans if I didn't join up. I didn't join and he came to me again and said if I didn't come to the next meeting and join he would wipe my name off the map of the United States."

"Did Mr. Bergfeld ever use the term 'fishing'?"

"Yes, sir. He said that would happen to you if you ever revealed Lodge secrets. They'd take you fishing."

"And what did you take that to mean?"

"It meant they'd take you out and kill you."

A chorus of coughs and conversation came from the gallery. A baby began to cry and reluctantly the mother carried it from the room.

"So, Mr. Lewis, you were understandably concerned for your safety if you did not do as Bergfeld asked, is that right?"

Atwell sprang to his feet. "Objection! He is leading the witness, Your Honor."

"Sustained," pronounced Judge Jack.

"At that meeting in Haskell where you were finally forced to join, did Mr. Bergfeld say anything else that reflected a violent nature?" O'Dell asked this question as if he had not heard the judge's ruling.

Bill Atwell rose again. "He is still leading the witness. And Mr. Lewis is not a psychologist. He cannot evaluate a man's nature."

Judge Jack looked at Mr. O'Dell over his glasses. "Just ask the witness what Mr. Bergfeld said, Mr. O'Dell."

"After the initiation, do you recall what Mr. Bergfeld said about the draft?"

"He said that if the conscription officer came we were to turn around and shoot him."

Louise noticed the jurors lean forward.

"Did he use the word conscription? Let's be careful as we can about that."

"That's the way I caught it."

"If the conscription officer came, to turn around and shoot him?"

"That's what he said."

O'Dell thanked the witness and walked to his chair, scowling, shaking his head at the thought that such awful things could go on in the world.

As Atwell approached the witness, he studied the notes he had made of Lewis's testimony. Then he looked at him, studied his face until the witness looked away. Only then did he ask his first question.

"Mr. Lewis, have you ever been fishing?"

"Yeah, lots of times."

"Have family members or friends ever offered to take you fishing?"

"Yes, sir. My neighbor Moe Short and my brother Tibb, they ask me all the time."

"Did you ever think that Moe Short and your brother Tibb's offer to take you fishing meant that they were going to take you out and kill you?"

"No, I didn't have no reason to think that."

"Mr. Lewis, you have told us about the meeting at Haskell. Did you consider it an important and memorable meeting?"

"Yes, sir."

"And at that important and memorable meeting, you heard Mr. Bergfeld say if a conscription officer came after you to turn around and shoot him, isn't that so?"

"Yes, sir."

"What were his words as near as you can tell?"

"I told you. That if the conscription officers came for us we should turn around and shoot them."

"You will swear he said that, will you?"

"Certainly I will."

Atwell continued. "What else did Mr. Bergfeld say on that important and memorable night?"

"That was about it."

"Nothing else?"

"Nothing I can recollect."

"But you do remember his exact words when he said you should turn around and shoot the conscription officers, isn't that right?"

"Yes, sir."

"By the way, were you present there for the entire meeting at Haskell?"

"Yes, I was."

"How long did it last?"

"About three hours."

"Didn't Mr. Bergfeld say he had been to a meeting in Cisco?"

"Not that I remember."

"Wasn't the purpose of that meeting to report to the Haskell Lodge what had happened at the Cisco meeting?"

"I don't think so."

"Isn't it true that Mr. Bergfeld made a long report on the organization of a farmer's cooperative, a way to obtain better prices for your crops?"

"I don't remember that. No, sir."

"And isn't it so that Mr. Bergfeld talked about the establishment of FLPA stores where you could purchase seeds and equipment without paying an exorbitant markup to middlemen?

"He may have said something about it, but I don't recall it."

"Will you swear before this jury that he didn't talk about a meeting in Cisco and report what happened there?"

"I don't remember."

Atwell sighed heavily, turned to face the jury, hoping they shared his astonishment that Lewis's memory was so selective.

"Now tell us what you remember Mr. Bergfeld said down there at Haskell that night."

"He said we should shoot any conscription officers that came."

"That is all you can remember? A three-hour meeting. One of the most important meetings you've ever been to. Out of all that happened and all that was said on that memorable night, you want this jury to believe that you only remember that one thing you claim Mr. Bergfeld said?"

"Yes, sir."

"I have no further questions for this witness," Bill Atwell said, and the witness was excused.

A Texas Ranger walked Virginia and Will back to the boarding house where they were staying for the tenure of the trial. By now the crowds that shadowed the defendants' every move had thinned. But still, leaving the courthouse at the end of the day was like running a gauntlet through ranks of reporters, redneck ruffians, hucksters, curious children and pompous townspeople who considered themselves riding the high horse of history. Virginia tried to close her mind to the commotion around them, avoiding eye contact, clinging to Will's arm. She wondered why ordinary people could be so changed by a drama that had so little to do with themselves. At another time, these were people she might have liked. But now she saw them as the enemy. She wondered if she was being changed by the trial. Would she be a different person when it all was over?

When the girls were asleep, Virginia watched Will reading. She had always been amazed how he could lose himself in a book, his attention absolutely riveted on the pages. During the trial he had been reading *The Social Contract* by Jean Jacques Rousseau. She had learned about Rousseau in school and knew that his writings had influenced the French Revolution. In the dim light she could imagine the ideas of Rousseau streaming from the pages into Will's mind. She envied Rousseau his conversation with her husband. *Could it all be true, then? Had Will been preparing for revolution all these years? A new American Revolution? How could that be?* This was her Will. The grown wild boy who did magic tricks for his children and tinkered with the motor of his motorcycle and who sometimes accompanied the sunset on his grandmother's violin. He was an unknown rural mail carrier in a small Texas town in the middle of nowhere. *How could such a man even find time to be a revolutionary?*

For the past few days, she had sensed a strain between them. The evenings were filled with long silences. He read long into the night and when he came to bed she was usually asleep, or pretending to be. Now, as she watched him read, she knew if they did not talk, something would be forever changed between them.

"Will."

He continued to read, oblivious to everyone and anything but

Rousseau and his demand for equality among men.

"Will, please!"

He looked up and smiled. As usual when confronted by Will's smile, her heart did a small dance in her breast and she thought, *Let it be, accept him as he is and trust that when the trial is over everything will be all right again.* But she knew she could not let it go.

"Tell me about Anna," she whispered.

"Anna?" He seemed truly surprised. "What about Anna?"

"Tell me what everyone but me seems to know."

Will looked at her for a moment with those dark Bergfeld eyes, then looked down. After turning down the corner of the page, Will closed the book. He closed his eyes for a moment, then asked, "What do you want to know?"

"Have you been intimate?"

"I think you must know. I was very young and inexperienced. She was attractive and I must say available. She was more experienced and it was new to me. I was flattered that she was interested in me. Yes, we were intimate. But that was a long time ago."

"But not before I met you."

"No. But you lived in another world. Daughter of the prominent Henry King. It was you I really wanted all the time. But you lived in that big house on Court Street. It took a long time for me to work up the courage."

"What about now? These last few years? You never spoke her name."

"I saw Anna every day. I delivered her mail."

"Tell me the truth!"

Will stood and moved to the window. In a way, Virginia was glad she would not have to look in his eyes when he answered. But he did not answer.

"Your Honor," he said instead, "counsel is badgering the witness." Then he turned. "Don't you see how unfair this is, Virginia? I've spent the last weeks being accused of crimes I didn't commit. I was accused of treason when the things they accuse me of happened even before war was declared. Now I'm being accused of being unfaithful for something that happened before we were married! It's not right."

He came to her, reached for her, but she stepped away. "Why won't you answer me, Will? Why won't you tell me what happened in Cisco? Why won't you tell me what happened in Ludlow? Why won't you tell me what's in your mind? Why won't you tell me if the things they are saying in the courtroom are true? Why won't you tell me about Anna?" Virginia did not cry and she was amazed that her voice and body were under control even though she felt she was coming unraveled.

"I love you, Virginia."

"That's not what I asked."

Will sighed, returned to his chair, removed the book and sat heavily down. For a moment, he pressed his hands to his forehead, then looked up into her eyes.

"I have not touched Anna Bennett in nearly seven years. She was a rite of passage. I have spoken to her, yes. I delivered her mail."

"Do you speak to her about things you don't speak to me about?" *That was it*, she thought. *That is where Will goes to unburden his heart, to his soul mate.* Somehow that seemed worse than if their relationship was still purely physical.

"Virginia, I'm not going to swear. I am only going to say that we rarely speak at all. I don't even think she likes me. I get the definite impression she doesn't. Whoever is telling you these things is a liar. Somebody else out to get me."

Virginia sighed and stepped behind Will's chair. Before she realized what she was doing, she reached down and touched his shoulder. "What about Cisco? What about the testimony in court?"

"Everything you've heard from the prosecution is true," he said and she removed her hand. "To a degree. But nothing they say I did was a crime. They say I urged the men to arm themselves. In Ludlow, friends of mine were killed by Rockefeller's henchmen. Twenty union miners and their families murdered, machine-gunned in their tents. Do you think I want my union people to go unarmed? Don't you think it is natural and right for them to be able to defend themselves against murderers, some of them government officers and National Guardsmen?" Will was pacing now. Virginia had seen it before, his efforts to control his emotions when his anger began to boil over, his frustrations with a world he saw that she could not know.

Will walked to the window, looked out, his arms wrapped tightly around his chest as if to keep what he felt inside from coming out. "Do you really want me to tell you about these things? The dark things. The hate I feel. How I sometimes hate myself for that hate I have that won't go away! Do you really want to know these things?"

Virginia moved to the window and leaned against his back. "Yes, Will, I do. I need to know. I need to know what tortures you. It's the only way I can be more than just the mother of your children. You say you love me. But you must not respect me or you would tell me what troubles you so. Maybe it's time. Open yourself to me. Let me in, Will. I pray that you let me in."

Will turned and they embraced. She could hear his heart.

Across the street, beneath a dark canopy of elm, the man called Grimes watched the watchers. The government agents worked in teams, night and day, recording every move that Bergfeld made, not just during the period of the trial, but long before. They were cold-eyed, faceless men selected from some deep layer of bureaucracy in the Secret Service. Grimes watched from the shadows, wondering about the nature of justice and those who claim to serve it. He had studied Bergfeld's file carefully, a file compiled by the Secret Service, and he had read again the testimony at the Grand Jury. *Bergfeld and I have much in common. We both seek justice, but in order to find it, we both have broken laws. If Bergfeld is guilty,* Grimes thought, *and he may well be, his guilt was established by unjust means. Truth had been withheld from the prosecution. O'Dell has never seen the report of the investigation of Mrs. Thurwanger, for instance, or even of Anna Bennett's.* Grimes knew these reports had never seen the light of day. *Normally the prosecution leads the investigation, but in this case the investigation is lead-*

ing the prosecution, offering only that evidence that points to Bergfeld's guilt. If Bergfeld is guilty, Grimes thought, as he watched one of the agents draw on a cigarette cupped in his hand, *then I am just as guilty.*

Now he saw the agents leaning forward and he knew they were watching Bergfeld and his wife embracing in the window. Grimes felt a blush of shame as he watched, but he could not tear his eyes away. He envied the passion reflected there, what seemed a kind of desperation in their holding to each other in that lighted room. He wished they would move away or turn out the light so that the watchers could not see. Then the shade came down and two silhouettes, arm in arm, moved away, leaving an orange oblong in the night.

In an upstairs hall of the same Abilene boarding house, Louise Bergfeld Tewes listened on the telephone to the gruff, guttural voice of her father as he said cruel words she certainly did not want to hear. She was horrified that he refused to speak English and she could imagine what someone on the party line might think hearing the language of their enemy. She reminded him that a law had been recently passed against speaking German, but he was too stubborn and contrary to care. She imagined the large, robust man, sitting alone in the half-dark among his chemicals and beakers and German periodicals, his eyes filled with mysteries and, sometimes, she thought, with madness. It crossed her mind that her father was a stranger, had always been ever since she and Will were children. He spent his time with his pharmaceuticals and his experiments and the few old men he met each noon. Now, when they needed him most, when Will desperately needed the support of his father, he refused to come to the trial. She knew Will would never ask him to come, much less beg, but she also knew he was deeply hurt by his father's absence.

"You must come, Papa! Will needs you. I need you. Think how it looks. A father turns his back on his son!"

"I have my reasons," Arthur Bergfeld said in German.

"Speak English, Papa. The walls have ears."

"I speak German because I am German. It is my native language. I will not be bullied by frightened fools."

"Why won't you come?"

"You must know. I just told you. I am German through and through. I still have ties to the Old Country. I am the enemy of the people who would destroy Will. So I protect him by staying away."

Louise was thankful now that he was speaking German. And she wondered what he meant by Old Country ties. She shivered. But one thing that eased her mind was that no man on earth despised Otto Bismarck more. "You won't come?" she asked again.

"I will not!"

"So you are going to abandon us once again," she said, and she hung up the receiver, leaving Arthur Bergfeld alone in the half-light among his chemicals and his secrets.

VIII.

Berlin, Germany.
December 1881

Arthur Bergfeld had worked late into the night memorizing the periodic table of elements developed by Mendeleyev a few years before. He had worked alone in the chemistry lab at the University of Berlin. At midnight, he washed his hands, removed his fur coat from the student's cloakroom, turned out the light, nodded to the watchman at the door, then moved out into the snow.

He walked a few blocks along Unter den Linden, then north toward the River Spree where the diplomats lived near the Jewish Quarter, the beating heart of the old city. It was snowing, the flakes large and moist, and the mansions and embassies along the avenue loomed from the white gloom like ghosts. Most of the houses were dark, but here and there he could see the light of chandeliers, small golden constellations, within the lower rooms. There was no sign of life in the mansions nor along the street beneath the naked linden trees. It was not a time for Jews to be walking alone in the dead of night, certainly not since March when Czar Alexander II had been assassinated as he returned from the Winter Palace in St. Petersburg. In order to forget for awhile the troubled times, Arthur focused his mind on chemistry and its welcome absolutes. He thought about Scandium, the last element discovered, and he wondered how many other elements remained hidden in the physical world and if, perhaps, the basic components of nature were incalculable, infinitely divisible, like the mind of God.

He was surprised to see lights blooming from the windows of his house and the soft silhouettes of carriages in the falling snow. He supposed his father had returned early from his travels with the Blind Prince. Eagerly, he moved toward the light.

He knew what had happened the moment he entered the house. His father's closest friends stood in a motionless tableau, hands folded, eyes filled with both rage and sorrow. Antonie Bergfeld was seated, one hand cupped over her eyes as if shading her face from the sun. Although there were fires burning in the grate, Arthur felt cold. Then his mother stepped forward, placed both hands on Arthur's shoulders and told him his father was dead, killed while protecting the Blind Prince during an assassination attempt.

"He died boldly," she said. "Just as he lived."

Shocked, feeling weak and sick, Arthur embraced his mother, then helped her to a sofa.

When they were alone, Antonie stood, then moved to the fireplace.

"Arthur, I know you understand the danger you are in. The new leaders who are coming into power will be after all men who might be loyal to the prince. The men who killed your father could be on their way here now. You must leave immediately. Get out of Germany. Go to America. God willing, I will someday follow you there. Gott hilft uns."

In almost total silence, Arthur packed for his journey. Antonie had given him all the money she could find in the house and insisted he take his violin.

A month after Arthur arrived in New York, he received a letter from his mother. The paper made a sound like a sigh as he slit the envelope and removed the letter. He recognized his mother's large, disciplined hand. He held the letter for a long time, knowing what was inside could only break his heart.

He read the letter by the light of the afternoon sun as he sat by the window in his one-room apartment.

Liebe Sohn,

First, you must know that I love you beyond all measure, and I have loved you since that first moment I felt you move in my womb. How happy you made me then.

You must know that I have always cherished your presence and I miss you terribly now. Insisting that you leave was the most difficult thing I have ever done. I have wondered if it was any less difficult for the mother of Moses to hide away her son from the Pharaoh. Throughout history mothers have kept their sons alive by giving them up. Sometimes love demands letting go of the object of that love.

But now I am going to ask you to do something even more difficult. You must, for the sake of your life, erase from your mind who you are. You must forget you are a Jew, forget all of our history, the life we've led, our Jewish ways. To honor your father, you may keep your name. But you must change your religion. If you remain a Jew, hatred will follow you wherever you go. To remain a Jew is to be a target for the rest of your life. It would be to condemn the family you will eventually have in America to a life of running and hiding and fear. I suggest you become a Lutheran like so many other Germans in America. It matters not what it says above the altar, only what it says in your heart.

Will I see you again? Who knows what fate has in store. But for the moment, for the foreseeable future, we must be together only in our thoughts and our prayers. And I would say this, my son. Love God and listen to your conscience and you will be all your father and I wished you to be. How proud I am of you. How blessed I am to have such a son.

Remember me and feel my love over the miles and years.

The letter was signed in that same strong hand. Arthur Bergfeld read the letter until it was too dark to make out the words. Finally, he folded it carefully, closed his eyes and looked out over the rooftops of his new home.

IX.

Abilene, Texas.
September 1917

Bettie King had always awakened with a prayer of praise for the day. "This is the day the Lord Hath made," she would whisper as she climbed out of bed. "Rejoice and be glad in it." Then she would stride into the morning with full resolve and a high heart. There was nothing the day could bring, no problem, no obstacle, that could not be swept away by good humor, good sense and good manners. But on this morning, the start of the second week of Will's trial, she could not shake the feeling that there was something she had forgotten to do, some responsibility she had failed to meet. For one thing, she was homesick. She had seldom been away from Seguin this long and she missed her rose garden, the front porch and the familiar sights and sounds along Court Street. She wondered if the chickens were being fed, the plants watered, and who was looking after Peachtree now that she and Will, his only friends, were gone. She was also, for the first time, feeling a growing helplessness, a sense that her family was being assailed by ominous forces that she was powerless to combat; forces that seemed immune to good humor, good sense and good manners. It was, of course, the war and the almost joyous hysteria it was generating on the streets and in the public mind. It was almost, she thought, as though people were eager for America to join the French and the British in the trenches, eager for the great blood rite to shatter the complacency and monotony of their lives. She missed her son George, who was away at Texas A&M, and she refused to think about the fact that he would soon be going off to this same war that people seemed so eager to join.

Since arriving in Abilene, it had been her habit to go for an early morning walk, to drink in the sights and fragrances of an unfamiliar town. This morning was no exception, and as she wandered through the neighborhoods she came to a small frame schoolhouse that had been defaced by vandals. Someone had painted in large letters "DEATH TO WOBBLIES AND HUNS." The sentiment itself did not surprise her. After all, for months the newspapers had been filled with the most awful tirades against Socialists and German-Americans. What surprised and saddened her was that the words had been painted on the schoolhouse a week before and no one, not teacher, not parent, had had the decency to remove them. Now, each morning, as the children came to school, each recess, at noon, and again when they went home in the afternoon, the words remained there to poison their young minds.

When Bettie reached the Grace Hotel, there was a newsboy opening a small newstand by the entrance. He reminded her of Peachtree, the same tattered clothes, the same wild and wary eyes. The headlines of his newspapers read: "More Doughboys Off To France." But it was another front-page story that made her wonder if this really was a day the Lord hath made. It was about a young German-American man named Robert Prager who had been seized by a crowd, stripped of his clothes, bound with a piece of cloth torn from bandstand bunting, then lynched in front of five hundred or more people. The story had been first reported some time ago. This morning the newspaper reported the results of the trial of the alleged leaders of the mob that murdered the boy. The jury deliberated twenty minutes before acquitting each of them.

Bettie could see people on the porch of the hotel reading the story. By mid-morning it would be the talk of the town and she wondered how it would affect Will's jury. Would they applaud the twisted patriotism of that distant jury, or would they feel shame at the miscarriage of justice? Bettie wanted to purchase all the newspapers on the stand, then destroy them so good people could not see how terribly flawed God's children had turned out to be. But she only purchased one paper from the boy, then returned through town to the boarding house.

She sat down with the paper on the porch swing. She felt a bit ashamed, as if she were afraid someone would catch her reading a racy novel or someone else's diary. If the daily newspaper was a sort of journal of society, then she was in fact eavesdropping, for certainly it was not her diary, and the people and events upon its pages were as foreign to her as creatures and happenings on the moon. How could people created in God's image be so insanely cruel to each other? She read about scientists devoted to the creation of poison gases, one gas so deadly that it would "render soil barren for seven years and a few drops on a tree trunk would cause a tree to completely wither within an hour."

Now, a terrible feeling of helplessness settled over Bettie, a kind of vertigo. She wondered if she would faint, something she had never done a single time in her life. Then she knew she had been touched by some subtle harbinger of death. She began to realize that it was quite possible Will would be executed. That his death would be real. That he would be taken to the gallows and hanged. Perhaps it was the unbidden image of the gallows and Will standing there that had summoned her dreadful malaise. Then she felt, rather than saw, an image of her son George, in his uniform, moving through the trenches. *How different they are from one another, Will and George,* she thought. *One outspoken and unpredictable, the other quiet and gentle; the one dark, the other fair; one hating the war, the other seeing service as his duty. But now both might well be facing death, one on the gallows, the other in the trenches.*

I know death is not final, she thought. *When we die we are not condemned to eternal darkness. Some part of us lives on in some way in some place. I believe that with all my heart, mind and soul. But I really don't understand how it happens. If Will dies, what will happen to Virginia and the little girls? What will happen to all the love between them? Is it their love that lasts forever? I don't fear my own death, but I am overwhelmed by fear of the death of loved ones who are just getting started with their lives. Please God, keep these boys safe. And give me the strength and the faith to overcome this fear.*

Bettie heard someone coming down the stairs. She felt feverish, weakened by her fears. Quickly she folded the paper and tucked it beneath the cushion. War had come. A war as terrible as any the world has ever known. And Will was at the front lines. George soon would be. As she moved to the dining room where the family would have a breakfast of grits, eggs, ham, gravy and biscuits, she prayed that the slaughter of American boys in the trenches would not begin at all, but if it had to begin, not until after Will's trial was over.

Prosecutor O'Dell had apparently not been depressed by the morning's news. He seemed in high good humor as he called his first witness, G. T. Hughes, an affable, portly man with a round, pleasant face and comfortable manner. O'Dell and Hughes went through the preliminary questions like good old friends chatting on the front porch until O'Dell noticed Judge Jack beginning to fidget. Atwell was curious why his adversary seemed so charged with energy and good will. Except for the devastating testimony of Ned Earl Calhoun, the first witness, Atwell scored the defense and prosecution at about even. There had been no other huge surprises. But now he sensed that O'Dell had something up his sleeve. With what seemed towering confidence, O'Dell asked Mr. Hughes if he were a member of the Farmers' and Laborers' Protective Association.

"Yes, sir, I am," Hughes replied.

"Did you attend a meeting of that organization in Cisco, Texas, on May fifth of this year?"

"Yes, sir."

"In what capacity did you attend that meeting?"

"I was a member of the Cisco Lodge. We hosted the meeting and I was assigned by the president of the Lodge to make sure everything ran smoothly and that all the delegates had everything they needed."

"How many delegates attended that meeting?"

"About one hundred. They represented lodges from all over Texas."

"Can you tell the jury the purpose of that Cisco meeting?"

"Well, we had just declared war on Germany. Congress was debating the Selective Draft Act. And a lot of our members were against the war and against conscription. So the meeting was called to study what our stand would be. What we would do if the bill was signed by the President."

"Do you recall certain resolutions having been passed there?"

"Yes, sir. There were twelve or thirteen resolutions in all."

"Who was on the resolutions committee?"

"Mr. Webb and Mr. Bergfeld and Mr. Cathart."

"Who was chairman of the resolutions committee?"

"Mr. Bergfeld."

Prosecutor O'Dell moved to face the defendants. "Can you point to Mr. Bergfeld in the courtroom?"

"Yes, sir. That's him there," Hughes said, pointing directly at Will.

"Mr. Hughes, were you acquainted with Mr. Bergfeld at the time?"

"I knew him by reputation, but I hadn't met him."

"Was Mr. Bergfeld known for a series of speeches he made at lodge meetings around Texas?"

"Yes, sir."

"Can you tell us the general theme of these speeches?"

"He was against the war. Against conscription. He felt the rich and powerful were going to make cannon fodder out of the poor."

"I object, Your Honor." Atwell called, lurching from his seat. "If Mr. Hughes had never met Mr. Bergfeld, then he couldn't have been present at those speeches. If he wasn't present, he couldn't have heard their contents. Therefore his response is hearsay and inadmissible."

"Thank you for the lengthy explanation, Counselor," Judge Jack said. "A simple objection will do."

"I do so object," Atwell said, hoping that Judge Jack would

mellow as the day progressed.

"Your objection is sustained," the judge ruled.

O'Dell continued. "Mr. Hughes, of the twelve to thirteen resolutions proposed at the meeting, did one of them have to do with allowing women into the organization?"

"Yes. It was presented by Mr. Bergfeld. He said that women were laboring people just like men, especially telephone and telegraph operators."

"Did he specifically mention telephone and telegraph operators?"

"Yes, sir. It had to do with the secret code."

"Tell us about the secret code and what it had to do with the women?"

"Mr. Bergfeld wanted to assign members numbers instead of names. If any member needed help or was in trouble, or in case of a revolt or uprising, members could communicate anonymously through the women operators. The operators could also listen in on calls between government agents, conscription officers or soldiers and then alert members of their plans."

"And who introduced this resolution?"

"Mr. Bergfeld."

The prosecutor paused, as if to collect his thoughts. "Mr. Hughes, as I understand it, one of the resolutions proposed at the Cisco meeting was called the Haskell Resolution. Could you describe the general intent of the Haskell Resolution?"

"Yes, sir. The intention of the Haskell Resolution was to establish the membership's opposition to the war against Germany."

"Who introduced this resolution?"

"Mr. Bergfeld."

"Do you recall if he used the term 'Germany'?"

"Yes, sir, he did."

"Was this Haskell Resolution presented in writing?"

"Yes, sir, it was. Mr. Bergfeld read it to the entire assembly."

O'Dell walked to the prosecutors' table and returned to the witness stand with a sheet of paper. "I would like you to examine this document. Mr. Hughes. Is this the resolution offered by Mr. Bergfeld at the Cisco meeting? The so-called Haskell Resolution?"

"Yes, sir, it appears to be."

"Who wrote the resolution?"

"Mr. Bergfeld did."

"You saw him write it?"

"Yes, sir. I was in and out of the committee room and I saw him writing it."

"And you saw him read what he had written to the gathered assembly?"

"Yes, sir."

"There is no doubt in your mind that this is the resolution you saw him write and read?"

"I am absolutely certain. I saw him write it and I heard him read it in the hall."

"With the court's permission, I offer this document into evidence as Exhibit 9."

"Any objection, Mr. Atwell?" the judge asked.

Atwell rose. "May I please examine the document, Your Honor?"

The judge nodded and Atwell took the paper from O'Dell's hand. O'Dell turned away, his hands clasped behind his back. Atwell saw at once what appeared to be Will's handwriting and one glance was all he needed to know about the incriminating nature of what was written. It was a shock of immense proportion and it took every bit of focus at his disposal to keep his expression from betraying the anger he felt at that moment toward his client who had for some reason withheld from him the existence of this document. He longed to look into Will's eyes, to question why he had been so stupid as to put in writing evidence that seemed to prove that the very charges against him were true, evidence that just might hang him. But Atwell simply said, "No objection." He knew that the resolution would be admitted by the judge and any objection would only emphasize how harmful it was.

Prosecutor O'Dell walked to the jury box, faced the jury, then turned to the judge. "With the Court's indulgence, I would like to read the resolution Mr. Bergfeld wrote."

"You may."

For a long moment, O'Dell looked into the eyes of the jurors. Atwell knew what was coming. He knew that O'Dell had practically memorized the resolution so that he could recite it dramatically without breaking eye contact with the jury. In a rich, sonorous voice, with a touch of sadness that seemed to say that he regretted to reveal that a fellow man could sink so low, O'Dell recited, "Be it resolved that the membership of the Farmers' and Laborers' Protective Association firmly opposes war with Germany or any other foreign power. Such a war would spill the blood of the poor while enriching the Capitalist classes. Be it further resolved that the FLPA membership opposes conscription and if a draft law is passed and signed, we will not only refuse conscription, but we will offer armed resistence to conscription officers who seek to enlist or arrest our members."

O'Dell continued to gaze at the jurors. Then he lowered his eyes and shook his head. There was a rising buzz of conversation from the spectators. Their worst suspicions confirmed, their good judgment vindicated. Bergfeld obviously was guilty as charged. The Haskell Resolution was essentially a written confession.

"Mr. Hughes, I ask you again," the prosecutor asked. "Is this the resolution you saw Mr. Bergfeld write?"

"Yes, sir, it is."

"And this is the resolution you heard Mr. Bergfeld read at the Cisco meeting?"

"Yes, sir, it is."

"Mr. Hughes, isn't it also true that Mr. Bergfeld proposed a resolution concerning the purchase of weapons?"

"Yes, sir." Atwell waited for the second shoe to fall. What now? He risked a glance at Will. He was looking down. Atwell noticed that everyone in the courtroom had their eyes riveted on the witness, all but Will's family. They were, as one, looking at Will. Atwell could only guess what they were thinking.

"What was the substance of this resolution as you recall?"

O'Dell asked.

"Because war had been declared and drafting was probably going to be done, this resolution stated that each member should purchase a high-powered gun, something like a 30-30 and about two hundred rounds of ammunition in order to fight the conscription officers."

"Did that resolution pass as originally offered?"

"It didn't pass. An objection came up that most of the men were poor and couldn't afford these guns. So the resolution was rewritten to say that those who could afford the guns should buy them and the others should get them when they were financially able to."

"And who offered this resolution to buy high-powered weapons and ammunition to fight conscription officers?"

"Mr. Bergfeld."

"The same Mr. Bergfeld?"

"Yes, sir."

"Thank you, Mr. Hughes. Pass the witness." Prosecutor O'Dell walked back to his seat, still shaking his head, his manner subdued, as if he was sorry he had to be the one to reveal such evil deeds.

Atwell's inclination was to stay seated, to think for awhile before he began the cross-examination, to wait for inspiration. But he could feel the eyes of the jury watching for a reaction. What could he ask? He could not very well deny that the evidence existed. It was obviously Will's handwriting. But his hesitation lasted merely a second or two and then he was on his feet, striding confidently toward the witness, his mind whirling, his expression serious, but untroubled. He would have to develop a strategy on the fly. There was no way he could break down the witness's testimony. But he knew if he asked no questions that would send a message to the jury that the witness's testimony was unimpeachable. He had to come up with some questions and hopefully not make things worse.

"You have testified that Will Bergfeld made a speech at that meeting about conscription. Do you also recall that he made a heated statement denouncing the Kaiser? In fact, he said that he wanted to get the Kaiser, did he not?"

"Yes, that is the way he talked."

"What do you think he meant by 'getting the Kaiser'?"

"I suppose he wanted to capture him or kill him."

"Will you agree with me that when Mr. Bergfeld indicated that he wanted to capture or kill the Kaiser, those were not the feelings of a man who would support Germany in a war against the United States?"

"Yeah, I guess I'd have to agree with that."

Atwell noticed the witness was not quite as comfortable as he had been before. He kept cutting his eyes toward Prosecutor O'Dell who studiously avoided his gaze.

"Mr. Hughes, do you recall how Mr. Bergfeld voted on the Haskell Resolution?"

"I do not."

"So what you are telling this jury is that Mr. Bergfeld read the resolution but you don't recall whether he voted for it or against it. Is that your testimony?"

"Yes, sir. I don't recall how he voted."

"You do recall your testimony today in reference to guns. That Bergfeld said that every man should be prepared to defend himself if attacked, or if his family was attacked?"

"Yes, sir."

"Do you also recall that there were long discussions about the danger of an attack from Mexico?"

"It was discussed, yes."

"Didn't Mr. Bergfeld and others express concern that Mexico would become an ally of Germany and become a dangerous enemy right on our southern border?"

"Mexico was mentioned."

"In fact, Mr. Hughes, didn't Mr. Bergfeld state that members should purchase guns and ammunition to protect their families from an attack by Mexican soldiers, not authorities from the United States?"

"He did state that, yes. But . . ."

"I have no further questions, Your Honor." Atwell turned away, feeling he had pushed his luck with this witness as far as he dared.

It had been an unusual Texas September, the temperature in the nineties for more days than Louise could remember. The relentless heat was such a constant companion that it was not news anymore, only remarked by farmers whose water had been stolen away by the drought—or greedy landowners. Louise made her way through the clutter of folding chairs in the silent courtroom. She nodded to the old man sweeping out the discarded newspapers and paper fans and other refuse left by the spectators who Louise now regarded as Romans come to see the slaughter of the Christians. She mused about the nature of prejudice. Here in the courtroom there was obvious prejudice against Will because of his German descent. If the trial were in Spain or Rome, he would certainly be persecuted because he was a Lutheran. The thoughts made her smile in spite of the exhaustion she felt from being buffeted by punishing testimony all day.

She entered the small conference room where Atwell and Will were sitting quietly, both occupied by private thoughts. Atwell seemed tired, the rose in his lapel wilted, his usual composure somehow askance, as was his bow tie. Louise looked from one to the other and sensed there had been harsh words between the two. Atwell stood and held a chair for Louise.

"I thought it time we had a talk," he said as Louise settled down across from Will. She saw in her brother's eyes the chip he so often carried on his shoulder.

"Things are not going as well as I had hoped," Atwell said. "Your brother is misbehaving, withholding information from his attorney."

"Why, Will?" Louise asked.

"Why what?" he responded, innocently.

She remembered once as children when Will was in trouble for carving his initials on his teacher's desk. Louise had asked why, and he had answered, "Why what?" And she had said "Why didn't you carve somebody else's initials, then you wouldn't have been caught?" And he had answered, "Because that wouldn't have been right."

"Why did you write it?" she said, realizing there was a great deal of the boy in the man. "The resolution?"

"I've already explained that. I had to. It was my duty. As chairman of the resolutions committee I was obligated to bring every resolution to the floor, whether I agreed with it or not. That was the rule, Louise!"

"Why didn't you tell Mr. Atwell about it?"

"I didn't think it was important."

"Our problem, Will, is getting a jury to believe that," Atwell said. "If I had known the written resolution existed, I could have prepared. If I had known why you wrote it I could have brought that out on cross-examination. But you left me hanging out to dry."

"Tell me this, Will," Louise said. "Did you vote against that resolution?"

"Yes. I thought it might be considered treasonous."

"But you didn't disagree with what it said?"

"Look, Louise, it doesn't really matter what I believe or don't believe. They've been after me ever since the Ludlow Massacre. I've been watched, followed and hounded. And the worst thing is they've won! Even if I'm acquitted, I'm no use to the labor movement. Rockefeller and his ilk will just go on killing innocent men, women and children. And I'll just have to stand by and watch it happen."

Atwell listened to the tirade patiently. Then after a pause he asked, "Are you finished, Will?"

"Looks like I am, doesn't it?"

"Whatever you've done or said doesn't merit a conviction in this case. But you will be convicted if you don't tell me every possible thing that they might use against you. Everything! You are a smart man, Will, and you know exactly what I'm talking about. Sometimes I think for some perverse reason you want to be convicted." Atwell sighed, then stood. "Look, I want you to think about what I've said, Will. And Louise, I want you to talk some sense into your brother's skull. Then we'll meet in the morning and you can tell me what I need to know if I'm to continue as your attorney."

Will grimaced as Atwell walked out of the room. "What got into him?"

"You did."

"I guess I am in a fix."

"So what's new? I've been getting you out of fixes for as long as I can remember. Little fixes and big fixes. Everything from the time you beat up that bully, Paul Brooks, to the thing with Anna Bennett. Are you going to tell him about that?"

Will shook his head. "No."

"Are you going to tell him about carving your initials on the teacher's desk?"

Will smiled. "Maybe," he said, reaching for her hand. "You know for somebody who's innocent, I sure have been guilty a lot."

Louise squeezed his hand. "Papa says 'no.' I'm sorry, Will. He won't come."

Will sighed, then straightened his shoulders. "I'm not surprised."

"What happened between you and Papa?"

Will was silent for awhile, as if searching for an answer. "He just changed. I adored him. Looked up to him. But then came that day at the Klein Opera House. He lost what he loved most and he was never the same again. At least not to me."

"I love you, Will."

"I know."

"And one way or another I'll get you out of this fix just like I got you out of all the others."

They rose and Will walked his sister to the boarding house where Bettie King, Virginia and the girls would be waiting for supper.

Sergeant Grimes was alone again. The room was barely large enough for a bed, a small table and a straight-back chair, its walls covered with floral wallpaper no ranger would have chosen for himself. He sat at the table covered with files and documents, a half bottle of whiskey, a glass, and a note pad with three names printed in large letters. Grimes circled the names, then sat back, sipping from the glass, saying the names aloud, one after another. "Calhoun. Crouch. Bennett." These, he knew, were the witnesses whose testimony had been, and would be, the most destructive to Will Bergfeld. He figured Atwell had checked them out, but the lead defense attorney was a good and decent man, a believer in the rule of law. Those qualities might not serve him well in an investigation of this sort. Grimes had watched all three of the named witnesses testify at the Grand Jury and he was fairly sure they were lying. Anna Bennett was unforgettable. She was still a beautiful woman, poised and sophisticated and comfortable on the stand. But there had been a certain hardness behind her words, a bitterness, even anger, that did not ring true. He knew there was more to her testimony than met the eye. Grimes underlined her name, and decided he would pay Anna a visit. After all, she was a beautiful woman and he was a very lonely man.

X.

Seguin, Texas.
April 1883

Elisabethe Jurcza sat beneath a spreading live oak. Her horse grazed nearby. She was reading about how Huckleberry Finn and Jim, the runaway slave, boarded a raft Huck built and headed out on a journey down the mile-wide Mississippi. She was falling in love with Huck, his wild innocence, his irreverence, his adventurous spirit, and she realized the book was such a sensation because Huck was the quintessential American. She thought about her own journey. *How far I have come from Bernau to this hill above the Guadalupe, a stream not as grand as the Mississippi but surely, drop for drop, the most beautiful and magical body of water on Earth. How eager I was to come to America, to Texas, the new and growing nation.*

It was an adventure of epic proportion. The immigrants had sailed the vast Atlantic, a sea greater than even Ulysses had sailed, had survived a plague and a hurricane in Indianola on the Texas coast, had trekked through a wilderness of hostile Indians, rattlesnakes and bandits, and then, at last, had come to this place on the Guadalupe. As they had struggled along the trail they had endured a life of hardship and simplicity. In order to survive the present, their past had been stripped away. When her family and the other Germans had at last arrived at Seguin, a town on the Guadalupe, they had decided to go no further. The future was a basket to be filled, a canvas yet to feel the touch of a brush. Here they had an opportunity to become new creatures, Americans, those most fabled of characters on the contemporary world stage.

Now, as she looked out over the lands her stepfather called *Song of Switzerland*, she realized they had not really become Americans at all. Over the years they had merely become what they had been before, had re-created what they had left behind.

The sun cast a mosaic of light and shadow down through the branches of the live oak. The day was balmy, the air soft and fragrant. Beyond the oak were fields of wild flowers and tall grasses, and beyond and below that was the river, a ribbon of jade winding through fields and trees toward the little town of Seguin, a town not unlike a small burg on the Rhine. Here were schools where lessons were taught in German, churches where the Lutheran God held stern sway, a town with five opera houses, more per capita than any town in Germany, where masked balls and Saengerfests and the music of Beethoven and Bach and Brahms nourished the romantic German soul. But it was a passive romanticism, not like the robust and daring romanticism that carried Huck and Jim down the Mississippi.

Elisabethe longed to ride that raft through the real America. From her reading she knew her adopted country was alive not only with the rogues Huck and Jim met, but with an array of bold heroes, with high adventure, surprise and delight. In Chicago, they were raising buildings ten stories high. In New York, electric lights made day of the darkest night. In the East, millionaires were being made overnight and a man like Cornelius Vanderbilt, who started life running a small ferry between Manhattan and Staten Island, could parlay that business into a one-hundred-million-dollar empire. From out West, Buffalo Bill Cody's Wild West Show, with its painted red Indians and stagecoach holdups and sharpshooters, was thundering across the land. And Huck was asking Jim where all the stars came from and Jim said, "the moon laid 'em."

Elisabethe knew she was not unhappy. She lived a life of gentility and grace, not unlike the one her mother had lived in Berlin. She had her loving parents and her friends and had earned a respected place in the community with her music, her performances and her theatrical productions in the Klein Opera House.

But she wondered now, beneath the live oak, if she was not unhappy, then what was this thing she felt, this small, soft pain, this formless anxiety that would not go away.

She thought of her mother, Maria Theresa, and her stepfather Frederick Naumann, and their great love. He had been her mother's first love and she his. After fifteen years apart, he had returned to rescue her and bring her halfway around the world to safety. Frederick had been a man of bold and reckless passions, had been a surveyor with Robert E. Lee before the Civil War. When war broke out, he went to Mexico to mine for gold. What he had taken from beneath a Mexican mountain had purchased their home, their *Song of Switzerland* high above the river and the town.

Now, she wondered, *where is my great love? Why have I rejected the suitors who have pursued me over the years?* She realized she was the last of her friends not to be married and it was the subject of comment in town. She longed for Huckleberry Finn to grow up quickly and come rafting along the Guadalupe and carry her away from her German town into America. But she knew the man she would marry would propose in the language of the Old Country. For a German farm girl or boy to marry an auslander simply was not done. In fact, the last time a German girl in Seguin married a Raggedy boy, her family held a wake for her as if she had died. No, she was going to marry a boy of German descent. He would be proper and decent and good. *I will teach my children to play the violin and pray to the Lutheran God, and celebrate our heritage each year. My life will be unremarkably fine. But will it be alive with the boldness, surprise and delight I longed for as we sailed on the little barque* Diana *from the Old World to the New?*

Elizabethe knew she would have to make a profoundly important decision. She was aware that her future depended on the utterance of a single word. She would have to decide whether or not to become the wife of Peter Gus Menger. His family was known for their hotel next to the Alamo. He had invited her to the masked ball on Saturday night, the night of German Heritage Day, and she believed that he would declare himself that night. They had been seeing each other for nearly a year and a proposal of marriage was due. Peter Gus was handsome, sophisticated, well-traveled, and the Menger family was widely known. They had been schoolmates at the German School in San Antonio. He had written love poems in her autograph book and they had recently been considered a couple at dances and Saengerfests. All she needed to do was utter one word and her future was assured. But what kind of future would it be? Maybe it would be adventure enough to satisfy her soul. Maybe this, and the children that would come, would be enough upon which to build a great love.

Elisabethe rode over the hills of *Song of Switzerland*, and followed the river toward town. Here and there the smoke of cooking fires wafted through the trees where people were camped on the Naumann land, and horses grazed and children played in the shallows or swung from vines into the river. The families had already begun to gather for the celebration of German Heritage Day now only two days away. They came from towns throughout Central Texas to honor their common, very uncommon past. Some were walking, leading their horses, most rode wagons, others even came by train from towns like Shiner and Schulenburg because few celebrations were as gala and spectacular as German Heritage Day in Seguin, Texas. Many of the men carried long rifles for the shooting contests to be held. Other horses had violin cases strapped to the saddle. Elisabethe remembered the refugees crowding the docks at Bremen, and she smiled when she realized these people along the Guadalupe were not fleeing away from Germany, but toward the memory of their native land.

She passed a wagon loaded with patent medicines and snake-oil and countless items of little value to be sold to the expected crowds. Signs on its sides were emblazoned with the name *Kickapoo Medicine Company*. When she neared the edge of the Naumann land, the south wind brought the sound of *conjunto*, that jubilant blending of German and Mexican musical styles that always made Elisabethe's heart beat faster. As she drew nearer to the source, a violin hurled silvery phrases above the guitars and concertinas. Here, beside the Guadalupe, a mariachi band and fiddlers in an oompah band joined to give a New World interpretation to an Old World hymn. She knew immediately that there was only one man in Texas who could play a fiddle with such reckless passion and absolute control. Elisabethe paused within the shadow of a sycamore to watch and listen to the gunfighter-pastor José Polycarpo Rodriguez, raise his fiddle in joyful prayer.

Pastor Polly had been among the first people Elisabethe had met when she had come ashore on the Texas coast nearly a dozen years before. He had lead a team of oxcarts out of Indianola. At the time, it seemed strange that the first American she would meet was a Mexican. He was a handsome, leather-tough man, with a fierce fur of a mustache. His eyes, when they could be seen beneath his battered, wide-brimmed hat, were black as night with a flame of sparkling light somewhere deep within the black. He wore an enormous revolver at each side and carried a rifle in one hand and a Bible in the other, or at least that is the image of the man she most remembered. He had been a frontier guide, a companion of her stepfather when they had surveyed the Mexican border for Robert E. Lee, and he was involved in the U.S. Army's experiment using camels across the West Texas desert. Frederick said that Pastor Polly had been a fierce Indian fighter before he was converted from Catholicism, but his conversion to the Methodist faith only improved his aim and his ferocity. In recent years he had answered the call to the ministry and he traveled Texas from the Rio Grande in the south to the High Plains, holding revivals that were part camp meeting and part musical extravaganza. José Polycarpo Rodriguez had ten brothers, all named José. Only their middle names, taken from saints and martyrs, were different. Pastor Polly was the namesake of Saint Polycarpo, the earliest of the Apostolic Fathers.

Pastor Polly was the most dangerous-looking man Elisabethe had ever seen, but he was also the most kind. On the trek from the Texas Coast to the hills of Central Texas he had taught her how to track wild animals, how to build a fire without matches and how to catch a fish without a hook. And he also taught her how to make a violin speak with a voice unlike any she had heard before. *Would it sound as pure and as perfect,* Elisabethe wondered, *in the concert halls of Berlin, or does it require the open air and the earth and the wild, rustic heart of an eccentric to create such a pure and transcendent sound?* She listened to the jubilant rhythms of *conjunto,* tapped her foot on a sycamore root, and was certain Huck Finn would approve of her friend José Polycarpo Rodriguez. *This is how America should be. A blending of the German-made accordions and flugelhorns, and the Mexican guitars, of polka and waltz, the folk music of the Old Country.* This was the future she longed for, not a cloying clinging to the past.

When Pastor Polly saw Elisabethe by the sycamore, he lowered his violin and walked toward her with his arms thrown wide, his bow in one hand, the fiddle in the other. His approach was accompanied by a torrent of Spanish, splashed with a word or two she could occasionally understand. She knew he was asking of her mother and stepfather and how she herself had fared over the years and how she had grown to be a beautiful woman. Held within the embrace of her old family friend, the words rolled on, question after question with no pause for an answer. She loved the sound of the Spanish language with its lovely lilt and musical rhythms, especially as spoken in the rich bass of a natural sermonizer. It was some moments before Pastor Polly remembered that Elisabethe did not speak Spanish, and he apologized and lifted her high and danced with her in a circle while the musicians picked up the beat and Elisabethe felt she was flying, round and round, in the arms of the fierce old man.

They sat on the riverbank, catching up on the news. He asked her why such a beautiful woman was still not married.

"The right man hasn't come along," she said.

"Then marry me!" he said. "We can have a dozen children. We will name them all José."

"And if we had a daughter?"

"José Maria, of course!"

She told him then about young Menger and how she thought he would propose at the ball.

"And do you love this young man?" Pastor Polly asked.

"I don't know."

Elisabethe smiled and blew the flaxen seeds from a dandelion toward the river. "Pastor Polly, is it true you are a seer, a Divine—you can see into Heaven and tell the future?"

"It is true. Sometimes I can with the help of God."

"What do you see for me? Will I marry? Have children? What will my life be like?"

"Sometimes it's best for the future to remain hidden," Pastor Polly said. "It is a serious thing you ask. The future is not a toy for our amusement."

"Please, Pastor Polly. It would help me make my decision."

"The decision has already been made. You just don't know what it is yet. The past, present and future are all one thing. They exist side by side in the mind of God."

José Polycarpo Rodriguez bowed his head and held Elisabethe's hand as he would hold a flower or a fragile cup or a holy relic. Pastor Polly prayed. The sun was warm. The river sang a treble melody as it ran by. A hawk wheeled overhead in a porcelain sky. The laughter of children rode the wind from the distance. Then Pastor Polly closed his eyes, sighed, raised her hand to his lips.

"I do not have the answer. We must continue to pray," he said.

Elisabethe could see there were tears in the old man's eyes and she felt a coldness cross the arc of her spine.

On the morning of German Heritage Day, the town of Seguin was alive with the spirit of festival. The hotels and boarding houses were full and tents had been set up on vacant lots, and country families camped in the backyards of their city kin. Prostitutes from San Antonio leaned out of windows of the bawdy house down the street from the Magnolia Hotel and Pastor José Polycarpo Rodriguez was spreading his huge gospel tent next to the jail, preparing to save souls with the Word and music. Along Austin

Street and Court Street, the red, white and black colors of the German flag were draped as bunting on porch rails and gazebos. The flag itself did not fly on the courthouse flagstaff because more than a few Confederate veterans remembered that German immigrants in Texas had adopted an antislavery resolution and had opposed secession from the Union. The bells of the German Methodist Church had not yet tolled the nine o'clock hour, yet the Seguin Civic Band was already bleating drinking songs from the city park bandstand with brass and gusto.

At the Klein Opera House preparations for the evening events were at a fever pitch. As chairman of the Heritage Day committee, Elisabethe was in charge of the decoration of the ballroom. She and the other women of the committee had selected nature and the natural world as a theme for both the play to be presented prior to the masked ball and for the ball itself. A forest had been painted on flats. Men were bringing in cypress branches and elephant ears from the river's edge. The women brought gray Spanish moss from ancient oaks, flowering lantana in lavender and gold, and armloads of green branches to augment the flats. All in all, Elisabethe was pleased with the effect. The idea was to create a wooded glen within the opera house, a setting as close to Eden or to a magical mysterious corner of the Black Forest as could be imagined.

The play's last rehearsal had been the night before and Elisabethe thought the cast of children and neighbors was as prepared as they would ever be. She had wanted to do a stage presentation of Tom Sawyer, but the town fathers felt that Tom and Becky and Huck were unsavory characters at best, with nothing at all to do with German heritage, and certainly were not good examples for the children of Seguin. Instead, she wrote a musical version of Hansel and Gretel, a play that perfectly suited the forest setting they were creating. Although the play was light and amusing and featured excellent parts for children and the church choir, there were a few darker moments inspired by her memory of fleeing Bismarck through mysterious forests where people still believed in witches and demons.

Elisabethe saved for herself two contrasting roles, a water sprite and a witch. For the water sprite's violin solo, she could have used the *Water Sprite Waltz,* composed by her great uncle Krug, but chose instead a contemporary piece by the American composer Sidney Lanier. She had heard him perform his *Field Larks and Blackbirds* in San Antonio and had been haunted by the piece ever since. She selected Wagner for her witch's final solo, to be performed just before she was cooked in the oven by the featured children—*a rather dubious happy ending,* she thought.

In the afternoon, most of the town was marching in the Heritage Day parade, watching horse races and shooting tournaments, moving on to booths selling pretzels and pickles out of barrels. The air was permeated with the aroma of sauerkraut, and home-brewed beer poured into pottery steins. Elisabethe prepared her costume for the ball and worked at not thinking about Peter Gus Menger and what she would say if he proposed. Most of the women attending the masked ball were from families of moderate means. Their costumes would be created from things they had at hand or garments they could make. Most of the women had saved their masks from previous balls. This evening's ball, with its natural theme, would probably be attended by women with the masks of animals, like rabbits or cats.

As the evening approached, Elisabethe decided to attend the ball as a wood nymph, not unlike the water sprite she would play in "Hansel and Gretel." She selected a gown of hunter green silk that her great-uncle had shipped from Berlin. She had removed the fashionable bustle, believing it not appropriate for wood nymph attire. The beautiful elfin mask was also of silk, but silver rather than green.

Peter Gus Menger was coming to the ball as Odin, the Norse god of wisdom, poetry and war. He was certain to win "Best Costume" for men because his carriage was being drawn by Odin's mythical steed Slepnir, with his two hunting hounds bounding along behind.

By nightfall, Elisabethe was beginning to feel trapped. She was caught between her fear of never marrying and her fear of marrying a man she did not love. Maybe she would say "yes" to Peter Gus Menger, but if he expected ideal and unquestioned devotion, he was in for a big disappointment.

At the ball Elisabethe was invisible. This was the appeal of a masked ball, the ability to move about anonymously, to see others without them seeing you, to be someone else for a while. The mask also made it impossible for others to see how flushed her face had become from the wine she had been secretly sipping from a decanter behind the stage. Elisabethe rarely drank at all, but with the echo of applause for her performance filling her mind, exhilarated by her play's success, dreading the decision she would soon have to make, she accepted a glass to toast the cast. Then she accepted another. Perhaps more, she could not remember for certain. But she was certain that the ballroom was not in the Klein Opera House, but in the magical depths of the Black Forest. Beyond, in the shadows, the spirits of the ancient trees and a host of legendary beasts moved with her. She felt weightless as a myth, spinning and gliding with Odin, who was actually rather handsome and not nearly as overbearing as she had sometimes thought him to be. Her operatic God danced beautifully, and it was good to be invisible in an enchanted forest, dancing in the arms of a god.

Later she would not recall the stranger asking her to dance, but she found herself moving with him across the forest floor while Odin reluctantly backed away. Through the stranger's mask she could see eyes as black as those of José Polycarpo Rodriguez. He was tall and lean and strong, and there was something familiar about him.

"You don't remember me," he said, as they waltzed by a hunter dancing with a rabbit.

Elizabethe shook her head.

"I remember everything about you."

Elisabethe looked into his eyes and she knew and she reached for his mask. He took her hand away.

"Not yet," he said. "Let's keep the masks for a while. I want to imagine what you look like now that you're grown."

"Arthur?" the question was whispered. Then louder, eyes wide, "Arthur Bergfeld!"

Now instead of dancing, they were holding each other beneath the linden trees, swaying, remembering, and the years peeled away to reveal two youngsters on the docks of Bremen watching the waves rising and falling in iron-gray ranks.

Arthur Bergfeld and Elisabethe Jurcza danced and talked and laughed until the rose of dawn when he asked her to be his wife. They were married before the first norther came down from the plains. After a decent interval, a daughter was born. They named her Louise.

XI.

Abilene, Texas.
September 1917

Defense Attorney Atwell watched the jurors file into the courtroom. They were now as familiar to him as old friends and he felt a special fondness for them as they took their places in the jury box and settled down for another day of testimony. He studied John Hallock, the lean farmer with his deep-set, brooding eyes and his craggy sun-savaged face; R. T. Hamilton, the balding storekeeper who sometimes napped when the testimony became repetitive and wearisome; Roy Don Budge, the railroad man who was quick to see fragments of irony and humor hidden from the others. When they and the others glanced his way, Atwell nodded at each and smiled in a way that meant he was pleased to see that they were well and glad to have their company for another difficult day.

Atwell took comfort in the fact that these were decent people, good folks placed in an extraordinary situation. Over the years, there had been times when he had inadvertently selected a scoundrel as a juror. But even then, there was something about the courtroom experience that was ennobling, that made a juror a better person than he had been before. The same was true of judges he had known. They might have been rogues as lawyers, but the bench often brought out a finer, more reasonable and humane component of their personalities and they rose above their former imperfections.

Atwell knew the jurors were going to remember this trial for the rest of their lives, and the story of what happened in this place, at this time, would be told and retold in their families for generations. He wondered for a moment how those stories would end. *What were they thinking now, these good people plucked from their own lives and placed in a position to shape the lives of others?* It was an enormous responsibility; to sift through all the facts and lies, information and misinformation, passion and boredom, and somehow to determine precisely where the truth could be found. Before it was all said and done, these jurors were going to hear the testimony of more than one hundred witnesses. Atwell tried to project himself into the jury box. *How would I feel if I were a juror? What would I believe? Could I put aside the concerns and prejudices and the pressures of my own personal life to concentrate on my duty as a juror?*

He tried to see behind each juror's eyes and into his mind and conscience. Ordinary people placed in an extraordinary situation. Decent people. But how could they not be affected by what was happening out in the streets, where war hysteria was raging like a fever and hatred of anything German was commonplace? In communities throughout Texas, committees called Councils of Defense had been organized to fight the disloyalty supposedly inherent in German culture. The Councils were especially eager to root out disloyalty in German newspapers, schools and churches. In fact, many German-language newspapers in Texas had indeed defended the Central Powers, when Germany, the Austro-Hungarian Empire, and Turkey began fighting the Allies—Russia, France and the British Empire. And they criticized President Wilson for favoring the Allies. These editorial policies changed when America entered the war, but the Defense Councils wanted to forbid the circulation of any German newspaper and periodical. What the Councils of Defense called "the enemy language" was completely eliminated from all schools. Laws were passed prohibiting the German language even in churches. In Castroville, west of San Antonio, the local council claimed that "if a man's religion couldn't be taught in English there was something wrong with it."

Surely the jurors were not blind and deaf to the rampant anti-German hysteria that was sweeping Texas. In Bastrop County, vigilantes shot a German farmer who had supposedly interfered with a war bond drive. Then they beat the victim's widow. In San Antonio, six Germans who declined to join the Red Cross were flogged. In Bishop, Texas, a Lutheran minister was flogged after he had held a German-language revival service. A West Texas German minister narrowly escaped a lynching from a mob that claimed he baptized a baby in the name of the Kaiser. Throughout Texas, German homes were smeared with yellow paint and "heinie" became a racial slur. Atwell wondered if the fever infected the jurors he saw before him. Or would the mysterious, ennobling power of the jury system act as an antibody to the disease of prejudice and misplaced patriotism that ruled the times? Atwell believed the American legal system had failed by bringing the case to trial in the first place. Now it was up to twelve jurors to set things right.

But Atwell knew that time was running out. It was imperative that the trial end before American boys started dying in the trenches, when even the most decent juror would find it difficult to render a just verdict. This sense of urgency would limit the number of character witnesses Atwell should call. In one sense, this would not be a problem because he had found, to his surprise, that there were very few effective character witnesses available, none in Weinert, with the exception of Dr. Cockrell and his wife, the postmistress. Will Bergfeld was well known, and well liked, but he had very few really close friends whose testimony would favorably impress a jury. And there was another problem that troubled a far corner of his mind. Why did Will's father refuse to attend the trial? Atwell was wondering what *that* was all about when O'Dell called his first witness of the morning.

Old Man Crouch wore a tailor-made linen suit and an unmistakable aura of prosperity. As he strode to the stand, it was apparent he was a man of consequence, a person confident of his place in the world.

After the witness was sworn in, O'Dell began his questioning. His manner was relaxed, his tone conversational. Atwell had an impression of two powerful men conversing at their club.

"Mr. Crouch," O'Dell began, "you are from Weinert, Texas.

Isn't that right?"

"Yes, sir. Up in Haskell County."

Prosecutor O"Dell smiled and scratched his head, as if confused. "Weinert. An unusual name for a town, is it not?"

"The town was named after Senator F. C. Weinert."

"Why was that, Mr. Crouch?"

"It was his land. When the railroad came through, people settled, and a town grew up around the railroad stop."

"And when did you settle in Weinert?"

"Early on. I came to supervise Senator Weinert's land. And I've lived there ever since. We run cattle, grow some cotton, a bit of grain."

"You were one of the original settlers?"

"Yes, sir, I was. I organized the immigrant train that brought the first families."

"So one might fairly say that *you* were cofounder of the town. Isn't that right?"

Old Man Couch straightened in his chair and appeared pleased with the prosecutor's logic. "Yes, I suppose that could be said."

O'Dell paused. Atwell knew he was now going to ask Crouch about Bergfeld.

"Mr. Crouch," O'Dell asked, "how long have you known Will Bergfeld?"

"I guess I've known him most of his life. As a boy in Seguin and then when he moved to Weinert."

"Mr. Crouch, are you aware that Mr. Bergfeld was a local organizer for the Farmers' and Laborers' Protective Association?"

"Yes, sir, I am."

"What do you know about the activities of that organization?"

Old Man Crouch crossed his arms over his chest and hunched his shoulders. It was a protective gesture, one that Atwell recognized as the prelude to a lie. "Bergfeld was a Socialist. He was foursquare against the American way of life. Still is. He was always making speeches about labor unions and blasting Rockefeller and how the rich were exploiting the working man. If he wasn't making a speech himself, he was bringing outside agitators in to speak.

Once he even brought that Jones woman. It didn't set too well with the town."

"Do you mean Mother Jones, of the Workers Defense League?"

"Yes, sir. She was just one of the agitators he brought in to make trouble. He was forcing local farmers to join that farmer's union against their will. Intimidating good men who only wanted to be left alone."

"What happened when a farmer declined to become a member?"

"It was common knowledge that Bergfeld kept a .45 pistol, a Bowie knife and a whip at those FLPA meetings. He told new members if they quit he would slice their backs with the whip like a woman slices a cake."

Atwell rose to object. "I doubt Mr. Crouch attended those meetings. This can only be hearsay and inadmissible."

Judge Jack sustained the objection.

"Mr. Crouch, did you ever have a personal, face-to-face conversation with Will Bergfeld about politics?"

"Yes, sir. On several occasions."

"Did he ever say anything to you about purchasing high-powered weapons and dynamite?"

"Yes, sir, he did."

"Could you tell the jury the general substance of those conversations?"

"He said the working man should arm himself so that they wouldn't get massacred like the miners in Ludlow, Colorado. He was always railing about Ludlow, Colorado."

"When did this conversation take place?"

"It was more a series of conversations over a long period of time."

"What was his manner during these conversations? Was he angry?"

"I'd say so. Abusive. Disrespectful. Because I had a good deal of land and a prosperous cattle operation, I don't think he liked me much. I was the enemy, like Rockefeller, damned because I wasn't poor."

"More recently, did you have a conversation with Will Bergfeld about conscription?"

"Yes, sir. He was against conscription. He said if the conscription officers came he would fight them to the death. He also said he had purchased two cases of dynamite."

"Did he tell you why he purchased the explosives?"

"No, sir. That's just the thing. When I asked, he just grinned and wouldn't answer. If he'd had a legitimate reason he would have told me."

"Why do you think he bought the dynamite?"

"To blow up bridges, bank vaults. That was the talk."

Atwell jumped to his feet as Crouch was responding. "Objection. Heresay and speculation. Mr. Crouch cannot read Mr. Bergfeld's mind."

Judge Jack sustained the objection.

O'Dell cast his eyes toward the ceiling as if he might find a new line of questioning there. "Mr. Crouch, your friend and business partner and cofounder of the town is German, isn't he?"

"Mr. Weinert? Yes, sir."

"And you admire this man, trust him?"

"Certainly."

"So you don't have any ill feelings toward Will Bergfeld because he is of German descent, do you?"

"No, sir. Absolutely not."

"The ill feelings toward Will Bergfeld you have expressed here are due purely to his political sentiments, isn't that true? Not because he's a German."

"That's true."

"Thank you, Mr. Crouch." O'Dell turned toward the defense attorney. "Your witness, Counselor."

Bill Atwell had always tried to maintain an entirely impersonal attitude toward witnesses. But as he approached the witness stand, he realized he did not like Old Man Crouch. The man was pompous, vain, and certainly not telling the truth. Yet, because he was pompous and vain, it just might be that he did not know he was not telling the truth. Atwell had known such men to be enormously self-deceptive. They often began to believe their lies. The defense attorney fought to disguise his dislike of the witness with a pleasant, friendly manner.

"Mr. Crouch," Atwell began. "You mentioned you have a cattle operation. Isn't that so?"

"Yes, sir."

"You own quite a lot of land?"

"Some eight thousand acres."

"How would you describe that land?"

"Well, it's prairie. Good soil when it rains."

"But it doesn't often rain, does it?"

"Not often."

"But your cattle need water, don't they? Your crops too. Your garden. How do you manage that?"

"There's a few streams. We build dirt dams, make tanks."

"You mean ponds or reservoirs where the cattle can drink? Water you can divert into the fields?"

"Yes, sir. We have several here and there on the land."

"Mr. Crouch, don't you have a number of neighbors, small farmers up there in Haskell County?"

"I do. Yes."

"Don't they have the same problem with water that you do?"

"I suppose so."

"And isn't it true that those streams that used to flow from your land onto theirs have been dammed?"

"Objection!" O'Dell called. "What possible relevance?"

Judge Jack looked at Atwell over his glasses. "Counselor? Could you tell us where this is going?"

"I intend to show that animosity exists between Mr. Crouch and Mr. Bergfeld and that this affects the witness's credibility."

"All right," Judge Jack said. "But please get to the point."

Bill Atwell looked into Old Man Crouch's eyes. What he saw was a blending of hatred and righteous indignation. Here was a man who was used to having his way.

"Mr. Crouch, wasn't one of these water reservoirs created by damming Lake Creek?"

"It was."

"And isn't it true that you built a water tower between the reservoir and the town?"

"On my land, yes."

"Isn't it also true that you formed a water company and you sold this water to local residents and farmers for a monthly fee?"

"Yes, a small fee."

"Farmers paid a monthly fee for water that at one time flowed freely onto their land. Isn't that right?"

"I had a contract from the Townsite Company to supply the town of Weinert with water."

"From the Weinert Water Plant?"

"That is what we called it."

"Tell me, Mr. Crouch, what was the reaction of your neighbors when you cut off their water supply and then made them pay for water that was once their own?"

"It was not *their* water, Mr. Atwell. This is my land and I have a God-given right to anything on that land. That includes water."

"Isn't it true that Mr. Bergfeld approached you on behalf of the area's small farmers? And that he wanted to negotiate a solution to the water rights problem?"

"Will Bergfeld is a rural mail carrier. Water is none of his business."

"But as a rural mail carrier he could observe firsthand the plight of the farmers along his route, couldn't he?"

"I suppose he could."

"Wasn't it his obligation, then, as head of the local Farmers' and Laborers' Protective Association, to help ease their plight?"

"I don't recognize Socialist organizations."

"So you refused to negotiate?"

"I can do with my land what I wish."

"So you and Mr. Bergfeld had words?"

"More than words. He was acting like a madman."

"Is that when he told you about the dynamite?"

"I don't know. He was out of control."

"Isn't it true that he told you the dynamite was for blasting wells and cisterns? Didn't he tell you he would continue to fight you over water rights, but in the meantime he had purchased two kegs of dynamite so there would be enough to dig cisterns and wells on all your neighbor's farms so they could survive the summer? Isn't that so, Mr. Crouch?"

"Will Bergfeld said a lot of things. Most of it didn't make sense."

"You don't like Mr. Bergfeld, do you, Mr. Crouch?"

"I make no secret of that fact."

Bill Atwell was finding it terribly difficult to mask his ever-growing disgust. He glanced at the jury and was certain he saw the same distaste reflected in their eyes, especially those of the farmer John Hallock, a man for whom water was life. The other jurors were motionless, their attention riveted on the witness. Shaking his head, Bill Atwell walked to the jury box, then turned back toward the witness.

"Mr. Crouch," he continued, "what is the Haskell County Defense Council?

"It is a patriotic organization."

"Isn't it true that you are chairman of the Haskell County Defense Council?"

"I'm proud to say it is true. Yes."

"Could you tell the jury the purpose of the Haskell County Defense Council?"

"It's to support the war effort. To get rid of anti-Americanism in all its forms."

"Does that mean getting rid of Socialists?"

"Certainly."

"You say Will Bergfeld is a Socialist. Does this mean getting rid of Will Bergfeld?"

"If the shoe fits, Mr. Atwell."

"Well, then. It all becomes clear. If Will Bergfeld goes to prison or is hung, you probably won't ever have to share your water. Isn't that so, Mr. Crouch?"

Old Man Crouch remained silent just long enough for Defense Attorney Atwell to throw up his hands in a gesture of disgust and say, "No further questions." He then turned on his heels and walked away, dismissing Old Man Crouch from the stand and from his mind.

The red touring car fairly flew toward the sunrise. In the passenger seat, Bettie watched Louise navigate the rutted road and marveled how times had changed. Here were two women, alone, roaring through Texas at nearly twenty miles an hour in a magnificent machine the color of an apple. It was good to get away from Abilene, free of the pressures of the trial for a while, and headed—*oh blessed be!*—home to Seguin. Because one of the jurors had a death in the family, Judge Jack had called a few days' recess, just enough time to drive to Fort Worth, catch a train for San Antonio, then Seguin, and restore her soul in God's country on the Guadalupe.

But blending with the sense of freedom and joy she felt as they sped through the countryside was a touch of something sad, a feeling a bit sharper than sorrow. For Henry and George would be meeting her in Seguin, her son coming home for the last time before shipping out to Camp Travis to be trained in the violent arts of war. She had dreaded the moment of his departure for months, praying that George would change his mind about volunteering. But she knew her son and he would do his duty to his country. It was his nature. But, then, wasn't Will also doing his duty to his country as he saw it? Sometimes she simply didn't know.

Bettie had been surprised when her husband had agreed to her and Louise making the automobile trip alone. Louise had insisted on the trip, even if she were to go by herself. She was eager to spend time with her husband in Karnes City, a few miles from Seguin. Louise also wanted to persuade Arthur Bergfeld to change his mind about attending his son's trial. And Bettie just wanted to be home, to feel the familiar rhythms of Court Street and tend to things too long neglected. And, of course, to tell her son good-bye.

Bettie was also surprised to find that she loved riding in an automobile. The speed was mesmerizing and she felt that she was an orbiting planet passing by strange and unknowable worlds. In the few houses they passed, people were starting their day, clearing away breakfast, beginning their chores and labors. *Who were these people?* she wondered. *Strangers of flesh and blood, spirit and dream, each the center of their universe. How odd that they don't even know I exist,* she thought. *They go about their lives unaware that Bettie King has passed through their world in a machine the color of an apple.*

In Fort Worth, Louise parked the car in a garage near the depot and they boarded the southbound train. They passed through rolling grasslands, raced flocks of geese wheeling in ordered patterns through wide pale skies. They crossed rivers where only a few years ago Indians had camped and families in wagons had forded on their way to the frontier. Now they leaped the rivers in a long, flying carriage of thunder and fire. *My, how the world is changing,* Bettie thought. And they flew on. The prairie gave way to limestone hills and forests of cedar and juniper, rough country, the Hill Country, where the Guadalupe was born. After a stop in the teeming, sophisticated city of San Antonio, they rumbled along a softer way, into the sweet, low hills of Guadalupe County and the little town of Seguin.

The house was there. Standing on Court Street as if it had been the world's first house, ageless, solid, fine. Bettie walked onto the porch, touched one of the high white pillars, looked up at the pale blue porch ceiling, a color that tradition claimed brought good luck to the home, and she had never felt more secure, more protected from the slings and arrows of the fast-changing world. The house on Court Street never changed and would be there, breathing, living, guarding the family, generation after generation forever. She opened the front door and entered the place where she was born to be.

Just before dusk, when the sound of wagon wheels and hoofbeats on Court Street grew distant, then still, and the world outside her window seemed softly painted blue, Bettie heard the call of an owl and she knew that Peachtree had come from his cave to see who had lit the lights within her rooms.

As usual, Peachtree remained in the shadows until she opened the back screen door, a signal that Henry was not at home and that he was welcome to come visit in the kitchen. As usual, Bettie felt a light tug of guilt that she would keep her strange friendship with Peachtree secret from Henry, but her husband simply would not understand that the hermit, although frightening, was almost harmless, not nearly as dangerous as his reputation.

When Bettie fed a passing hobo or poor soul like Peachtree, she was following the admonition of her favorite verse of the Bible: "Be not forgetful to entertain strangers for thereby some have entertained angels unaware." Peachtree approached the house slowly, cautiously, walking crablike, one shoulder turned to where he was going, the other to where he had been. His clothes were the same rags he had been wearing when she last saw him several weeks ago. His eyes were bright black within an unkempt wreath of hair and beard. At the door, he tied his pet owl to the boot scrape, removed his ruined derby hat and presented Bettie with a late-blooming rose, certainly stolen from her own garden. As she opened the screen door, he passed her like an ill wind, sat at the kitchen table and said, "What?"

Peachtree was a gatherer of information, yet a disseminator of none. His vocabulary consisted primarily of five basic one-word questions. He would ask what, where, when, who, and especially why. He seemed insatiable to know what was going on in the world that had rejected him so completely. Bettie was certain that explained why he was sometimes found prowling in people's houses, why he wandered the night streets, listened to the stories of the prisoners through the windows of the jail and traveled widely, riding the rails with hoboes, always returning to his cave in the Guadalupe bottoms. Bettie wondered what he did with all that information about people. Maybe by knowing the details of other people's lives he could come to terms with his own. She realized he was waiting for news about Will who, besides herself, was probably his best friend in the world.

Bettie dished out a piece of the apple pie her neighbor had

delivered when she learned of Bettie's return. She knew better than to provide a fork. To her everlasting dismay, Peachtree would, of course, eat with his fingers. Once she had criticized his table manners and he had growled at her and abruptly left, not returning for several weeks.

"The trial is not going well," she said.

"Why?" he asked, his eyes roaming the room. Bettie wondered if he had been in the house while she was gone. The thought disturbed her and she realized she was not altogether unafraid of her visitor.

"Witnesses are lying. And we can't prove it."

"Why?"

"The prosecutor and his witnesses think Will is helping the enemy. You know how Will talks. And he's German of course, and there's the war with Germany."

"Who are the witnesses?" he asked.

As Peachtree licked his fingers and drank a glass of buttermilk, Bettie told him about the testimony of Ned Earl Calhoun and Old Man Crouch and that she feared more bad testimony was coming from Anna Bennett. Atwell had told her that these would be the three most damaging witnesses. Although his eyes continued to wander the room, she was sure he was listening intently.

When Bettie finished, the room was still. Peachtree wiped the buttermilk from his beard with a sleeve. He rose and put on his derby. Then, without another word, he retrieved his owl and left. Except for a lingering aroma of wildness, the night swallowed him whole.

A handsome Bergfeld Drug Store, on the corner of Court and Crockett, smelled of cinnamon and licorice, alcohol and sulfur, vanilla and hemp. Louise watched her father, Arthur Bergfeld, work with his chemicals, grinding grains and particles of matter with his mortar and pestle, blending liquids of exotic colors in glass beakers, preparing medicines to cure everything from rheumatism to a broken heart. In his white coat, she thought he looked a bit like a mad scientist or an ancient alchemist in search of the philosopher's stone. His hair was almost pure white now. He was lean and erect, undaunted by years of bending over his chemicals and the weight of the nameless demons that apparently marched through his memory. Even though Louise could not remember when she had last seen him smile, she could remember how much she still loved him.

The walls were lined with bottles and vials of every size and color, most corked and carrying labels written in Arthur's bold hand. The labels on his own preparations were in German. The glass-fronted cabinets and shelves of rich, dark mahogany rose to the pressed-tin ceiling. In addition to his own concoctions, the shelves held large brown bottles of sweet oil, camphor and rose water. A countertop displayed exotic cures for chills and fever. Along one wall a dozen shelves contained what Louise had always thought were the most amazing mysteries. For a long while, Louise watched her father work.

"Why won't you come?" Louise asked, once again, refusing to give up easily.

Arthur Bergfeld kept his eyes on his work. He removed a small object from a leather bag, placed it in the mortar, hammered it to pieces with the heavy stone pestle, then began to grind it to powder. After a long while he said, in German, "I can't leave the pharmacy."

"Please speak English," Louise said, exasperated, and hugely disappointed in her father's intransigence.

Arthur sighed and turned. His eyes were haunted and old as poisoned wells. "You know why I can't go! I've told you." His voice cracked, as if it had been a long time since he had spoken. "I am German! I speak German! Germany lives in my soul! I am the enemy! Can't you see that? Can't you see that my presence at the trial would kill Will?"

"There is something else, isn't there?"

"There is nothing."

"Something you're not telling me. Tell me about your father."

"He's dead."

"Grandmother Antonie. Why don't you ever talk about her? She's not dead. What happened back there in Germany?"

At the mention of Antonie, Arthur looked up. "You should go now."

"He needs you, Papa."

"Will has never needed anybody." Arthur turned back to his work. The gritty sound of the moving pestle grated on Louise's nerves.

"Well, he needs you now," she said.

"There are things you don't know. Life is not always as it appears." Arthur removed the powder from the mortar and funneled it into a small jar of amber liquid. Then he lay down the pestle, dropped his arms to his side and his eyes to the floor. "Go now," he said. "Tell Will I love him." The words seemed to be dragged from somewhere deep in his heart. Then Arthur Bergfeld turned and walked from the room.

Louise sighed and took one last look at the familiar surroundings, this darkly mysterious place that had been the center of her life. And she wondered what it was she did not know.

In a farmhouse outside Weinert, Sergeant Grimes listened to Anna Bennett talk about Will Bergfeld and about the hard, sharp corners of fate that can bruise a life and a soul. It was nearly dusk. Outside the wind swept the prairie like a broom, and dust so filled the air that the falling sun was a dull orange, like a rotting pumpkin. Tom Grimes could taste the dust on the rim of his wineglass. He had not meant to stay so late. He had simply wanted to gather some sense of who this woman was and why she might have lied to the Grand Jury. But Anna was hungry for company, a single woman alone too long. When he had arrived she offered him a glass of wine that she said was left over from a friend's birthday. As they sipped their wine and it grew darker, she turned up the lamplight and he could see that she was still beautiful. Grimes had never seen such flame-red hair and such absolute contrast between that scarlet fire and the pure white of her throat. Yet, Grimes thought there was a hardness in her eyes and more than a touch of bitterness in her voice as they talked about the trial and her relationship with Will.

"We were in love," she had said, her face first glowing with the memory, then saddened by it. "We were to be married, you know. He was going to take me away from this God-awful place. I thought our love would last forever. But it ended."

"What happened?"

"Things end, that's all."

"Do you still love him?"

She had nodded. There was something terribly tight about the woman. Some inner tension, like a clock too tightly wound.

"But you would still testify against him?"

"It's larger than what's between two people. It's the war. The life of the country. It's just something I have to do. After all, he said he was going to kill President Wilson."

"When was this?" Grimes asked.

"I don't know exactly. Every day is the same." There was that bitterness again. Grimes could feel her unhappiness flowing from her like a poisoned stream.

Anna Bennett walked to the window and looked out at the night. "Do you know what it's like to live in a place like this?" She shivered, stepped back slightly from the window as if repelled by some unseen force. "It is to be half alive. And to be half alive is to be half dead." Still gazing out the window, she asked, "Have you ever been to San Marcos, Sergeant Grimes?"

"Yes."

"That's where I lived when I was young. A beautiful place. Green and fresh. The river clear as an angel's eye. But then we moved here. It's like the Sahara. Or the surface of the moon. Nothing green as far as the eye can see. Just listen to that wind." She turned from the window. There were tears in her eyes. "I hate the wind! It parches your skin, howls in your dreams. And the dust! It gets into your mouth, your eyes, your hair, everywhere."

Anna tilted her head and ran one hand through her hair as if to shake out accumulated dust. Grimes had the feeling that she was talking more to herself than to him. She might have even forgotten he was there.

"When the wind comes it sweeps the dust and sand into your life. It cuts your face like bits of glass and there's no defense. You come in the house, close the windows and doors, yet it creeps in somehow, through every tiny crack and crevice and you can feel the dust in your bed and in your food and in the air you breathe. I hate the wind! The naked wind! Will was going to take me someplace where the air is still. But he lied to me and left me here with the wind."

"Why didn't you just leave?"

"A woman alone? Besides, I have a good teaching job and kin folks all around the county. And then," she added, "I always hoped that Will. . . ." She let the sentence trail away.

Grimes listened, politely waiting for an indication that the interview was over. But it did not come. Anna Bennett poured more wine, began to pace, to rail against the fates that had brought her to her present situation. "I had everything," she said. "Youth, a prosperous family, a future. Then this! Years and years following one after the other like bad dreams. I might as well be dead! And you know who killed me! He might as well have used a gun! He was my way out of here. Promised me. But he lied."

Grimes considered going to the woman and holding her, telling her he understood how she felt. But she seemed almost dangerous, a bomb that could easily explode. He knew that her love for Will was a lingering fiction. What she really felt was hate. Hate enough to lie before a Grand Jury. Hate enough to send the man she loved to the gallows. It was the wrath of a woman condemned to life imprisonment on the empty prairie. And so, feeling somehow that she had been asking for help he was unable or unwilling to give, he rose, thanked her for the wine and her time, and left.

As he stepped from the porch, Tom Grimes paused and looked back. Framed in the lighted window, he could see Anna Bennett glaring out into the night, her lips speaking words to the darkness and he knew she was cursing Will Bergfeld and the wind.

Bettie King, her husband Henry and their son George sat on the front porch listening to the gathering night. It was late, no wagons or buggies or automobiles stirred on Court Street. George talked for a while about life at Texas A&M, how he had sailed through his classes with little trouble, how to his surprise he had enjoyed his military training and was looking forward to Camp Travis and his life as a commissioned officer in the regular Army. Henry had been unusually silent, and Bettie knew he was thinking of the boy George had been and the man he had become. It was a leap that had seemed only an instant's duration. Bettie felt her son had grown up so fast, had moved through life so smoothly, that she had hardly come to know him. It came to her that he had never broken a bone and she had never seen him cry. She looked at him now, in the light that spilled onto the porch from the living room, and she realized this tall, good man was almost a stranger. They had lived in the same house, loved each other profoundly, but he had never been in trouble, had always obeyed his parent's wishes, had always taken the straight path and done the right thing. George had always been there at the center of her life, but she realized she had no idea what he was like inside, the private person dwelling within. *Was he afraid of the dark?* she wondered. *Was he afraid of what would happen in the war?* So self-contained, so self-controlled was her son that she had never thought to ask. And she did not ask now, as they rocked on the porch, their love hanging unexpressed in the air, strangers waiting for the morning.

XII.

Seguin, Texas.
November 1889

On an early November morning, Bettie stepped from her front porch into a morning alive with mystery and delight. A light southerly breeze whispered through the naked limbs of the tall elm trees rising above the sunlit spaces along Court Street. In the distance, she could hear a train wailing its warning that it was about to leave the depot for New Orleans. It was a mysterious sound, the train, a machine-made cry that seemed as eerily natural as the call of a coyote or an owl. The whistle hinted of adventure in distant exotic places. But Bettie was glad it was someone else traveling east because walking down Court Street in Seguin, Texas, was where she would rather be than anywhere else in the world.

The air was ambrosian, the sky crystalline, the white piles of cloud defined so precisely that they seemed cut from cotton cloth and pasted there against the absolute blue of the heavens. The pale ghost of a new moon remained aloft, as if reluctant to relinquish her place to the ascending sun. *It was a delightful morning*, she thought, *safe and clean and good.*

The mystery of the morning had to do with who she might see on her walk downtown to purchase a medication for Henry's ailing leg, a limb he had broken years before that had never properly healed. Bettie had begun to think about the mystery over breakfast. On her walk to the Bergfeld Drug Store, she would pass the homes of three women who had become legends in their own time, women whose lives proved absolutely that God did not make Eve from Adam's rib. Together they were women who made their own way in the world and were so strong and different one from the other that it would have been impossible for them all to have been constructed from the same overly praised and brittle bone.

The first of these women was her mother-in-law Euphemia Texas Ashby King. When she was young, she had been able to ride and shoot like a man, had survived Comanche raids, and was near the battlefield when Sam Houston defeated the villainous Santa Anna at San Jacinto. Tough as she was, Euphemia had been a lifetime defender of civility over savagery. Her house was there, on the right above the springs where King Branch flowed toward the Guadalupe. Euphemia was in the garden, beside her new house, already preparing the soil for her spring planting. When Bettie called to her, Euphemia waved and offered a rare smile. The frail little woman did not appear to be the fierce warrior of her legend.

On the left, hard against the bank of the river, was the small frame house where the woman called Idella Lampkin lived. She was a Negro girl about Bettie's age who was reputed to be able to find things lost and hold long conversations with the dead. Nearly every night the horses and wagons of her clients were tied to a post by her house—people who came to contact departed loved ones or to find a lost ring or lost person. Of course, as a Christian woman, Bettie did not believe in the occult. But she did believe in Idella. Too many people she respected had observed that the girl could see what was hidden from others, could tell what the future held in store. Too many visitors from all over Central Texas had come to her house for too long. There had to be something to her growing legend and to her amazing gifts. As Bettie passed, she thought she saw Idella out back by the river. But maybe it was a trick of light and shadow. Idella was probably still sleeping, exhausted from her sojourns among the lost and the dead.

A few blocks from the courthouse, Bettie walked south so she could pass the venerable Magnolia Hotel, where stagecoaches had stopped for thirty years. Nearby was the naughty house where the redoubtable Pink Rosebud entertained her clients. The notorious lady of the evening fascinated Bettie, and she wondered, *How could a woman so beautiful, so graceful, have fallen into her disreputable profession? Or perhaps she was pushed.* Sometimes, when she saw Pink Rosebud walking downtown in her hard-earned finery, she was amazed at the woman's aplomb. She seemed oblivious to the stir she caused, not noticing how women crossed to the other side of the street, their noses in the air, or how men cast their eyes everywhere but where they really longed to look, which was at Pink Rosebud's shapely form. She went about her day, her face a lovely mask, and only the Devil knew how she went about her nights. *What did Pink Rosebud think about,* Bettie wondered, *and what did she feel in the early morning when her visitors had gone and she was alone? What did she dream or dread?* Bettie believed in the perfectability of the human heart and although she had never spoken to Pink Rosebud she did not bear her ill will. She was certain there was a room in one of Heaven's many mansions even for a woman of the night.

Euphemia Texas Ashby King, Idella Lampkin, Pink Rosebud—three women who proved the amazing diversity of the descendants of Eve. And they all lived in a row, in one small town in the middle of Texas on a small, coiling river the color of smoke and jade. Bettie walked past the Bergfeld Drug Store and strolled onto the town square. She paused to admire the stately courthouse with its towers and spires and eight great chimneys. She had been told that European towns were built around cathedrals or churches, while towns in Texas had courthouses at their center. Old World towns were anchored by faith, while towns in the New World were anchored by law. She was not sure which tradition she preferred, yet she was pleased to realize that both depended on a constant and continuing search for truth.

As always, Bettie loved the energy and activity that enlivened the town square. In the orderly formation of businesses along the streets bordering the square there were people living their lives and making their way in so many contrasting yet complementary ways. Bankers, bakers, storekeepers, preachers, doctors, mule skinners, teachers, cobblers, milliners, seamstresses, restaurateurs, bootblacks, all strolling players on the stage of human community. Here were heroes and rogues, the rich and the poor, wise men and fools, all essential to the heartbeat of the town Bettie loved.

She turned back, past Vivroux Hardware and the Masonic Lodge and back to Court Street and the Bergfeld Drug Store, where she was sure to find Elisabethe Bergfeld, another strong woman who was becoming a Seguin legend as a violinist, composer and teacher.

Elisabethe was waiting on customers. Her husband Arthur was due back from one of his frequent trips to Germany. There were those in town who wondered how a man who came to Texas penniless could afford to buy and stock a drugstore and take his many sojourns abroad. The gossips whispered that Arthur Bergfeld had a secret source of money hidden somewhere in the pharmacy or buried beneath the fountain in the small courtyard between the drugstore and his living quarters.

Bettie agreed that Arthur was a man entirely too opaque and intense for her taste, but she absolutely adored his wife Elisabethe. She was a singularly beautiful woman, a good and loyal friend, and one of the town's most popular and active citizens. Like her mother, she was an accomplished musician, and Bettie had enjoyed many of her performances at the Klein Opera House.

Elisabethe's four-year-old daughter, Louise, was playing with one of the magnificent porcelain dolls that Arthur imported from Germany in addition to his confections and pharmaceuticals. Elisabethe was beginning the last month of her pregnancy. Bettie thought she looked rather tired, and there were shadows beneath her eyes Bettie had not seen before. Elisabethe was making change for an elderly gentleman who had purchased *The Guadalupe Times*, one of the five Seguin newspapers.

As the gentleman departed and Elisabeth was reaching her hand out to Bettie, her welcoming smile suddenly froze and became a grimace of shock and pain. Wide-eyed, she staggered from behind the counter, gasping, clutching her abdomen, blood pooling at her feet. Bettie half caught her as she fell and eased her to the floor. Elisabethe was trying to scream, but pain tore the sound from her throat. Blood now soaked Elisabethe's dress and her hands where she had pressed them against the pain. Bettie felt as if she herself had been struck by lightning, her vision wavering, her heart racing, yet she willed herself to think of something, anything, to stop the terrible bleeding, to ease the agony she could see in her friend's eyes.

"Louise!" Bettie shouted, then saw that the little girl was standing at her shoulder, her eyes filled with terror and confusion. "Run next door! Get Dr. Meyer! Tell him the baby's coming! Quickly now!"

The little girl raced from the room, petticoats flying. Bettie had delivered calves and knew she could deliver a human baby. But this was different, somehow. Something was terribly wrong. It was happening too fast. When she removed Elisabethe's lower garments, it was apparent the placenta was beginning to emerge with the blood.

Then a large Negro woman was kneeling by Bettie's side. "Heat some water, Miss Bettie. And we'll need something to put the baby in. Dr. Meyer is out of town so we'll have to do. See if you can find something for the pain. Likely on those shelves." Then the woman lifted Elisabethe in her arms and carried her from the pharmacy, across the courtyard, into the home, through the parlor and into the bedroom.

The woman was Virgin Annie Jackson, a local midwife. It was no less than a miracle that she had been passing by and Bettie told her so.

"Weren't no miracle," Virgin Annie said. "It was Idella. She saw you pass and she saw this happening before it did and sent me quick. She said go to the Bergfelds cause the Missus has a sudden bleed."

Virgin Annie laid Elisabethe on her back at the foot of the bed, one leg supported high by a table, the other on a treadle sewing machine. Beneath where the blood was flowing from Elisabethe's body, Virgin Annie placed a tin pail. "Most times both mama and baby go," she whispered to Bettie, as the first sign of the baby began to appear. "It's called placenta previa. The placenta comes out first.

Then the baby. The mother loses too much blood. The baby swallows so much it drowns in its mother's blood." Bettie hoped that Elisabethe could not hear what Virgin Annie was saying. She seemed unconscious now. Bettie grasped her friend's hand, wiped the sweat from her forehead with a cool, damp cloth, and listened to the sound of blood falling on tin.

"I need you," Virgin Annie said. "Get that child. She can help, too."

Bettie called little Louise into the bedroom. Virgin Annie was beginning to guide the baby into the world. "Now listen, Child. Miss Bettie and I are gonna try to save your mother. We need you to save the little one. Now we don't have time to get it all cleaned up. But when it comes out, you gotta hold that baby and rock it in that little rocking chair as fast as you can. That rocking will keep the baby breathing. Can you do that, Child?"

Little Louise nodded her head, stepped closer, her eyes riveted on the emerging life.

Bettie feared this was too much to ask of one so young. "Maybe I should do that," she said.

"I can do it," Louise said.

"I need you here by me," Virgin Annie said to Bettie.

Then she lifted the baby free. "It's a baby brother," she said, severing the umbilical cord and placing the infant in an enamel basin. The midwife reached into the baby's mouth with a crooked finger to rake out blood and placenta tissue. Then she slapped him soundly on the bottom. The baby sucked in a gasping, rattling lungful of air and began to kick and wave his arms. But he did not cry. After wiping away much of the blood with a wet cloth, Virgin Annie placed the slippery infant in Louise's arms. "Now rock your brother, Child. And keep slapping him on the back like you would a doll, but harder. Maybe you can keep him alive until his little body can tend to himself."

Bettie helped Louise settle into her child's rocking chair. The little girl's face was white as magazine paper and her eyes were filled with tears of fear. "You can do it, Sweetheart," Bettie said.

Then she returned to where Virgin Annie Jackson's attention was now on saving the life of the mother.

"Here's what we do," Virgin Annie said to Bettie. "I'm gonna see if I can get this bleeding stopped by massaging the womb. Sometimes that seems to help. And what I want you to do is to lay your hands on this woman's heart and pray to God Almighty. Pray with all your might. Ask the Good Lord to let some of your life pass into the heart of this woman."

For the next hour there was only the sound of the rocking chair, clattering and creaking on the board floor. Now and then, Virgin Annie hummed an old Gospel tune as she worked tirelessly through the morning. Sometimes, as she prayed, Bettie thought she might hear the wings of angels that God sent to see what all the commotion was down here in the small bedroom in a Texas town. With her hands pressing Elisabethe's heart, Bettie talked to God. *Dear Lord, one of Your finest creations is in mortal danger. It would be a terrible waste of Your labors if this woman were to die. Surely You know that she is exactly what You had in mind when You decided to make woman. Dear God, let her live. Please give her a little more time so she can be a mother to these beautiful children.*

Then the sound of wings was gone. All Bettie could hear was Virgin Annie Jackson's deep contralto and the chatter of the rocking chair. After what seemed like an eternity, Elisabethe Bergfeld opened her eyes. As if this sign of life were a signal, the baby in Louise's arms began to make a sound his big sister would later swear was laughter.

"What's the baby's name?" Bettie asked little Louise.

"Will," she said. "His name is Will."

For Bettie King, watching Will Bergfeld grow up was an adventure beyond compare. Because she had been present that desperate day when Will was born, she retained a keen and personal and loving interest in how he fared. She now had a daughter of her own, Virginia, and Bettie had this strange, unexplainable notion that fate might have something in store for them to share. Virginia and

Will seemed so absolutely opposite—he impulsive and dark, she graceful and composed and fair—and Bettie was mindful of the old adage that opposites attract. And Will was something to behold. A beautiful and gifted child.

By the time he was six years old, it was apparent Will had extraordinary talents, especially in mathematics and music. Waiting at a railroad crossing with his father one day, a long freight train lumbered by and Will counted the cars before declaring, "I've watched five trains with a total of 239 cars since Sunday." Arthur realized that the boy had kept a running total in his head. Later, Arthur tested Will and found that his son could perform long division without the aid of paper and pen. Performances of this sort provided high entertainment for customers in the pharmacy. They were performances that little Will loved every bit as much as his audience.

As is often the case with those gifted in mathematics, Will was also a musical prodigy. Both his mother and father were violinists and they often played after supper and even after Will and Louise had been tucked into bed. One day, Elisabethe heard Arthur playing and she wondered why he was not in the drugstore. When she went to see, she found it was not Arthur playing, but little Will. Astonished, she remained in the hall shadows, listening, thrilling to the primitive, unseasoned sound. But as time passed, his notes became more precise, his tone less raw. Soon, he was not merely producing sound, but playing music. Elisabethe began giving him lessons every day, and soon, as a schoolboy, Will was performing with his mother at the Klein Opera House.

There was another activity at which Will excelled. He also had a gift for mischief that was extraordinary. If there was trouble to get into, Will would find a way to be in the middle of it, not just as participant, but as instigator.

Across the street from the Bergfeld Drug Store was Humberto Hertado's Mule Barn, a gathering place favored by stagecoach drivers, unemployed cowboys, and those with a tendency to avoid honest work or honest ways. It was exactly the kind of place where a little boy with an adventurous spirit would find towering inspiration. Here, among the minions of Hertado's Mule Barn, little Will learned a third language, the language of humor, to add to his German and English. He became adept at telling traveling salesman jokes, and the tales of the horsebreeding crowd. It was at Hertado's that he learned to perform rope tricks and to crack a bullwhip with such uncommon precision that he could flick a horsefly off a mule's withers without touching the mule. He also learned the dubious art of spitting for distance, and an imperfect but thrilling awareness of what Pink Rosebud did at night. It was at Hertado's that a man from a medicine show taught Will how to palm a coin and make it appear again unexpectedly.

Will was also a favorite of those who raced their mules on Saturday afternoon. Though large for his age, he was fearless and lighter than the older boys and he became a mule jockey much in demand. He had learned how to use his knees to get the most speed and endurance from a horse or mule, and his mounts won a great deal of money for his betting friends until his father caught him at it and fast ended his string of victories. Will would later say that it was the flying mules at Hertado's that generated his lifelong love of speed.

Will's most constant companion was the wild boy Peachtree. Bettie, who had also befriended the orphaned child, applauded the strange friendship and, ever the optimist, hoped for the best. But the best was not always forthcoming.

The two boys often conducted epic expeditions down in the bottoms, searching for Santa Anna's lost treasure, trapping skunks whose skins they sold at Hertado's, and digging endless secret passages leading to lost worlds in the riverbank.

Bettie observed Will's escapades from a distance. He was often the subject of conversation among the tenant families on Henry King's land. Indeed Will's exploits, both laudable and lamentable, were discussed wherever people gathered. Will seemed to be everywhere at once, his behavior always winning high praise or deep censure, sometimes both on the same day. Bettie also observed the boy up close. Since she and Will's mother had become fast friends, Bettie and her daughter Virginia often visited Elisabethe at the drugstore. Although Virginia was a few years younger than Louise, they both delighted in playing with the German dolls Arthur displayed on the shelves.

Over the years, Bettie could not help but be aware of a tension in the Bergfeld household. Arthur Bergfeld insisted that the family maintain its Old World culture, language and traditions. One wall of his drugstore was filled with books and periodicals published in Germany and the walled courtyard outside was a meeting place for gentlemen who seemed unaware that they had left Germany at all. In the home, Arthur only spoke German, and when the children reached school age, they were packed away to a German school. It was on the occasion of Will's first day of school that he ran away for the first of many times. He claimed that Raggedy boys were more fun than the square-headed German boys, and he wanted to go to school with Texans or not at all. But, Elisabethe pulled the children toward things American. She always spoke to them in English and when Arthur was out of earshot, she urged the children to speak English with others.

It occurred to Bettie that her own life represented the two poles existing in the Bergfeld family. She was, after all, a woman of German heritage who married a man from a Scotch-Irish family. But her father's outlook had been shaped by the American experience after he was orphaned at age twelve and taken in by a Raggedy family. This is why she understood Elisabethe's desire to lead her children to become Americans. But it was so much harder for Elisabethe because of the stubborn resistance of her husband.

Bettie also noticed another dimension of tension in the family. Arthur often chastised Will for wasting his God-given gifts. Although Will loved his music, he would only practice when forced. He would much rather listen to the stories of cowboys and wagonmen over at Hertado's Mule Barn. "You'll amount to nothing!" his father would shout. "You're no better than those

Raggedies at the livery stable." Silently, Will agreed, rejecting his father's implicit belief that the German immigrants were better than the other Texans. The more Arthur tried to force his son into a mold, the more Will resisted. Secretly, Bettie feared that Will might be wasting his potential. She was afraid his rebellious nature was going to be his downfall. But she also realized there was plenty of time for him to get his feet on the ground.

Another thing Bettie observed during her visits with the Bergfelds was their exuberance. They pursued life with a sense of joy and rare good humor that was fun to see. Whether it was playing music or organizing a supper at the church, or simply working around the house or the drugstore, Elisabethe and Louise seemed to rejoice in each and every moment. And Will's bright and capersome spirit was legend. Even Arthur pursued his chemistry experiments and his myriad mysterious errands with a vigor one could only admire. And best of all, the Bergfeld home was filled with love abundant. Louise and Will were inseparable and they both adored their mother. It was obvious that Arthur was very much in love with Elisabethe and that he was often brusk and demanding of his children only because he loved them and was concerned about their future.

But of all the things that filled the Bergfeld home and overflowed into the community, the most remarkable was music. The entire family was gifted at both violin and piano. Elisabethe continued to write and direct productions at several opera houses in town, one of which, the Dietz Opera House, had been established nearly a decade before the Metropolitan in New York. Elisabethe's favorite Seguin venue was the Klein Opera House on the corner of Austin and Court Streets, only two blocks away from the Bergfeld home. Upstairs from the saloon of Ferdinand Klein and the law firm of Tips and Campbell, the Klein was the most important of the opera houses in Seguin. It was, in fact, with the possible exception of the Bergfeld Drug Store, the most frequented social center in town. Over the years, its impressive, high-ceilinged stage held such productions and performers as the San Geronimo German

Singing Group, The New Braunfels String Band, and even Chicago's Schubert Symphony Club. But it was the locally produced entertainment that captured the heart and the support of the town. Elisabethe often adapted an opera, such as Wagner's *Parsifal*, or works such as a tone poem by Strauss, or *Opus 80* by Brahms for presentation on the Klein stage.

During the summer when Will was seven years old, Elisabethe was asked to produce an evening of entertainment at the Klein Opera House to raise money for the City Park. She rebelled at the thought of producing yet another adaptation of a German classic, and decided on something completely American. At the time, the most popular stage production in the country was the burlesque extravaganza, *Adonis*, a totally American review that had been a hit on Broadway for three years running. The music was written by the American composer Edward E. Rice. Although Elisabethe had never seen the production, she had purchased the sheet music and loved its energy. She thought the review format with its skits and magic and song-and-dance routines would offer a wonderful opportunity to combine the talents of a wide range of local performers, including children. It also would offer an excellent opportunity for the Bergfeld family to perform on the same stage together.

As the day of the production drew near, it seemed the entire town was involved in rehearsals. They were held on the stage of the Klein Opera House. By popular demand, Will's magic and Wild West act, accompanied by the Bergfeld-Rodriguez String Ensemble, was rehearsed more than any other routine, not because the act needed polishing, but because it was so popular with the townspeople. The open rehearsals attracted crowds nearly as large as those expected at the performance itself.

One late afternoon, as the light softened and a pleasant stillness began to fall on the little town, Elisabethe, her mother, Maria Theresa Naumann, Arthur, the children and Jose Polycarpo Rodriguez gathered on the stage of the Klein to rehearse. Beyond the stage lights it was dark and because the rehearsal had been called at supper time, the hall was nearly empty. As Elisabethe cradled her beloved violin, she suddenly realized that most of what she loved in life was here on this stage, and her mind traveled leisurely back through time. It was like a series of warm images projected by a magic lantern. She remembered her mother's great love with Frederick Naumann and Arthur as he was when she first knew him, gallant and mysterious and even dangerous. She remembered the grand adventure of escaping from Bismarck's agents twenty years ago when she was only nine and how when they got to America her dear friend Pastor Polly had kept them safe from bandits and Comanches on the road from Indianola. She recalled the night of the Masked Ball when Arthur had come back into her life and as she looked at him now, his bow poised above his violin, she realized how much she still loved the strange man who swept her off her feet that glorious night. And there were Louise and Will, the living evidence of that love.

As Elisabethe raised her violin, Pastor Polly reached over and touched her arm. "No," he said softly.

Elisabethe hesitated, a confused smile on her face. "Why?"

"I don't know why," Pastor Polly said.

"Well, then, let's make music," She raised the violin to her chin and began to play.

At first it was a very small pain, a sharp piercing sensation on her lip. She lowered the violin and swept her hand across her mouth. Everyone stopped playing except Pastor Polly, who had never started and was looking skyward, his lips moving in prayer.

"What is it?" Arthur asked.

Elisabethe's face was ashen. "Something bit me. It was in the violin." She touched her lip with her fingers. There was a slight swelling. She tried to say more, but her tongue and lips seemed paralyzed and she could not form the words.

"It's a spider," Will said, bending down, turning the spider over with his foot, seeing the red hourglass design on its abdomen. "A black widow." Will ground the spider into the stage floor.

Louise ran for Dr. Meyer. Arthur carried Elisabethe in his arms across the courthouse square to their home a block away.

He placed her on the bed, loosened her clothing. Within minutes, Elisabethe began to feel the paralysis spreading into her chest. Her diaphragm seemed partially paralyzed and she found it difficult to breathe.

By the time Dr. Meyer rushed into the bedroom, the pain had extended from the bite down to her hips and legs.

The doctor examined the whitish spot on Elisabethe's swollen lip and then began to pinch her, first her arm, then her hand, then her thigh. Each time he asked her if she could feel what he was doing and each time she shook her head.

"What can we do?" Arthur asked.

Dr. Meyer looked at his empty hands, then at Arthur and shook his head.

Arthur grasped the doctor's arm. "Do something!"

The doctor pulled Arthur's hand away, not roughly. "You're a pharmacist, Arthur. You know there is nothing I can do. The venom has spread too far. It's in the hands of God."

The pain grew excruciating and Elisabethe began to cramp, severe nausea sweeping over her in angry waves. As the pain extended now to all parts of her body, it seemed to clear her mind and she could see on the faces of those around her that she was dying. She felt an immense and abiding sorrow. *How quickly it comes.* She remembered those few times when she had realized the hour of her dying would come. That there would come a moment when she would know it was her dying day. But it was always a fragment of thought that was vanquished by the fact of youth. What was it Pastor Polly had once said? The past and the future exist side by side in the mind of God. She began to feel less pain now and it filled her with momentary terror. As long as she could feel the pain she knew she was alive and she wished to celebrate the pain, hold it close. But she could feel it slipping away and she was growing cold. Her vision was growing cloudy and all she could see of her family were shapes around the bed. She knew she must look terrible with the huge swelling on her lip and her pillow soiled by her nausea. Elizabethe smiled to herself when she realized that she could feel vanity in the face of death. She thought about last words, the proverbial utterances by which one is remembered. *More vanity,* she thought. She wished to tell Arthur how much she loved him and to tell Will to stop going over to Hertado's and to tell Louise to make sure Will stays out of trouble. But her lips would not move and she decided the sum of her life would have to be last words enough.

The pain was gone now. Elisabethe listened to Pastor Polly praying and she heard all the music she had ever played. With her family gathered near, her young heart stopped and the music faded away.

XIII.

Abilene, Texas.
October 1917

The Methodist church seemed almost lonely on the edge of the prairie, a white ghost of what it must have been before the heart of town passed on by. Like most American towns, expansion was almost always northward and westward, toward the prevailing winds. In this way, families sought to avoid much of the wind-blown soot and smoke from the railroad tracks and the sewage deposited by neighbors upstream. Anyway, that was a theory Henry King had and Bettie supposed it was fact. He also had a theory about why American churches, like the one Bettie now approached, often had two towers of unequal height. He said it was a reflection of the fact that Medieval cathedrals took so long to build that the towers were often unfinished or their construction delayed by warfare or plague, or some other disaster. Somewhere along the line, the builders of American houses of worship decided that this was the way churches were supposed to be and that it was pleasing in the sight of God. Bettie supposed this was true.

Although the church seemed weather-worn, and it had one tall slim bell tower and one squat square one, Bettie noticed that it had been tended with loving care. The frame structure had been recently whitewashed. What grass there was in the dirt yard and in the small fenced graveyard behind had been mowed and she could smell a trace of the sweet just-cut grass aroma in the dusty air. Bettie was curious why there were so few headstones in the graveyard.

Maybe the church elders simply refused to be buried in such a desolate place and had asked to be buried where there was some shade, at least. Yet, there was about the church that feeling of transcendence that seemed to dwell in the deep woods or invade high hilltops or cling to even the most homely of churches. It was a sense that, at least here, during these few hours, on this particular day, God has come by to see what's what.

Bettie had arrived early. She had come alone. Upon awaking she had felt a deep need to be by herself, away from the trial, even the family, somewhere, anywhere, to empty her mind for awhile. On one of her morning walks, she had noticed this little church on the edge of the prairie and, although she would not be alone there, she thought she might be able to lose herself among strangers. Soon the worshipers began to arrive. It was a Sabbath scene repeated a thousand times throughout American towns. Families dressed in their Sunday best, children freshly scrubbed, the pastor at the door greeting his flock, people he has known most of their lives, men and women he had married and would bury one day.

Bettie had hardly entered the churchyard before she was spotted by several women who approached and embraced her with effusive welcomes. After introductions, one of the women, Emily Thomas, took her arm and they walked together toward the door.

"Are you visiting?" the woman asked.

"Just passing through," Bettie replied. She wondered what Emily would think if she knew she was talking with the mother-in-law of Will Bergfeld, the celebrated German sympathizer. Or if they knew her father was German-born. "I'm on my way to Colorado," she said, astounded at the lie that had escaped her lips, on Sunday, in the front yard of God's house. It was the greatest sin she had ever committed and she was both shocked at her unbidden audacity and thrilled by how easy it would be to create an entirely new identity among strangers.

As they approached the door where the pastor waited with outstretched hand, Bettie noticed a woman with three small children standing apart from the other families. She was dressed in an old, worn frock, clean but ragged. Her children were barefoot. The mother's face was gaunt, her eyes desperate. The children clung to her skirts, solemn, silent, and Bettie wondered when they had last eaten a solid meal.

Bettie paused, turned toward the sad little family. "Who are they?" she asked Emily.

"Some of those Germans camping near here," she said.

"Those children look hungry."

"It's a sad story, Bettie."

"Why doesn't someone help them?"

"What could we do?"

"Something, I would think," Bettie said, taking a step toward the family.

Emily Thomas took her arm and steered her away, toward the church door again. "It's tragic for the children, of course. But as a visitor you wouldn't know what those people have done."

Then they were into the church. It was as plain inside as out. The congregation half filled the pews, families taking their accustomed places, Bettie sitting next to Emily, Mr. Thomas and their two teenage girls. The sermon was on the application of the Book of Revelations to everyday life, a topic that would have made little sense to Bettie even if she had not been thinking about the impoverished German family outside. The visions of St. John did not include how to feed hungry children or dress them against the chilly winds soon to come. As the collection was being taken, Bettie risked a glance toward the back of the church. The mother and her children were there, huddled alone together on a back pew. When the collection plate reached the back row, the deacon was about to pass on by the German family, when the mother rose and dropped a coin into the plate. The coin rang like a clarion, the sound filling the church and resonating in Bettie's mind. Although terribly poor, the woman had saved something for the Lord.

After church, Bettie followed the woman and her children. They crossed the prairie into a hollow, between two hills. Here, protected somewhat from the North Texas winds, was a community built of wagons and rude tents of muslin. The wagons were formed up in a circle, some turned on their sides as windbreaks. A few people, including the family she had followed, were gathered around a small fire at the center of the circled wagons. Bettie saw only women and small children. Suddenly she knew she had come upon wives and children of the FLPA defendants who, unlike Will's family, could not raise the ten-thousand-dollar bail. She had met only a few relatives of the other defendants in court, and now she knew why. Seeing these people now, in their woeful condition, was like a physical blow. She felt pity for them and at the same time she was vexed with herself for being so blind that she had not realized the predicament these families were in—abruptly deprived of their husbands and fathers, as well as their livelihood and their dignity.

Bettie walked toward the wagons. The women and children watched her come, their eyes empty, probably dreading what new calamity this strange woman was bringing into their midst. She reached the fire. It did not give off much heat. No one spoke. Bettie nodded to the woman she had seen in church. "My name is Bettie King," she said. "My daughter is married to Will Bergfeld."

"You are welcome here," the mother said. "My name is Hilma." The woman did not smile, although Bettie thought she might have if she had had the energy. But she made a place by the fire for Bettie to sit. Then Hilma introduced the others, including Frieda Boelt, wife of one of the defendants who had been unable to make bail. Frieda and her six little girls were barely managing to survive.

"What people don't realize," Frieda said, "is that when they put the breadwinner in jail, we have no bread. So imagine, fifty breadwinners jailed, and each one supports maybe four or five, that's two hundred people without food."

"And no one helps?"

"Some do. They do what they can. But these are hard times for everybody."

Bettie felt a brush of shame that she and Henry had been able to make bail for Will while these other families had nothing. It was an illogical shame, but she felt it just the same.

"I'm so sorry," Bettie said. "I mean Will is free and your husband is. . . ."

Frieda grasped her hand. "Don't be sorry, Bettie. What else could you have done?"

"That's a question to hide behind," she said. "Something can always be done. What about the churches?"

"No," Frieda said, shaking her head. "Most look the other way. Or they look right through us as if we weren't here. Even some of the German families don't want to be associated with us. I think they're afraid. 'There but for the grace of God go I.'

"The worse thing is that we've lost our land," Hilma said. "We're mostly farmers. Our farm was near Ranger. And what happens is that we're always beholden to the banks. We have to borrow each year to make crops. With the men in jail, the crops failed so there was no way to meet our payments to the banks. So they foreclosed, and our land is gone. Our homes are gone. All we have left are our wagons and a few animals."

Bettie thought about the irrelevant sermon on Revelations and her frustration grew.

"This is what your Will was trying to fight," Frieda said. "What Mr. Powell was fighting for. They were trying to help the farmers be shut of the bankers. Cooperatives, they called it. He's a good man, your Will. But those who opposed him were too strong."

Hilma and Frieda took Bettie for a tour of the community. Conditions were deplorable. A good many of the women were in advanced pregnancy and some of the children were seriously ill. A few children, she learned, had already died and were buried in unmarked graves nearby. The tents and hovels offered little protection and Bettie shuddered. *What will happen when the northers sweep down from Canada with their sleet and freezing winds?* When the people learned who Bettie was, they welcomed her with genuine warmth. She had been afraid they might resent her, a woman who must seem to have everything when they had nothing. After all, Will had gotten them into this awful situation by being among the most outspoken members of the Farmers' and Laborers'

Protective Association. But as the afternoon progressed, she realized that Will was universally respected in the community and they obviously accepted his mother-in-law as well.

"I'll bring a doctor," she told Frieda. "And I'll see if I can't get something started with the churches."

"Bless you," Frieda said.

"I'll be back when I can," Bettie said.

As Bettie moved across the prairie into town, her resolve began to build. After all, she had the ability to organize church suppers and head up charitable events in Seguin, so why not use her God-given talents to get help for these people?

On Monday morning, Judge Jack excused the jury and announced to both the defense and the prosecution that he was ready to hear arguments on the admissibility of evidence related to the so-called German List. The spectators crowding the hall, aware that this issue had led to some entertaining fireworks the week before, crowded forward, eager for action or at least heated argument. With Sergeant Grimes back on the witness stand, Judge Jack asked the defense to begin the questioning.

"Your Honor," Bill Atwell said, "in order for me to properly explain why this document should be admitted before the jury, I need to develop some background information from Sergeant Grimes."

"Your witness," Judge Jack said.

"Sergeant Grimes," Atwell asked, "tell us about the train that you used on the night you arrested Will Bergfeld."

"Well, it was not a regularly scheduled train. It was a special train put together solely for these arrests."

"Who made the special arrangements for the train?"

"People in Washington. The Justice Department."

"Wasn't there a feature on this train that most trains don't have?"

"It had a jail car to hold the people we were going to pick up in Haskell County and some of the surrounding areas."

"Who was on that train, Sergeant Grimes?"

"When we entered Haskell County the only people on it were law officers and government agents."

"How many officers were on that train?"

"There were thirty-two in all."

"Were they all armed?"

"Yes, sir."

"How did you know who you were supposed to pick up and put in this rolling jail?"

"We had lists with names and addresses."

Atwell removed papers from the defense table and approached the witness stand. "Let me show you this document and ask you to tell us what it is."

Sergeant Grimes thumbed through the document. "It's one of the lists we used to arrest some of the defendants."

"Please read to the judge the exact title of this document."

"Alphabetical List of Subjects of the Teutonic Order."

Defense Attorney Atwell stepped next to the witness stand, leaned over and pointed out a particular passage on the document. "For the record, let me direct your attention to what it says here, below the title. Would you read this line for the judge?"

"It says, 'Enclosed herewith is a list of those investigated in connection with German affairs.'"

"Sergeant Grimes, the document also mentions that some of the people on the list were involved in 'socialist activities' and that some were members of the Farmers' and Laborers' Protective Association. Isn't that so?"

"Yes, sir. That's all written there."

Atwell asked Sergeant Grimes to turn to page two. "At the top of this page, is there anything indicating that government agents were spying on Will Bergfeld before he was even charged with any crime?"

"Yes, sir, I can see that it does."

"And doesn't it refer to Will Bergfeld as German born?" Atwell pointed out the statement. "Here. It says 'William A. Bergfeld was born in Germany.' "

"Yes, it says that."

"In fact, Sergeant Grimes, isn't it true that Will Bergfeld was born in Texas?"

"I don't know that."

"Can you agree with me that if the government's lengthy and in-depth investigation was dead wrong about such a fundamental fact, they could be dead wrong about a lot of things. Isn't that so?"

"That could be."

Bill Atwell took the document from the witness. "Sergeant Grimes, from what you have seen of this document, do you agree with me that it appears to list people who the Department of the Army feared might sympathize with Germany in our war against that country?"

"Yes, sir. In fact, some of the officials on the train referred to it as the 'German Enemies List.'"

"Were these officials you're referring to from Texas?"

"No, sir, I don't think so, because their orders regarding the arrest came from the Department of the Army and then through the Justice Department in Washington."

"Did they ever share with you the evidence they had against the people they were asking you to help arrest?"

"No, sir. All I knew is that they wanted some Texas Rangers to help arrest the people on the list."

"So it is correct that none of the Rangers had any personal knowledge of any evidence of any crimes charged against these defendants?"

"All I can say for sure is that I had no personal knowledge. And I don't think any of the other Texas officers did either. As I said, we were just there to help make the arrest."

"Do you recall any conversations or comments by any of these federal officers about their duties here in Texas?"

"Yes, sir. One of them, who seemed to be in charge, said, 'We've got to get these goddamn trouble-making Germans off the streets before they undermine this country's war effort.' I can't swear those were his exact words, but that's sure enough close to his exact words. I know that."

O'Dell rose to object.

"Do you object to the statement of Sergeant Grimes?" Judge Jack asked. "Or to the statement of the federal officer he quoted?"

"I object to everything I've heard in this procedure," O'Dell answered. "Not only is Sergeant Grimes's last statement hearsay, it's entirely irrelevant."

"Mr. O'Dell, in the absence of the jury, I'm allowing some latitude here. Now just sit down. You'll get your turn."

As O'Dell reluctantly took his seat, Atwell studied the lean and angular Texas Ranger. That he would voluntarily quote the words of the federal officer on the train was quite unexpected. He could have easily avoided such an inflammatory response. No wonder O'Dell was in such a funk. *If only the jury could hear this testimony,* Atwell thought. He looked at the judge who also seemed to be studying the witness. Atwell stepped forward before the judge.

"Your Honor, at this time the defendants respectfully suggest that this testimony that Sergeant Grimes has just given should be allowed in evidence and repeated in front of the jury. The jury is entitled to hear this testimony and review the contents of the document."

The judge was still looking at the witness. Atwell could see that Judge Jack was also confused by the Ranger's apparent leanings toward the defense. The taciturn lawman who had at first testified with one-word answers now was offering evidence injurious to the prosecution without being asked.

"Tell me why this man's testimony should be heard by the jury," Judge Jack asked, his eyes now on Atwell.

"Because it shows why these defendants are here. These men have been arrested, not because they committed the crimes charged against them, but because certain people in Washington don't like their national heritage and their political associations. The jury needs to know what this case is really about. It is about prejudice and a flagrant violation of these defendants' rights under the United States Constitution. If these facts are kept from the jury it will be like blindfolding the jurors at a time when we're asking them to make a decision, through their verdict, which will forever affect the lives of these men. In fairness to the jury, they need to know all of the facts, and so I respectfully ask you to overrule the prosecution's objection and allow me to present this evidence."

"Mr. O'Dell," Judge Jack said, "now you may offer your objections to the motion."

O'Dell positioned himself squarely behind the podium facing the judge. "May it please the Court," he began, "the government objects to this testimony given by Sergeant Grimes and we also object to the document containing the so-called German List. All such evidence is irrelevant and immaterial to any of the issues in this case. It matters not one whit what these documents say or how they were used in connection with some of the arrests. The questions before the jury in this case are whether or not the defendants are guilty as charged. The testimony just given by Sergeant Grimes does not shed any light on the guilt or innocence of any defendant. In fact, Sergeant Grimes has admitted that he was not a part of the criminal investigation and that he has no knowledge of the evidence against the defendants. And so, Your Honor, the government respectfully requests that our objection to this evidence be sustained and that all of it be excluded from the jury."

One of the world's most mysterious and unknowable places is that province existing within the mind of a judge, absolutely enigmatic in its inner workings, Atwell thought. *The mind of a judge should be little different from the mind of the lawyer he had been before. But often a beguiling metamorphosis takes place between lawyer and judge, not unlike the transformation of caterpillar into moth. Here is a blending of reason and emotion; decisions influenced by legal precedent, political expediency, personal conviction and blind hunch; and of course, there are always those human failings such as vanity, mulishness, and prejudice, recognized or not. Just when you think you have figured out the judge and know how he will respond,* Atwell thought, *he rules in an altogether surprising way.*

In this case, as Judge Jack pondered, eyes nearly closed behind his spectacles, arms folded across his chest, Atwell thought he could have been listening to music, or remembering some nearly forgotten event from his youth. *What was going on in that mind?* Perhaps O'Dell was right and Grimes's testimony was irrelevant to the case. Surely, this would be running through the judge's mind. But there was also the broader issue of justice and what was right and what was wrong in a larger sense. Atwell also had a growing awareness of the presence of the spectators. He glanced behind him and saw that every eye was on the judge. Everyone in the courtroom understood the import of his ruling and the impact it would have on the case. If Grimes were allowed to give this testimony before the jury, it would be a major plus for the defense. If Grimes's testimony were disallowed, it would mean that the defense was still in an uphill battle for a favorable verdict.

Then Judge Jack opened his eyes, moved uncomfortably and looked toward the empty seats in the jury box, then toward the witness and the two lawyers. "It is the order of the Court that the government's objection is sustained. The evidence pertaining to the so-called German List will be excluded from the jury."

Judge Jack called a recess.

Atwell examined the hollow feeling beneath his ribs. He wondered if he had done all he could have done for his clients, if he had advanced every possible argument on this issue. He glanced toward Will and his family, feeling not only disappointment, but what could only be described as guilt. Will was expressionless. Virginia was holding his hand, their daughters gathered around them. *An American tableau*, Atwell thought. *A family in search of justice.* He met Louise Bergfeld's eyes. Unlike the other members of the family, they were bright with more anger than disappointment, and before looking away, she clenched her fist, a gesture that renewed Bill Atwell's resolve to fight for these good people in his care.

What happened in the courtroom that morning was a severe blow to the defense and to the effort to save Will Bergfeld's life. But it was not nearly as disastrous as what would happen out in the street in the afternoon.

Louise Bergfeld left the courthouse and walked across the lawn to her apple-red touring car. For weeks now, her exit from the courthouse had become a familiar ritual and she was followed by the catcalls and leers of young boys and some men old enough to know better. It was as if the passing of this beautiful and exotic stranger, said to be the sister of the chief German agent, was the highpoint of their day. Apparently, the fact that she was the hated enemy gave them license to be rude and abusive. At first, the behavior of the courthouse loafers and redneck rowdies disturbed Louise, but as the days passed, she began to ignore, even pity, the rabble that followed her to her car and then stood around as she settled into the soft leather seats.

She started the car, shifted into gear. But as she began to pull away, she was blocked by her entourage of admirers. They had surrounded the car, young boys running their hands lovingly over the fine smooth curves of the hood and fenders, older boys admiring the curves of the driver. Louise honked the horn. The crowd just laughed, crowded closer. Louise began to feel the first icy touch of alarm.

"Hey boys, little lady gonna give us a ride!" one of the men called.

"You ride the car," another called, "I'll ride the little lady!" This was followed by a chorus of hoots and whistles. A red-faced man, obviously drunk, was staggering toward her. One of the boys climbed up on the hood and leered obscenely at her through the windshield. Louise was deciding whether or not she should gun the engine and speed away, risking injury to the fools tormenting her, when she was aware of a sudden change in the mood of the small crowd surrounding the roadster. She followed their eyes to a large man standing several yards away. She recognized him as Spec Davis, one of the witnesses for the prosecution.

"Better leave her be, boys. You, too, Kennemer." The man's voice broke as he spoke. He seemed outraged, but afraid, as if confronting Louise's tormentors was something he simply had to do regardless of the risk.

"Well, if it ain't the Judas," said the man who had tried to get in her car.

"Let the woman go," Davis repeated. "She done you no harm, Kennemer."

"You done more harm than any man alive, Spec! For what you done you gonna suffer in Hell!"

The man called Kennemer stepped away from the car and the group's focus shifted from Louise to the confrontation between Spec Davis and Luke Kennemer. The crowd in the street grew larger, drawn by the expectation of trouble. After all, the fight in the courtroom had been merely symbolic, hurled words. Here was the promise of real action. The car was now surrounded, trapped, and Louise was a reluctant witness to the unfolding drama.

"I did what was right," Spec Davis said.

"What you done was stupid! You knew what would happen to you if you broke your blood oath! We all knew. We all took that oath. But you sold us down the river, and some good men are settin' in jail because of rats like you."

Luke Kennemer slammed his fist down on the hood of the red roadster. The voice of the crowd rose. A small boy, then another, began to beat on the fenders. Others began to rock the car. Louise pressed the horn, desperately seeking to attract the attention of law officers. Hands reached into the car, Louise slapped them away, spat in a face that had drawn close, lips pursed in a pantomime kiss. The air was filled with shouts mixed with the blaring of the horn.

Then there came a sound that shut out all other sound like a door slammed shut. And in the silence, in that suspended instant, Louise saw something that would remain in her mind for the rest of her days. Kennemer's smoking revolver pointed to a crimson flower blooming on Spec Davis's shirt, just above his belt. Davis stood for a long moment, staring at his stomach in disbelief, then he slowly folded to the ground. Kennemer stood over the bleeding body and spoke. "Now die, you son of a bitch. You betrayed us all. So die and while you're dying think what you've done to your brothers."

The silence following the gunshot was shattered now by voices calling and the pounding of footfalls and horses' hooves and the screams of those who had witnessed the shooting. Soon Texas Rangers and sheriff's deputies were surrounding Louise's car and the fallen witness. A doctor was summoned. What had been a small flower of blood was now a sodden red bouquet and Louise noticed that Spec Davis's eyes filled with tears as if he mourned his own passing. As he was lifted and carried away, he looked toward Louise and their eyes met and held. Louise wondered what message those eyes conveyed. Did he blame her? If not for her, he might have passed on by, unnoticed by Kennemer and his drunken rage. Or was he seeking to prolong his life by holding on to the living eyes of another? In any event, Louise was saddened and sickened and then she was unable to hold back the tears that came and the pummeling sobs of grief for Spec Davis and for all of humanity that was sentenced to die by the simple fact of life.

Kennemer was one of the fifty-two defendants, along with Will, who was out on bond. But this time when he was arrested for murder, he was jailed without bond. Spec Davis survived several days and was able to make a lengthy statement, naming Kennemer as one of a number of FLPA members who had threatened him if he testified. Luke Kennemer had specifically told Spec Davis that if he revealed lodge secrets he would be killed. Now Luke had made good on his threat.

Davis's deathbed statement was an Indictment of the Farmers' and Laborers' Protective Association. Newspapers were filled with accounts of the murder and editorials damning the FLPA, a secret fraternity that harbored not only German sympathizers and socialists, but now murderers, as well. "Not exactly your Sunday school kind of organization," Bill Atwell said, as he tried to assess the damage done to their cause.

Louise felt violated to read story after story connecting her to the murder, suggesting that the beautiful sister of the infamous Will Bergfeld had been the cause of the quarrel between Davis and Kennemer.

Several days after Spec Davis was shot, Bettie King led a column of women and children to a Methodist church on the edge of the prairie. She had begged and cajoled and shamed the Methodist Women's Missionary Society to shift some of their focus and resources from Asia and Africa to their desperate sisters suffering in the shadow of their own church. Now, in the churchyard, tables had been set up where two physicians were preparing to examine the sick. Stacks of clothing and bedding had been collected. Other tables labored under the weight of tins of butter and lard, vessels of milk, bags of sugar and flour. Some goods had been bought with contributions from the men and women of the German Methodist Church in Seguin.

Charity begged and cajoled and shamed, is charity just the same, Bettie thought, as she and Emily led the women through the dust. Sometimes you just have to dig a little to find the good in folks.

XIV.

Seguin, Texas.
Spring 1907

Louise Bergfeld could not count the number of times she had reread Will's letters since the last time he had run away. Although he had spent much of his childhood running from home or hiding out with Peachtree in the Guadalupe River bottoms, only to be dragged back by the sheriff, she feared that this time he was gone for good. She lifted the stack of letters, felt their heft, a measure more in meaning than in weight, and she marveled that he had expressed more of his feelings in writing than he had ever expressed in person. They had always been close, brother and sister, two against the world, but never as close as when divided by distance.

She missed Will terribly. In a sense she felt he had abandoned her, left her to deal with the grief that had divided the family ever since their mother died. But the family was shattered now, no longer really existed, so maybe the anguish would dissipate into the air like the smoke from a grass fire.

After her mother's death, her father, Arthur Bergfeld, sank into deep mourning. For a year, he descended into a private hell where no one else was allowed. He spent his days and nights at the drugstore, working in his chemistry lab, often until late at night. He seldom spoke, and when he did, it was expressions of frustration and remorse. He ignored Will and Louise completely. They spent most of their childhood in the homes of neighbors and kin. Will had once claimed that he "had more mothers than any boy in Seguin." But the many different women who had doctored his bruises, washed his tears and comforted him with thick slices of homemade bread, heavily coated with fresh churned butter and preserves, could not replace his real mother.

Then came Emma Greifenstein. Suddenly she was there. When Emma Greifenstein entered the Bergfeld family, it had shocked the community. Over clotheslines and back fences, the women of Seguin gossiped about the improbable match. Emma was in her early twenties, Arthur was old enough to be her father and so sour and taciturn that it seemed impossible any young girl in her right mind would want to spend even a day with him, much less a lifetime. It was argued by some that she was after his money. After all, his pharmacy was flourishing and he was quite prosperous. And since Arthur was such a recluse, hiding out in his drugstore, his bride could have his money and the house without bothering about having much to do with the man. Why Arthur would want Emma was something else again. Some said he needed a woman, any woman, to run the household. Unspoken was the fact that Emma Greifenstein was a voluptuous young woman and Arthur must have been a very lonely man.

Louise never found Emma attractive. In contrast to the soft curves of her body, her face was hard and angular. She had a beak of a nose and eyes that regarded the world and its inhabitants with haughty disdain. And there was certainly nothing attractive in her relationship with Will. Although Emma simply ignored Louise, Emma did not like Will from the start, and a simple word or gesture from her stepson sent her into a fury. She never spoke a civil word to him, only demands and orders, recriminations and reprimands. Because of Will's lively temperament and his dubious gift of attracting attention to himself, Emma often accused him of embarrassing her before the whole county.

One summer day, near Peachtree's cave and below where Idella's house backed up to the Guadalupe, the boys began construction of a sailing ship. The model Will had in mind was the *Santa Maria*. The hull was fashioned from boards gathered from abandoned picket fences and outhouses and from a pile of lumber behind the Mission Hotel. A large piece of canvas, formerly a cover for a pioneer's wagon, was borrowed from Hertado's and patched by Louise who, in return, had been invited to sail with them to the mouth of the Guadalupe and then on to the Indies, a destination even Columbus had failed to reach. Louise declined the invitation, but agreed to keep the voyage secret from their parents. With the boards and lumber the boys made a box frame and then wrapped the frame in canvas. The result, Idella said, was not unlike a coffin, which it nearly turned out to be.

One sunny and sweltering morning, the two explorers set out on their epic and star-crossed voyage. Their crude craft, which they had named *Old Ironsides,* moved out into the Guadalupe, the course set for Gonzales and eventually Cuero, Victoria and the Gulf of Mexico.

A few days passed before they consumed the last sausage and bread stored on board, but friendly farmers along the way always gave them food. A bigger problem was that they had become food for the swarming mosquitos that lurked in every quiet and dark place along the path of the placid river. The boys at first welcomed the rapids that from time to time stirred the water, but they soon tired of hauling their boat over the gravel bars that interupted the stretches of navigable water. Once *Old Ironsides* got caught in an eddy spinning in the current until Peachtree got sick to his stomach. Finally, Will took a board from the boat itself to push off from the high bank and to break free of the eddy.

When they came to a navigable stretch in the river and floated for a ways, the boys started to debate which was worse, the days with their skin raw from sunburn or the nights being eaten alive by mosquitos. Once Peachtree went overboard in deep water, and because he could not swim Will went in after him. Holding Peachtree's head above water, Will struggled for the shore, but the current was so swift that they were swept on downstream. Later Will would say the Peachtree was as buoyant as an anvil. But first they had to follow *Old Ironsides* down the river to where it had run aground in some shallows.

Two weeks passed before the boys approached their first goal, Gonzales. As the exhausted youths floated around a bend in the river, they came upon a small crowd gathered in front of a man preaching by the riverside. As they were swept closer, Will saw it was the Reverend Polycarpo Rodriguez, his mother's dear friend, leading a revival and about to begin playing his holy music. Pastor Polly spied the boys and recognized Will. He promptly waded into the water and pulled their boat ashore. Instead of saving souls Pastor Polly had saved their hides. He delivered the waterlogged explorers back to Seguin.

After this celebrated event all evening meals were torturous, conducted almost as punishment. The only words spoken were strained or angry or ugly. And Will always addressed his stepmother as Miss Emma, as if refusing to acknowledge that she was married to his father.

On Will's birthday, Emma sent him from the table before the cake Louise had made could be served.

"It's his birthday!" Louise protested.

"I will not stand for that look on his face!" Emma said, continuing to butter her sweet potato.

"What look?" Will asked, innocently. Louise knew. In one look Will could say a thousand words, half of them striking like physical blows. *And that was certainly a part of the trouble,* Louise thought. *Will could drive a person crazy with that look.*

"I told you to leave the table, young man!" Emma said, now picking at her sweet potato.

"I'll give you more than a look," Will whispered, as he got up and walked from the room.

In the terrible silence that followed, a silence that always accompanied the intervals after Will left the dinner table, Louise tried to put herself in her stepmother's place, to see the world from her point of view. *What could have made her so mean and despotic? Certainly Will was difficult, but he was essentially a good boy with a generous spirit. There must be something else.* Maybe it was because

Emma was so young when she married Arthur, only a few years older than Louise was now. Maybe she was simply trying to assert her authority. Or maybe she had deep regrets about marrying Arthur and believed that she was wasting her youth with an unpleasant and unappreciative middle-aged man.

After bedtime, when she was sure everyone was asleep, Louise crept into her brother's room and got him to follow her into the kitchen. She divided what was left of Will's birthday cake between them. They ate in silence. Louise knew what she had long dreaded was about to happen. Tears filled her eyes even before he said what he had to do.

"If I stay here I will kill her," he said softly, after he finished his cake. "It's more than I can handle. She provokes me and makes me want to wring her neck. I've got to go before something terrible happens."

"Where will you go?"

"Herman Weinert started that new town up on the Wichita Valley rail line. Ashby McCulloch is putting together another immigrant train of homesteaders. Maybe that's what I need. A whole new start in a new place, away from Miss Emma. Just think, Louise, I would be like a pioneer. Building a whole new life in the wilderness. Like Mama and Papa did before things turned bad."

"What would you do there?"

"There'll be a lot of work for a young man. My friend Wayne McCulloch is going with his brother, Sam. I can live with the McCullochs. On the train we'll take care of the animals. And there'll be plenty of work once we get there."

"You have only three months until graduation. You can't go now."

"Chances like this don't come twice. Besides, Miss Emma and Papa will be glad to see me gone. They'd be glad to see you go too. You can come with us, Sis."

A small thrill danced at the back of Louise's neck. What an adventure that would be! But she answered, "I can't go, Will."

"Why not? There's nothing for you here."

"I have a contract to teach school at New Berlin. And there's my music. I want to be a performer like Mama and Grandma Naumann. I can't do that out in the wilderness."

"Please?"

"My life is here in Seguin, Will."

"We've never been apart," Will said. "Except that time Peachtree and I took that cruise down the Guadalupe." They laughed, images of their life together sliding behind their eyes.

"When will you go?" Louise knew the answer.

"Before morning. I'll stay with the McCullochs until the train leaves."

"Wait, it's your birthday, and I have a present."

Louise went into her room and returned with the gift. It was a tin of watercolors. Will had demonstrated talent as an artist, especially lifelike portraits he had sketched in pencil. Louise was confident he could do equally well in color.

Will's eyes grew large as his fingers touched the tray of colors and tested the softness of the brushes. "I love the names they give the pigments—burnt umber, indigo, white, French nude, damask, dahlia blue. They're like words in a poem." He leaned over the table. "It's really nice. Thanks."

"I knew you would leave. But not so soon. I wanted you to paint my portrait so I can always be where you are. But there's no time now."

"I have your image in my mind. I'll paint the portrait as soon as I get settled."

Will left just before dawn.

Now, nearly a year after his departure, Louise looked at the stack of his letters. She picked up his first letter. It was dated a few weeks after he left.

Dear Louise,

If this land wasn't so cheap, I sure can't imagine why anyone would want it. Not a tree in sight and the wind blows dust into town and into your eyes and into your supper. I doubt even the Indians lived in this area because the only game I've seen is prairie dogs, jack rabbits, and rattlesnakes. But there is something exciting about watching a town spring up in the middle of nowhere. When you build from scratch you get to do it right. The main street is very wide and the buildings facing it are built with the heart pine brought up on the train. They are square, like boxes, with large covered porches to keep you out of the rain if it were ever to rain, which I have my doubts. Some of the buildings, like the Weinert Hotel, are two-story with railed balconies overlooking the activity in the street. Other buildings pretend to be two-story, but the second floor is just a big false front to make it look larger and more important than it is. They are nicely proportioned, raw looking and new.

I helped paint the lettering on businesses like L. A. Crouch Fry Goods and Grocery. This is the main store in town for everything, Lefty Crouch is certainly one of the owners, but rumor is that Weinert and Crouch are partners in almost every business here. They run the town, that's for sure. Old Man Crouch controls the water. People got really miffed at him when they found the water was salty. It seems he is trying to profit from this water business by damming up the only creek and then selling the water to folks who don't have any. Now there are some people, including yours truly, who wonder how Old Man Crouch got the land in the first place. What was once given to the people as school land, suddenly ended up in Crouch's pocket. Maybe it is politics. I used to think politics was dull, but I've changed my mind. It seems to be a system that can make a difference in people's lives. I miss you. I'm working on your portrait. If you see Peachtree tell him Howdy.

Your brother,
Will

Louise tried to imagine Will in a place that was raw and new and devoid of the natural beauty that was so abundant in Seguin. *How could he exist without the magical Guadalupe and the mysterious bottoms where he and Peachtree had lazed away the afternoons? How could he be happy in a land without the great oak canopies that lined the streets of Seguin, away from the wildflowers, and the monarch butterflies and the soft fragrant air? How could Will exist without music? Maybe he will create his own beauty in the arid desert.* Louise recalled that the poetry of the Psalms was written by scribes wandering the desert solitudes, and the prophets and sages of many of the world's great religions were inspired by pilgrimages into the wilderness. *Maybe my brother will find his way in the wilderness.*

She recalled a letter he had written shortly after the first in which he praised the prairie nights.

Dear Louise,

If only you could see the stars, it would take your breath away. The sky is so much larger here and the stars are like diamonds God spilled from a cup. They fill the heavens. Sometimes when I look at all those billions of worlds up there it makes me feel we are not alone in the Universe. I wonder if there is someone looking back at us from one of those glimmers of light. It's almost impossible to imagine this isn't so.

No, this is not a joyless place. You misunderstood me. We often have musicals. Most families have violins, mandolins, banjos, harmonicas, or accordians and when you get them all playing the same tune on a back porch it's something to hear. And there's also the high entertainment of rushing to the depot each day to meet the train. Plenty of joy here in old Weinert, Texas. And if you want beauty, just walk out at night and look up.

Your brother,
Will

Louise pictured Will out in the desert night. In another letter he told of his new motorcycle and the joy of riding it full out through the moonlight.

Dear Sis,

Living with the McCullochs I was able to save almost all of my earnings. And I made some extra money repairing bicycles. With what I saved I bought what I've always dreamed of having one day—a motorcycle. But not just any motorcycle, it is the fastest and best motorcycle in the world. The Indian dominates racing. Of course there's no racing here because I'm the only one in town, besides Dr. Cockrell, with a motorcycle, and he just rides his to visit patients. But, what a thrill to take off over the prairie, the engine making a sound like thunder, speeding along fast as a train. Nobody for miles around but you and the wind and the stars and the magical thrill of speed, of moving fast on the slow-turning earth.

I miss you,
Will

Louise turned to the last letter she had recieved.

Dear Louise,

Did you hear that Mama's friend Pastor Polly has married again? He's eighty-four and he married a girl who is fifteen. That means a difference in their ages of almost seventy years. I wonder if the marriage will last? Ha. Ha. I mention Pastor Polly because he recommended me to the sheriff here. He wrote Sheriff Mose Parks saying I'd make a good deputy because I'm a pretty good shot and good with a whip. This is not boasting, it's just what Pastor Polly wrote to the sheriff. So I was hired, got a tin star to wear and I'm the law.

It's not the easiest job in the world because this is a pretty rough and tumble town, especially on Saturday night when the boys from

Lone Star come to celebrate pay day at the end of their week. This wild bunch comes in, all busting for a fight, and they put on a rodeo in the middle of Main Street. There's no saloon in Weinert, so folks buy their liquor from barrels Mr. Weinert keeps at Old Man Crouch's store.

Last week a bunch of these rowdies from Lone Star bored holes in the barrels and drained off great quantities of whiskey into their canteens which they forthwith consumed. It was my unhappy chore to run the Lone Star boys out of town, which I did, much to the entertainment of the local citizens. I don't mind telling you that it made me a hero of sorts. But the boys from Lone Star were so drunk on Weinert's whiskey that a little old lady could have done what I did. Just hope the boys from Lone Star won't be sober next time they come into Weinert. I miss you.

Your wandering brother,
Will

Louise moved to her desk, opened her school atlas and made a finger voyage across Texas to where she imagined Weinert must be. She could almost feel the distance widening between Will and her. *Where will his wanderings end? How can we cling to family when we are so far apart?*

XV.

Abilene, Texas.
October 1917

On the day Spec Davis died, the Abilene newspaper carried a front-page story under the banner, "Death of An American Hero." There was a photograph of a much younger Spec Davis, smiling, his arm around his mother, his other arm extended toward the camera as if inviting someone, the reader, to join the intimate group. Obviously, the story had been rushed to press, researched, written and composed as the murdered man lay dying. It listed every award and achievement, from first grade to his charge up San Juan Hill at the side of Teddy Roosevelt. As Bill Atwell scanned the front page, he wondered if the editor had prepared another layout to publish in the event Spec Davis had survived.

The story suggested that Spec Davis had given his life in the cause of liberty and justice. He had been warned not to testify, told that he would be killed if he did, but he stepped courageously to the witness stand to preserve the American way of life. Atwell had to admit that much of the story was true. Spec Davis was warned, he did ignore the warnings, and he was killed. Testifying had been a courageous thing to do. But the worst thing about the story was that it made it appear that Will Bergfeld was the murderer, not the low-life Kennemer. The murdered man had been a witness against Will. And even though Will had been inside the courthouse at the time of the shooting, anyone who read the story would believe that Will pulled the trigger. In a small sidebar on page two, questions were raised about Louise's part in the affair. What was her role in the deadly quarrel that resulted in Spec Davis's death? Atwell wondered if the prosecution had anything to do with the story. He knew it would be more effective than any witness O'Dell might bring to the stand.

In a brief morning conference with the family, Atwell reviewed the damage the murder of Spec Davis had done to the case. "There are times," he said, "when court cases are won or lost outside of the courtroom. The jurors will read the papers and they will be affected. It is simply human nature. Even if they don't read the papers they will hear the talk, which is really worse." Atwell paused, looked at the faces around him. *Was it defeat he saw in their eyes?* "Look," he continued. "I know things are not going well now, but we haven't had our chance on the stand. I have a feeling the prosecution will wind up its case, if not today, tomorrow. Then it's our turn. Don't let the jury see you as I see you now. Let them see you as people confident that the truth is on their side. And, folks, let me warn you. I'm certain O'Dell will save some of his big guns for last. These final witnesses are going to make things look a lot worse before they get better. We will probably hear a lot of lies that sound remarkably like the truth. I promise you, when our turn comes, we will get momentum going our way. But I need you to make a promise to me. I need you to promise to fight along with me. I need your support, your energy and your prayers. All we can do is seek the truth, have faith in each other, and place our trust in God."

Virginia heard the words, and she knew what she was supposed to feel, but what she really felt was empty. *He can't know how hard this is, so hard, so hard. And how ashamed I am that I can't be stronger, that I can't face up to people like Louise or quote the scriptures like my mother or laugh in the face of fate like Will. All I can do is try to fake confidence I don't feel. I am a character in a masquerade, but the mask doesn't hide my feelings because I don't have any. It is like my foot is asleep, without feeling, but it isn't my foot, it is my soul. And I am so afraid that when the feeling comes back it will be pain. Maybe it's better to continue to feel nothing to keep the pain away. I wish I could talk to Will about my sleeping soul, and I'm sure he would say soothing words and touch me tenderly in that intimate way that makes me forget everything but that touch, that intimacy, that moment. But in that secret closet of his mind, what would he think of me? After all, he is the one at risk. It is his life that might be taken, not mine. And that is the lie I am living. It is the loss of my own life I fear. For if they take Will away, they carry my life away as well. Perhaps I feel nothing now because I am seeking to hide how ashamed I am that I am more afraid for myself than I am for Will.*

The first prosecution witness of the day was a pale, heavyset man with the appearance of great strength. Virginia could see how the sleeves of his jacket could barely contain his muscular arms. After a moment, she realized that his pale face was due to a lifetime spent in the coal mines.

When he was seated, O'Dell asked, "Would you please state your name to the jury?"

"A. C. Ferguson."

"Where do you reside, Mr. Ferguson?" O'Dell paced in front of the witness. The man's eyes followed.

"Henryetta, Oklahoma."

"How long have you lived in Henryetta?"

"Off and on for many years. My work takes me away."

"What is your work, Mr. Ferguson?"

"I'm a driller."

"In the mines?"

"Yes, sir."

The prosecutor paused, his hand to his chin, as if seeking to remember a detail. Virginia decided the gesture was to make the questions and answers seem unrehearsed. "Where were you employed in May of 1917?"

"I was secretary of the local branch of the Industrial Workers of the World."

"Now, Mr. Ferguson," O'Dell continued, his eyes now on the jurors. "As secretary of that organization, do you recall meeting the defendant Will Bergfeld?"

"Yes, sir, I do."

"Could you tell the jury the circumstances of that meeting as near as you can recall?" The prosecutor walked to the jury box, then turned back to the witness, giving the appearance that he, like the jury, was hearing this testimony for the first time.

"Bergfeld and another man named Cathcart came up from Texas to join our organization."

"And they were initiated, weren't they, Mr. Ferguson? They became members of the IWW?"

"Yes, sir."

"Who initiated these men?

"I did."

"You did?" O'Dell pretended surprise.

"Yes, sir. In the office there."

"Mr. Ferguson, are you still a member of the IWW?"

"No, sir."

"Could you tell the jury why you are no longer a member of the Industrial Workers of the World?"

"I decided to quit."

"You no longer believed in IWW goals?"

"It wasn't their goals I didn't believe in. I still believe in those. It was their methods. Especially with our country at war."

"Now, Mr. Ferguson, could you be more specific? What were the IWW methods that caused you to terminate your membership?"

"Well, sabotage, for one. Making things break on purpose. Destroying company property."

"And you felt these actions worked against the war effort?"

"The coal mines and shipyards and steel mills are the strength of this country. The IWW worked to weaken them."

"I would like you to examine this document, Mr. Ferguson. It has been marked and entered as exhibit number 30. Could you tell the jury what this document represents?"

"It's the preamble to the Industrial Workers of the World official membership book. Each new member is given one of these books. You can see that this was given to W. A. Bergfeld. Here is his name and his membership number."

"If it please the court, I'd like to read a portion of this document that Will Bergfeld signed."

"How long is this document?" the judge asked.

"About three pages, Your Honor. But I only wish to read several brief paragraphs."

"Go ahead then," Judge Jack said. Virginia sensed that the judge suspected the prosecution was about to rest its case, and he was eager to move the trial along. She wondered if that meant he had heard all he wished to hear, and was bored with the constant repetition. *After all, what new information could there possibly be?*

Pacing before the jury, O'Dell began to provide several new verbal assaults that hammered away against Will. He read, "The working class and the employing class have nothing in common. There can be no peace so long as hunger and want are found among millions of the working people and the few who make up the employing class have all the good things in life.

"Between these classes a struggle must go on until the workers of the world organize as a class, take possession of the earth and the machinery of production and abolish the wage system.

"It is the historic mission of the working class to do away with capitalism. The army of production must be organized, not only for the everyday struggle with capitalists, but also to carry on production when capitalism shall have been overthrown. By organizing industrially, we are forming the structure of the new society within the shell of the old."

O'Dell paused and lowered the document. "Now, Mr. Ferguson, does this fairly state, as you understand it, the mission of the IWW?"

"Yes, sir."

"Doesn't it state that the IWW struggles to overthrow capitalism?"

"Yes, it states that clearly."

"Is America a capitalistic society?

"Yes, sir."

"Then wouldn't it follow that the goal of the IWW, this organization that Will Bergfeld traveled hundreds of miles to join, is to overthrow the United States of America?"

"Objection, your honor," Atwell called. "He knows better than that. He is not only telling the witness what he wants him to say, he's telling him what conclusions to reach."

"Sustained," Judge Jack said, with a slight smile. "I think you do know better, Counselor."

Virginia could tell that O'Dell had cleverly lured the witness into false testimony. But false or not she could tell it had an impact on the jury. Each of the jurors seemed to be following O'Dell's accusing stare, a stare that led directly to Will.

"Your witness," O'Dell said, still looking at Will and shaking his head sadly.

Atwell rose. He knew Will had a good explanation for his membership in the IWW. But it was, like most of Will's explanations, rather convoluted and, quite frankly, hard to believe. Bill Atwell thought Will was telling the truth, but the truth was rather strange. The problem was that Will did not live his life in a linear, predictable manner. His enthusiasms and convictions led him into situations that were beyond an ordinary man's experience. Then he was hard-pressed to explain to others what he often could not explain to himself. Atwell decided to save Will's explanation for later. Now he would take another tack.

"Mr. Ferguson," Atwell asked the witness, "how many members are in the IWW organization?"

"I can't say offhand."

"But you would say thousands, perhaps tens of thousands?"

"Yes, sir. It is very large."

"And did each of these tens of thousands of members sign this official membership book?"

"Yes, sir. It was required."

"Do you think all of these members were involved in sabotage?"

"Objection," Prosecutor O'Dell called. "Conjecture. How can

the witness possibly know?"

"Sustained."

"You signed the membership book, did you not?"

"Yes, sir."

"During the period of your membership were you ever involved in sabotage or any other unlawful act?"

"I was not."

Bill Atwell turned toward the jury. He paused until he was certain he had their attention. "So, let me ask you this, Mr. Ferguson. Since you were innocent of any unlawful act during the period of your membership in the IWW, isn't it possible, quite likely even, that other members of the IWW could remain faithful to the laws of the United States of America?"

"Yes, sir. I suppose that's true."

"Isn't it possible, then, that Will Bergfeld's membership in the IWW was motivated by his desire to improve the conditions of the working man and that he, like you, Mr. Ferguson, is entirely innocent of any unlawful act?"

"It's possible," Ferguson responded.

"That's all I have for this witness." Ferguson remained for a moment in the witness chair, looking out toward Wilmot O'Dell, as if expecting more questions from the prosecutor. O'Dell ignored him completely.

The prosecution's next witness was L. T. Barrow. He was lean and weathered and walked forward with one hand extended as if he was afraid of tripping over some unseen obstacle. He looked to Virginia like a man who had spent a lifetime following a plow in the field. His trousers and jacket, though ill fitting, appeared new. He seemed terribly uncomfortable as he folded his lanky frame into the witness chair.

Prosecutor O'Dell quickly got to the heart of Barrow's testimony. "Mr. Barrow, did you have occasion to travel by train to Dallas, Texas, in June of 1917?"

"Yes, sir."

Atwell glanced toward Will, their eyes met, and Atwell raised his eyebrows. Will shrugged and looked back toward the witness stand.

"What was the purpose of that trip?" O'Dell asked.

"I was summoned as a witness before a Grand Jury."

"Was that the Grand Jury hearing evidence against these defendants?" O'Dell's gesture swept the area where the defendants were seated.

"It was."

"Isn't it true that Will Bergfeld was one of the defendants in that Grand Jury investigation?"

"Yes, sir."

"Do you recall some of the other passengers on that train?"

"There were some other witnesses from Haskell County. Mrs. Thurwanger, for one. Miss Bennett, for another. I remember her."

"Isn't it true that Will Bergfeld was also a passenger on that train?"

"He was."

"Did you have a conversation with Mr. Bergfeld on that occasion?"

"Yes, sir, I did."

"Could you tell the jury the substance of that conversation as near as you can recall."

"He said he wanted to give me some money. He had fifty dollars in a roll and said he wanted me to have it."

As the implication of his words became clear, the crowd in the courtroom grew restive. Chairs rumbled. Whispers rose, a breathy chorus in which there could be distinctly heard the one-syllable word "*bribe*."

Judge Jack pounded his gavel. "Quiet!" he shouted. He pounded his gavel again and the whispers ceased.

"Did you ask him for money?" Prosecutor O'Dell asked.

"No. I certainly did not."

"Did he say why he wanted you to have the money?"

"I think that's obvious."

"Objection," Atwell called as the spectators came alive again, some laughing derisively.

Judge Jack again wielded his gavel. "Sustained," the judge said. "Mr. Barrow, please answer the questions put to you. What is obvious and is not obvious is up to the jury to decide."

O'Dell reworded his question."Did Will Bergfeld state that he knew you were to testify before the Grand Jury?"

"Yes. He said he hoped I would be a good witness. He said that as he tried to push the money into my pocket."

"Did you take the money?"

"No, sir. That would have been to accept a bribe."

"Objection!" Atwell called, rising this time.

"Sustained," the judge said. "Mr. Barrow, just answer the questions and avoid these voluntary comments." The judge looked toward the court reporter. "Strike the statement about the bribe. The jury will disregard what the witness said in that regard."

O'Dell continued. "Did you have further conversations with Bergfeld after you arrived in Dallas?"

"No, sir."

"Isn't it true that you saw him in the courthouse having conversations with other witnesses?"

"Yes, sir. Everybody saw it."

"Did you overhear any of these conversations?"

"Yes, sir. He was trying to find out what the witnesses knew. What they would say."

"Isn't it true that Bergfeld was led away from the witnesses by Assistant District Attorney Allen?"

"Yes, sir."

"Did you hear the words that passed between Bergfeld and the officer?"

"Yes, sir."

"Do you recall those words?"

"The officer said if Bergfeld didn't stop trying to sway witnesses, he'd lock him up."

The crowd moved and murmured. Will Bergfeld looked down

at his hands.

"One last question, Mr. Barrow. Did you testify against Will Bergfeld before the Grand Jury?"

"Yes, sir, I did."

Prosecutor O'Dell turned toward the defense table, a smirk on his face. He seemed to be struggling to keep his elation from showing on his face. "Your witness, Mr. Atwell."

Defense Attorney Atwell rose and moved forward. "Mr. Barrow," he began, "how many other witnesses were on that train?"

"I don't know. Several. There were some I didn't know. There might have been others in different coaches."

"Did anyone hear the words that passed between you and Mr. Bergfeld?"

"I couldn't say. The train made a lot of noise."

"When you had that conversation with Will Bergfeld, did you approach him or did he approach you?"

"He approached me. I was sitting alone and he sat down beside me."

"Had you met him before?"

"Yes, we both lived in the same town."

"Were you friends?"

"We knew each other."

"Are you married, Mr. Barrow?"

"Yes, sir."

"Have a family?"

"Yes. Three daughters."

"Would you say that the Bergfeld family and your family were neighbors?"

"We lived close by. It's a small town."

Atwell walked away from the witness, then turned. "Back to that train ride, Mr. Barrow. When Will Bergfeld sat down beside you, what did he say? Try to recall everything, leave nothing out."

"He said he had this money he wanted to give me."

"What were his actual words?"

"He said that he heard I'd been down and out for a while and he had some money to see me through."

"What do you mean 'down and out'?"

"I've been down on my luck. Lost my job. My wife has been ill."

"You worked at a hardware store, isn't that right?

"Yes."

"For how long?"

"Nearly fifteen years."

"How long have you been out of work?"

"Nearly a year now."

"Times must be pretty hard for you and your family?"

"Yes, sir."

"How old are your daughters?"

"Four, five and six."

"How is your wife doing? Is she improving?"

"She is bedridden now."

"I'm truly sorry, Mr. Barrow. These must be very difficult times for your family."

The witness nodded, his eyes moist.

"Mr. Barrow, isn't it just possible that Will Bergfeld, a longtime neighbor, might have offered you money because he genuinely wanted to help a family down on its luck? Isn't it possible he offered you that money out of sympathy for your family, your little daughters and your wife? Isn't this what Texans try to do? Offer a helping hand to neighbors when they can? Isn't this what really happened, Mr. Barrow?"

The witness looked back at Atwell, his eyes unfocused. "It's possible," he responded. Then the tears that had been pooled in his eyes began to flow. Bill Atwell stepped forward and helped Mr. Barrow make his way down from the stand. For the first time in a long time, there was absolute silence in the courtroom. Atwell could feel Barrow's sorrow and he sensed it might be mixed with another emotion that he could not quite identify.

After Mr. Barrow, O'Dell offered several other witnesses who expounded upon Will's alleged crimes in great detail. Although Defense Attorney Atwell diminished the impact of their testimony with logic, intelligence and wit, the mountain of evidence against the accused steadily grew. But as each witness stepped down from the stand, Atwell knew that the prosecution's star witness reserved for the close of evidence was yet to come.

Louise thought Anna Bennett looked like a movie star as she moved to the witness stand. She was dressed conservatively, yet she still caused a stir as she took her place and then gazed out over the courtroom. Tall and slender, with her cloud of Titian hair, she was still quite beautiful. Atwell had warned that the prosecution would probably save Anna for last. He had also warned that if she repeated what she had told the Grand Jury, her testimony would be devastating. Not that she would be offering anything new, but that every red-blooded man on the jury would want to believe her story. Louise wondered how much of the story she would tell. She also wondered how much of the story Will would reveal. She felt a hollow pain at her center when she realized Will would never tell what really happened, even to save himself from the gallows.

"Would you please state your name to the jury?"

"Anna Bennett."

"Are you married?"

"No, I am not." Louise thought there was just a touch too much force in her answer. She glanced at the jurors and knew they must wonder why a beautiful woman like Anna never married.

"Where do you reside, Miss Bennett?"

"I live near Weinert. In Haskell County."

"How long have you lived in Weinert, Miss Bennett?"

"I moved there when I was about fifteen. We lived originally in San Marcos." Her voice was firm and clear. She seemed confident. Louise watched to see if she glanced toward Will, but it seemed her responses were directed only to Prosecutor O'Dell.

"Tell me, Miss Bennett, are you acquainted with the defendant Will Bergfeld?"

"Yes, sir."

"Under what circumstances did you meet Mr. Bergfeld?"

"He delivered my mail. I suppose I met him at the mailbox." *Now it begins*, Louise thought, *the lies, the omissions, the revenge. How can she be so calm, so assured?* Louise wondered if Anna actually believed she hadn't known Will before. *Maybe she has blocked the humiliation and the hurt out of her mind.*

"After that first meeting, how often did you see Mr. Bergfeld?"

"Quite often. Generally every day."

"Did he stop by whether you had mail or not?"

"I suppose it became a sort of routine. He came by the same time every day in the late afternoon. On his motorcycle, usually."

"How long would he stay?"

"Just a few minutes."

"And you met there at the mailbox? You never invited him into the house?"

"Oh, no. Sometimes, on a very hot day, I'd have a jar of iced tea for him. We'd chat, then he'd be off again with a roar."

"Did you and Mr. Bergfeld become friends?"

"Yes, I suppose so. He is an interesting man with unconventional views. I enjoyed talking with him."

"What was the general subject of your conversations? Did they center on any one field? Like the weather, for instance?"

Anna smiled, suggesting that weather was the last thing they talked about. "We talked about politics, Mr. O'Dell. Mostly he talked, I listened."

"During these discussions at the mailbox, did he ever mention the war?"

"Oh, certainly. He had very strong opinions about the war."

"Could you tell the jury the general substance of these opinions?"

"He was against the war. He said the war was a way the capitalist class could enrich themselves at the expense of working people. He said that President Wilson had promised to keep us out of war, but he was going back on his promise."

"In these conversations by the mailbox, did Will Bergfeld ever talk specifically about President Wilson?"

"Often. It was an obsession."

Atwell rose to object. "Miss Bennett is not a psychiatrist."

Judge Jack sustained the objection.

"Can you recall any specific comments Will Bergfeld made concerning President Wilson?"

"He said he should be shot." The plural voice of the crowd rose and Anna looked up, surprised.

"Were these his exact words?" O'Dell asked. "I want you to be very sure about this."

"Yes, sir. I'm quite sure. He said President Wilson should be assassinated before it was too late. He should be shot like a rattlesnake."

"Did he use the exact phrase as you state it? That President Wilson should be assassinated before it is too late? That he should be shot like a rattlesnake?"

"Yes, sir. This and more. Not just once, but over and over."

"What was his demeanor when he made these threats? Was he angry?"

"Objection," Atwell called. "The prosecution is leading the witness."

"Sustained," Judge Jack said, looking over his glasses at the witness.

"Miss Bennett, did there come a time when your relationship with Mr. Bergfeld changed?"

For the first time, Anna looked at Will. "Yes," she replied.

"Could you tell the jury what happened?"

"For some time I had been uncomfortable with his comments about President Wilson. At first, I thought he was merely making conversation. Trying to shock me. But as time went by, I realized he really meant what he was saying. And his anger frightened me. I didn't enjoy his visits anymore."

"Was that the end of it then?"

"No, sir."

"What happened?"

"He started coming to the door, demanding to come in. Once he drove his motorcycle up on the porch."

Louise wondered if the judge who had surely listened to many lies from the stand could recognize Anna's testimony for what it was.

"Miss Bennett, how did you feel about this behavior? What was in your mind at the time?"

"At first I was frightened, as you might imagine. Then I realized it was in part my fault. Somehow I must have misled him. He must have thought our friendship was more than it was. I felt bad about that."

"Did Mr. Bergfeld continue to try to force himself into your home?"

"For a while. Then he stopped. He would deliver the mail, then pass on by."

"How do you feel about Will Bergfeld now?"

"He was a friend. Everyone hates to lose a friend. Everyone hates to see someone they have cared about in trouble. I just wish he hadn't done what he did."

"And what is that, Miss Bennett?"

"I wish he hadn't threatened to assassinate the President."

"Thank you, Miss Bennett. Your witness, Counselor."

Judge Jack made a show of pulling his pocket watch out from beneath his robe. "As it is nearly supper time, let us recess until nine o'clock sharp tomorrow morning." There was an immediate chorus of coughs and conversation and rattling of chairs as the crowd rose. There was even a scattering of applause as if an especially dramatic scene had been played and the curtain was sweeping closed. Louise would not have been surprised if O'Dell and Anna Bennett had emerged from behind the curtain, holding hands, bowing and blowing kisses.

The wooden ticking of the clock filled the small room in the basement of the courthouse. Will Bergfeld and his defense attorney leaned over a table filled with a miscellany of documents, files and newspaper clippings. Beyond the closed door, Atwell could hear the metallic ringing of meal trays against the iron bars confining the defendants who had not made bail. Atwell rose, moved to the door, checked to make sure no one was listening, then returned to the table. For a long moment he looked down at Will, seeking again to fathom the depth of this strange man's mind. "She's good," Atwell said.

"I know." Will was reading an editorial about American troops at last moving into the trenches. "But it's all absolute rubbish."

"Look at me, Will!"

Will looked up from the paper. Atwell thought he saw challenge in Will's eyes.

"Did you say these things to Anna Bennett? Even in jest? Or an offhand remark that you've since forgotten?"

"We've been through this, Bill. How many times do I have to tell you?!"

"Then why would she lie? I have to know. Give me something, Will! In the morning I've got to cross-examine this witness and I can't just stand up there with egg on my face! Somehow I've got to prove she's a liar."

"I don't want you to be hard on her, Bill."

"Now what's this?" Atwell wondered how many curves Bergfeld was capable of throwing. "What happened between you and Anna Bennett?"

Will looked into Atwell's eyes, seeming to come to some kind of decision. "What happened between me and Anna is between me and Anna. It's nothing the jury should hear."

"I've got to know, Will."

Will looked up at the clock on the wall, watched the second hand creep 'round and then imagined time slowing, moving backwards, gaining speed, dragging him physically into the past. Then he began to tell Bill Atwell why Anna Bennett might lie.

Far to the south, Peachtree emerged from the Guadalupe River bottoms, passed the house where Idella talked with the dead, then moved rapidly up Court Street toward the town square. It was nearing midnight, the moon was a crescent cutting through piles of black cloud, the streets were empty of all but slow-moving shadows cast by the branches of wind-blown oaks. With his owl on his shoulder, the strange man skittered from shadow to shadow, like a soldier taking cover from enemy fire. He passed the ancient Magnolia Hotel, paused stock still at the sound of the night's last revelers in an upper room, then moved on toward the jail. He crept to a barred window, stood with his back against the stone wall. His owl called. A face appeared behind the bars. Peachtree remained at the window for some time, listening, listening, then he moved on into the night, toward the railroad tracks and the hobo camps where he would hear from the outcast and the lawless what regular people might never learn.

XVI.

Weinert, Texas.
June 1908

Anna Bennett knew the moment she saw Will Bergfeld that he was the one she had been waiting for. Not that he was rich or famous, as she herself intended to be one day, but he was as handsome as any movie star and there was about him a sense of purpose, so unlike the local farm boys whose greatest ambition was to dig in the dirt and survive until they died in the fields. It seemed their only other ambition was to get her to go with them to church or behind the barn, neither invitation appealing to her at all. Both led to the altar and she would burn in Hell before she surrendered to the kind of prison that held the women of Weinert in its cruel kitchen cells, cooking, scrubbing, bearing litters of children, growing dry and old and weary. Somehow she would escape this life, this terrible place, this prairie prison, and Will Bergfeld held the key.

Setting her cap for Will had nothing of the thrilling happenstance of the romance novels she devoured by lantern light. It was more a strategic campaign, a series of planned moves based on the awareness of her own beauty and what she sensed in Will to be absolute innocence when it came to women. With her flame-red hair, porcelain complexion, her lithe figure and a maturity beyond her years, she knew she had a powerful effect on men, even some of the husbands whose roving eyes proved their interest. In fact, she found this power she had to turn men's heads terribly exciting. It was a game she played to make her lonely life bearable. She would select a young man as a target and then create situations in which he could only believe she was interested in him. Then she would lead him along, meting out favors, allowing him to touch her, kiss her, seeing how long it took to drive him out of his mind, pleading for further intimacy or marriage. Then, when the men grew desperate and she grew weary of the game, she would find an excuse to end it. *How strong I am*, she thought. *How amazing that I can get a man to do anything I want him to do. I am Jane Austen's heroine, able to manipulate lives any way I choose. I am Jane Austen herself, a novelist of real life, creating plots not on paper but in flesh and blood and dream. It is only right. Just think how many millions of women over the centuries have been manipulated by men. Why shouldn't I even the score a little? Because I can and it's amusing and there's nothing else to do in this wasteland of a town.*

For a while, Anna merely observed Will from afar. He lived with the Cockrells and spent his days at a bicycle shop in a shed he rented from Dr. Cockrell. On occasion she would make sure to pass him on the street and she would meet his eyes, but not smile, then pass on. She had discovered that the more aloof she seemed, the more men's interest grew. It was in these brief encounters that she learned a great deal about Will Bergfeld. Everything about him suggested strength and self-assurance, yet there was something about the way he looked at her, a kind of wistful, lingering longing that suggested he was both lonely and unsure of himself. She knew he wished to approach her but was afraid of rejection. She was once again amazed by the way a woman could easily bring out the weakness in the strongest of men.

It was there, in his shop, surrounded by dismantled bicycles, wheels, gears and strange machines Will was inventing, that she spoke to him for the first time. She had planned her outfit, a simple thin cotton frock, and she made sure the morning sun was behind her, setting her hair afire and silhouetting her body in the sunlight. The effect she had in mind was a sprite, a creature of the earth, natural and mythic.

"Teach me to ride," she said.

For a long moment, he simply looked at her, as one might look at a rose or a butterfly. "Do you have a bicycle?" he asked, wiping grease from his hands with a rag.

"No."

"Why learn to ride if you don't have a bicycle?" Now he was smiling. Anna stepped closer. She thought what a handsome couple they would make. And there was that strength! A truth quick as a will o' the wisp passed through Anna's mind—she knew in an instant that this was no game. It was real.

"I'll ride yours."

He asked her name.

"Anna. I know yours is Will."

Will looked down at her for a moment more, then looked around, searching for a bicycle that was not all apart. "Tell you what, Anna. If you promise to buy one of these bikes, I'll teach you to ride."

For the rest of the morning, Will instructed Anna in the intricacies of the cyclist's art. For much of the time, he ran alongside, with one hand on the handlebar and one hand on Anna's back. She struggled to remain mounted, the bicycle weaving dangerously along the street, an expanse of leg beneath her frock shocking those they passed. Once, she fell, and Will lifted her up and Anna was surprised how little effort it seemed to take. He began to help her brush the dust from her frock, then, embarrassed, he picked up the bike. Then, they were off again, careening down the street, their laughter echoing off the storefronts.

"Don't think about it," Will said. "Just let your mind go. Your body knows what to do. You're thinking too much."

At last, she was riding on her own, feeling the thrill of silent motion, balancing naturally, yet missing the touch of Will's hands. When they returned to the shop, Will showed her his motorcycle. "Now *this*," he said, "is what you should ride."

"When?" she asked. "It's something I've never done."

"How about after I close the shop? We can ride out to watch the sunset."

"I'd like that, Will." Anna knew she had him now. But she also felt something she had never felt before. It wasn't until she got home and looked into the mirror that she realized what she felt was the first sweet tremulous stirring of love.

Years later Anna would recall that night not only as a wild ride across the prairie, but the beginning of a wild ride through life. They became inseparable, she and Will, exploring all that a man and woman can experience together, holding onto each other, so close that it was like they were the same person. They told each other the story of their lives. She told him of her loneliness and of her dreams of leaving Weinert forever. They planned a journey across America on Will's Indian motorcycle, a pilgrimage to California where Will would make a fortune from his mechanical inventions and Anna would get a leading part in a D. W. Griffiths movie. They would marry, have beautiful children, live on the edge of the sea. On some nights, she secretly met Will and they would go into the hayloft and spread a blanket so they could make love beneath the moon and promise each other that they would love each other forever.

Will became something of a local celebrity when he raced the passenger train from Haskell to Weinert, arriving on his motorcycle ahead of the train by a good measure.

After a year, Mrs. Cockrell, his landlady and the Weinert postmistress, offered Will a position as a mail carrier. The pay was much more than he had made as a deputy sheriff or that he earned at the bicycle shop and it allowed him to save for their trip to California. When the weather allowed, he delivered the mail on his beloved Indian motorcycle, often at breakneck speed. He ran his rural route of twenty-seven miles and seventy-three mailboxes, stopping at every box, in an average of one hour and thirty minutes. In addition to his mail route, Will made extra money by renting motorcycles, a buggy, a wagon and several horses. His entrepreneurial activities also included operating a tennis court, a boxing ring and a mule racing track out from town. The *Weinert Enterprise* called Will "a good hustler." Will's savings mounted. Anna could almost feel the soft sea air of the California coast.

That July, the mail carrier delivered himself a letter that would change many lives. It came from Will's sister Louise, in Seguin.

Dear Will,

I want you to know that a wonderful man has asked me to be his wife and I have accepted. His name is Robert Tewes. I'm sure you know his family. They are an old German family with stores, gins and banks in San Antonio, New Berlin and Marion. After the wedding, Rob will manage the family's store in Karnes City where we will live. I never imagined I could be so happy. For our engagement he gave me a diamond the size of a barn and the flashiest bright red roadster automobile you ever saw. Now I understand your fascination with speed. The wedding is planned for October 27 and I would be honored if you could provide the music at the ceremony. I'm sure you remember Virginia King. She has agreed to play the organ and I believe you two would get along fine, musically and otherwise. Please respond as quickly as you can, dear Will.

I love you.
Louise

"I still don't understand why I can't go," Anna said. Her head rested on Will's chest. She could hear his heart still racing from their recent passion. "Give me one good reason why."

Will said nothing. She wondered where he went when he was so silent, how he could be so close and so distant at the same time. She rose on one elbow and kissed his neck, then his lips. "Just tell me why, Will."

"It is not the right time."

"Time for what?"

"For us. This is Louise's time. And Rob's. If we came together it would steal their thunder. Besides, it's a family thing."

Anna felt something heavy fall inside, a throb of anger. She sat up, brushed hay from her hair, looked down at Will. "Look at me, Will!"

Will seemed to drag his eyes toward her. They were opaque, unfathomable. "I am family, Will," Anna said. "We are family! I have given myself body and soul to you. Don't tell me I'm not family." She felt the coming of tears. In her mind, the picture of his family began to coalesce, a portrait of terribly proper German generations, standing stiff as boards, their haughty, accusing, unforgiving eyes riveted on the little Irish prairie girl who had stolen away their favorite son. Then they all, as one, turned away and she was left alone, naked in the hayloft. "Are you ashamed of me, Will? Is that it? Is the little Raggedy girl too far beneath your family's standards?"

"Anna. I would be proud of you. You are the most beautiful girl in Texas. But I wouldn't have time to be with you. I'm a member of the wedding party. All the plans have been made and if you came with me, it would confuse things. Where would you stay? We couldn't stay together. How would I explain who you are? How we are?"

"You would introduce me as your fiancee. The woman you love and have promised to marry. This is the perfect time for me to meet your family. They'll all be together." She rose and stood between Will and the moon, knowing what he would see, knowing the effect her silhouette would have.

"Come lie beside me," Will said. He pulled her down next to him, held her. Anna felt her anger fade. Maybe she did not want to go to Seguin anyway. What a bore that wedding would be. Certainly not as exciting as a summer evening in the hayloft. Not as exciting as the prospect of California. Then, as Will kissed her, she felt her power over him once more ascend. She was Eve and it was from her rib that Adam would be created.

Anna was both shocked and outraged when Will left for the wedding in Seguin without her.

The day of the wedding dawned perfectly. The sky was hung like a great cameo, an easy, soft blue with clouds the color of an angel's wing. As the clouds moved and billowed and slowly tumbled above the earth, they formed celestial faces, visages of Heaven's most virtuous gods. A cool breeze from the east stirred the oaks along

Court Street, and when the wind's breath stilled, the voice of the jade-green Guadalupe could be heard murmuring musically against its banks.

The wedding itself mirrored the perfection of the day. *The Seguin Enterprise* reported that the Emanuel's Lutheran Church was beautifully decorated with white and yellow chrysanthemums, palms and ferns. The bride wore a dress of pink coral silk with a long lace veil. Miss Amy Bernhard sang *Beauty's Eyes.*

But most of what happened in the church was missed entirely by Will Bergfeld. All he would remember was the girl who joined him to play Mendelssohn's *Wedding March* as his sister Louise and Rob Tewes entered the church. All he could remember was how beautiful little Virginia had grown up to be.

The reception was held in the ballroom of the Klein Opera House. The guests danced almost 'til dawn to the rhythms of old Pastor Polly's Mexican band. And as often as seemed appropriate, and as often as she would allow, Will danced with the beautiful daughter of Bettie and Henry King.

Louise was not certain whether to feel sorry for Will's predicament or to celebrate the fact that he had fallen in love with her good friend Virginia King. As was usually the case with Will's adventures, his current dilemma, as outlined in an unusually revealing letter, was enormously complex. Not only would he have to extricate himself from his relationship with the girl in Weinert—a relationship she suspected was one not of the heart but of other more unmentionable body parts—but he would have to court Virginia secretly. Neither Arthur Bergfeld nor Henry King would favor the match.

She looked back over the letter Will had written after he had returned to Weinert from the wedding.

My dear sister,

I thought I knew what love was, but when I saw Virginia, heard her voice, I realized I was wrong. She is an angel. There is in her every gesture a grace that I have only seen in the willows along the river. I feel we speak to each other in our music and we are comfortable with our silences. Do you know how rare that is? To be perfectly at ease with another person in silence? I wonder if she has spoken of me. Dare I ask? Does she know about Anna? How would she feel if she knew? I'm terrified to tell her. And what of Bobby Wuest? How serious are they? I know I cannot express my feelings for Virginia until I break with Anna. I am tormented by the promise I made her. But I am certain neither of us could be happy now. My heart would always be with Virginia.

Your brother,
Will

Louise looked at the letter, not at the words but at the graceful, bold lines that formed the words. Will's letters were a kind of art, soaring, sweeping forms, suitable for framing on the wall. She wondered if he had made any progress on her portrait. For a long while he had admitted that he could not get it quite right. Now he avoided mention of it at all. *Dear Will. In another world, another time, I wonder what you could have been. A great artist, a concert musician, an inventor. Why the fates led you to be a mail carrier in a dusty, joyless town like Weinert, I'll never know. What will happen to all that talent if it is left unfinished like my portrait? Will it just waste away, fade like a painting left too long in the sun?* She held his letter to her breast and began to rock, remembering, remembering rocking life into her infant brother as Virgin Annie's voice rose in contralto prayer.

The day exploded into near silence. The motorcycle made small metallic complaints as its engine cooled. Anna pulled herself from the sidecar Will had built, wishing they could have ridden forever, and she hated the absence of the engine's thunder because now she could hear the wind and she hated the wind. It moved in the mesquites and in her hair, bringing to her nerve ends the near pain of a cat scratching glass. Will removed a blanket, spread it on the ground, then removed their basket of braunschweiger, cheese and bread from the saddlebags. The little grove of mesquites was the only feature in a vast and treeless spread of prairie. *If there is any beauty in this dreadful country,* Anna thought, *it is the mesquite tree. Farmers spend their lives clearing them from their fields, hacking them to pieces, burning them in fragrant fires. Yet the leaves are as delicate as any flower, like green lace in a world of hard, sharp edges.*

They ate in silence. Anna could feel the tension between them. It had been growing ever since Will had returned from his sister's wedding. The silence grew into something hard and substantial, a weight bearing down, and Anna again longed for the blessed concealing thunder of the Indian's motor.

"Say something," Anna said. She was not hungry. The smell of the liverwurst made her feel slightly sick.

Will seemed to be watching a buzzard wheel in the distance.

"There's someone else, isn't there?" As the question left her lips she longed to retract the words, knowing the answer, hating the wind, hating this man who was ruining her life.

"I didn't want it to happen," Will said.

"What to happen?"

"I met this person and we got along."

Anna was amazed that she felt so calm, even superior, as if she were listening to the confession of a child. "So what are you telling me, Will? Why don't you look me in the eyes and tell me what you've done? Why are you such a coward?"

"It's not what I've done, Anna. It just happened."

"What happens we make happen, Will." Anna wondered where all Will's strength had gone. He seemed weak now, hardly the man to whom she had entrusted her life, her love, her soul. "What's her name?"

"Does it matter?"

"It matters."

"Virginia."

"Virginia what?"

"Virginia King."

Now her enemy had a name. "Why, Will?" she said. "Does this mean we have been living a lie? I'm trying to understand what this means. What did you feel all this time? I know what you said. But you never really told me what you felt. Tell me now, Will. Did you love me?"

"Yes, of course I did."

"Do you love me now?"

Will looked down, searching for an answer in the picnic basket. "Yes, but in a different way." He reached up to move a wisp of Anna's hair that had fallen onto her forehead. She pushed his hand away.

"I know your kind of love," Anna hissed. She was still calm, but a cold calm, as if her blood had been replaced by a blending of fury and quicksilver. "It is a deceitful love. You are a deceitful man. You pretend to be one thing and you are actually something else."

"Don't," Will said. "I don't want it to end like this."

"What do you want? To be friends? Maybe we can all be friends, you and me and what's her name. My God, Will! I gave you everything! We were one person, inside each other, we were each other. And now you've destroyed all that. You've destroyed me. You've taken something from me that can never be replaced. You are a thief!"

"Have you finished, Anna?"

"No, I have not! I'll never finish as long as I live. You will be sorry, Will. You will suffer for what you've done."

Bettie and Henry King looked toward the King family cemetery where Will and Virginia were nested on the drooping branch of an oak tree. It was late afternoon and Henry's cattle were heading toward the barn where Peachtree was sharpening shovels. Bettie felt unusually comfortable with the day, comfortable with life. She watched her husband try not to look toward the motte of oaks, knowing he was trying to come to grips with the fact that his beloved daughter, his treasure, was in love with a man he considered a marginally acceptable suitor.

"What do they do up there?" he asked, his voice little more

than a growl.

"Henry!" Bettie smiled, remembering their own courtship. "Is your memory so short?"

"Whatever we did we didn't do it in a tree, like chickens roosting."

"They think they're hiding."

"Why would they hide?"

"Mainly because of you. And Will's father, too. It's plain neither of you approve."

"They are just so different. Different backgrounds."

"I seem to remember you fell in love with a little German girl one time. Your father had an attitude similar to yours. So did my father." She took his hand and squeezed. "Well, we got married anyway and I'd say things worked out pretty well."

"He's just so unpredictable. And I'm not sure I agree with his politics."

"The farmers' union? I think that's just talk. Besides, I'd say your politics and Will's are pretty close. I seem to remember that you started the first farmers' union in Guadalupe County. You've always fought for the rights of the little man. Just like Will. I'd think you'd respect what Will is trying to do."

"I respect him, but he worries me. He's not . . . practical," Henry King said.

"And they make such a beautiful couple. Think of the children they'll have! Our grandchildren!"

Henry King looked out toward the cemetery where so many generations of Kings had been buried. In the motte of oaks he saw the future was beginning. "You've worn me down, Bettie. Tell them it's safe to come out of the trees now."

After Will asked Virginia to marry him, and was given consent by Bettie and Henry King, he took his wife-to-be to the Bergfeld Drug Store. There Virginia heard Arthur Bergfeld speak German to his son once more, asking him, "Will, why not choose a good German girl?"

Will Bergfeld and Virginia King were married on Christmas Day, 1910. The ceremony was in the living room of the King homeplace on Court Street. After a reception and refreshments, they took the afternoon train to Weinert and to the house Will had built for Virginia with the money he had saved to go to California.

XVII.

Abilene, Texas.
October 1917

Bill Atwell drifted in and out of sleep all night. An autumnal wind rattled through the window frames and crept beneath his threadbare blanket, disturbing his dreams with its cool breath. He was not certain of the boundaries between his waking and dreaming; the two seemed seamless, speaking to him side by side. He dreamed he was at home with his wife, arguing about his obligation to the truth. Oddly, they wore togas and were in a columned amphitheater surrounded by cloud. His wife claimed that there was no such thing as a moral dilemma regarding truth because in human affairs there is only one right course of action, and to contemplate another, to pursue another, is to diminish truth. Truth is absolute, she argued, adjusting her laurel crown, and if altered, it becomes something else. In his wakeful hours he recalled his last conversation with Will Bergfeld and he wrestled with the possibility that there might be times when truth must bow to decency.

"You will not question Anna about those times!" Will had been adamant. "I forbid it. I've done her enough harm. And think how it would hurt Virginia. There are just too many people involved."

"You are tying my hands, Will! I appreciate your noble sentiments, but this woman's lies can send you to the gallows! I'll be as gentle as I can, but I can't allow her to destroy you."

Near dawn, Atwell's wakeful dreaming was interrupted by a battalion of snare drummers marching by and he rose to stuff newspaper around the windows to quiet their rattling. Now he lay fully awake, deeply troubled by what Will had told him about his youthful affair with Anna Bennett. It certainly explained why she had lied on the witness stand. It was revenge, pure and simple. She had perjured herself when she told O'Dell that she had met Will while he was delivering mail. If she lied about that, it probably would not be difficult to show that she had lied about other things as well. Atwell knew, if he were careful, he could probably tangle Anna in the web of her own lies and show the jury how the woman was motivated by revenge, how she was punishing Will for what he had done to her a long time ago. He could bring out the truth, but there was also the matter of decency, the point Will had been trying to make. What Will had done would be seen as reprehensible from a number of standpoints. He and Anna had engaged in behavior that was simply beyond the pale of accepted community standards. Even if Will had been led on by Anna, he had behaved badly. He had taken advantage of a young women, promised marriage, then broken his promise. The truth would prove Anna a liar, but it would also reveal Will in a terribly unfavorable light. The jury might not see Will simply as a man who had made a youthful mistake. Rather, the jurors might believe that if Will could be disloyal to this beautiful woman, he might be equally capable of being disloyal to his country. This was certainly one of those cases when the truth might not serve justice. Besides, Will insisted that the story of what happened between him and Anna remain secret, that Atwell put the whole thing out of his mind and pursue another line of questioning. Will had expressed profound remorse, was deeply sorry for what he had done, and he wanted to protect Anna from further injury. To bring out the truth would be devastating to her and it would be equally devastating to Will's family. Atwell had to admit that Will had a point. Maybe the decent thing to do would be to let the whole sordid business alone. Maybe he would be serving his client best to keep Will's unsavory rite of passage a secret.

A crowd had already gathered in and around the courthouse when Bill Atwell arrived. He was aware of a heightened excitement, generated partly, it seemed, by the distribution of printed handbills. They were being passed hand to hand, causing laughter and raucous comment, some flying like winged litter along the courthouse lawn. When Atwell reached the defense table, one of the other defense attorneys handed him a copy of the handbill. It was a year-old reprint from the Weinert newspaper, dominated by a photograph of a smiling Will Bergfeld, rifle beneath his arm, posed before a fence festooned with dead rattlesnakes. Beneath the photograph the cut line read: *Local man kills fifty rattlers in three hours.* The relevance to Anna Bennett's testimony was obviously not lost on the courthouse crowd. Here was a man famed for shooting rattlesnakes who had apparently threatened the President of the United States with the same fate.

Anna Bennett seemed as fully composed as she had been the day before. She was dressed in gray, with white lace at the collar and on the long sleeves. She wore no jewelry and her striking red hair was pulled back in a severe bun. She could have been a schoolteacher, albeit an extraordinarily beautiful one. Surely this did not seem to be a woman so crazy for revenge that she would risk perjury to condemn an innocent man. As Bill Atwell approached the witness, she waited for him with serene and innocent eyes, as if eager to reveal all that was in her heart. He realized he was probably more nervous than she was. He could feel his heart beating. For one of the few times in his career, he had been unable to decide on a strategy. He had no idea what he would ask, and he decided he would just have to wait, like the jury was waiting, like the judge was waiting, like Anna Bennett was waiting, to see what came to his mind.

He stood for a moment, looking into Anna Bennett's eyes, seeking inspiration there, wondering if it was possible everything she had said on direct examination had been the truth. Maybe Will had, in one of his reckless, passionate moments, made some outlandish threat against the president. But as he recalled her testimony, it occurred to him that what she claimed Will had said was not actually a threat at all.

"Any time now, Counselor," Judge Jack said, placing his gold pocket watch before him. There was a soft scattering of laughter around the courtroom. Anna Bennett smiled.

"Miss Bennett," Atwell began. "Yesterday when you were questioned by Mr. O'Dell you told the jury that Will Bergfeld made certain threats against a high official in government. Would you repeat for us now the actual words of that threat?"

"He said that President Wilson should be assassinated before it was too late. He should be shot like a rattlesnake."

"Those were his exact words?"

"Yes, sir."

"You are absolutely sure?"

"Yes, sir."

"That he should be shot like a rattlesnake?"

"Yes, sir."

"Did he say *who* should shoot the President?"

"Well, no, sir."

"He didn't say that he—Will Bergfeld—was going to shoot the President?"

"No, sir, not really."

Atwell thought for a moment, then asked, "Miss Bennett, do you have a garden?"

Anna smiled. "Yes, I do."

"Some flowers. Some vegetables."

"Yes."

"Lettuce?"

Smiling wider, "Yes."

Atwell glanced toward O'Dell who was smiling expectantly, as if waiting for the punch line of some joke. "Let me ask you this, Miss Bennett. Suppose you looked out at your garden and saw a jackrabbit eating your lettuce. And you said, 'I'm going to shoot that rabbit.' Now that would be a threat, wouldn't it? A threat to take action against the rabbit?"

"I suppose so, Mr. Atwell."

"Now suppose you said, 'That rabbit ought to be shot.' Now, would you consider that a threat? Or would that be merely an expression of your opinion?"

Anna glanced toward the judge. "I don't believe I understand the question."

"If Will Bergfeld said that the President should be shot, that is not a threat—that is an expression of his opinion, isn't that right, Miss Bennett?"

The remnant of her smile faded. "It was spoken in a threatening manner."

"But he didn't say that he—Will Bergfeld—was going to shoot the President, did he, Miss Bennett?"

Prosecutor O'Dell objected. "He is badgering the witness with these trivial differences, Your Honor. Asked and answered."

"I am just trying to show that there is a great deal of difference between a threat and an opinion. This is America and every American is free to express an opinion, no matter how unpopular that opinion might be."

"I'm going to overrule the objection," Judge Jack said, after a pause. "But you've made your point, Counselor, and I wish you'd move on."

Atwell knew that jurors sometimes resented such semantic juggling, and he sensed their patience was growing thin. He knew he needed to come up with something better or he would lose them entirely. Should he go for the jugular? He glanced at Will. He looked toward Virginia and the little girls. Will shook his head. Atwell decided he might be able to discredit Anna without going into the carnal aspects of her relationship with Will.

"Miss Bennett," Atwell continued. "You also testified yesterday that you met Will Bergfeld when he was a rural mail carrier. When he delivered your mail. Wasn't that your testimony?"

"Yes, sir."

"Now I would like you to think carefully about this. Isn't it possible that you had met Will Bergfeld before he was a mail carrier? While he was still a single man?"

"I don't think so."

"But it's possible?"

"Anything's possible, Mr. Atwell."

"Weinert is a small town, isn't it, Miss Bennett?"

"Yes."

"And I'd say Will Bergfeld was one of the town's most noticeable citizens and most eligible bachelors. He raced motorcycles. An accomplished musician. A good-looking man. I'd say everybody in town knew Will Bergfeld, wouldn't you, Miss Bennett?"

"I didn't say I didn't know who he was."

"So you did know Will Bergfeld before he became a rural mail carrier, isn't that correct?"

"I knew of him."

Atwell sensed that Anna was not quite as composed as she had been. She was rubbing the fingers of one hand against her thumb. When she realized Atwell was staring at her hands, she lowered them into her lap.

"Tell me, Miss Bennett, do you like living in Weinert?"

"Weinert is my home."

"But haven't you expressed many times that you would like to move away? Isn't that something you have told your friend Mrs. Thurwanger?"

"I may have."

"Haven't you always wanted to move to California?"

"When I was younger, yes."

"Miss Bennett, isn't it true that you and Will Bergfeld had planned to go to California together? Isn't it a fact, Miss Bennett, that you knew Will Bergfeld quite well? That you were, in fact, engaged to be married?"

"Objection!" shouted O'Dell as he rose to his feet. The voice of the spectators also rose, a harsh whisper of surprise.

Before the prosecutor could give a reason for his objection, Judge Jack silenced him with a raised hand. "I would like to hear an answer," the judge said.

Bill Atwell was astounded that Anna Bennett could remain so calm. She was like a woman carved from ivory.

"That's simply not true. We were not engaged."

"Then how would you characterize your relationship with Will

Bergfeld?"

"I knew him. We did things together sometimes."

"What things did you and Will Bergfeld do together, Miss Bennett?"

"There's not much to do in Weinert, Mr. Atwell. We talked. Went riding."

"Horses?"

"Motorcycle. He had a motorcycle with a sidecar."

"Wasn't it your plan to ride that motorcycle to California? The two of you?"

"It was just talk. A game. Young people dreaming."

"Isn't it true that you wanted desperately to leave Weinert? That you hated Weinert and saw Will as a means of escape?"

"It was more than that. I cared for Will."

"Isn't it true that you planned to be married?"

"It wasn't a plan. We were young. Attracted to each other. We saw a future together."

"But Will Bergfeld fell in love with another woman. He married someone else, isn't that true?"

"Yes."

"What was your state of mind when you learned the man you planned to marry was going to marry someone else instead?"

Anna Bennett turned toward the judge as if to ask if it was necessary for her to answer. O'Dell seemed poised to object, but remained silent.

"I was not pleased."

"In fact, weren't you furious?"

"That was a long time ago," Anna replied, still icily calm. But Atwell noticed a slight tremor at the corner of one eye. He wondered why O'Dell wasn't objecting to his questions. He decided to take a risk.

"Isn't it true that you promised revenge and you are testifying against him today because 'Hell hath no fury like a woman scorned'?"

Now O'Dell did leap to his feet. "Counsel is testifying, Your Honor! If he wishes to testify, let him take the stand!"

"Sustained," Judge Jack said over his glasses. "Limit yourself to questions, Mr. Atwell."

"Isn't it true you promised Will that one day he would be sorry for deserting you?"

"Objection!" shouted O'Dell.

Before Judge Jack could rule on the objection, Anna turned to the judge. "I want to answer, Your Honor." As she spoke, her clear voice had just an edge of indignation. "No, it is not true. I cared for Will. I still do. I would never wish him harm. I pray to God that he had never said those things about President Wilson. But he did and that's wrong."

Atwell could feel the jurors leaning forward to embrace the lovely woman with their sympathy. She had been wronged by his client and was facing her plight bravely and with compassion for the one who had wronged her. Atwell also realized his examination of the witness was about to end in disaster. But he could think of nothing else to ask that would not make things worse. He felt he had shown that Anna Bennett lied about her relationship with Will, but the jury didn't seem to care. A beautiful liar, it seemed, was preferable to a traitorous Lothario.

"I have no further questions, Your Honor."

O'Dell rose. "If I may redirect, Your Honor."

"Go ahead, Counselor."

O'Dell walked slowly toward the witness, apparently deep in thought. "Miss Bennett, when I asked you yesterday when you had met Will Bergfeld, didn't you respond within the context of this trial?"

Anna stared into O'Dell's eyes, seeking the response he wanted. "You didn't ask me when I *first* met Will Bergfeld. If you had, I would have answered differently."

"You didn't think I was asking about the distant past, did you?"

"No, sir."

"And again, when Mr. Atwell asked the same question a moment ago, you were reluctant to mention your youthful friendship, weren't you?"

"Objection! He's leading the witness." Atwell wondered if a jury could possibly swallow this transparent misdirection.

"Sustained," called Judge Jack.

"Why were you reluctant to bring up these matters from the past?"

"It didn't seem relevant. And I've tried to forget those times. They were not very pleasant for me. If my answer was misleading, I apologize. A lady doesn't like to admit that she has been rejected."

O'Dell reflected the height of sympathy. "I, too, am sorry this unhappy incident from the past has been revisited. But as long as the defense counsel has taken us there, let me ask you this: Did you ever hear of someone called Moses?"

"Oh, yes, sir. It was how Will referred to himself."

"Would you please explain for the jury?"

"He considered himself a leader in the labor movement. That was his code name. Moses."

"A secret code name?"

"Just about everything about Will was secret," Anna said, her eyes looking boldly toward where Will was sitting among the defendants, his eyes averted, looking not at all like a leader of men.

As the witness was excused, O'Dell announced that the government would call no more witnesses. "Your Honor," he said, his eyes sweeping across the jury, then resting on Bill Atwell. "The prosecution rests."

As Louise watched Defense Attorney Atwell walk toward the jury to make his opening statement, she felt an almost overpowering impatience. In all these weeks, it seemed Will was no closer to freedom than he had been the night his family was terrorized and he had been arrested. It seemed as if everything had gone downhill from there. One witness after another had come forward with accusations that seemed to prove her brother's guilt. Calhoun and his fantastic story of his conversation with Will in Cisco. Old Man Crouch, the pompous and arrogant water thief. Anna Bennett, the consummate actress. Especially, Anna Bennett. When Louise had listened to her testimony, at first she had been enraged, but helpless to vent the anger she felt. Louise had feared she would explode right there in the courtroom. In another time, if she had been a man, she would have challenged the woman to a duel. But then she began to see that there was just enough truth woven into the fabric of lies to confuse even Louise's own mind.

Louise knew all three had lied through their teeth. But the problem was this: a jury might believe one was lying, or perhaps two, but what are the odds that all three were not telling the truth? And from the jury's standpoint the prosecution would not spend all this time, money and effort, basing its primary case on the testimony of three liars. Bill Atwell had revealed innumerable inaccuracies in their testimony, had found ways to discredit their memory or their interpretation of events. In the case of Anna Bennett, he had actually caught her in a lie, but it didn't seem to make much of an impact on the jury. It was understandable that a woman who had been treated cruelly and humiliated would not want to relive the experience in public.

Louise sincerely believed that more lies had come from prosecution witnesses than truth. In fact, the government's entire case was based on an elaborate mosaic of lies. Then she wondered, *Is a lie a lie if the one telling the lie believes it is the truth? What if Anna and Calhoun and Old Man Crouch actually believe in their hearts that Will is a German agent? What if all three are convinced that Will is a dangerous man, a man who has done great harm to his country? Then perhaps the details don't really matter. If the facts don't build a foundation for that belief, then change the facts, juggle them around, so the foundation is strengthened and the belief structure doesn't fall.*

Atwell stood for a moment, smiling at each of the jurors. He was wearing the late summer rose Louise had given him for his lapel. She noticed, for the first time, how much the defense attorney resembled her husband Rob. They both were slender, were immaculately groomed, wore their gray suits with stylish elegance. Instead of a rose, Rob wore a diamond stickpin in his lapel. Louise thought that Rob Tewes and Bill Atwell were two of very few men who could wear a rose or a diamond stickpin without it seeming an affectation. Then Atwell began. He spoke conversationally to the jurors, as if across a backyard fence.

"May it please the Court, Counsel, Gentlemen of the Jury. At this time I have the opportunity to briefly relate to you the position of the defense in this case. I think for you to understand this position, we should focus on what the defendants are *not* charged with and precisely what crimes they *are* alleged to have committed.

Get on with it. I know you said that the worst is over and now it's our turn to make points with the jury. But why so slowly, why such courtly language? Get on with it! Louise's impatience had not abated.

"First," Atwell continued, "consider those things the defendants are not charged with. They are not charged with opposing the war. They are not charged with conspiracy to oppose the war. They are not charged with conspiracy to oppose conscription, or the draft as we often call it. They are not charged with joining or helping to organize the FLPA or the IWW. They are not charged with buying or owning weapons or explosives. And, of course, the obvious reason they are not charged with doing any of those things is because none of the things I mentioned constitute crimes under the laws of the United States. If indeed there is evidence that these defendants were engaged in these activities I just mentioned, I submit to you that such acts or conduct on the part of the defendants is meaningless. So much of the testimony offered by the prosecution is irrelevant because this testimony offers evidence of activities that might be unpopular, but are completely within the law. We are in a court of law where all of these defendants are charged with specific crimes. They are not charged with conducting themselves in a way that might be unpopular with some people."

Louise studied the jury, concentrating first on one juror, then another. Each seemed to be listening attentively, eyes following Atwell as he paced slowly and thoughtfully before them. *What are they thinking? Maybe one is thinking about a subtle pain felt recently in his chest, wondering at its cause, fearing that it might be the heart, the first dread signal of its failure to sustain life. Or another is thinking of a lost love, or a humiliation endured, or a sorrow that keeps life uneasy and unbalanced and makes full joy impossible. One may be thinking of the death of a child or a parent, an event impossible to forget or to anticipate. "What is the life of this Will Bergfeld or all these farmers," each juror must think, "when balanced against my own life? I am the center of the Universe. Will Bergfeld is at its edge, a stranger, and when his story has been told, I will still be here, battling against pain, struggling to know joy, railing against the night."*

"Now let me focus your attention on exactly what these defendants are actually charged with." Atwell made a sweeping gesture that carried the jurors' eyes over the seated sea of defendants. "The U.S. District Attorney in this case is claiming that all of these defendants unlawfully, knowingly, wickedly and feloniously conspired among themselves to overthrow, put down and destroy by force the government of the United States. And gentlemen, if that is not enough, further the prosecution has alleged that they conspired to levy war against the United States.

"To be even more specific, these defendants are charged with conspiring and agreeing among themselves to oppose by force the raising of an army by the United States. It is alleged that these defendants conspired to assault and kill officers and agents of the United States who were engaged in raising that army. I submit to you gentlemen of the jury that these charges are ludicrous, they have no basis in fact, the prosecution has not proven these charges and they never will prove these charges against the defendants."

Louise had always been able to make Will look her way. It was a talent they had practiced as children, concentrating on each other's mind, sending a message through the air, speaking the other's name like a whispered mantra. Now her silent lips formed the word, her brother's name. Again, she thrilled as his head turned and his eyes found hers and he smiled that smile that swept away all but their love for each other. Once again she felt the towering impatience. *What can I do? How can I help him? There must be something. If the witnesses are lying—and I know they are—what can be done besides sitting here in a stuffy courtroom before a hostile crowd listening to lawyers show off their vocabulary? I know my brother better than he knows himself. When he denies the testimony of Old Man Crouch and Anna Bennett, I know his denial might be overstated. Not that he would lie. But he has always been a master of evasion, of letting the truth slide by like a bullfighter evading a bull, cape flying, sidestepping gracefully. But when he talks about Ned Earl Calhoun and denies that he ever met the man or talked with him, I can see absolute truth in his eyes. This is the key. Ned Earl Calhoun. Why doesn't Atwell concentrate on Calhoun and stop this infernal double-talk?*

Atwell continued. "I am sure you will understand that in a federal criminal case like this, the prosecution has the burden of proving the guilt of each of the defendants named in the Indictment beyond a reasonable doubt. Under our system of justice, a defendant who is charged with a crime has absolutely no obligation or responsibility to prove his own innocence. Under our laws these defendants do not have to present any evidence in their own defense. They do not have to present witnesses in their defense. They do not have to testify themselves in their own defense. The entire burden is on the Federal Prosecutor to prove that each of these defendants is guilty beyond a reasonable doubt.

"However, the defendants in this case have decided that they will present some evidence. We will bring witnesses to testify that these defendants enjoyed a good reputation as law-abiding citizens in their own communities. In the days ahead, several of the defendants will personally testify in this case. It is important for you to understand that defendants do not have any obligation to testify and if some of them choose not to do so it should not be considered by you as any presumption of their guilt."

Get on with it.

"As you listen to the defendant's testimony, I am certain that it will become clear that these men are innocent of the charges against them. They are merely good and decent men caught up in a fiction created by the prosecution in its zeal to eliminate all opposition to the war. Now, you will have an opportunity to hear not the fiction, but the true story of what these defendants did and did not do.

"Gentlemen of the jury, you have been very attentive to all the testimony presented by the prosecution and I hope you will continue to show the same interest in the testimony presented by the witnesses called on behalf of the defendants."

Bill Atwell then called the first of 161 witnesses for the defense.

For the next several days, as Atwell and the other defense attorneys presented their witnesses, Louise's impatience only grew more intense. It seemed to go on forever. First came numerous character witnesses all testifying to the defendants' sterling qualities of truth and veracity. Louise was certain she saw the jurors' eyes glaze over. Those who testified concerning Will's character followed the same script. Only Dr. Cockrell's testimony had a ring of unrehearsed praise of a good and caring and trustworthy neighbor. But this was not what the jurors wanted to hear. A person's flaws and failings are far more interesting than their virtues. The prosecution had made points because it had sole ownership of Will's flaws and failings.

Get on with it.

Following the character witnesses, the defense paraded an impossibly long roster of defendants to the stand, gaunt farmers with empty eyes, the husbands of the poor women Louise and Bettie had been helping to survive until their men could get back on the land. The men were pale from their imprisonment and seemed defeated by forces they could neither understand nor control. All they had wanted was to coax a living from the soil. All they had wanted was a better life for their children in communities so small and remote they sometimes had no names. Then came strangers with promises. Professional organizers like Mother Jones and Risley and Powell. *Men of conscience like Will. Like Moses? Follow us and things will be better. Your children will have something to eat. Your cows will not die of thirst in the pasture. Your women will not grow old before their time. The meek shall inherit the Earth.* It was a promise as old as the Bible. Louise's heart went out to these impoverished farmers and their families and she wondered if the jurors felt the same. She thought this must be Atwell's strategy: to win empathy for the farmers' plight. Louise could see no other reason to bring so many witnesses to the stand to tell the same story over and over again.

In the third week of the defense's presentation, Z. L. Risley, President of the Farmers' and Laborers' Protective Association, took the stand. He was followed by Samuel Powell, the Secretary. Unlike many of the other defendants, both men were well-dressed, composed and articulate. As organizers and paid officers of the FLPA, both men had either the resources or, like Will, the connections to make bail. Unlike the farmers they had recruited, they were not led in chains to a barren cell each night. Unlike the farmers they had recruited, their lives were not in ruin.

Louise could not muster any sympathy for Risley or for Powell. *Fat cats*, she thought to herself. *Why is it that leadership always carries an inherent inequality, even demands it? The General rides behind the lines on a fine horse while the Private approaches the enemy on foot. Senators nearly always retire wealthy. The Bishop wears a cross of pure gold. The company President makes in a month what his laborers will not earn in a lifetime. Now I sound like Will. The world needs to change. And I guess it takes people like Risley and Powell to make change happen. And people like Will.*

During their initial questioning, the testimony of Risley and Powell was relatively uneventful. They offered a general description of their union's goals and philosophy and an absolute denial that anything remotely illegal had been done in their meetings. But in one memorable session, when Secretary Powell was being questioned by O'Dell, he was asked where the minutes were that he had taken at the meetings. Powell at first said that they had disappeared, then said they had been destroyed by burning them up. Prosecutor O'Dell was aghast.

"You faithfully took minutes of these meetings, then destroyed them?"

"Yes, sir," Powell had said, as if the destruction of minutes was a routine activity.

"As I understand it," O'Dell had said, "the purpose of taking minutes is to have a permanent record of what was said, what was done, isn't that so?"

"Yes, sir."

"Then why on Earth would you burn the minutes?"

"We just had too much paper around. Too much to keep track of."

"So you destroyed them. Who burned up the minutes of the Cisco meeting?"

"As I recall, it was me, Mr. Risley and Mr. Bergfeld."

"Isn't it true, Mr. Powell, that those minutes were destroyed because they were compelling evidence of criminal activities?"

"No, sir. We just had too much paper to keep track of."

Louise had shuddered at the mention of Will's name. She also knew the jury would have trouble believing that the minutes were burned up because there was too much paper.

Then, on a Friday afternoon in October, Defense Attorney Bill Atwell asked Judge Jack for an early recess so he could prepare for his next witness. On Monday, he planned to bring Defendant Will Bergfeld to the stand.

"It's about time," Louise said softly. "Let's get on with it."

Late that night, in the Fort Worth railroad yards, the man called Peachtree climbed aboard a westbound freight. He sensed there were others in the boxcar's deep shadows, but he could sense no threat, no danger, no trap set by railroad police. Carefully, he found an unoccupied corner and settled down for the ride to Abilene. He began to empty his mind of thoughts as he often did to make time disappear. It was not an easy task because thoughts pelted around in his head like frightened birds in a cage. They were living things and he had no control over their content or direction. Only with great care and concentration could he still the chaos in his mind.

He thought back to his earliest memory, a time when he realized he was not like other people and never would be and that he would always be alone. It was not a moment remembered with sorrow or regret; it was, in fact, a moment that filled him with calm, blessed calm. Then from the calm came the sound of his heartbeat and the soft call of his owl and a thought that was not really a thought, but an awareness of why he was on the train and what he had to do. His heart beat faster as he realized his urgent task would take him within that most terrifying of places, the community of human beings.

XVIII.

Ludlow, Colorado.
March 1914

Virginia could hear Will's motorcycle long before she saw the rooster tail of dust it cast up from the road. The babies were taking their nap and she hoped he would cut the engine before entering the yard. But, of course, he came on like a clattering comet, scattering chickens, speeding on the thin edge of control, skidding to a stop in a cloud of dust and decibels. In their bedroom, the little girls began to fret, but they did not cry, and Virginia left the porch to welcome her man back from work.

She tried to guess what surprise this astonishing man had in store on this day. In the years they had been married, every day had been a marvelous adventure. Apparently, as Will drove his rural mail route, his mind was free to wander, to create, to invent. If it was not some new way to generate electricity, or a new theory for perpetual motion, or a means of organizing the state's farmers into a union, it was some other ingenious newfangled idea that had never been imagined before. *How I love this man*, she thought, as they embraced. *How good he feels, how strong. Will I ever tire of his touch, his voice, his laugh, the love in his eyes as he sings to his daughters? Will I ever tire of the way he feels against me, within me?* She felt absolutely naughty as she wondered what day it was that God created love. *Maybe He dreamed it on that seventh day as He rested, just before He imagined how nice babies would be.*

All through supper, Will seemed preoccupied. *It was not like him,* Virginia thought. Usually he filled the air with tales of what he had seen or thought during the day, making even the most humdrum occurrences seem magical and alive with whimsy or irony or mystery. But now, he ate in silence.

"Is something wrong, Will?"

He looked up, smiled a thin ghost of a smile. "I don't know. It depends on what you think."

"About what?"

"About what I have to say."

He was looking deep into her eyes, yet there was nothing there she could read. A chill of uneasiness touched her breast.

"What, Will?"

Will put down his fork, pushed back his chair. "I need to know how you feel about my leaving Weinert for a few weeks."

"Where? Why?" Virginia could not imagine being apart from Will even for one day.

"Sheriff Parks stopped me today," Will continued. "There's an opportunity for me to take a job in Ludlow, Colorado. I'd be able to earn more than double what I get now. And I could get my old job back when I come home."

"What kind of job is it?"

"There's some kind of trouble in the mines up there. They're looking for experienced lawmen. Sheriff Parks remembers how I handled the boys from Lone Star."

"But why you, Will?"

"Why not me?"

"Because you have two little babies in there, that's why." Virginia paused, realizing they were on the verge of their first argument. "What kind of trouble?"

"I don't know exactly. But they're paying real good money and, well, it just seems like something I ought to do."

"What kind of trouble? Is it dangerous?"

"No, I doubt it."

"What about us? What if something happens and we need you?"

"You'll be fine. The Cockrells are right across the street."

"What do you want me to say, Will?"

"I want you to say you're not mad at me."

Virginia sighed. "I don't know what I feel, Will. I think I'm surprised. A little hurt maybe. A little scared."

"Virginia, you know how much I care about you and the girls. If you insist, I won't take the job. I'll stay."

Virginia sighed. "When will you leave?"

"On the morning train."

That night, as Virginia was on the verge of sleep, she felt Will climb quietly from bed. For a while, she heard nothing, then the sounds of Will packing his valise. She knew she could say one word and Will would stay. She longed to call out to him, but did not. She was certain the Colorado job had little to do with money. It had more to do with that part of Will he did not share with her, his wanderlust, that wild side that longed for adventure and risk and novelty. One word and he would stay. But she knew that would make him unhappy. So Virginia said nothing, pretended sleep, despite the metallic sound of Will removing his pistols from the trunk in the hall. Then she heard the slide of the bolt of the long gun. It was a sound that spoke volumes about what she did not know about this man who had fathered her daughters.

The old woman watched the stranger standing guard from the shoulder of the arroyo that runs into Ludlow, his rifle carelessly over his shoulder, his eyes on the distant Santa de Christo Mountains. She could tell he was a man unaccustomed to high country; he had the look and manner of a flatlander, a man who distrusted mountains, creations so much larger than himself. She had observed the young man for several days now. She had seen him first racing his motorcycle across the plain, daring the rocky earth, seeming to relish the pure and thrilling fact of speed. At first she was attracted by his physical beauty, so much in contrast to the ugliness all around and to the other guards hired by the Baldwin-Felts Detective Agency, outlaws and compromised lawmen mostly, the rabble of the West. Although he was a large man who, in addition to his 30-30 rifle, carried a coiled whip, he did not seem to belong in the company of the other hired goons. She had noticed that he did not really take part in the beatings and evictions ordered by the mine bosses. His participation was a kind of pantomime, a pretending, as if he were going through the motions of preserving law and order in the Ludlow coal camp. He seemed to be drinking everything in, soaking up the experience, observing, watching. And she had seen something else. Once she had seen him playing with some children, doing magic with a coin. She had heard his laughter, a sound rarely heard in the coal country of Southern Colorado. *Would a man who gives pleasure to a child do harm to its parents?* After a few days, the old woman became sure he would not. *But would he help?*

The old woman's name was Mary Harris. Those who knew her called her Mother Jones. Some called her the "Angel of the Coal Fields." In her seventies, with ice-blue eyes and hair the color of cloud, she could have been anyone's great-grandmother rocking away the years on her porch. But despite her fragile demeanor, she was a self-proclaimed "hell-raiser," a well-known union organizer, and a fighter for the rights and the very lives of coal miners and their families.

Beyond the fire, where Mother Jones sat with a man called Louis the Greek, the coal camp shanties and tents littered the ground like things thrown away. It was an awful world devoid of trees or color or grace, a broad pasture of dreadful hovels, like stunted roots or rotting teeth rising from the mud. Here, nearly a thousand miners and their families suffered a life even more desperate than the life they had fled in their native Poland, Ireland, Italy or Greece. Whole families were packed into one-room shelters with only tarps or blankets hung from the low ceilings for privacy. They lived in abject poverty, most deeply in debt to the company store, enduring the bitter winters with little heat and less hope, the men laboring from dark to dark in the earth like moles. And everywhere, in the air, ground deep into the flesh and into the soul was the indelible black grime of the coalfield. No matter how a woman scrubbed her bedding and clothing and children in the camp's single acid-polluted stream, the coal dust remained as a signature of the world's most difficult and dangerous occupation.

And beyond, down a mud road through a windswept upland slope of buffalo grass and scrub pinion, was the killer mine. It had killed twenty-nine men only a week before. They were consumed in a preventable firestorm of exploding methane gas. If it had not been the gas, it would have been a cave-in or a bullet from a guard's rifle or eventually tuberculosis or black lung disease. *Death,* Mother Jones thought, *has easy pickings in the Colorado mines of Mr. John D. Rockefeller, the world's first billionaire.*

"Is that the one?" Louis the Greek asked. He, too, had been observing the young guard. Louis Tikas was a small, wiry man with slack patches of flesh beneath his eyes and an overall appearance of exhaustion. His eyelids drooped half closed as if sleep might overtake him at any moment.

"His name is Bergfeld. From Texas."

"Have you spoken to him?"

"Briefly."

"Will he come?"

"Says he will. Tonight."

"Can you trust this Bergfeld?" Louis wanted to know. "He could turn you in, you know."

"I can see in his face that he hates what he has seen here," Mother Jones said. "Hate is a rare and useful thing in a good man."

They met beneath a makeshift oilcloth shelter in a canyon by the hobo road, the rail tracks running between Trinidad and Pueblo. Mother Jones was there, Louis the Greek, the Irishman O'Leary and two other miners, their faces black as minstrels, their boots caked with the mud from the flooded rooms and shafts underground. It was near midnight. A light rain was falling. Mother Jones could feel the exhaustion and tension within the group as she introduced Bergfeld and she watched the miners search the young man's face for signs that he could be trusted.

"Where do you stand?" the Irishman asked.

"I stand on the ground," Bergfeld said, after a pause. He apparently didn't like the question.

"What the hell does that mean?" O'Leary asked, his fists balled, apparently not liking Bergfeld's answer or Bergfeld, for that matter. Mother Jones knew that trust was a concept the Irishman had lost long ago. It had been stripped away by years of broken promises, lies and greed on the part of the mine bosses. He had seen his companions die needlessly to cut costs and leverage a bit more profit for the owners.

Mother Jones smiled. "This is not easy for us, Will. There have been company spies before. If you are not the man you say you are, it could have disastrous consequences. Our lives are at stake here. So you can understand why we must be careful."

"You asked me to come and I came. I promised to listen and to keep what I heard to myself. That's all I can say, unless you want me to take some kind of oath. And I won't do that."

"Why not?" O'Leary asked.

"Because I gave my word. That's enough."

Mother Jones wasn't surprised that Bergfeld was quick to show his temper. "Tell us what you've seen here, Will."

Will thought for a moment, then said, "I've seen I'm on the wrong side of things. I've seen men treated worse than mules. I've seen sick children who shouldn't be. I've seen I don't belong where I am."

"Then why are you here?" This from Louis the Greek.

"It was a mistake. I'm waiting for my first paycheck. Then I'm heading home."

"Maybe you should stay," Mother Jones said.

They talked on toward dawn. The rain ceased and stars slid from behind clouds as black as the coal the men mined. The Greek and the Irishman smoked their pipes. The aroma of tobacco blended with the smoke of the pinion fires kindled by the miners' wives up before day to prepare breakfasts of turnips and black bread and barley soup. Mother Jones talked about an America that was far different than the land envisioned by the Founding Fathers.

"The company owns the coal, they own the mines that produce the coal, the mills where the coal is used to make steel and the plant that makes things like rails and rods from the steel. They own everything."

The Irishman tamped out his pipe, sharp blows reflecting his fury. "And they own the only store where we can buy food and supplies. Charge twice what we could buy those goods for anywhere else."

"But there isn't anywhere else," Louis the Greek added. "Except Trinidad or Pueblo. But how we gonna get there? I get paid $1.68 for a twelve-hour day. I can scarcely feed my family with that. Especially after paying rent at the company rates for housing."

"And we don't get paid in cash," one of the miners who had been silent said. "They pay us in company scrip. The only place you can spend scrip is in the company store."

"The company owns us. Like we were horses or dogs," Louis the Greek continued.

"Why don't you just quit?" Will asked. "Go somewhere else."

"Most of us don't know any other type of work." Louis said. "Some speak little or no English. Their families can't afford to miss a week's pay, meager as it is. Where would we go? How would we go? Anyway, they'd just replace us with some other poor soul and nothing would change."

"We want things to change, Will," Mother Jones said. "And the only way we can do that is to stay here and fight." She could see that Will was deeply moved by their plight, had probably been since he first laid eyes on Ludlow.

"Where do I come in?"

"We need someone who can command the respect of the workers. Somebody on the inside who can help us find company officials who might listen to our grievances. We've formed a labor union, Will. I need someone to help me organize. There are more mines like this scattered throughout the foothills of the Santa de

Christo Mountains, even into New Mexico. There might be as many as ten thousand miners in these hills. If we could organize all of them into a union, what a mighty force that would be. We need someone who has free access to all the mines and can direct us to the most reasonable company officials we can negotiate with."

"From what I hear," Will said, "Rockefeller hates the unions."

"It's the only way," Mother Jones said. "If we all stand together we might be able to make some changes. Maybe we could force better wages and better working conditions where there won't be so many widows and orphans. We're not asking for much. We're simply asking to be treated like human beings."

"What if the company doesn't listen or turns you down?"

"Then we strike," Louis the Greek said.

Silence. Mother Jones watched the pale intrusion of dawn on the eastern horizon. She knew the miners would soon be trudging up the slope for another day of labor for the Rockefellers. In the new light she could see the dismal landscape of the coal fields take shape. She looked at Will Bergfeld, wondered what he was thinking, wondered where his heart was. *Maybe he is afraid to face the awful odds the miners are up against. Maybe he is afraid of O'Leary.*

"So, Bergfeld," the Irishman asked. "Are you with us or against us?"

Will smiled. "I'm not against you. I promise you that." Then he reached over to the glowering Irishman to pull a coin from his ear. Before O'Leary could react, Bergfeld flipped the coin high into the air and as it arced down, Will's whip suddenly appeared, uncoiled, cracked, and the coin went spinning, singing off into the canyon. "I'm not against you, O'Leary," he said, still smiling, as he recoiled the whip. "Just don't you be against me."

Mother Jones watched Will Bergfeld walk away. She knew she had the right man.

During the next week, Mother Jones watched Will Bergfeld win the hearts of the miners and their families. He accompanied Mother Jones on her nightly visits to the shanties, listened as she explained the importance of the union and how it was the only way to make life better. Often he managed to bring something he had purchased at the company store, candy for the children or a bit of cloth or ribbon for the women. He learned the names of the children and talked with them as equals. On two occasions, late at night, there were meetings where the miners' demands were discussed. They argued about what they could realistically expect from the owners and bosses and what would merely further the bosses' resistance to the idea of the union. Usually Will reported on the progress of organization at other nearby mines. At the second meeting, in the shanty of a Polish family named Yeskenski, Will was shown the family treasure, a violin they had brought from Poland. For the next hour, Will played and the music of Beethoven flowed like a prayer through the camp, and for a while beauty found its way where little beauty had ever been before. Mother Jones marveled at the power of music when she saw tears streaming down O'Leary's coarse and grimy face.

As the days passed, Mother Jones and Will were often together. He listened intently as she talked about social justice and how political revolutions around the world had merely exchanged one kind of tyranny for another. She felt the American Revolution had banished the British from the land, but had created a state ruled by those who became rich by subjugating others. She railed on about how a small elite group of men had always possessed most of the country's wealth and power. With the industrial revolution, enslavement was passed from the Negro to the immigrant. Although the immigrant cannot be sold like a slave, he can be sold out by the slave masters of the Industrial Revolution—the Rockefellers, the Morgans, the Vanderbilts. She called them the pirates of the new age. Mother Jones recounted the long struggle of Colorado miners to form a union, a fight that began as early as 1884. Yet, each time they managed to organize, the operators crushed their efforts by firing the leaders, burning their homes or deporting them from Colorado like so many cattle in boxcars. Will rarely asked questions. He seemed to drink in her political philosophy and her outrage as if starved for something to believe in and fight for.

Although she recognized Will's strength, Mother Jones perceived that he was somehow adrift, a young man half formed. Although he was quick to laughter, there was something sad about him, something that stirred her maternal instincts. When he told her about his mother's death and how his father essentially abandoned him and his sister, she recognized that he might easily want more from her than she had to give him. She was already a parent to thousands and she certainly did not need this grown child consuming her energy and commitment.

When she asked him what he intended to do with his life, Will replied that he did not know. "I'm happy with my life in Texas, with my family. But sometimes I think there's more. I don't know, something I need to do."

"How about your music? You're very good, you know."

"It isn't enough. Music is a pleasure. It is not a life. There has to be something more," Will said. "I want to make a difference. I want to be remembered as more than a name on a headstone."

"We all want to be immortal, Will."

"Not immortal in that sense. I want my life to have meaning while I'm living it. Not when I'm gone."

"If you ask me, I think you've found what you're looking for."

"What do you mean?"

"I think you know. I see it in your eyes when you are with the families. You could do a lot worse in life than devoting yourself to these people. You could do a lot worse than fighting for the God-given rights of the common man."

"Where? How? I have my family to consider."

"Working people and farmers are hurting everywhere. You can fight for them in Texas, too."

"How would I know what to do?"

"For now, I'll teach you what I know during the next few weeks."

Mother Jones watched Will's face as he considered her offer. She believed this might be one of those defining moments when a person sees clearly where life's road leads. *What a fighter he would make. How quickly he has won the miners' trust. Even O'Leary has been won over by whatever quality it is that draws people to Will. Perhaps his best quality is the way he loves the miners and their families.*

Will and Virginia wrote to each other almost every day, but the letter that meant the most to Will came the third week of his stay:

Dearest Will,

You know how much we love you and miss you. We can hardly wait for you to come home, but I can tell from your letters that Mother Jones and your work there has rekindled your spirit and love for life. I thank God that I did not insist that you stay here.

We are doing fine.
You will know best when to come home.

Love from all of us,

Virginia

Will and Mother Jones were able to recruit the company doctor into the movement. Dr. Bollinger was a lean, haunted man who seemed hopelessly defeated by conflicting responsibility. He was a widower with three grown daughters and many grandchildren.

"I do what I can to treat the sick, but I know the motives of the mine owners are wrong. All they want me to do is get the men healthy so they can get back to work in the mines. They pay me to keep the workers on the job so profits can continue to roll in. But I can't leave. These people need what little help I can provide." Dr. Bollinger was bitter and disillusioned, ashamed of the fact he was being paid not for healing, but as a tool for making profit. As he became more involved in the miners' plans, he seemed to regain some of his purpose and his pride.

After a few late-night meetings, the miners agreed on those

things they would demand from the mine operators. First, and most important, they would demand recognition of the union. They would ask for a 10 percent increase in wages; the right to trade in any store, not just the company store; and abolishment of the armed mine guards. Currently, miners were paid by the weight of the coal they mined and that coal was weighed by a company man who often tipped the scales in the favor of the operators. Now, the miners were asking for the right to elect a check weight man, a trusted one of their own.

One of Will's duties as a company guard was to see that the workers arrived and left work on time and that they did what they were ordered to do by the mine bosses. But his main job was to break up fistfights and make sure the workers did not get out of line. The company approved of his association with the miners; it was a way he could command their respect. The presence of Mother Jones was rumored, but unsubstantiated. So certain of their power, the mine owners did not really care if she were there or not. After all, they ruled the mine with an iron fist. What was there to fear from an old gray-haired woman?

When the miners' demands had been refined and written into a formal document, it was decided that the union's position would be presented by Dr. Bollinger and Louis the Greek. Mother Jones would remain in hiding. Her presence as an outside agitator might only reinforce the resistance of the local bosses. Will and Dr. Bollinger decided which of the local company men should be approached. Will would accompany the representatives to the office of the Colorado Fuel and Iron Company, a frame building that also housed the company store, a saloon and the dormitory of the company gunmen. Here, the initial contacts would be made. Mother Jones believed that Dr. Bollinger would legitimize the committee, and the local Ludlow operators would pass their demands along to the Rockefeller headquarters in New York. She believed that the enslavement of the miners was no longer a secret tyranny, but was a national shame that the public could no longer ignore. Upton Sinclair and other muckraking writers were exposing the inhumane and criminal activities of such barons of industry as Carnegie and Rockefeller. The government was moving against monopolies, and she was certain that public opinion, and the inherent fairness of the average American, would now come to the rescue of the Ludlow miners.

On the appointed day, Will Bergfeld, Dr. Bollinger and Louis the Greek moved up the slope toward the company office. A north wind had come in the night and the road of ubiquitous mud was coated with a layer of ice that crunched underfoot. The three men walked with their collars up, shoulders hunched against the wind that still swept down from the mountains. The steel of the rifle was cold in Will's hand.

Will led the others to the office of Lieutenant Eugene Billy, head of the Ludlow guards and bartender of the company saloon. It was a small room, plain board walls made from rough cut lumber, no windows, devoid of decoration of any kind. Lieutenant Billy was a large bald man, gone to fat, his round face seeming to emerge directly from his heavy sloping shoulders. From his seat behind a desk far too small for his great body, he looked at the doctor, the miner, then back at Will.

"What you want, Bergfeld?"

"Need to see the boss man," Will said.

Lieutenant Billy's eyes were almost consumed by the surrounding fat. They were tiny in his massive face, suspicious. "What's it got to do with?" he said, eyes cutting from Will to the others.

"Something he needs to know."

With great effort, a struggle consuming a full minute, the lieutenant hauled himself up from behind the desk. "This better be important," he said, each word releasing a small cloud of his breath into the cold room. "You wanna tell me what it is?"

"I mean no disrespect, Lieutenant," Will said. "But it's something MacGregor ought to hear first."

"Don't matter. I know anyway." The lieutenant's eyes disappeared almost entirely as he grinned.

They moved down a long, windowless hallway past large rooms filled with iron cots and the smell of tobacco, sweat and unwashed bodies. They passed the armory where racks of rifles stood and where several guards were cleaning disassembled Gatling guns. They moved on down the hall, footsteps loud on the board floor, then came to a stairway leading down. Lieutenant Billy paused at the top, sighed, then one step at a time, holding tight to a rail along the wall, hauled himself down. At the bottom of the flight of stairs was another hallway and rooms that must have been carved from the hillside.

It was almost as if Angus McGregor had expected them. He stood in the door to one of the rooms that could have been his office. Will did not know, for he had never visited this basement level. McGregor was a man of average height, wearing a suit that seemed out of place in such rustic surroundings. He did not look like the ogre of camp legend, a man who ordered beatings and evictions and even murders, some said. He looked more like a schoolteacher, Will thought, *maybe math or some other science not requiring much imagination.* His face was absolutely devoid of expression. It could have been a wax mask. Nodding at Lieutenant Billy, Will and the doctor, he ushered them through the doorway. He ignored Louis the Greek as if the miner did not exist.

They stepped into the room and immediately the door closed behind them. The first thing Will saw was O'Leary. He was on the ground, his head in a pool of blood. Two armed guards stood nearby.

"Gentlemen," MacGregor said, his voice calm, almost a whisper, "I'd like to call this collective bargaining session to order."

The doctor bent over the still form of the Irishmen. He felt for a pulse, found none, looked up at MacGregor. "He's dead."

"Any other old business?" the mine boss asked. "If not, let us move on."

At a signal from MacGregor, Lieutenant Billy put a gun to Louis the Greek's head. "Take Bergfeld's rifle," MacGregor ordered. "And Bergfeld, any nonsense from you and you'll be responsible for another dead man." Will had no choice. He allowed Lieutenant Billy to take his gun.

"Now let's negotiate," MacGregor said. "There will be no union here now or ever. Now that's my position, what's yours?"

Will remained calm, realizing that all three of them had been led into a trap. "Since it appears we can't have serious negotiations," Will said, "we'll be on our way." As Will reached to retrieve his rifle, he felt an explosion behind his eyes and he fell to his knees. He seemed paralyzed, kneeling but not falling. Then, as he sank to the floor next to the body of the Irishman, he felt consciousness slip slowly down like the curtain of the Klein Opera House in Seguin.

Mother Jones listened to the sound of the iron wheels, pulled a blanket up around her shoulders, then felt once again for Will's pulse. It seemed stronger now. As she once again changed the rag dressing on the back of his head, she felt him stir. It was the first real sign of life since she had found Will with the bodies of O'Leary and Louis the Greek, half-buried under mine waste by the tracks.

Will groaned, then opened his eyes.

"Are Dr. Bollinger and the Greek all right?"

"The doc is fine. The Greek is dead."

"What train is this?"

"We're on a freight headed to Weinert."

"Why didn't they kill me?"

"The doc told them you were dead. They let him live with the promise that they'd kill his daughters if he goes to the authorities."

Then Mother Jones told him how Rockefeller's hired assassins had surrounded the camp and had opened fire with machine guns. The tents had been filled with women and children and they were slaughtered. Those who tried to run were cut down. Some escaped into pits dug beneath the tents, but they had been doused with gasoline and set afire by Angus MacGregor and his uniformed murderers.

"How many dead?"

"Nobody knows. Dozens maybe."

"I'm so sorry."

"I know," she said, sighing, squeezing his hand. "Some of the men saved your motorcycle. It's here."

"I didn't save anything. Or anybody."

"Don't blame yourself."

Will began to cry. Mother Jones remained silent and prayed that he was strong enough not to have lost his commitment to the cause or to life.

"There is only one thing to do now, Will," she said at last. "All we can do is mourn the dead and fight like hell for the living."

Virginia and Dr. Cockrell waited at the Weinert depot. As Virginia watched the eastbound grow larger, then fill the depot with screams of steel and steam, she reached into her pocket and touched the telegram from Mother Jones asking her to meet Will at the station. When the train stopped, Virginia and Dr. Cockrell helped the old woman load Will and his motorcycle onto his wagon. Then Mother Jones climbed back into the cattle car and looked back, without waving, and then was gone.

XIX.

Abilene, Texas.
October 1917

Bettie King watched Will Bergfeld approach the witness stand and prayed he had no surprises in store. She had anticipated his testimony both eagerly and with dread. Though she loved her son-in-law dearly, she knew he was entirely unpredictable, never able to let events flow on their own without putting a foot out to trip them up, setting them spinning in some new direction. She wondered, *how does Virginia endure this bewildering uncertainty? I suppose the years by his side have inured her to her husband's gift for caprice.* Bettie had heard Defense Attorney Atwell lecture Will on the necessity to control any impulse to embellish the facts and to answer only the questions asked. With his characteristic wide-eyed innocence, Will had promised to behave. She recalled evenings when the family would be together for supper and Will would dominate conversation with long and often hilarious tales woven around characters on his rural mail route. Some of the characters were certainly fictional, but others were based on real people. The little girls especially loved his stories about Mrs. Thurwanger and Old Man Lefty Crouch, two larger-than-life villains whose meddlesome exploits were always discovered and set right just in time by the arrival of the heroic rural mail carrier. Bettie wondered if Will could possibly separate fact from fancy in the hours ahead. She refused to wonder about the other villainous character on his mail route, the woman Will never spoke of at all. Bettie was still irritated with Bill Atwell for bringing out that old story. *It was nobody's business, certainly not mine,* she told herself trying not to think about it. But she could not stop it from coming to mind because she had seen the hurt in Virginia's eyes and had felt Henry bristle by her side when he, too, had seen that hurt.

Will took his seat as if he owned it. Bettie knew this was the moment the crowd had waited for. Here was the German agent! The traitor in our midst. The deadly neighbor. They leaned forward on their benches, silent now, as if in church, waiting for the promised sermon on the wages of sin. Will looked back at them, his handsome face composed, his slate-gray eyes innocent as a child's, his arms crossed across his chest. There was just a touch of belligerence that Bettie wished was not so visible. Humility had never been one of Will's virtues.

Bettie's mind filled with thoughts. *Was Will too handsome for his own good? Maybe it would go better for him if the jurors could see some flaw, some imperfection. Perhaps if his dark, wavy hair was tousled, or if he were not wearing a tooled leather vest over a striped wine-red shirt, or if he had left his onyx ring in a drawer for the duration of the trial, then this extraordinary man might realistically expect more sympathy from this jury of ordinary men.* She wished Bill Atwell had advised Will to dress more conservatively for the trial. Then she realized he probably had and Will had simply ignored the advice. When she had tried to understand why so many people in Weinert seemed to be lying about Will, she decided that much of the resentment was due to envy. After all, he had come to town and had taken it by storm. While most of the town's residents merely struggled to survive, he had a coveted job, a successful business and a good life. He seemed to have everything when so many had so little.

"State your full name for the jury," Atwell instructed, breaking the silence.

"William Adolph Bergfeld." A collective sigh escaped the spectators. Now it begins, the sigh seemed to say.

"How old are you, Mr. Bergfeld?"

"Twenty-eight."

"Where were you born?"

"Seguin, Texas."

"Born in Texas?"

"Yes, sir."

"Not in Germany?"

"No, sir. Guadalupe County, Texas."

"Tell us about your parents."

"My mother and father were born in Germany. They each came to America over forty years ago. They were married in Seguin, Texas. My mother died of a black widow spider bite when I was a small boy. My father still lives in Seguin and owns the Bergfeld Drug Store."

"Are you married?"

"Yes, sir."

"Married to Captain King's daughter Virginia, of Seguin?"

Will motioned toward his family, smiled. "Yes, sir. That's my wife and our daughters right there on the front bench."

Bettie divided her attention between Will and the jurors. They seemed to soften as they listened to the simple exchange between Atwell and Will. Maybe for the first time they were seeing a person and not a defendant. In a few moments, Atwell had created a flesh-and-blood person of his witness, a man with a family and a long history in Texas. But she knew there were those who would insist that Will was loyal to Germany even though he had been born and raised in America.

"Where do you reside?" Atwell continued.

"Well, my home was broken up. It was in Weinert when I was arrested, but I'm living in a boarding house in Abilene for the present."

"You own your own home in Weinert?"

"I think so. I'm not sure."

"Have you sold it?"

"Well, I own it. But it's mortgaged and since I've been unable to work. . . ."

O'Dell rose to object. "I don't think that is material."

It was clear to Bettie why O'Dell objected. Atwell was trying to establish that an injustice had been done when Will was arrested—that a man's home had been lost, his family uprooted. The judge sustained the objection.

Atwell nodded his head, almost in apology, then asked, "Mr. Bergfeld, we have heard a great deal of testimony here about conscription, or the draft. Do you have any personal convictions one way or another concerning conscription?"

"Yes, sir, I do. I'm against it. I think it's wrong because it takes away the freedoms guaranteed by the Constitution of this country."

"But your country is at war. If called, would you have served in the Army?"

"Yes, sir, I volunteered. I wanted to serve in the Aviation Corps. I made all the arrangements. Got permission from the postmistress where I worked. Wrote a letter to the Postmaster General."

"Of the United States?"

"Yes."

"And you also had the postmaster at Haskell to write for you."

"Yes."

"Did the postmaster receive a response from the Postmaster General?"

"Yes, sir."

Atwell produced a letter and showed it to Will. "Is this the letter?"

"Yes."

"What is the gist of the letter you received from the Postmaster General?"

"He said I would be granted leave. He said they would hold my job until I got back from the war."

Atwell spoke to the judge. "I would like to offer this letter in evidence, as Exhibit 13."

After asking if Prosecutor O'Dell had any objection, Judge Jack said, "Exhibit 13 will be admitted into evidence."

Atwell walked toward the jury, then faced back toward Will. "When did you correspond about going into the Aviation Corps?"

"It was this past spring when war was declared," Will answered.

"Tell the jury why you volunteered to go to war."

"Well, I was opposed to conscription. But I felt I should do my duty, and I thought with my knowledge and experience as a mechanic I could quickly learn to be a pilot."

"Did you go to a recruiting office?"

"Yes, sir. In Fort Worth."

"Were you accepted?"

"No, sir. He said they didn't take married men."

"But it was fully your intent to serve your country as an aviator in the Aviation Corps?"

"Yes, sir. It was fully my intent."

At first, a thin cloud, like a mist of gray or a lace curtain, crossed Bettie's mind. *I've never heard this Aviation Corps subject mentioned. It would have been big news in the family, the subject of much discussion.* But then she remembered that Will always wanted to take flying lessons, and had once actually written to Marjorie Stenson's flight school in San Antonio. But the cost had been too high and he could not take the time off from work. Bettie had watched Will closely as he told of his wish to volunteer. *Nothing in his eyes nor manner would make a jury doubt what he was saying,* she concluded.

Prosecutor O'Dell was making a note, smirking, as if he thought Will's story had been contrived. Bettie feared he would challenge it on cross-examination.

Defense Attorney Atwell changed the subject. He also changed the timbre in his voice. While previously he had spoken with Will on a personal level, as friend to friend, now his voice took on an edge of authority. He became an official of the court, not seeking to defend, but to determine the truth. "Mr. Bergfeld, are you a member of the Farmers' and Laborers' Protective Association?"

"Yes, sir."

"Have you ever been an officer in that organization?"

"I was president of the Weinert Lodge."

"Did you not, in fact, organize the Weinert Lodge?"

"I did."

"For what purpose was the lodge organized?"

"Well, farmers were having a hard time. We were trying to help the brothers better their lives."

"What were you trying to do to help them?"

"Get the farmers to cooperate with each other. We wanted to develop a method of barter between growers. A farmer over here grew beans. A farmer over there had potatoes. Their crops would become a medium of exchange. The high cost of living would be reduced." Will began to speak with his hands. Bettie had seen this before when he was getting steamed up about the plight of the farmer.

Atwell interrupted. "Were you also trying to establish a store?"

"Yes, sir. The idea was to cut out the middleman so the farmer could earn more from his crops."

"Did the farmers in Haskell County form a county organization?"

"Yes, sir. And the Weinert Lodge was a part of it."

"How many lodges went in to form that county organization?"

"Maybe seven."

"Tell us whether or not the Haskell County Organization had a meeting in February 1917?"

"Yes, sir, we did."

"What was the business transacted at that meeting?"

"Well, the main purpose was to establish a store. We had to decide on how much stock to carry, where the store would be located. We had to select someone to manage the store."

"At that time, had the United States severed diplomatic relations with Germany?"

"I don't think so."

"At that meeting, was there any discussion of the war?"

"Yes, sir. Some of the brothers thought we ought to take an official position on the war. Sentiment ran pretty high against it. They didn't want America to get into a European war. They thought somebody was trying to force President Wilson into a declaration. A couple of the boys said they would write up a resolution on the subject of the war and then place it before the members."

"What did your meeting do in reference to that resolution?"

"Well, I told them we should take a recess until they wrote it out. We did, and they came back and read the resolution."

"And was the resolution adopted at that meeting in early February of 1917?"

"Yes. As far as I recall it was adopted in about a minute."

"Was the next convention of the state Farmers' and Laborers' Protective Association in Cisco, Texas?"

"Yes. There were two Cisco conventions. The first was right after the Haskell meeting in February. The second Cisco convention was about three months later, on May fifth of this year."

"Were you elected as a delegate to the first Cisco convention? The one in February?"

"Yes, sir. A delegate from the Weinert Lodge."

"Was the resolution we just discussed presented at that Cisco convention?"

"Yes, sir."

"Tell the jury how that came about."

As his testimony progressed, Will seemed to be enjoying himself more and more. Bettie knew he had always loved to be center stage, the focus of attention. But she also sensed there was a core of loneliness about Will, as if his need to be surrounded by admirers was to fill some sort of void he felt inside. Sometimes she wondered if he must feel like a failure in life. All his life people had assumed that he would be a famous musician, a concert violinist, and that he had fallen short of his promise. Such talk had always infuriated Bettie and she defended Will, if only in her own mind. After all, he had made quite a success of his life. Until recently, he had a fine house, a good government job and a growing rental business. But what a man did to earn a living was only a fraction of his worth as a human being. What was important was the love and care and devotion he tendered to his family and the way he treated his fellow man. And in these areas Will had no shortcomings.

And there was also a person's inner life, that silent behavior of the mind and spirit that was hidden from all but the self. And here was a mystery. What transpired in Will's mind was rarely revealed. He would talk incessantly about what he thought and what he knew. *But not once, except for flashes of temper, have I ever heard him say how he felt, how he really felt. But there are times when I have gotten a glimpse of what is within his mind. I have even looked into his soul. I have heard him play his violin when he thought he was alone. There was no audience to please, no one to judge the quality of what he played. He played only for himself and what I heard was the sounds that must sing in Heaven. What poured from his hands and his soul was as pure and fine as any sound I have ever heard. But there was also sorrow. A deep and abiding sadness that was like tears given the gift of melody. Is it possible that this robust man who laughs so heartily and goes through life with such reckless abandon is suffering the malaise of deep sorrow? Is he mourning for the shortcomings of his fellow men, of those beings God created on the morning and evening of the Sixth Day? Does he sorrow because people have mean spirits? Because people are cruel one to another? Because God's finest creations are flawed? Because the rich and powerful trample on the lives of the poor and powerless? Is that what his life is all about? Is that what this trial is all about? If Will is guilty, he is guilty of caring too much, of loving too deeply. He is guilty of sorrow.*

On the stand, Will was explaining his first trip to Cisco, a convention about which others had previously testified. "I was instructed to take the Haskell County resolution to present to the boys in Cisco. And it was carried to Cisco by me in person."

"Where did you get that resolution that you took to Cisco?"

"Well, it was written by a couple of committeemen in Haskell. I think they were Mr. Robertson and Mr. Stoval. But I'm not sure."

"What did you do with it when you got to Cisco?"

"They were looking for a good resolution to state our position on the war. I merely remarked that I had a war resolution in my pocket and I believed it would be all right. And if I am not mistaken I gave it to them to read. After they read it, they said, 'That's good.' And I simply put it back in my pocket."

"I will ask you to look at Exhibit 14 and tell us whether or not that is the resolution that is called the Haskell County Resolution and the one you took to Cisco and about which you have just testified?" Atwell passed the document to the witness.

Will examined the resolution. "Yes. That is the one. Yes."

"In whose handwriting is it, Mr. Bergfeld?"

"Mr. Robertson's, I suppose."

"Whose name is signed to it?"

"Mr. Robertson's, Mr. Williams and Mr. Stovall."

Atwell looked toward the bench. "We formally offer this in evidence, Your Honor." After examining the document, the judge nodded and asked that it be marked and filed.

"Now, Mr. Bergfeld," Atwell continued. "In regard to this Haskell County Resolution, were you on the committee that drafted it?"

"No, sir."

"Had you seen it before it was read to the members?"

"No, sir."

"Your Honor," Atwell said, "with the Court's permission, I'd like to read this Haskell County Resolution."

"Go ahead," the judge said over his glasses. Bettie thought he would just as soon not have to listen.

Atwell read the resolution. The jury seemed more attentive than the judge.

To the President of Haskell County Farmers' and Laborers' Protective Association of America:

Whereas the citizens of this great Republic are a peace-loving people, we wish to announce to all the world that we stand for the principles of Peace on earth and Goodwill toward all men. We are opposed to all false patriotism and ask for cooperation of all the pure liberty-loving people to cry out with a mighty voice against militarism.

We do not approve of the action of the Governor of Texas in his war maneuvers and we oppose the United States Government in the prosecution of a foreign war.

We therefore resolve to refuse to invade a foreign country at the commands of the Capitalist Class and refuse to shoot our fellow man.

Resolved also that should war be declared against the will of the people we request that all elected officials, from the President down to Constable, resign and go to war and leave the American people in peace.

Resolved further that should the American people be forced to go to war, we will fight for Liberty, Justice and for the Brotherhood of Man.

Atwell lowered the document, stared at the jury for a moment, then turned to Will. "Did the resolution I have just read pass at the Cisco convention?"

"No, sir. The words 'United States Government' were scratched out and replaced with the words 'Capitalist Class.' The version we adopted read: 'We oppose the Capitalist Class in the prosecution of a foreign war.' It didn't say that we oppose the government of the United States."

"Tell the jury why that change was made."

"Someone raised an objection. If I'm not mistaken, it was Mr. Glidewell. He said, 'Boys, that might be treason against the United States government.' So it was amended and it passed."

"Did you vote for the resolution?"

"Yes, sir. I thought it fairly summarized my view."

"That you were opposed to the war?"

"Yes, sir."

"But not that you were opposed to the United States government, isn't that right?"

"Yes, sir. That is certainly right. That's why we changed the way it was first written."

"One more question about this resolution and we'll move on," Atwell said. "What in your mind does the last paragraph mean? 'Resolved further should the American people be forced to go to war, we will fight for Liberty and Justice and for Brotherhood of Man'?"

"It means should war come, and we were called, we would go to war. You've got to remember this resolution was written about two months before war was declared."

Atwell walked to a position directly in front of the jury. His next question was directed more to the jurors than to Will. "So you and your fellow members were resolved to going to war if indeed war was declared? You resolved to do your duty as citizens of this great country?"

"Yes, sir. That is certainly what we resolved to do."

Bettie felt that the jurors were impressed by the last exchange. Will seemed absolutely believable.

After a pause to check his notes, Defense Attorney Atwell returned to the witness stand. "Now I want to direct your attention to the second convention in Cisco. The one you said took place on May 5, 1917. What position did you hold at this second Cisco convention?"

"I was elected Secretary of the Resolutions Committee."

"What time did you arrive in Cisco for this May fifth convention?"

"My train came in about eight o'clock the night before."

"It has been testified that you had a lengthy conversation with a man named Ned Earl Calhoun. Can you recall the substance of that conversation?"

"No, sir. It never happened."

"Never happened?"

"No, sir."

"Did you have any conversation at the Cisco convention with the government witness Ned Earl Calhoun?"

"I've never had a conversation with the man at any time or any place."

"Do you recall ever seeing Ned Earl Calhoun before he testified here?"

"No, sir, I have never laid eyes on the man."

"How do you account for the fact that he testified, under oath, that he had this long, heartfelt conversation with you in Cisco?"

"Objection!" O'Dell called. "He can't look into Mr. Calhoun's mind."

"Sustained," said Judge Jack.

Atwell looked at the jury and shrugged, as if to say he would have gotten to the truth of the matter, but the judge had tied his hands. Then, to Will, "You testified that you were elected Secretary of the Resolutions Committee. Do you know why you were chosen for this position?"

"Well, I suppose it was because I had experience with resolutions at the local level. Also I could write fast."

Several jurors smiled. Will smiled back. *How can you not love and trust this man*, Bettie thought as Will's smile brightened the room. She reminded herself to advise him to smile at every opportunity.

"Whose idea was it?"

"Actually, it was Mr. Risley's. He first mentioned it when I ran into him at the train station the night before."

"Did you know Mr. Risley before you met him at the train station?"

"I had seen him at a few lodge meetings. He and George Bryant and Sam Powell came around pretty often because they were state officers."

"As the Secretary of the Resolutions Committee, what resolutions were you to present to the membership?"

"All that were given to us."

"How were they given to you?"

"Some were brought in verbally. One of those boys would come in and tell us what he wanted and I'd try to write it down. Others brought in scraps of paper. What I'd do is try to put the words in good shape where the resolutions made sense."

"What were your instructions as to these resolutions brought in?"

"Mr. Risely instructed the committee to present every resolution to the convention, even if they were improper or radical or treasonous. He said if they were illegal or treasonous he'd rule them out. He said we shouldn't worry."

"Tell the jury about the one time you disregarded Mr. Risely's instructions."

"One old boy came in with a resolution that was surely treasonous. After I read it, I tore it up." Will made the motions of tearing up the paper with his hands.

"Was that the end of that particular resolution?"

"No, sir. He came back to me and said. . . ."

"Who was the man?"

"Well, I could recognize the man if I was to see him."

"Is he on trial here?"

"No, sir."

"Go ahead."

"He came up and he says, 'What did you do with my resolution?' And I said, 'I tore it up.' He says, 'What did you tear it up for?' I said, 'Well, the committee decided it was unlawful.' And he says, 'You try to dig up that resolution.' I says, 'It is tore up.' And he says, 'Well, you are under an obligation to present everything before this convention that comes before you.' And I says, 'I know that, but. . . .' And he says, 'I'm going to write it out again. I want it done.' And I went on to explain that I would not put my name on a document like that. So then Mr. Risely came up to me and says, 'Will, that man wants his resolution presented.' I said I wouldn't sign it. So we decided the only thing to do was present it without anyone on the Resolutions Committee signing it. So the man talked out his resolution again and I wrote it down and read it to the members."

"Was the resolution voted on?"

"There was no vote taken. When I presented it before the convention, I turned around hoping and expecting Mr. Risley would rule it out of order. But he wasn't there, must have been called out for something. So I had this other resolution, one we called the moderate resolution, and I quick started reading it before the traitorous one could come to a vote."

"Tell us about this second resolution. Not the radical one that you tore up—not the one that opposed conscription, but the one that actually came to a vote."

"Well, it wasn't as tough. It was more moderate and it didn't mention conscription at all."

"What was the purpose of this moderate resolution?"

"We wanted to offer something for the more levelheaded boys in the membership. Something they could back without worrying that it might be considered unlawful down the road."

"Who presented these resolutions to the convention?"

"I did."

"Did you make any recommendation concerning which ones should be passed?"

"No, sir."

"But you did present the radical resolution?"

"It was my obligation."

"Now, Mr. Bergfeld, tell the jury which of these resolutions you voted for."

"I voted for the moderate resolution. The one that did not call for action against conscription."

"Did you, or anyone there at the convention, champion the radical resolution?"

"No, sir. A vote was taken and the moderate resolution carried. The vote was sixty-three to forty."

"Could you tell us as near as you can recall the language that was in this moderate resolution that was adopted?"

Prosecutor O'Dell rose to object. "Testimony shows that this resolution was last in the possession of the defendants. Before the witness states what was in it, the original should be produced or its absence accounted for."

"Mr. Bergfeld, did you ever have this document in your possession?"

"Only when I read it to the convention."

Judge Jack asked, "Do you know where it is, Mr. Bergfeld?"

"No, sir."

"Proceed," the judge said.

"My objection," O"Dell continued, "is that the document is the best evidence of the contents of the resolution. The witness should not be allowed to give his best guess as to its wording. I believe the defense should offer the document itself."

Bettie realized that Prosecutor O'Dell was planting the seed in the jurors' minds that the missing document might never have existed at all. He wanted the jury to think Will was making it up after the fact to suggest that the membership was not against conscription.

"I understand," Judge Jack said. "I want the defense to redouble their efforts to produce this document. But for now, Mr. Bergfeld, as best you can, I will allow you to detail the contents of this moderate resolution."

"It came down to the point that the Farmers' and Laborers' Protective Association take no action whatever in regard to conscription. No drastic action whatsoever. The word 'drastic' was in there. We further recommend that we cooperate with all other labor organizations to see about perfecting our organization. Or substantially like that."

"Was there any action taken on this notion of the FLPA cooperating with other labor organizations?"

"Yes, sir. It was decided that we'd check out the possibility of joining up with other unions. Somebody says, 'How about the Industrial Workers of the World?' Somebody else mentions the Working Class Union and the United Mine Workers. We decided to send a committee to Oklahoma to see if we couldn't join together, amalgamate, cooperate."

"Who was selected on that committee?"

"Mr. Cathcart and myself."

"At the time you were selected, did you know anything about the purposes of the IWWs? What the IWWs stood for?"

"I knew it had a purpose similar to ours. To work for better conditions for its members. At that time I also thought they were opposed to any unlawful acts." Bettie wondered if the jury would believe that a man as informed as Will on labor matters would not know what the infamous Wobblies were all about.

"Did you and Mr. Cathcart make this trip to Oklahoma?"

"Yes, sir."

"When you got there, did you join the Industrial Workers of the World?"

"Yes, sir."

"Would you tell the jury how you became members?"

"I think it was the night we got to town. In Henryetta. We got about five or six of these IWW union men together and they said, 'We can't tell you nothing about our organization, it's secret!' And I said, 'Well, we can't tell you anything about ours.' George Cathcart spoke up and said, 'Possibly if you would initiate us and we initiate you, then we can reveal our secrets and see whether anything can be done to make our organizations one.'"

"Was that done?"

"Yes."

"They initiated you and you initiated them?" Smiles from the jury. One juror joined the general laughter with the spectators. Even the judge found it difficult to keep a straight face.

"Yes. They initiated us first. After we were initiated and heard an explanation of the organization, we were told to sign a card and we paid twenty-five cents."

"Well, did you learn anything about the IWW?"

"In the end, we learned that they wouldn't join up with our organization. They were industrial and we were farmers. They didn't want to join up with farmers."

Atwell approached the stand. "I hand you Exhibit Number 15. Is this the card you signed evidencing your membership in the Working Class Union?"

"Yes, sir. We joined the Working Class Union, as well."

"In order to learn more about their organization?"

"Yes, sir."

"And what did you learn?"

"We didn't like a lot of what we heard. They were for sabotage. Where they'd throw sand or emery dust in machinery and they'd let a car roll down the rails and break up things or cripple a man. We didn't want to be a part of that."

"What did you do then?"

"It was all off, and I told George, 'It is all off and we can't do anything. We can't amalgamate with either of these organizations. And there's no use going around where we might be suspected of doing something dirty. And we had better get on back home.'"

"How long were you a member in the WCU?"

"About fifteen minutes." Again, chuckles from the crowd. Will joined in and there was that smile again. Bettie could almost see a bridge of good will between the jury box and the witness stand and she was grateful for the power of laughter. Also smiling, Judge Jack gaveled the laughter to silence.

"How long were you members of the IWW?"

"We signed up for two months. After two months our membership expired."

"Have you had anything to do with either organization since?"

"No, sir. Absolutely not."

Atwell returned to the defense table and thumbed through his notes. "Now Mr. Bergfeld," he said when he returned to the witness stand, "I am going to ask you about some of the things that have been mentioned by the prosecutor's witnesses—dynamite. Did you have dynamite in your barn?"

"Yes, sir. Two kegs."

"Why did you have it?"

"Some of the farmers were going to need dynamite for blasting, to make more water wells on their land. Since I had a good-paying job, I bought it for them. They were going to use it and pay me back when they could."

"It is charged in this Indictment that you got a gun and pistol, or some sort of firearms to carry out this conspiracy against the United States government. Tell the jury whether or not that is true."

"I had two pistols. A small automatic .32 and the other was an automatic .45. The small gun was for my wife. I always like to leave her with it when I'm gone at night. The .45, I carry in the motorcycle. And the reason I bought these guns is because I was told that I was liable to be shot."

"You were threatened?"

"Yes, sir. Some boys drove by my house and told me that some fellow said if war was declared that I would be the first to be killed because I was a German. I said, 'Well, I'm not German. I was born in Seguin, Texas.' They said I was at the top of the list of some folks who hated Germans."

"What did you do?"

"I took the threat seriously and I ordered the guns the next day."

"And these are the only guns you possess?"

"Yes, sir.

"No high-powered rifles?"

"No, sir."

"Now let me ask you this, Mr. Bergfeld," Atwell said, after letting the jurors reflect for a moment on the great arsenal with which Will was going to launch a revolution. "Earlier in this trial, evidence was introduced that referred to the word, or name, Moses. It was testified that Moses was a code name you used as a leader in the labor movement. Is that true or untrue?"

"It is untrue. I referred to Moses because in my speeches and writings I try to use Biblical references to make a point. Most of these boys are grounded in the Good Book and they understand."

"Did you, in fact, consider yourself a leader in the labor movement?"

"I was a leader in Weinert. But that's all."

Atwell turned toward the seated defendants. "Now, Mr. Bergfeld, let's get to the heart of the matter." He gestured toward the fifty-two defendants. "Have you ever had any agreement with any of these men, either direct or indirect, to rebel against the United States government?"

"No, sir."

"Or its authority?"

"No, sir."

"Or to oppose the laws of the United States?"

"No, sir."

"Have you had any agreement, directly or indirectly, remote or close, to resist the laws of conscription of the Army or to resist the government of the United States in any way whatsoever?"

"No, sir."

"Or to blow up bridges of the railroads or anything of the sort?"

"No, sir."

The continuing exchange between Will and Atwell had a certain ascending rhythm. Bettie felt it was almost like music. Atwell's voice rose with each question, the intensity of the exchange rising, the responses heartfelt and believable. It was thrilling, Bettie thought, and she could tell the jurors were also moved.

"Have you had any agreement, direct or indirect, approximately or remote, to commit treason against the United States of America?"

"No, sir."

"Or its authority?"

"No, sir."

"Either in private conversation or public speech, have you ever threatened the life of the President of the United States?"

"No, sir, I have not."

"Not in speeches at the various union halls?"

"No, sir."

"Not in private conversation with Ms. Bennett or Mr. Couch or Mrs. Thurwanger?"

"Absolutely not."

"Tell the jury whether or not you are a loyal American citizen."

"I am. Certainly. I am."

Atwell paused, dropped his arms to his side. "That's all I have for this witness." Bettie felt flushed and proud and relieved and assured for the first time that Will was, if not entirely innocent, at least on the side of the angels. *It went well,* she thought. *Will has behaved. Guided by his lawyer, he has parried or defused most of the charges against him.* Yet, there remained the powerful testimony of Ned Earl Calhoun. All Will could do was deny that the conversation had ever happened. It was Will's word against an extremely believable witness who had no apparent motive to lie.

The judge called a recess until the following morning.

The man called Peachtree watched the crowd leave the courthouse. He was extremely uncomfortable, feeling ill and weak. It was the crowd that poisoned his breathing, that made him feel he would suffocate. All those people with their staring eyes and voices blaring like trumpets. He longed for his cave and the solitude of the river bottoms, the gentle sound the river made sliding by, speaking its name—*Guadalupe, Guadalupe.* If he remained in the city, among all these people, he knew he would die. But there was Will. His friend from childhood, who understood his loneliness, the confusion in his mind, the chaos of his thoughts.

Peachtree had found out something that might help his old friend. He heard it first from a prisoner in the Guadalupe County Jail, not a quarter-mile from his cave. Then he traced down the hobo trail, whispers in the night from prisoners and the forsaken and lost. He was not sure what that meant. But he knew it was important. Important enough to suffer the trip to the suffocating city, to leave for a while his life of blessed solitude.

Peachtree watched from the shadows. Suddenly, from behind, a strong hand gripped his shoulder. Peachtree wondered if God had come down to punish him for living among the lower animals and not among his own kind.

"What's going on here, fella?" the tall man asked. He wore the star of a Texas Ranger. Peachtree, terrified of being locked up, began yelling and fighting to get away. The owl screeched and clawed at the Ranger's arm.

Tom Grimes had no choice but to drag the deranged vagrant to jail and lock him up.

XX.

Abilene, Texas.
October 1917

It was cold. The leaves of the live oaks along Main Street rattled in a wind that had swept dust in from the northern prairie. Bettie King wished she had brought a warmer coat and she also wished she was back in Seguin, where the winds of October seemed less fierce than this earlt norther that now besieged the town of Abilene. Although it could get quite cold in Guadalupe County, it seemed the river there somehow gentled the air, dulled the blade of the wind. Now, in the pale amber light of the new day, the streets were empty. Bettie moved alone through the dusty haze, her footsteps a brittle cadence on the walk. She had long realized that she was a slave to this early morning routine of greeting the new day with motion. *Get moving,* she thought. *In motion there is life. It is one of God's fundamental principles. The heavens revolve, the planets speed on their journey around the sun, the blood flows, the molecules in our body are in constant motion, everything grows and changes, the rose, crops in the field, the love that moves in our hearts. In motion there is life.*

Pulling her collar closed more tightly, Bettie turned her back to the wind, walking sideways, avoiding the cracks in the walk out of obedience to a children's rhyme. It was then she saw the Ranger coming her way. She remembered his name was Grimes, Sergeant Grimes. She had seen him testify, a tall man with melancholy eyes and a courteous manner. He had been among those who arrested Will.

The Ranger approached and tipped his hat. "Mrs. King?"

"Yes?"

"There's a man in the jail asking for you."

"For me? Are you sure?"

"He is quite insistent."

"Who?"

"Well, he won't say his name. No identification. He's a hobo. Wears ragged clothing. Has a pet owl."

Bettie smiled. She knew only one man in Christendom who matched that description. "Peachtree."

"Ma'am?"

"He's called Peachtree. His name is Petrie, but folks call him Peachtree."

"I didn't know if I should bother you with this. If you don't want to see him, I'll certainly understand. He seems a little crazy."

"I suppose he is. But he's harmless."

"His owl isn't harmless." Sergeant Grimes grimaced and touched his arm where Peachtree's owl had apparently attacked him.

Again Bettie King smiled as she imagined how it must have been when Grimes apprehended Peachtree. "One riot, one Ranger" was the famous saying. But that had been before Peachtree's owl came to town.

The courthouse was slightly warmer than the air outside but gave protection from the dust. Bettie felt sorry for the prisoners she saw huddled in their cages, awaiting day. Most were awake, restless and bored, and with empty eyes they watched her pass. From somewhere a man was moaning, perhaps in his sleep, perhaps not. Bettie felt enormously conspicuous and her heart went out to these desperate men who had been too poor to make bail. *What kind of justice is this?* She thought. *A system where you can be free if you have enough money to buy it.*

Peachtree cowered against the back wall of his cell. He seemed insubstantial, colorless, a formless bundle of bone and rags and hair. As always, Bettie wondered how a person could come to such a pass. He seemed so pitiful there, with his wide frightened eyes. She knew it must be torture for a man who lived free as a wild animal to be locked away in a cell.

"Peachtree?" Bettie said his name gently.

Peachtree merely stared. He was trembling from the cold.

"He won't say anything. Only your name."

"What did he do?" Bettie asked. "I mean, is he charged with anything?"

"Vagrancy."

"Can you let him go? I'll vouch for him. He's an old friend." Bettie could tell that Grimes was puzzled, curious, even slightly amused that a prim and proper woman would call this wild and uncouth creature an old friend.

"I suppose I can. If you're sure."

"How about his owl?"

"Free to go," Grimes said, smiling. *He has a nice smile,* Bettie thought. And she loved the idea that this tall, rawboned Ranger had a sense of humor. She decided she liked him even if he was the one who broke into Will's home and carted him off to jail.

When they reached the boardinghouse, Peachtree refused to come inside. "I'll get you some food," she said.

Peachtree shook his head. Then, for a while he seemed to be dozing. Bettie wondered what must fill the strange, wild man's mind. Suddenly, he looked up, seemingly confused, as if he was trying to understand where he was, why he was here in a strange town where it was so dusty and dry. Over the years Bettie had seen Peachtree like this, when he seemed virtually unable to speak. "Lometa," he finally said, his voice little more than a rasping whisper.

Bettie's heart suddenly began to race. "Lometa? What about Lometa?"

Peachtree closed his eyes. "I don't know."

"Do you mean the town?"

Peachtree nodded his head. "Get hold of Deputy Sheriff Draper there. For Will."

"Please come inside," Bettie pleaded. "I'll get you something. We can talk to Will and Louise about this." She reached to touch his shoulder and he pulled away, as if her hand held a weapon.

Peachtree stared into Bettie's eyes. His eyes were hard as metal, then they softened and he looked away. After a moment's pause he turned and with his herky-jerky gait, he moved away toward the railroad tracks and home.

Although it was early, every seat in the courtroom was filled and people stood along the wall and on wooden stands that had been raised beneath the windows. This was the day Prosecutor O'Dell was going to cross-examine Will Bergfeld. There would be fireworks for sure, and the crowd sensed that the long trial was coming to a climax and the traitors in their midst would soon be found guilty and carted away to prison or the gallows.

In a small room near the cells where the prisoners were being fed a meager breakfast of coffee and oatmeal, Virginia held Will's hand as Bill Atwell gave his client final instructions. "The most important thing is to stay calm," he said. "O'Dell will try to get you rattled or angry. He'll make it seem that everything you say is untrue or unbelievable. He will be argumentative. He will call you a liar."

"He can't do that!" Will said, heatedly.

"He will call you a liar in a hundred different ways without actually using the word. He'll say, 'Do you expect this jury to believe . . . etcetera . . . like that?'"

"Can't you object?" Virginia asked.

"I can. And I will. But there can be a problem if I object too often. Even if my objections are sustained, the jurors might think I'm trying to hide something or that I'm whining or being petty. Being overly defensive."

"You are a defense attorney, after all," Will said. "How can a defense attorney be overly defensive?"

"If I object too often, it could also irritate the judge. Judge Jack is not the soul of patience, and I think he's eager to get this whole thing to the jury."

"So what are you saying?" Will asked.

"I'm just saying that I'm not going to object to every abusive or argumentative thing O'Dell says. I'm saying that the judge will probably give the prosecution a great deal of leeway and O'Dell will frame his questions in a way to make your answers seem like lies. But you can't react angrily. You just have to sit there and take it. Trust in the jurors' good sense. Just be calm and tell the truth."

Will sighed and looked down at Virginia's hands. He traced her wedding ring with his finger. Virginia was suddenly chilled by the realization that Will was afraid. That power, that aura of invincibility and confidence that always accompanied his touch, was diminished, was failing. She could feel only his hands, not the power of his spirit. *It was,* she thought, *as if a flame in his heart was burning low, wavering. Maybe it was the awful wind and dust, maybe only that. For the first time in his life he is not in control. There is no way for him to fight back against those who would take him down. Always before there were his fists, his whip, the power of his words hurled in anger. But now, all that has been taken away. He is almost chained in the witness chair, a Samson shorn, a fighter without fists, a strong man whose greatest strength—the focus of his righteous indignation—could now be the very thing to bring him down.*

Will looked out toward the courtroom as if he could see through the walls. "Why do they want me to be found guilty?"

"I'm not sure they do," Atwell said.

"They want my blood," Will said.

"What they want is drama in their lives. That's what you're giving them. What constitutes a good drama? A character you like is threatened. The threat becomes greater and greater until it seems the character is doomed. Then, suddenly, dramatically, the character is saved. If you were to be found guilty, it would break the laws of good literature, of a good story, whether fiction or real life. No, Will, in spite of their actions, deep down inside they want you to be found innocent. I'm certain of it."

"What about the jury? How do they want the story to end?"

"When you confront O'Dell on the stand, I'm certain they will be pulling for you. They will want your answers to be plausible. They will want to be on your side. But there is also this. Whether they remain on your side depends on you and what you say and how you say it. If you speak the truth and speak it with calm conviction, the jury will believe you."

During the first half-hour of Will's testimony, the exchanges between him and O'Dell had been benign, even warily friendly, a kind of sparring, as Will reviewed the high points of his life, his work as a rural mail carrier and his involvement in the Farmers' and Laborers' Protective Association.

The only tense moment was when O'Dell asked Will about his occupation after he moved to Weinert.

"I was a deputy sheriff," Will had replied with pride.

He answered, Virginia thought, *as if boasting.*

"An officer of the law. I'm impressed," O'Dell had said. "How long were you a deputy sheriff?"

"Well, I'll have to think on that."

"Five years? Ten years?"

"More like six months."

O'Dell chuckled, spread his arms toward the jury. "And that was the whole of your career as an officer of the law? Six months?"

"Yes, sir." Virginia could tell Will was bristling, angry at himself for making a big thing out of such a little thing. And he was stinging from the laughter O'Dell had coaxed from the crowd.

"Do you have any kinfolks still living in Germany?" O'Dell asked.

"Yes, sir, my grandmother."

"Since your parents both came from Germany, did you speak German growing up in Seguin?"

"Yes, sir."

"How about at school? Were you taught in German?"

"Yes, sir, for the first few grades."

"What about the textbooks? Were they in German?"

"Yes, sir, for those early grades."

"As a child, you were actually educated by German teachers?"

"No, sir. They were Americans. They just spoke the German language."

O'Dell abruptly changed the subject and began asking Will

about his activities as an organizer of the Farmers' and Laborers' Protective Association.

"You testified on direct examination that a committee was appointed at the Cisco convention to confer with the IWW and the Workers Union?"

"Yes. A committee was elected to visit these organizations in Henryetta and Tulsa."

"That committee consisted of you and Mr. Cathcart?"

"Yes, sir."

"You returned home after that meeting in Cisco, didn't you?"

"Yes, sir."

"What did you do when you got home? What did you do to prepare for this trip to Henryetta and Tulsa?"

"I repaired my car. I saw the postmistress and told her I'd be off for a week. That's when I was trying to make arrangements to join the Aviation Corps."

"Arranged with Mrs. Cockrell so she could provide a substitute during your absence?"

"Yes."

"What did you tell her the purpose of your trip was?"

"I told her I was going to Fort Worth to try to get in the Aviation Corps."

"You didn't tell Mrs. Cockrell you were going to other places to confer with the IWWs and the WCUs?"

"No, sir."

"So you really did not tell Mrs. Cockrell the whole truth about your trip, did you?"

"What I told her was the truth. I was going to Fort Worth to try to join the Aviation Corps. But I didn't think it was necessary for me to tell about my plans to visit the unions."

"So you agree that you deliberately misled Mrs. Cockrell about the full reason for your absence?"

"I didn't tell her the whole truth if that's what you're trying to get me to say."

"So what we know is that even with your own boss you

sometimes hid part of the truth?"

"Objection," called Atwell. "Argumentative. He is badgering the witness. Also asked and answered."

"Sustained," Judge Jack ruled, eager to bring the long trial to a close. "Let's move on, Counsel."

"When did you get to Fort Worth?"

"Tuesday, about eight or nine o'clock at night. I was one day making the run."

"Are you a pretty good reader, Mr. Bergfeld?"

"Yes."

"Read the daily newspaper? Keep up with current events pretty well?"

"Yes."

"What newspapers do you read?"

Defense Attorney Atwell rose to object. "This line of questioning is immaterial and prejudicial, Your Honor."

Judge Jack considered for a moment. "You may show that he read the daily newspapers and kept up with current events."

"In the newspapers you read, you must be pretty well posted about matters incident to the war?"

"Yes." Will was obviously becoming uneasy. Atwell was poised to object. Virginia could tell O'Dell was up to something.

"On the way to visit the IWWs and the WCUs you stopped in Fort Worth to make inquiries about this aviation thing?"

"Yes."

"Who did you talk to there at the recruiting station?"

"I don't remember his name."

"You don't remember?" O'Dell feigned surprise.

Will shifted his position. "I don't know if he gave me his name."

"You have testified that this man told you that the Aviation Corps didn't take married men, isn't that correct?"

"That's correct."

O'Dell turned to the jury, held out his arms, shook his head in utter disbelief. "You mean to tell this jury you selected for your inquiry a branch of the service that did not admit married men?"

Virginia knew Will had walked into a trap. O'Dell was making it seem Will had never intended to join the service. Will's face reddened. Virginia was not sure she had ever seen her husband blush.

"I didn't know about that at the time." His answer lacked conviction.

"You hadn't seen it stated in the newspapers before that?"

"No, sir."

"Anyway, that is the branch of the service that you talked to—this branch that didn't take married men?"

"Objection, Your Honor. Mr. Bergfeld has already answered this question. Several times, in fact."

"I will sustain the objection," Judge Jack ruled.

"Did you then make inquiries at the Signal Corps? A branch that *does* take married men?"

"No, sir."

"The Ambulance Corps?"

"No, sir. I don't think I did."

"You made no further effort to enlist in any other branch of the service except the one that did not take married men?"

"No, sir. I don't think I did."

"Volunteering to go to war is an important thing in a man's life, isn't it, Mr. Bergfeld?"

"Yes." He spoke the word softly.

"Would you please speak up, Mr. Bergfeld."

"Yes!" Will almost shouted the word. Virginia prayed he would hold his temper in check.

"And you are telling this jury that you can't remember whether or not you volunteered for any service other than this one that you knew full well didn't take married men?"

"Objection!" Atwell called. "Asked and answered."

"Sustained."

"Let me put it this way, Mr. Bergfeld. Isn't it true that it was never your intention to volunteer in the Aviation Corps? And, in fact, this whole story is a sham? A feeble attempt to convince this jury that you are something you are not: a loyal, patriotic citizen?"

Atwell's objection was drowned out by Will's shouted denial, the rising voice of the crowd, the pounding of Judge Jack's gavel and the chaos of despairing thoughts that coiled behind Virginia's eyes.

The small room was filled with a heavy, heaving layer of gloom. No one spoke. Bill Atwell drummed his fingers on the table. Virginia stood behind Will massaging his shoulders. Bettie had taken the little girls home for a nap during the recess. Outside, on the courthouse lawn, a parade honoring the first soldiers from the county to depart for training at Camp Travis was taking shape under a warming sun. Escorting the young men to the depot were the town's new fire truck, the women of the Red Cross and the Abilene High School marching band. It had been the loud patriotic music of the band that had caused Judge Jack to call a recess. Louise wondered if he had also recognized the irony of the two simultaneous courthouse events—a parade honoring men conscripted to go to war, and a trial of those accused of treason. Inside the walls cowered the traitors, outside marched the heroes. Now the sounds of the music and shouting were fading. The silence in the room grew uncomfortable. After a while Louise thought if someone didn't speak she'd go mad. "I don't know why everybody is so glum," she said.

"It's my fault," Bill Atwell said. "We should never have brought up the Aviation Corps. I knew better."

"But what Will said is true," Virginia said.

"Sometimes the truth is less believable than a lie."

"It's also that blasted parade," Will said. "I bet it was orchestrated by O'Dell."

"It just wasn't our morning," Atwell said.

"What do we do now?" Louise asked.

"Well, it's still O'Dell's move," Atwell answered. "We just have to wait and see how the rest of Will's cross-examination goes."

"Waiting for something to happen isn't my favorite thing to do," Louise said.

"I'll have a chance to redirect," Atwell said.

"In the meantime?" Louise wanted to know.

"We wait."

"I keep thinking about what Peachtree told Bettie. Maybe there's something there."

"But what?" Will said. "He just mentioned this god-forsaken little town down near San Saba. Then he clammed up like he usually does."

"He mentioned a Deputy Sheriff named Draper," Louise said. "Maybe he knows something that would help. I think we should go."

"To Lometa?" Will asked.

"Why not? It's worth a try," Louise insisted.

"Do we have time?" Will asked.

"Not much." Atwell said. "When O'Dell finishes his cross-examination, I can redirect. Stall for a while. Maybe bring another witness or two. Then the judge will read his charge to the jury and immediately after that the lawyers will proceed with closing arguments."

"How far is Lometa?"

"About one hundred and fifty miles. Maybe a little less."

"How long by train?"

"Too long. You'd have to go through Fort Worth for sure, but I doubt any train goes there."

"How long can you stall?" Louise asked Atwell.

"Maybe two days and that gets us to the weekend recess. But if the jury senses I'm stalling, we'll be doing more harm than good. And then if you come up empty, we might be in worse shape than we are now. Besides, what do you expect to find?"

"I have no idea," Louise said.

"I do know this," Bettie chimed in. "Peachtree may be looney and he may not say much, but what he does say usually has something to it."

"I think it's worth the gamble," Louise said. "How about you, Will?"

Will took a deep breath, straightened his shoulders, smiled. Louise was glad to see a trace of the old fire return. Will always had been a gambler at heart, ever attracted to the long odds. "Who goes?" Will asked.

"I'll go," Louise announced. "I can be there in a day."

"You can't go alone," Will said.

"Why not? I've got a fast car. The rest of you belong here. Virginia with Will. Bettie watching the little girls."

"How about your husband?" Atwell asked.

"No time. Rob's in Dallas on business. Besides, I'm the only one who really can go. I probably have the best car in Abilene and I am not needed here, not for the next few days anyway," Louise insisted.

"You're going even in this weather?" Will asked.

"Look, I'm going," Louise declared, her mind made up. "I may find something. Besides, a wild goose chase is better than no chase at all."

"I'd like to return to your trip to Henryetta and Tulsa," O'Dell said to Will, as he paced before the witness chair. "Your purpose was to visit the Industrial Workers of the World and the Working Class Union?"

"Yes, sir."

Bettie could hear the wind howling outside. The morning paper had reported a record low temperature for the month of October. Now it had begun to rain. She said a brief prayer for Louise who was now a few hours into her journey.

"The idea was to see if you could amalgamate your local organization of the FLPA into these national groups?"

"Yes, sir."

"Where was it you went to confer with these organizations?"

"The first place was Henryetta, Oklahoma."

"Who did you talk to there?"

"I don't remember the name."

"Who did you see when you got to Tulsa?"

"I don't know his name either."

"You testified yesterday that one of the men you talked to admitted that the Working Class Union had been accused of some pretty violent things."

"They might have mentioned something about the Working

Class Union being accused of so and so. I think there was something mentioned about a water tank being destroyed. But they said they didn't do it."

"But he told you they had been accused of things of that kind?"

"Yes."

"Who told you these things?"

"I don't recall his name."

"You cannot give the name of any man you talked to?"

"No, sir. Except Mr. Ferguson who testified earlier."

"You were initiated into the Working Class Union?"

"Yes. By Mr. Ferguson."

"So what you did was join the Working Class Union without reading the application, isn't that what you testified to yesterday?"

"Yes, sir."

"And you joined the union even though you knew that it had been accused of sabotage? Isn't that right?"

"That's what I've said. But he said they didn't do it."

"What did the application of the WCU say about juries?"

"They requested that if a working man was brought to trial, we should all try to get on the jury so we could sway the verdict, even hanging the jury, if possible. Also, if a working man got into trouble during a strike or something like that and there were thugs around, we were to circle around him and protect him. And if you saw a member making a speech, you were to do the same thing, protect his life and such as that."

"Now let's talk about the IWW—the Industrial Workers of the World. You said you joined for two months, right?"

"Yes, sir."

"Within a day or two after you joined, you learned that the IWW engaged in sabotage, right?"

"That's right."

"What kind of sabotage did you learn the IWW engaged in?"

"In case of a strike, they would make a coal car run off the track and cause damage. Things like that."

"This is something you learned a day or two after you joined?"

"Yes, sir."

"Did you immediately send in your resignation?"

"No, sir."

"In fact, by your own testimony, you have admitted that you continued to be on the membership rolls for two months after you knew the IWW engaged in sabotage, isn't that right?"

"Yes, sir."

O'Dell nodded his head and began to pace. Then he paused and held up one finger, as if suddenly remembering something important.

"Mr. Bergfeld, didn't you testify that at the time of your arrest you had two kegs of dynamite in your barn? About one hundred sticks. Right?"

"Yes, sir."

"You have also admitted that this dynamite was not for your own personal use, correct?"

"Correct."

"In fact, your testimony is that you bought all this dynamite so it could be used by the members of the FLPA. Isn't that what you testified yesterday?"

"Yes, sir. So they could use it for water wells."

Again, O'Dell shook his head, then looked skyward. "For water wells, Mr. Bergfeld? What were they going to do? Drop a few sticks in a hole and 'poof'—water would spring up out of the ground?"

Atwell rose to his feet to object, but then sensed that O'Dell had overstepped, trying to impress the jury with his sarcasm. He decided to let Will field the question himself and he sat back down.

"No, sir, Mr. O'Dell," Will said. "It's not that easy. I don't know where you're from, but in these parts water is not a joking matter. It can mean life or death to a family."

Bettie felt like applauding. She looked out at the people in the courtroom. Many were farmers who had been struggling against drought, and she felt a subtle shifting of sentiment away from O'Dell. The prosecutor was searching his notes for a way to recover, regain his momentum. It was clear he was going to move on to another subject and avoid any more exchanges with Will about water.

"Now, Mr. Bergfeld," O'Dell continued. "I'd like to direct your attention to the second Cisco Convention of the Farmers' and Laborers' Protective Association. The convention that met on May fifth of this year. You testified that you were secretary of the Resolutions Committee, isn't that correct?"

"Yes, sir."

"You also testified that a resolution concerning the war was presented to your committee, isn't that so? The so-called radical resolution."

"Yes, sir."

"And you found this resolution to be treasonous and you tore it up?"

"Yes, sir."

"What was in this resolution that was presented, Mr. Bergfeld?"

"It was my conclusion after reading it that it was almost the same as open revolt. That if the government forced the American people into an unpopular war, then we were to use any means to resist it."

"Please state all you can remember that was in that resolution."

"It said in there that we were opposed to conscription, that it was against the Nineteenth Amendment to the Constitution. There was something about what we would do if conscription was passed."

"What was that, Mr. Bergfeld?"

"Something about a general strike and we would refuse to fight. That we would resist conscription even unto death."

"Even unto death," O'Dell spaced the words out dramatically. "What else?"

"There was a part about electing Mr. Risley as provisional President."

Judge Jack leaned forward. "Elect Mr. Risley President of what?"

"The United States might have been in there, but I would not be positive."

"In place of President Wilson?"

"Yes, sir."

"What was in your mind? What did you mean by electing Risley President?"

"It was not in my mind at all. I'm not sure what was meant by it. This man just handed it to me. Then I showed it to the other members of the committee. Mr. Webb says, 'That is hell,' or 'That is a hell of a note to bring in here.' I remember he used the word 'hell.' And Mr. Williams was reading it at about the same time and he says, 'This is plain treason, boys.' And like I told you, this is when I tore it up."

"You testified that the resolution was handed to you by one of your members. What was the man's name?"

"I don't believe I ever knew his name."

"You are not very good with names, are you, Mr. Bergfeld? Is he one of the defendants in this trial?"

"No, sir."

"After you tore it up, then Mr. Risely has the man dictate his resolution again and you wrote it down, isn't that what you testified?"

"Yes, sir."

"And you read it to the convention?"

"Yes."

"After your own committee members had denounced the resolution as treason, you went before the convention and presented it, didn't you?"

"It was the rule. Every resolution brought to the committee had to be presented before the convention. I was simply following the rule."

"But you have admitted that this resolution that you knew was treasonous was in your handwriting when you presented it to the convention."

"Objection, Your Honor," Atwell called out. "This question has been asked and answered. The witness has testified on this particular point. Now Counsel goes over it once again with an inflected voice. The question itself proves it is repetitive. 'But you have admitted. . . .' Well, that's my point. If he's already admitted it, we shouldn't be going over it again."

"Objection overruled," Judge Jack said. "It may be somewhat repetitive, but this is cross-examination and I am going to allow a wide latitude. I have allowed that same latitude to the counsel for the defendants. You may proceed."

Strutting before the witness stand, O'Dell continued. "Mr. Bergfeld, isn't it true that you presented a resolution at that Cisco convention that you knew was treason against the United States government?"

"As I have explained . . ."

"Just answer the question 'yes' or 'no.'"

"I can't answer it yes or no. It isn't that simple."

"I believe you can," Judge Jack said. "I insist you do. Please answer the question as instructed."

"Well, ask the question again," Will said.

O'Dell turned his back on the witness and faced the jury. "Isn't it true, Mr. Bergfeld, that you presented a resolution at the May fifth Cisco convention—a resolution that you had written in your own hand—a resolution that you knew was treason against the United States government?"

Will looked toward the defense table, seeking there some way out of his trap. Atwell looked away. Will turned his eyes toward the jury, seeking their understanding. The jurors, as one, stared back, waiting. Then Will responded with the only answer he could truthfully give. "Yes," he said, softly.

"Was that a 'yes,' Mr. Bergfeld?"

"Yes. That was a yes, Mr. O'Dell."

O'Dell crossed his arms across his chest. Bettie thought he looked like a politician who had just demolished a rival in debate. Then he lowered his arms and began pounding his right fist in his left hand. He was again strutting, as he moved from the witness stand to a position before the jury. It was clear he was about to go for the jugular.

"Mr. Bergfeld," O'Dell began anew. "You have heard all the testimony from several witnesses about your threatening and conspiring to kill President Wilson, haven't you?"

"I heard it all, but I know I never threatened or conspired to kill anybody."

"You do admit that in these FLPA meetings dozens of people heard you say harsh and hateful things about President Wilson, don't you?"

"It was no secret. I don't like the man and I have said so."

"More specifically, in this courtroom Ned Earl Calhoun, Lefty Crouch and Anna Bennett have all testified in one way or another that they heard you threaten to kill the President. You heard this testimony, did you not?"

"Yes, sir."

"And they gave that testimony under sworn oath to tell the truth, didn't they?"

"Yes, sir. I heard them if that's what you're asking."

"Did Ned Earl Calhoun lie about what he heard you say?"

"Yes, sir. He sure did."

"How about Lefty Crouch? Did he lie under oath about what he heard you say?"

"Yes, sir. He sure did."

"How about Anna Bennett? Did she lie under oath about what she heard you say?"

Will started to answer, then remained silent, looking down at his hands.

"Pass the witness," O'Dell announced to the entire courtroom with a great flourish. Then he strode back to his seat.

Sheets of dust like champagne curtains were blown by the wind across the road. Louise listened to the rumble of the tires on the roadway, a sound not unlike an orchestra of drums accompanied by the rumble of the engine, the sharp clatter of gravel on the iron undercarriage, and the pounding of the touring car's springs when it bottomed out on ruts. Somehow she had hoped the roads to be better. In this almost flat and wide-open landscape the roads were little more than pounded sand, only slightly improved since they had been cattle trails leading north to the railhead in Abilene. Here and there hand-rolled gravel filled a stretch, but more often wagon ruts left in mud had hardened into fearsome canyons.

She drove on, as she had since first light, following a map Will had filled with annotations. He had come this way many times on his motorcycle and had marked the preferred routes, notes that pointed out landmarks to guide her way. *One day*, Louise thought, *Texas will mark its roads with signs.* But now, her way was marked only by Will's memory, scrawls on a rough map. The hours passed more quickly than the miles. Because of the condition of the roads and a number of wrong turns, she began to fear she would not be anywhere near Lometa by dark.

What if I cannot find my way? Why was I so impetuous? Was it vanity? I will save my brother. I will do this heroic thing! But maybe I've put him more at risk. Instead of saving him, I am killing him with my vanity. What will I do when it is pitch dark? How will I find my way? What if it starts to rain? Why did I ever believe I could do this thing?

Her worst fears were confirmed when Louise saw a darkening of clouds gathering where the cool winds were colliding with currents of warm air. Soon the rain was like a solid wall, while donder and blitzen ruled the sky.

The touring car's fabric top was designed more for style than comfort, and the icy wind and veils of fine spray spilled through cracks and onto Louise's coat and hands and hair. She was almost numb with cold, especially her hands, and she tried for a while to drive with one hand warming in her pocket, but soon she realized the rough road required both hands on the wheel. The rain had turned deep dust to mud and she was in constant danger of sliding into the cavernous wagon ruts that were the main feature of the road.

Louise tried to force her discomfort from her mind by reveling in the sensation of speed and power. *How alike we are, Will and I,* she thought. *It is as if we were the same person. We love the same things and some of the things we love are entirely opposed one from the other. The speed and thunder of a machine hurtling along the earth despite the elements. An etude played perfectly on a violin. How could two sounds, two sensations be more contradictory? Will loves confrontation, risk, the high-hearted possibility of adventure. If I had been a boy, what brothers we would have been. We would have conquered the world.*

She had begun shivering by mid-afternoon. Often when the road would cross from one ranch to another, she had to climb out of the car to open gates, return to the car, drive through, then go back to close the gate again. This, too, took more time than she had planned. By early afternoon, Will's map was ruined, the notations smudged and unreadable. With an ascending sense of dread, she realized the creeks were rising. There were few bridges. As the touring car approached a creek flowing across the road, Louise would stop the car and survey her chances of making it across. The rushing of floodwater was louder than the engine. But there was only one decision to make: to pray and then go on. She would give the engine full throttle and, with leaping heart and nearly closed eyes, she would roar ahead, her prayers pulling the machine through, the wheels hurling spray high as the creek banks. A few of the larger creeks had low-water bridges of warped planks that shook and trembled as she passed over.

As the afternoon leaned toward dusk, the light began to fail early. It was as if God, upon deciding to go to bed early, had blown out the day's lamp. The road ahead filled with ghost images, the touring car's lamp lights pushed weakly through the curtains of dust. The world narrowed until all that existed on earth was the small red machine and the dark-haired woman who leaned forward, staring through the mist-fogged windshield, singing now to chase the fear she had begun to feel.

Occasionally, when she came to a small town or a ranch, Louise would ask directions. She would be told to turn at this windmill or that live oak or at a wooden bridge or some other landmark. Generally, when she came to a crossroads, she learned that the road with the deepest ruts was probably the main road, but she was never sure that she was not lost. By late afternoon, she was exhausted from shaking and concentrating on the road and from her doubts concerning the way. Then when she thought she could no longer bear the cold and the wet, she felt a strange warming. Her forehead felt hot, her eyes burned in the sockets, and she knew she was feverish and must find shelter from the cold.

She drove on. It grew dark. Ahead was another pool of water covering the road. She could not see its depth or current, but she could hear its voice, a chorus of wildly singing baritones. Once again, she coaxed the machine to its full speed. Later she would recall how much the moment was like coaxing a horse to ford a stream. The machine had seemed just as reluctant. The engine roared, the car leaped ahead into the waters, then stalled. The engine fell silent. Louise felt the car slide slowly sideways, pushed by the hidden current. Night fell like a black stone.

XXI.

Abilene, Texas.
October 1917

Defense Attorney Atwell sat in the empty courthouse listening to the rain and watching an old man mop the floor. It was not yet light, and there was a chill in the air and in his mind. He was still worried about some of the testimony O'Dell had so skillfully pulled out of Will the previous day. He was also discouraged by an encounter with the press on the courthouse lawn after the close of Will's testimony. Since the trial had begun, Atwell had been careful to walk a fine line with reporters—to offering them as little of substance as possible while appearing to be helpful and forthcoming, and suffering their most stupid questions with patience and calm. It was a technique that had always worked well in the past, but the furor surrounding this trial—the misguided patriotism, the possibility of the defendants being put to death, the public hunger for insights into the mind of this band of traitors—made it difficult to sidestep the questions of the Fourth Estate. No detail seemed trivial to either the reporters or to their readers.

A reporter had asked if this trial was similar to the Aaron Burr trial, both in its import and substance, especially as it related to Will Bergfeld. Atwell had been impressed with the question and had paused to consider before answering that he thought the two trials were not similar at all. It is true, both Burr and Bergfeld were born in America, not in England nor in Germany. Both had rebelled against authority all of their lives. Both loved a good fight, evidenced by Burr's duel with Alexander Hamilton. It could be said that both worked for the United States government, Bergfeld for the Postal Service and Burr as Vice President. Both had been indicted for treason. And the outcome of both trials had great implications for the future of the nation. But the charges were altogether different. Burr had been accused of scheming to carve out a new country, a vast empire, in the American South and West. Atwell told the reporter that the greatest similarity between the two cases was that Burr had been acquitted and Bergfeld would certainly be when all the facts are known.

"Maybe they both will be acquitted," the reporter had said. "That doesn't mean they are both innocent. History has shown that Aaron Burr was guilty as sin. What will history say about Bergfeld? And what about the grandmother in Germany? And where is Bergfeld's father? Don't you think it strange that he is not here supporting his son?"

Atwell lay awake most of the night thinking about what the reporter had asked. How clever of O'Dell to bring out that Will had a grandmother still living in Germany. It was one more negative link between Will and the enemy. Atwell had searched the far corners of his mind for any strategy that might turn things around. But he had come up empty.

The absence of Will's father was also puzzling to Atwell. Several times he had asked Will about Arthur Bergfeld. But he could tell Will was deeply hurt by his father's refusal to attend the trial, and he had not pursued the question. Still, he wondered if there was something in Arthur Bergfeld's background or in his recent activities that might be relevant to the trial. And he thought O'Dell probably had similar suspicions.

Atwell's brooding was interrupted when one of the other defense attorneys entered the conference room. Randall Morris was a young man, small and rail thin, yet possessing an obvious store of energy that made him seem much larger than he was. Standing stock still he seemed in motion; only his intelligent eyes were still and calm. Morris shook the water out of his cap and coat. As he settled down at the table, he and Atwell talked a while of the rain and the crowd already gathering outside in the dark, eager for the next act of the unfolding drama.

Then, Atwell revealed why he had asked the younger man for a conference. "I need some time," he said. "I need some distance between Bergfeld's testimony yesterday and the judge's charge to the jury. O'Dell's cross-examination made Will look bad. Right now it's fresh on the jurors' minds. I need something to take their minds off yesterday's testimony. Have you got a witness we can bring to the stand? A little misdirection? Somebody with a good story to tell?"

"Ross Fee," Morris said smiling. "A real character."

"One of the Fee brothers? The boys who mistook the Rangers who arrested Will for conscription officers?"

"Right. He doesn't have much upstairs, but he's very believable. It's not that he's dumb, he's just illiterate and hasn't had much experience in the world."

"Good. Anyone else?"

After a pause, Morris smiled again and offered the name, "Sprayberry."

"Sprayberry?" Atwell didn't recognize the name from among the defendants. "He's not a defendant."

"No. But I think the jury will like him," Morris said. "He's really funny. Not that he tries, he just naturally is. A little comic relief. Besides, he can testify to the fact that Will's life was threatened and that's why he bought the guns. He also has some fairly strong things to say against Old Man Crouch."

"Sounds good," Atwell said. "Meanwhile, we're trying to find some new evidence that might shake the foundation of O'Dell's case. It's a long shot, but it's just about all we've got. I need a day or two to see what develops." Atwell looked out at the rain pelting down and wondered if Louise had found anything in Lometa. A miracle would be nice.

When Louise awakened, she saw a great light blooming beyond the cloud where she lay. It was warmer than she thought Heaven would be and far wetter; in fact, the cloud was drenched in what seemed like perspiration. She was also surprised that pain was a concept that migrated upward through the Pearly Gates, as was the aroma of cooking bacon. Then, seeing Louise was awake, one of the angels came, lifted her head onto pillows and offered her a cup of warm milk.

"Drink, *Schatzi*," the woman said. The great light became the sunrise beyond the window, the cloud a featherbed, the angel a woman whose hands were gentle and whose face had become worn and furrowed by a life both hard and long.

"What is this place?" Louise asked as she sipped the milk.

"Our home. We call it *Heimat*," the woman said. "It is a German word that cannot be easily translated into English. It means homeplace—not a place exactly, but an idea—a place without boundaries where you feel comfortable."

Little by little the horrors of the night began to return. Louise saw a swollen river, the engine roaring then falling silent, the claws of the torrent seeking to drag her down. She saw herself fighting to the bank and crawling to higher ground. The images were strangely distant, impersonal, as if she were watching the struggles of another less fortunate woman unfolding, yet the images were too real to be a dream. For a moment she wondered who that woman was she watched, then she knew she was watching her own torment in the night. She recalled the cold, the blackness all around. She remembered the light in the distance, a small star in the gloom, and how she had set off through the storm, guided by the star as the shepherds had once been guided to Salvation by a star. She remembered strong arms and hot water and the featherbed cloud and she could still taste the bitter bite of whiskey she had been given to drive away the cold.

The woman said her name was Hilda Merten and she told Louise that her husband and her son had gone to fetch the car. They would drag it from the stream with a team of mules, then see what they could do.

Louise tried to rise and was driven back down by a pain behind her eyes. She felt terribly weak and was burning with fever.

"Lie still, Sweetheart," Hilda Merten said.

"I can't," Louise said, her voice a weak whisper. "I have to go." Then she told her new friend what she had to do, how it was important to get to Lometa to try to save her brother's life. Helda Merten recognized the name Bergfeld and she was aware of his predicament. Few people in Texas had not heard of the trial.

"When my husband gets back, we will see."

As she closed her eyes to sleep, Louise realized they had been speaking in German.

When the Merten men returned, dragging the touring car along behind their mules, Louise managed to climb from bed. Mrs. Merten gave her clean, dry clothes—overalls and a plaid shirt last worn by her son. Feeling weak and disoriented, Louise went to the door.

Hans Merten was behind the wheel, beaming with pride. He was obviously at the wheel of an automobile for the first time. His father, Deter, was at the traces of the mules. The rain had ceased in the night, yet the world seemed drenched and heavy and gray. When Louise stepped out on the front porch, Hans seemed embarrassed to see such a beautiful woman wearing his clothes.

Louise walked to her car and nodded to the men. "Thank you," she said.

"It might still run," Deter said. "The motor wasn't under the water."

"Not for the car," Louise said. "Thank you for my life."

"At first we thought you were a ghost out spookin' in the rain."

"Another hour or two and I would have been a ghost," Louise said.

It was apparent that neither Hans nor Deter had ever started a car. Painfully stiff, her head still throbbing, Louise climbed behind the wheel, set the spark and throttle, then climbed down again. Taking the starting crank from the trunk, she moved around to the front of the car. "The engine wasn't under water?" she asked, surprised. The last memory she had of the car was of it disappearing into the black current.

"Wasn't," Deter said. "The automobile slid in backwards."

Louise bent to insert the crank and the pain in her head drove her to her knees. Hans rushed forward and took the crank from her hand. "Just tell me how," he said, as Hilda Merten's strong arms raised Louise to her feet again.

On the fifth crank, the engine exploded into life, a sound like a joyous iron anthem. Hans beamed, waved the crank in the air. Louise was sick with relief and she smiled in spite of her pulsing temple. She cut the ignition and leaned back in the driver's seat. Her eyes closed in a quiet prayer of thanksgiving.

Over a hot breakfast, feeling somewhat human again, Louise began to insist that she had to leave immediately.

"You can't drive," Hilda Merten said. "You'll end up in another creek."

"*I* can drive," Hans announced. He spoke as if driving a touring car across Texas was a most natural thing to do.

"You can't drive an automobile, Son."

"Well, I never have, but that doesn't mean I can't."

"Could you?" Louise asked. "I could show you how. It's not really hard."

And so it was decided. With Hans Merten at the wheel, Louise swaddled in his farmer's clothes, the automobile careening through the mud, they thundered on down the rutted roads and the settling pools of water toward the little town of Lometa where Peachtree said they should seek a deputy sheriff named Draper.

Ross Fee was a small, sandy-haired man with a pleasant face and a relaxed manner. He seemed comfortable on the witness stand, polite and eager to please. He looked like a schoolboy admitting to some minor mischief for which he felt no remorse. Randall Morris began his questioning.

"Mr. Fee, so the jury will know, I'm Randall Morris and I represent you, your brother Sam and your father J. R. Fee. All three are defendants in this case, correct?"

"Yes, sir." He spoke with an accent shaped by his rural experience.

Atwell figured the Fee boys had rarely, if ever, attended school.

"Tell us your age," Morris continued.

"Twenty-four."

"Are you single?"

"Yes, sir."

"Where do you live?"

"With my parents in Weinert, Texas."

"Sometime in May, did you leave home for awhile?"

"Yes, sir."

"Did your fear of government conscription have anything to do with that?"

"Yes, sir."

"Tell the jury what experience or knowledge you and your family had regarding conscription."

Ross Fee settled deep into the witness chair. "Well, I growed up knowing all about conscription because way back when my pa was two or three years old, before I was born, conscription officers came to their house during the Civil War. They says to my pa's papa that he had to fight with them for the South. When Grandpa tolt them he had crops to tend and wouldn't go, they says they gonna rape his wife right before his eyes if he don't go. So he went. He went alright, but he never came back. Nobody ever see'd or hear'd tell of him again. Spose he's kilt but nobody knows for sure. I heard that story all my life."

"Were there any other experiences you had in your family in regard to conscription?"

An assistant prosecutor named Allen rose to his feet. "Objection, Your Honor. All this is irrelevant."

Judge Jack looked over his glasses at Ross Fee, then at Randall Morris. "Counselor?"

"The relevance will become clear in a moment."

"I hope so," Judge Jack said, seeming bored with the testimony. "You may answer the question."

Ross Fee took a deep breath and continued.

"My mama, too, done told us about conscription from a big ol' history book we had in our house. She tolt about folks in Germany a long time ago, in all their wars, when the conscription fella came to a house to take a thirteen-year-old boy, his mother grabbed a knife and hollered, 'He's my only child. You'll have to kill me if you take him.' And so they did. My mama read that one to us about a dozen times."

Atwell glanced at the jury. A few of the jurors were smiling, apparently amused by Ross Fee, a boy who seemed totally sincere and guileless. It would be impossible to believe this country bumpkin could be guilty of anything more serious than truancy.

"Tell us about your leaving home on May 23 of this year. What happened that night?"

"Well, the Jeter boys, my brother and me went to town to get a drink or two from Mr. Weinert's barrels at Old Man Crouch's store. On our way back home we saw a train comin' into town. Strangest thing was, no whistle like it usually does. A whole bunch of men got off, all of 'em movin' fast, runnin' down the street, all of 'em carryin' one or two guns. First thing we knew they was haulin' Will Bergfeld out of his house. Lem Jeter says, 'Them's conscription officers,' and we lit out for home."

"How old are the Jeter boys?"

"Eighteen or nineteen."

"Single, like you?"

"Yeah."

"Tell the jury exactly what was said and what you fellas did that night."

"Well, to tell you the truth it was all kinda settled on before."

"Settled? You mean planned?"

"Yeah. My brother, the Jeters, Luke Kennemer . . ."

Randall Morris held up his hand, interrupting the testimony. "Now when you mention Luke Kennemer, are you talking about the same Luke Kennemer who was a defendant in this case, but is not here now?"

"Yes, sir."

"In fact, the judge instructed the jury that they should not consider anything they have read or heard about him. Is this the same Luke Kennemer you are talking about?"

"Yeah, the one that done the murder."

Morris turned pale. He knew that Judge Jack had tried hard to keep out of evidence the fact that Defendant Kennemer was charged with a murder commited during the trial. Wanting to quickly change the subject he said, "Let me direct your attention back to that night. Tell us what you had planned to do."

"We'd been goin' to meetings of the farmers' union, you know. They heard conscription officers would be coming soon as it was law. So we bought up some 30-30 rifles, a few pistols, lots of ammo, cases of shells and bullets. We was ready to take off into Swisher Canyon to wait it out."

"Wait out what?"

"'Til the conscription officers done come and gone. Then we'd head back home."

"Were you going to shoot the government conscription officers if they came after you?"

"No, sir. When we bought all that stuff, we was thinking about goin' all the way to Colorado. Didn't know how long we'd be gone. We figured if folks saw us we'd look like hunters and no one would suspect we were running away."

"Did the conscription officers catch up with you in Swisher Canyon?"

"Well, somebody sure as hell did. I'm not sure just who it was."

"What happened?"

"Long about midnight of the second night in the canyon, we heard horses and voices. We could see lanterns comin' down the trail. I remember it was pretty lit up by the moon."

"Then what happened?"

"We split up, took to opposite sides of the canyon. Jeters on one side and Kennemer, my brother and me on the other. We hid in the boulders and the brush and watched the men down below. They found our camp from the ashes of the fire."

"What then?" Morris asked.

"They wandered all around, lookin' and hollerin' for us to come out, but we never moved or spoke a word, and they gave up when they couldn't find us."

"Did you have your guns with you?"

"Sure did. Could've shot them all a hundert times over. We could see them, but they couldn't see us. They had lanterns, you know. Sometimes they'd be only twenty feet from us. Sure could have shot them if we'd meant to."

"What happened next?"

"Not too long after they left, Pa and two friends showed up lookin' for us.They said they'd already been arrested by the Rangers and released. Pa said that half of Haskell County done been arrested and all but a few were still in jail. Sheriff told Pa if he'd get us to give up quick-like he'd get us released, but if not, no tellin' what might happen. So we went back to Weinert and looked up the sheriff and turned our ownselves in."

"Were the Jeter boys arrested?"

"Only Kennemer and us Fee brothers. When the Jeters turned themselves in, Sheriff Allen looked at his papers and says, 'Git out of here and git on home. Hell, you ain't even on the list.'"

"So, you ran away into the canyon because you thought you were being chased by conscription officers, isn't this true?"

"Yes, sir."

"And you never had any thought about shooting anybody?"

"No, sir."

"It was all a kind of misunderstanding, isn't that right?"

"Yes, sir."

"And the sheriff understood and he let you go without any bond?"

"That's right."

"But then the U.S. Marshals and Texas Rangers came and re-arrested you, this time for treason, right?"

"That's what they did."

"Another big misunderstanding, isn't that right, Mr. Fee?"

"Objection!" called Prosecutor O'Dell.

"Sustained," said Judge Jack.

Morris thanked the witness and said, "I have no further questions, Your Honor."

As Morris took his seat, Atwell was certain Fee's testimony had made a favorable impression on the jury. It was not his specific answers to specific questions that impressed, but the general aura of innocence that accompanied the words. All Ross Fee was guilty of was innocence. Atwell looked out over the other defendants, men with little, if any, experience in the larger world. With a few exceptions, here were men who probably could not point out where Germany was if you showed them an atlas. Surely, the jurors must realize this. Surely they must know that most of these men, people whose lives were lived close to the earth, were unjustly accused. Like Ross Fee, they were only guilty of their innocence.

O'Dell rose and approached the witness. "I have a few questions for this witness, Your Honor."

"Proceed, Counselor," Judge Jack said.

"You have testified you are a member of the Farmers' and Laborers' Protective Association, isn't that right?"

"Yes, sir."

"Do you know the defendant G. T. Bryant?"

"Yes, sir."

"What position does he hold in the FLPA?"

"He's head of it, I think."

"Did he ever talk against conscription at a meeting you attended?"

"Wasn't nobody for conscription. Everybody talked agin' it."

"Did you ever hear Mr, Bryant advise FLPA members that if the conscription officers came you were to rise up in revolt, take up high-powered rifles and take over towns and blow up bridges and trains?"

"I'm not fully sure I did. Sometimes we didn't listen too close to them speeches. They went on some."

"Isn't it true that, like a good soldier, you followed your leader's orders? That you and the others bought high-powered rifles and took to the canyons, fully intending to shoot the conscription officers when they came?"

Before Fee could respond, O'Dell waved his hand as if shooing a fly and said, "I have no further questions for this witness."

R. S. Sprayberry was tall and spare, weathered by the seasons. His hands were the color of his land, his blue eyes faded from looking too long at dry, empty, cloudless skies. Once again, Randall Morris handled the questions.

"Where do you reside, Mr. Sprayberry?"

"I live in the northwest of Haskell County."

"How long have you lived in Texas?"

"I've been here about thirty years."

"How old are you, Mr. Sprayberry?"

"Forty-six."

"What part of Texas were you born in?"

"Down near Temple, in Bell County."

"What business are you in?"

"I am in farming and writing hail insurance."

"Are you a man of family?"

"Yes, sir."

"Do you know the defendant Bergfeld?"

"Yes, sir."

"What report, if any, did you carry to Mr. Bergfeld in the Spring of 1917?"

"I was traveling through O'Brien and a gentleman came up to me and told me this fella told him that in case of war the first thing he was going to do was to kill Bergfeld and Old Man Crouch, and he seemed to be so earnest about it that I decided maybe I'd better tell Bergfeld, and I went there and told him about it."

"Do you know whether Mr. Bergfeld then ordered his six-shooter?"

"I advised him to, yes."

Randall Morris thanked and excused the witness. When he arrived back at the defense table, Atwell whispered, "Is that all? He didn't seem to have much to say."

"I'm hoping O'Dell will take the bait," Morris said, as the prosecutor rose and approached the witness. "Just wait. This could be interesting."

"Mr. Sprayberry," O'Dell began, "where did this conversation between you and Mr. Bergfeld take place?"

"At Weinert. At Mr. Bergfeld's garage where he kept his car. I went to his house."

"When was it?"

"The later part of March, this year."

"So you went around and told Mr. Bergfeld about this man who threatened to kill him and Mr. Crouch?"

"Yes."

"Did you warn Mr. Crouch?"

"No, sir."

"Why didn't you warn Mr. Crouch?"

"Because I and Mr. Crouch were not intimate friends, and I and Will Bergfeld were."

"You didn't think that was a matter of sufficient importance to tell Mr. Crouch?"

"No, I didn't consider I had anything to do with Old Man Crouch."

"Is this the Mr. Crouch who has testified in this case?"

"Yes, sir. The gentlemen that lives up there in Weinert."

"What does he do?"

"Mostly farmers, I think."

There came a scattering of laughter from the crowd, especially from the defendants, most of whom had been done by Old Man Crouch. "What do you mean by that?" O'Dell asked. "What do you mean that he *does* farmers, Mr. Sprayberry?"

"I mean he sells them water, runs a little pump station. I don't know what all he does."

"Is that *doing* the farmers? Is that what you call *doing* the farmers?"

"Yes, to a great extent."

"He owns a water tank and furnishes the farmers with water.

You call that doing the farmers?"

Atwell watched in amazement as Wilmot O'Dell blundered on. It was obvious the prosecutor had no sense of humor and could not understand why so many people in the courtroom were finding the testimony so amusing. Several jurors were grinning. Even Judge Jack wore a smile. O'Dell just would not let it go.

"Well, I don't know as I can hardly tell you more," Sprayberry responded. He was playing it straight, unsmiling, a bit impatient with the prosecutor. "Look. I've done explained it all. He pumps this water, that would be runnin' down to the farmers' lands, into a tank and then sells this water to farmers at extortionate prices. That's what I call *doing* the farmers."

This time there was laughter out loud, a rare moment in the trial when the tension was broken. O'Dell's expression never changed. If he was embarrassed by the exchange and by the laughter at his expense, he did not show it. Still the bull charging into the china shop, O'Dell continued his questioning.

"So you say you heard somebody make threats against the life of Mr. Bergfeld?"

"No. A man came to me and told me about a fella who threatened Will Bergfeld and Old Man Crouch. And he asked me to go down there and tell Will Bergfeld."

"Did he ask you to notify Mr. Crouch?"

"No, sir. He asked me to notify Will Bergfeld."

"He said that threats had been made against both?"

"Yes, sir."

"Did you take what he said seriously? Did you think there was really serious danger that those men would lose their lives?"

"I didn't know. All I knew was what I was told."

"Now if you thought that threat was serious enough to warn Mr. Bergfeld, why didn't you also warn Mr. Crouch?"

"I told you Mr. Crouch and I are not really enemies, but Mr. Crouch and I are not close friends like Mr. Bergfeld and I are. And I have to tell you that Mr. Crouch sure charges farmers a lot for that water."

"Why do you think Mr. Bergfeld's life was threatened?" Judge Jack glanced at Morris to see if he would object. Morris just smiled.

"Because he's German."

"But Mr. Crouch is not of German descent. Why do you think Mr. Crouch's life was threatened?"

"Because he *does* the farmers."

O'Dell excused the witness and walked back to the prosecution table, still shaking his head about what Old Man Crouch does to the farmers.

Louise watched Hans Merten drive. He had been tentative, at first, creeping along, oversteering, his expression a blending of joy and terror. Now, as they moved onto the northern skirts of the Hill Country, he was gaining confidence. The bright red touring car thundered up the rises and then flew down again, careening from one side of the road to the other, scattering wild turkeys and an occasional jackrabbit. Hans was a gangly, lanky teenager with hair like straw and a smile so shy it departed almost before it arrived. Louise knew Hans had fallen in love with her the moment they had met. She knew well the impact she had on men, and she could imagine the effect she must have had on this young man—a beautiful, mysterious stranger walking into his life from out of a storm, handing him the keys to a gorgeous motor car. Now she wore his clothes. She imagined, in the future, he would be swept up in fantasy each time he wore them, or until a real girl came along.

The day was gray as smoke, the clouds heavy, leaden, filled with rain not falling. Louise was not quite as cold as she had been and she supposed it was the fever that pressed against the back of her eyes and made her face feel tight and hot. A sharp pain pressed her ribs, and she tried to take shallow breaths to ease its bite. There was a sense of unreality about the journey, the strange red car moving into a rolling vista of grass-covered limestone hills, broken by cedars and mesquite. For a while, she imagined she was a sister to the hawk she saw wheeling above the hills and she watched the passage of the automobile as a hawk might see it gazing down from the base of the clouds. She soared softly on the wind, slowly, easily, drifting, her mind moving in and out of reality, almost sleeping.

She felt a presence next to her, around her, not exactly in the car, but with her and the hawk, moving above, keeping pace, watching young Hans experiencing a ride that would be a major memory in his life. Louise looked up at the hawk and thought about Will saying that the Creeks believe a hovering hawk means God has a message for you. Again, she felt the presence. *What is it? Who is there?* Then she knew. Her mother, young and alive as she had been before the spider came. And her mother's mother, performing on the Berlin stage. And behind them, a host of women all the way back to Eve, the women whose blood beat in her heart, whose thoughts shaped her own, whose spirit they had passed down through the generations.

I welcome you who have created me and I thank you for my life. What a miracle is your gift to me. I am all that has been before and all that will come. We are sisters and mothers and daughters of time and we live forever. The Good Lord created the world in seven days. But we are the custodians of the eighth day of Creation. The Lord labored six days and rested the seventh. The eighth day is ours. For it is our labor that gives birth to the future.

Then, in her fevered dream, Louise looked into the future for the flesh and spirit she would bring into the world and what she saw was an empty hall that stretched to the end of time. And what she heard was someone sobbing in that hollow hall, a sound so jarring and painful that she was awakened instantly.

The engine rattled, but the car was still. Hans watched her, his eyes sad and soulful, his hand reaching to give comfort, then retracted again as Louise opened her eyes.

"Why have we stopped?" Louise asked.

"You were crying."

"I never cry."

"Well."

"May we drive on?"

"Yes."

They drove on.

Lometa was a primitive scattering of frame and limestone structures rising at a crossroads. Wooden sidewalks skirted the main street. Beneath the boards, dogs scratched away their boredom in the dust that had evaded the recent rain. Storefronts announced the availability of hardware, dry goods, livery and whiskey. When they asked for Deputy Sheriff Draper, they were directed to the jailhouse, little more than a roofed cage with a porch. Hans helped Louise from the car and they walked through the drying mud to the porch where an old man was whittling on a stick. At the other end of the porch, Louise could see another man asleep on the stone floor.

"Deputy Draper?" Louise asked the old man.

"Not hardly," the old man laughed.

"Do you know where . . . ?"

"Sure do," the old man said, jerking his thumb toward the sleeping man. "Over there. Sleeping off one helluva bout with old John Barleycorn."

XXII.

Abilene, Texas.
October 1917

"Your Honor," Defense Attorney Atwell called, "With the Court's permission, I'd like to recall Ned Earl Calhoun to the stand." There was a murmur of surprise from the spectators and heads craned, benches scraped, as the crowd turned to watch the bailiff leave to fetch the witness. Atwell tried to read O'Dell's face, but whatever he was thinking was not written there. The defense attorney glanced at the jurors and they, too, revealed little more than a mild curiosity. The judge appeared to be sleeping, his eyes closed behind his thick glasses, his hands folded across his ample stomach. Atwell smiled to himself, knowing that this quiet courtroom was soon going to erupt into chaos and confusion.

If Calhoun was concerned about being recalled, it didn't show. As pale and anonymous as before, he carried a slight smile on his round face. Atwell sensed the jury's renewed interest. They seemed to lean forward, as one, eager to hear what this mild-looking man could say that was so important to the defense that they would bring him back again.

"Mr. Calhoun," Bill Atwell began, "I believe earlier in this trial you testified that you went to Cisco at the request of the prosecutors in San Antonio to try to obtain some information about Will Bergfeld and about the FLPA, is that correct?"

"That's correct."

"Do you remember when it was that you went to that convention?"

"Yes, sir. The convention was scheduled to begin on the evening of May fifth and I arrived about mid-afternoon."

"So you are absolutely sure that it was at this convention that occurred May fifth when you spoke to Will Bergfeld?"

"I'm absolutely positive of that. I spoke with him a few hours before the convention was to begin."

As Atwell phrased his questions, he was amazed Calhoun could remain so apparently at ease. Like Anna Bennett, he seemed a master of the undetectable lie. Atwell wondered if it was an art developed over a lifetime, beginning in childhood, maybe with white lies about homework or chores not done, then escalating in import to these more recent blood-red lies that could take away a man's life.

"How did you get to that convention?"

"I drove a vehicle owned by my father-in-law."

"Drove from Gonzales all the way to Cisco?"

"Yes, sir."

"How long did it take you to make that drive?"

Calhoun seemed to calculate. "If I'm not mistaken, I wanted to take my time so I allowed two or three days."

"Did you make any stops along the way?"

"Yes, I just pulled off the road a few times and took a nap. I don't recall any other stops."

"Is it correct that one of the places you passed through on your way to Cisco was Lometa, Texas?" Atwell watched Calhoun's face carefully and noticed a small pulse at the corner of his left eye.

"Yes, sir, that's true."

"Is it fair to say that you probably arrived at Lometa on May third, 1917?"

Calhoun paused, thinking back. "That's probably the day I passed through there."

"Do you remember stopping there?"

"I may have, but I don't recall." The slight pulse beside Calhoun's eye grew stronger. He blinked, as if to make it stop.

"Mr. Calhoun, do you recall that as you were passing through Lometa, Texas, you were stopped by two sheriff's deputies and arrested on a stolen car charge, because your wife had charged you with beating her up in Gonzales and stealing her father's car? Do you have any recollection of that arrest taking place in Lometa on May third, 1917?"

"I'm not sure I know what you're talking about." Calhoun's face was reddening now and he was shifting uneasily in his chair. The crowd in the courtroom began to stir. The judge opened his eyes.

"Well, Mr. Calhoun, let me clarify it for you," Atwell continued. "I have here in my hand some jail records sworn to by the sheriff, indicating you were placed in the Lometa jail on May third and that you remained there until May ninth of 1917. And so you couldn't possibly have talked with Will Bergfeld in Cisco because you were in jail at the time."

O'Dell was on his feet, shouting his objection. He was obviously stunned, as was everyone else in the courthouse, from the men of the jury to the huckster who had come to the window from where he sold miniature gallows on the courthouse lawn. The crowd in the courtroom made a sound like that heard when a circus aerialist falls from the high wire. Even the judge seemed astonished as he pounded his gavel for order. Reporters wrote furiously on their pads. Atwell glanced toward Will's family. They were beaming, holding hands. Virginia was weeping, dabbing at her eyes with a handkerchief. Out among the defendants, Will seemed to be suspended between anger and elation, anger that Calhoun had lied and elation that he had been found out.

After the courtroom quieted down, O'Dell continued his objection. "Your Honor, we object to the reference to any records that have not been properly proven up or identified. In fact, such records have not been shown to the U.S. Attorney."

"Your Honor," Atwell responded, "these records are certified by a Deputy Sheriff from Lometa, who has sworn that they are true and correct records reflecting that Ned Earl Calhoun was in jail in Lometa from May third to May ninth of 1917."

O'Dell remained standing. Atwell knew the prosecutor was grasping at straws. "We object to the introduction of these records or any further mention of these records for they constitute hearsay. Further, these records should not be allowed into evidence unless we have the opportunity to cross-examine the deputy sheriff regarding their authenticity."

Atwell responded. "Well, Your Honor, Deputy Draper, the man who signed these records, is waiting out in the hall. He's going to be our next witness, and you can bet your life he's going to verify these records."

Judge Jack gaveled down the rising clamor in the courtroom. "I overrule your objection, Mr. O'Dell. You may continue, Counselor."

Atwell turned to the witness and said, "Mr. Calhoun, isn't it true that you were in jail in Lometa, Texas, continuously from the afternoon of May third until the morning of May ninth, 1917? Isn't that true?"

Calhoun looked toward O'Dell for help, but O'Dell did not respond. "I refuse to answer," Calhoun said to the judge.

"Unless you are invoking your Fifth Amendment rights and refusing to answer on the grounds that your answer might incriminate you, then I'm going to order you to answer the question."

"That's right, Your Honor. I'm invoking those rights, my Fifth Amendment rights."

Calhoun kept looking to O'Dell for help. But the prosecutor merely glared back with eyes so filled with fury that they actually seemed on fire.

Atwell continued to tear into Calhoun's story. "Isn't it true that on the morning of May third, 1917, you and your wife had a violent argument which resulted in her filing assault charges against you and also charges that you stole her father's car? And isn't it correct that as a result of the charges she filed that you were stopped in Lometa and arrested and placed in jail there for almost six days, and then you were released from jail because you persuaded your wife to drop the charges? Isn't that what happened?"

"I refuse to answer on the grounds of the Fifth Amendment."

"Isn't it true that the reason you could not tell us anything about the meeting that took place in Cisco on May fifth is that you were never even near Cisco on May fifth, isn't that a fact?"

"I refuse to answer because of the Fifth Amendment."

"Isn't it true that it was impossible for you to have had a conversation with Will Bergfeld on May fifth, as you testified under oath, because you were in jail in Lometa at the time?"

"I refuse to answer."

Atwell turned, looked at O'Dell and said, "No further questions."

"No further questions," O'Dell said, avoiding Atwell's eyes.

After Deputy Draper testified to the authenticity of the jail records, Judge Jack asked, "Mr. Atwell, does the defense have any further witnesses?"

"No, Your Honor, the defense rests."

"Mr. O'Dell, what says the prosecution?"

"Your Honor, we have no further witnesses. The prosecution rests."

Judge Jack turned toward the jury box. "Gentlemen, both sides have rested their case. This means that all of the evidence to be presented in this trial has now been presented by all parties. This afternoon it will be necessary for me to take up some legal matters with the lawyers outside the presence of the jury; therefore, you are excused until nine o'clock in the morning."

As the spectators rose and commented noisily on this unexpected development, Judge Jack turned back to address the lawyers. "Gentlemen, I want all of the attorneys back in the courtroom at one o'clock to review the Court's Charge and Jury Instructions that I have prepared. I will expect you to submit your objections and any motions you may have at that time. Court is adjourned until one o'clock."

It was mid-afternoon of the same day when Arthur Bergfeld answered the telephone in his drugstore. He was pleased to learn that it was Louise, but he immediately asked, "Are you ill? You don't sound right."

"I'll be fine. I called to tell you the evidence in Will's case has ended. We think it will be over in a few days."

Louise quickly related the details of Calhoun's testimony. "I helped prove he was a liar by driving the deputy from Lometa to the courthouse in Abilene. That part of the trial went well, but Mr. Atwell is worried about the anti-German protesters who keep marching outside the courthouse. He said he's afraid the atmosphere of hate in the street will permeate into the courtroom and infect the jurors."

Louise asked her father one more time to come to Abilene.

When the call ended, Arthur knew that he had deliberately not told her what he had to do the next day.

Arthur Bergfeld was furious. It was a kind of smoldering anger, the hard edges softened by sorrow, a mourning for something stolen away. It was a feeling he had not had since the murder of his father. He knew what he mourned was the plunder and loss of his freedom. U.S. Marshals had ordered that every German-born person in Seguin was required to register as an enemy alien.

The new laws were published on handbills and in the newspaper. Germans must carry their enemy alien card at all times, and were forbidden to travel more than one hundred miles from home, or step within twenty feet of a government building. It reminded Arthur of the Germany he had left behind, the Germany that killed his father. The sound of boots in the night, enemies without faces, a ubiquitous fear that no dimension of courage could rise above. Now this fear was loose in America, in Seguin, in his heart.

Arthur knew it was almost impossible for him to even consider going to Abilene. Now, to do so, to travel more than one hundred miles from Seguin, would break the law. *It was no wonder,* Arthur thought to himself, as he walked to the courthouse to register, that he could not control his heartbeat. The world was unraveling, the faceless enemy was on the march.

The line around the Guadalupe County Courthouse was obscenely long. It reminded Arthur of the refugees on the road from Berlin to Bremen. He sensed their anger, their outrage. And he sensed something else, a kind of shame, an embarrassment that they were singled out so unjustly and were so powerless to assert and defend their rights.

Arthur joined the line. It moved forward. Whispers. Indignation. Incredulity. Arthur stood behind Johann Kristoff Koehler, who turned and asked if Arthur had heard what happened to Erna Wentzel, a woman they knew who takes in sewing. When Arthur shook his head, Johann said, "Yesterday two men with some kind of badges came into the house and tore things up. They said she stitched secret codes into the clothes she made. Then they took an axe and chopped her sewing machine into pieces. That sewing machine was her livelihood. Now it's destroyed."

"What will she do?" Arthur asked, knowing the answer.

"What can any of us do?" Johann replied.

The line moved on.

Arthur saw Otto and Meta Repschlagle join the line. Those nearby stepped aside to let them in. Several women embraced Meta, hoping to give her comfort, for it was well known their country home had been burned down by arsonists a few days before. "They burned us out," Otto said. "Men wearing flour sacks over their head. Everything's gone. Our house, our barns, the horses."

As the line moved forward, Arthur began to realize the enormity of the hatred and persecution directed against his neighbors. And many of them were now being further humiliated by the order to register as enemy aliens. He recognized Mr. Halm, a much beloved photographer who had come up from Mexico with nothing but a camera and a tripod and had built a good business taking portraits of Seguin families. Then, last Tuesday, the door to his studio on Austin Street was broken down and two Marshals ransacked the place searching for what they implied was evidence of espionage. They burned all his photographs, many of his family that were irreplaceable.

Up ahead, Arthur recognized Rudolph Tschoepe. Until recent weeks he had been a highly respected member of the State Legislature. He had come to America from Germany with his parents when he was four years old. Now, half a century later, he was ousted from the Legislature because he could not prove he was an

American citizen. Yet, no man Arthur knew was more loyal to America than Representative Tschoepe. The faceless enemy was on the march.

The line moved on. Arthur Bergfeld took pen in hand and with a sick tightness below his heart forced his fingers to sign his name to the enemy alien registration.

Later in the day, Arthur and Emma attended a prayer service for the first two Seguin boys to land in France. Then they proceeded to a dinner honoring C. T. Schawe, a new trustee at Texas Lutheran College. The banquet was hosted by the president of the college. As Arthur sat with friends, his anger began to subside. He was able to still his heartbeat and even enjoy this pleasant time among people he knew and respected.

Arthur's mood was shattered when four U.S. Marshals strode through the crowd and onto the platform where the honored guest was seated. Before anyone knew what was happening, the Marshals pulled Schawe from his chair, handcuffed him and roughly dragged him from the hall.

The fire broke out in the old Bruns-Hey building, which had been an early Guadalupe County courthouse. It was three o'clock in the morning, a few hours after Schawe's arrest, and all Seguin was sleeping, except for a few furtive figures carrying cans of gasoline from place to place in the shadows. A flower of fire bloomed, then spread in crimson tributaries along the old wood floor, exploded up the walls; the flames sucked out through the windows carrying smoke blacker than the night and constellations of small frenetic stars high into the air. Nearby, in the firehouse, the smell of wood smoke woke old Fritz Schildroth, the night watchman. Then seeing the fire itself, he rushed to the bell rope, pulled with all his might, and the rope broke, the bell pealing once, but not again. The town slept on. The fire hungered and feasted.

Arthur Bergfeld thought at first he was dreaming the fire, a dream so real that the smoke was burning his eyes and lungs. When he waked, the first thing he saw was the reflected towers of flame in his bedroom window. The first thing he knew was unfathomable dread. His heart pumping, still not entirely believing his senses, Arthur hurriedly dressed and rushed outside into a scene from Dante. His first thought, as he rushed toward the town square, was that this must be what Hell is like. The fire raged entirely out of control, a living thing, feeding, consuming the town. In the fitful, staccato light the fire cast, people were rushing about, some toward the fire, others away from it, some seeking to fight the flames, others to surrender and save what they could. Arthur passed women with robes over nightgowns rushing with their children to join bucket brigades at the center of town. Volunteer firemen were filling the buckets from a hose that snaked down from the tall water tower in the city park. Others had attached hoses to fireplugs, the crystal arcs of water so slim, so meager against the enormity of the inferno. He passed nuns from the Seguin Catholic School, raising buckets of water from their wells. Horses and mules released from the livery ran wild-eyed through the streets. The heat burned like the summer sun.

When Arthur reached his drugstore, he found his prayers had been answered. The building was still untouched by the flames. The volunteer firemen had retreated from the blocks of Court Street north of the courthouse, leaving the fire to consume itself on the buildings already destroyed. Here, on the street in front of the Bergfeld Drug Store, they had decided to make their stand. Arthur joined the desperate men fighting against the fire, all but the whites of their eyes blackened by the cloying ash and soot. A roiling cloud of smoke soiled the air and invaded the lungs. Arthur fought on against the fire, against ruin, his mind empty of all but the effort to lift one more bucket one more time. No one noticed when day came, the sunrise was obscured by the smoke.

It must have been noon or later when Arthur realized the danger to his drugstore had passed. Exhausted, he looked around at the devastation. What had a few hours ago been a beautiful Texas town was now a ravaged wasteland. Here and there in the desolation a few fires still smoldered. Men and women wandered the skeletal remains of their businesses, assessing their loss. Gone were the Krezdorn Jewelry Company, Dr. Tegener's dentist office, August Hildebrandt Photography, George Levy Dry Goods, the Blumberg Brothers Store on Austin Street, the Schultz Saloon at the corner of Austin and Court Street, and many others. *It happened so quickly,* Arthur thought. *Fire is both the blessing and curse of mankind.* He breathed a prayer of thanks to Jehovah, then smiled thinly at the name of the deity he had not spoken in so many years.

Inside, Arthur surveyed what he could have lost. The walls and cabinets of medicines, the periodicals and books, banjos, mandolins, tea sets, boxes of paints, toy trains, the soda fountain, the apothecary, all the wares and facilities of a modern drugstore. Arthur was exhausted from his fight against the fire, but he did not want to go home. He wanted to be in this place where he had spent so much of his life, this place he had nearly lost. Once again, he thought of his greatest loss, of Elisabethe, and how not a day went by that he did not miss her terribly. He walked into the courtyard behind the drugstore, eased into a chair, listened to the shouts and cries of people mourning what the fire had taken away. He had never felt more alone, except for a few times when he was with Emma. The smell of wood smoke was still heavy in the air. Arthur supposed it would be days before the air was sweet again.

In Abilene, the family met in the small conference room where they had previously gathered throughout the trial. There was a powerful sense of quiet and prayerful celebration in the room, what a gladiator must feel after defeating a much stronger foe. Bill Atwell was consumed with mixed emotions. He was obviously elated with the evidence Louise had found. But he was concerned about the cost. He glanced toward where Louise was sitting, surrounded by her family. She was flushed, feverish, obviously ill, and Dr. Cockrell, who was attending the last days of the trial, had advised her to stay in bed. But Louise had steadfastly refused. She would not be denied the opportunity to see Ned Earl Calhoun's face when confronted by what she had found. Bettie had opened her quilting kit and began stitching her pieces of colorful cloth. Virginia was crocheting again, and Will had the satisfied look of a vindicated man.

Atwell was also concerned by his own reaction to Calhoun's new testimony. He felt a strange kind of release, a dissolution of resolve, a letdown in the level of tension it required to bring the trial to a successful conclusion. When he spoke to the family, he knew the words were meant for himself, as well as for them.

"First of all I want to say that I could not be happier with the way the evidence ended. It is obvious to the jury and everybody in the courtroom that Ned Earl Calhoun is a liar, and when the evidence ends with the main witness for the prosecution refusing to answer questions on the grounds that it might incriminate him, well . . . for our purposes, it just can't get much better than that.

"But I need to warn you, it can get worse. That was just a single battle in a long and difficult war. In the morning, when the jury returns, the judge will read his Charge and Instructions to the jury. Afterwards, Mr. O'Dell will present his first closing argument. Then the other defense attorneys and I will present our closing arguments. This will be our last time to speak to the jury. Unfortunately, Mr. O'Dell will have the last word. And there are few prosecutors more skillful, more forceful in a final argument than Wilmot O'Dell. He is a mesmerizing orator. I can assure you that he will save his most emotional, most convincing argument for last. And I won't be able to rebut his final argument. So when the jurors go back into the jury room to deliberate, his most powerful and eloquent words will still be ringing in their ears. Obviously, this is a big advantage for the prosecution."

Atwell also explained that another advantage for the prosecution might be Judge Jack's Charge to the jury. "He'll give a summary of the case, the evidence presented, and an explanation of the law as it applies to the case from his point of view. Although I can not predict exactly what Judge Jack will tell the jury in his Charge, I know that for years he was a prosecutor, and it would not surprise me at all if his Charge might lean heavily toward the prosecution's view of the case. So tomorrow you may hear some upsetting things from both Mr. O'Dell and Judge Jack. It won't be fair. But the main thing is not to appear upset. Just try to be calm and collected. I'll try to do the same."

Bill Atwell felt an almost overpowering fondness for these three strong women who were standing with Will, in what was truly his time of trial, listening so intently to his words. Atwell understood that their lives and well-being depended upon him so absolutely. Their absolute trust was humbling, and it was also disturbing. He had a renewed respect for Will, whose stubborn insistence that the charges against him were bogus was now more credible than it had been only a week ago.

In the weeks before, Atwell's task had been professional. Now it was personal as well. He had come to know this family. He wondered, *Is this personal dimension an advantage or a disadvantage? Does it make me better able to defend Will, or does this dissolution of objectivity diminish the effectiveness of his defense? Now I confront Wilmot O'Dell. The trial has narrowed down to a contest between him and me, a face-to-face struggle for the minds, the hearts, if not the very souls, of the jurors. Never have I met a more worthy opponent. And now, as a result of Calhoun's testimony, he's been bloodied. But never is a beast more dangerous than when wounded.*

Promptly at nine o'clock the next morning, the jurors took their seats. As usual, the courtroom was packed, many of the spectators who arrived hours before were jostling to obtain good seats. It had rained off and on during the night and there was a dampness in the air, as if the courthouse roof had leaked in the night. Defense Attorney Bill Atwell looked at each juror in turn, wondering how they would react to the judge's Charge. *Would they recognize the bias that was sure to come? Would they have the good sense to wade through all the verbiage and legal terms to get at what was real and fair?*

The bailiff called the court to order and Judge Jack entered, took his place, and after a few preliminary comments, he began to read the Indictment. His voice was high, like an Irish tenor, and although he tried to lend his reading dramatic inflection, he often stumbled, lost his place. Atwell supposed he might need new lenses for his glasses.

"The first count," the judge read, "charges the defendants conspired to overthrow, put down and destroy by force the government of the United States. The second count charges that the defendants conspired to oppose by force the authority of the United States." And so it went, count after count, a damning litany of criminal activity and conspiracy.

The judge reached the fifth count. "The defendants conspired to commit treason against the United States." Then he paused and removed his glasses. "In this connection, it is important for you to know how the law defines treason. The defendants are guilty of conspiring to commit treason if they gave aid or comfort to the enemy, the German Empire, or conspired to undermine the war efforts of the United States. It's that simple."

And so it begins, Atwell thought. He's given the worst possible explanation of treason. What is "aid and comfort"? And how does one conspire to offer "aid and comfort"? How can a definition be more vague?

Atwell did not have long to wait for this question to be answered because the judge immediately went into his definition of conspiracy. "Now a conspiracy," the judge explained, "is formed when two or more persons agree to get together to do an unlawful act. It is not necessary that the two or more persons should meet together and enter into an explicit or formal agreement for the unlawful scheme, or that they set forth in words or writings the details of such an unlawful act. It is sufficient if two or more come to a mutual understanding about an unlawful course of action."

Atwell had represented defendants in conspiracy cases before and each time was disgusted how terribly unfair the definition was under federal law. Judge Jack had explained the law properly, but under this loose definition, almost anyone present at a meeting could be charged with conspiracy if anyone at the meeting advocated unlawful acts. Atwell considered how devastating this instruction was to the defendants. Essentially, the judge was telling the jury that if any one member of the FLPA had advocated an unlawful act at a meeting, everyone who attended that meeting was guilty of conspiracy to commit that act. He thought about the Cisco meeting when Will read the resolution that advocated treasonous acts. By the law's definition, everyone at that Cisco meeting would be deemed guilty of treason, whether they agreed with the resolution or not. *Preposterous*, Atwell thought. *How can the jury return a fair verdict when given this instruction?*

Then the judge began referring to the FLPA as a "secret" organization. The judge told the jury, "In the year 1915, Defendant Bryant came to Texas from Oklahoma and began to organize lodges of a secret order known as the Farmers' and Laborers' Protective Association." Although there had been testimony about "secret" rituals, Atwell thought the judge should have been more sensitive as to how inflammatory the word "secret" can be. It suggested a den of spies or a coven of witches. Yet the FLPA was no more secret than the Masons or Elks or any other fraternal order.

Then, as Judge Jack continued, he made numerous references to the enemy, the German Empire, and he gave the jury a chronological history of the conflict with Germany and how it coincided with the activities of the defendants. "Early in 1917," he read, "the probability of war between the United States and Germany became a matter of general discussion. On February third, 1917, diplomatic relations between the United States and Germany were formally severed. About a week thereafter, February ninth and tenth, the FLPA held its state convention at Cisco. Defendants Bryant, Risley, Powell and Bergfeld were all present at that meeting and they all had official duties and responsibilities in one way or another."

The judge then reminded the jury of the evidence regarding the May fifth convention at Cisco where the treasonous proposals had been introduced by Will. He reminded the jury of Will's membership in the Industrial Workers of the World and the Working Class Union. In fact, he seemed to focus his comments primarily on Will Bergfeld, and he mentioned Will's name far more often than any of the other defendants, even Bryant, Risley and Powell, the acknowledged leadership of the FLPA. The judge made sure the jury remembered that Will had purchased guns and dynamite at a time when war between the United States and Germany was inevitable and the first conscription officers were expected to arrive in Haskell County.

Atwell leaned back in his chair and tried to appear calm. But he was furious and filled with a bitter sense of impending disaster. Atwell had feared that the judge's instructions to the jury would strongly favor the prosecution, and now his worst fears were being confirmed. For all practical purposes, the judge was testifying for the prosecution. He was coming as close as he could to instructing the jury to go out and find the defendants guilty. Atwell glanced at O'Dell and their eyes met and locked. Atwell was certain the prosecutor was hoping his closing arguments would be as prejudicial to the defendants as the judge's charge.

XXIII.

Abilene, Texas.
October 1917

n the morning of the day Wilmot O'Dell was to begin his final arguments before the jury, Bettie King awakened fleeing in terror from a nightmare. In the dream, her son George was face to face with a German soldier, in the trenches, somewhere in France. The sound of exploding shells and gunfire filled the air. She could see clouds of flame-reddened smoke and barbed wire and the bones of the dead. So real was the dream that her eyes burned and she could hardly breathe because of the poisonous gasses wafting into the trench. The German boy was George's age. His eyes were blue and he seemed too small for the heavy uniform coat he wore. His gloved hands held a rifle pointed at George King, who was no more than five feet away. George, too, was armed, his weapon pointed at the enemy. Strangely, no one else was around; the two boys stood alone, both frightened, uncertain, knowing that death was only moments away. But whose death?

Then Bettie was there in the trench, a ghost figure, behind her son. And through the smoke and gas another woman came and she stood behind her son, the flesh, blood and spirit she had brought into the world at great pain with great love.

"Shoot him," the other woman said. She spoke in German, the language of Bettie's youth. Bettie could understand the boy's hesitation. He had probably been taught all his life that taking a human life was wrong. After all, the Commandments clearly stated that "Thou shall not kill." There were tears in the boy's eyes.

When Bettie saw the boy's finger tighten on the trigger, she whispered in George's ear and the sound of the words she whispered were like knives cutting into her heart. For what she whispered to her son was this: "Kill him, Son. Quickly." They were words that she had never imagined she could say, especially to her son, but to lose him would be far more terrible than the dreadful guilt her advice would cause. There were tears in George's eyes. Then the trench, the room, was rocked by gunfire and Bettie woke weeping.

There was that flood of relief that always comes when the dreamer sees the sunlight and feels the familiar dimensions of the bed, the room, the wakeful heartbeat, Henry warm by her side. As Henry held her, Bettie struggled to regain her composure, and in a few minutes her breathing returned to normal, but the nightmare would not go away. It clung to her mind like a spider web walked into in the woods and she could not brush it away. Bettie lay in bed seeking meaning in the dream. *Since time began mothers have done whatever was necessary to save their sons. It is only the natural order of things. The mother bear kills to protect her cubs, teaches her young to kill in order to survive. If the dream had been real, would I have urged George to kill the other boy in order to save his own life? Or would I have said, "turn the other cheek" and then mourned his death? Love Thine Enemy is suicide, it is to invite death. It is only what saints and poets can do. But we are neither saints nor poets—we are sinners, born with a corner of our soul wild as an animal, wild as the bear, the hawk or the wolf. And when our sons are threatened by an enemy we say, "Kill him, Son. Quickly." What is the meaning of the dream here and now? I have stood by passively as my son went off to war. Although not with words, I have given him my permission to kill. It is what all mothers do the world over and what all mothers have done since the beginning of time. Now there are those who see Will as the enemy. He is the blue-eyed soldier in the trench holding a gun on their sons. His finger is tightening on the trigger. "Kill him, Son. Quickly," the mothers are saying and the jury might hear.*

"What is it?" Henry asked.

"I don't know," Bettie replied. She knew, but the dream had

been too terrible to tell.

As she dressed, Bettie could not shake her sense of foreboding, the feeling that events were spinning out of control. Always she had been able to rise to any occasion, no matter how difficult, but now she felt her family slipping away. George in the trenches, Will fighting for his life, Virginia and the little girls facing an uncertain future. And now dear Louise was ill, her fever high, her cough worse. Above her head, Bettie could hear the footsteps of Will and Virginia and the soprano complaint one of the girls raised, reluctant to begin the day.

Now Bettie's family had passed through her fingers into the hands of Bill Atwell, a man she had grown to trust and respect. But he was just one man against the enormous weight of prejudice that was aimed like a rifle at Will's heart. Both George and Will were at war and she offered a prayer for them both, and for Bill Atwell who would soon fight the biggest battle of his career, if not today, tomorrow.

The walk to the courthouse was not unlike the walk to church on a Sunday morning. From all directions, the people came, in family groups, in couples, some alone. Bettie recognized more than a few, the familiar faces of persons unknown, strangers she would only recognize in the context of the trial. They descended on the building like pilgrims to a cathedral or mosque or temple or holy mountain where divine mysteries dwelled, mysteries of life and death and redemption. Yet, unlike these places where pilgrims go, Bettie knew the courthouse lacked one profound principle. Nowhere in the elaborate rules of juris prudence was there anywhere mentioned the simple virtue of forgiveness.

The people poured into the courthouse and found their accustomed places, seats claimed as their own, as if reserved by custom, *not unlike the Methodist church,* Bettie thought. They entered with a kind of unruly awe. There was some jostling for a better view of the judge, the jury, and, of course, the more frequently mentioned defendants, like Bryant, Powell, Risely and Bergfeld. Some had climbed up into the window sills, blocking the view of those outside, causing shouts of anger and dismay. Perhaps it was the cold outside and the womblike warmth within that filled the room so with sound. Deep-mouthed voices and the wooden chattering of chairs, coughs like the call of small animals, fragments of laughter, all woven into a tapestry of sound, vibrating, pulsing, reverberating against the walls, filling the mind. And Bettie was instantly aware of the heightened expectation of the crowd. This was the day the two lawyers would do battle. This was the day when the mysteries of life and death would begin to unfold, when the truth would be known and served. The individuals who had entered the courthouse were now one being, one living organism, one beast. And it frightened Bettie because it was a beast that seemed out for blood. Then the bailiff came and called the beast to order.

O'Dell walked out center stage like a Shakespearean hero. He seemed to fill the room, his presence undeniable, and Bettie could not help making a comparison between the two laywers. Although O'Dell possessed a rough exterior and seemed to have risen from, but not above, the ranks of the common man, he spoke as the senators of Imperial Rome must have spoken, in an age when they ruled the world. He was a backwoods Caesar. His voice was sonorous, full-bodied, and he had a gift of sliding from an almost prayerlike softness to a deep, roisterous, full-throated aria of baritone passion or fury, all within a few heartbeats. He sought to influence the jury with the strength of his will and by teasing and prodding the emotions, in much the same manner as William Jennings Bryan. On the other hand, Atwell appealed to reason and what he considered the fundamental American virtue of fair play. While O'Dell lectured the jury, Atwell invited them to join him in trying to understand where truth could be found. While O'Dell seemed apart from the jury, Atwell presented himself as the thirteenth juror, struggling with them to do the right thing.

O'Dell began by thanking the jury for their service over the past six weeks. He acknowledged the hardship this service might have caused, how two jurors had suffered death in their families during the trial.

"There are those," O'Dell said, beginning to stride back and forth before the jury, "who subsrcibe to the great man theory of history. They see history as written by the lives of great men. The events that unfold around their lives are the chapters of the human experience. But I have a different idea of history and it is this: I believe a few good and ordinary people, of like mind, can change the world. In this time, in this place, a few good men have gathered. And although your names may not be widely known, it is in your power to write history. What you do here will not be contained within these walls, or even within this state. What you do here will write an important chapter in the history of this great country. It will define our tolerance of those who would destroy us. It will establish a line beyond which our enemies cannot go. It will say to young men who fight in the trenches that you are not alone. That we have taken a stand and that stand will be remembered as long as there are enemies at our gate, or worse, enemies within the walls."

O'Dell paused, removed a handkerchief from his pocket and wiped his brow. "I know most of you realize that in order for criminals to be convicted of their crimes in this country, it takes a team effort. No one man or no group can convict a criminal of a crime he has committed. First it takes investigating officers to dig out the evidence of the crime, then the office of the prosecutors has to draw up the Indictment and present the evidence to a Grand Jury. The next step in the road to conviction is the Grand Jury's Indictment of the criminals. Then the judge must see that the evidence against the criminals is properly presented to a jury. The final step of conviction, however, rests with the jury. It rests with you, gentlemen. Up to this point all of the necessary steps have been taken by the investigators, the arresting officers, the Grand Jury, the prosecutors and the judge, but it will soon be up to you to take the last step required by our criminal justice system. I know you will do your duty as all those before you have done in the process of developing and proving up the dastardly criminal acts committed by all of these defendants."

The prosecutor went on to explain that it would be his duty

and responsibility to summarize the nature of the evidence against all fifty-two defendants. He further explained that he would focus on those four defendants whose acts had been the most reprehensible, the most—and here he paused as if searching for the right word. "Despicable," he finally said as if spitting out a grape seed. "You know their names. They will echo in the halls of infamy. Bryant! Risely! Powell! Bergfeld!"

Never, Bettie thought, *had she heard more virulent hostility packed into the utterance of four last names.*

"The first defendant that I'm going to talk about is Mr. G. T. Bryant. As the judge told you, in 1915 Defendant Bryant came to Texas from Oklahoma to begin to organize the local lodges of the secret organization known as the Farmers' and Laborers' Protective Association, the FLPA.

"Before I go into details about Mr. Bryant's activities and the nature of the FLPA, I want to direct your attention to the Court's Charge—the instructions the judge read to you earlier today. I'm sure you realize that everything that the judge told you in his instructions must be considered by you as a fact or as the law applicable to this case. For example, when the judge told you that Mr. Bryant came to Texas in 1915 and organized this secret order known as the FLPA, you don't have to decide whether or not Mr. Bryant came here in 1915 and organized this secret order because the judge has told you it is a fact. If that were something in controversy the judge would not have given you that instruction. Now this is important because all of the other instructions he gave you, all of the other details that he related to you about all of these defendants, those are matters of proven fact. The judge's instructions are not open to speculation or debate. The instructions he gave you about the defendants in this case as a matter of law must be accepted by you as undenied, uncontroverted fact.

"Now with regard to G. T. Bryant, here is something very important about him that we know from the undisputed evidence, and we also know from the judge's instructions to you: On the night of May fifth, in Cisco, Texas, immediately preceding the convention, there was an informal conference of about twenty members for the purpose of discussing the work of the convention and particularly in regard to its action on the conscription bill, then pending in Congress. Defendants Cathcart, Munday and Webb, along with Bryant, Risely, Powell and Bergfeld, were all present and they all spoke against conscription. The uncontroverted evidence is that Mr. Bryant stated, among other things, that he was a member of the IWW and they had three hundred thousand members. He said that the members of the FLPA should join up with the members of the IWW and take charge of the towns on the day set for the beginning of conscription. And then march through the country, taking charge of the banks and using the money for buying provisions. Mr. Bryant went on to say that these men would themselves conscript others and force others to join them in the revolt and the plans were to cut off all lines of communication and blow up trains and bridges.

"Again, gentlemen, it is undisputed that Mr. Bryant said these things. This is not a matter for conjecture or debate. As a matter of law, you must accept this evidence as fact because it was given to you in the Court's Charge.

"Now let's talk about this secret FLPA organization that Mr. Bryant founded in Texas. What did it stand for? What were its purposes? You've heard witness after witness tell you about what happened at their meetings. Things the members stood up and said, resolutions that were read and passed. You heard it all. In some instances over and over again. Surely there can be no doubt in your mind that this FLPA organization was a Socialist organization that vigorously and openly opposed capitalism and in every way possible sought to undermine and deter the war effort of the United States.

"These defendants want you to believe that these were just the goals and ideals of the organization. Each one of them wants you to believe they are not responsible for the beliefs and activities of their organization. Gentlemen, common sense will tell you organizations don't talk, organizations don't act, organizations don't have ideas. People do, the members do. And these defendants before you were the men who were making this organization function. Surely you're not going to let these defendants get away with coming before you and saying, 'Oh, yes, I was a member.' 'Oh, yes, I went to a lot of meetings.' 'Oh, yes, I heard all these terrible things being said by everybody there, but I never really intended to participate in those things.'

"Gentlemen, I submit to you that every one of these defendants participated in the goals and ideals of the FLPA by joining and continuing to go to the meetings. I submit to you that under the judge's instructions the mere fact that these defendants continued to attend meeting after meeting where overthrow of the United States Government was discussed constitutes a conspiracy as that term has been defined to you by this Court.

"Gentlemen, I submit to you that if anybody is guilty of the charges in this Indictment it is G. T. Bryant, who was the undisputed initiator and organizer of the FLPA in Texas."

O'Dell paused, walked back to the prosecution table, reached for a sheath of papers, then returned to a place before the jury.

"Now gentlemen, I promised you that I would discuss the evidence against every defendant in this case. So at this time I will move on to other defendants."

Since O'Dell had begun with Bryant, Bettie presumed that he would immediately proceed to discuss the evidence against Risley and Powell and Will, the other three target defendants. She was somewhat surprised when O'Dell said he would next discuss the evidence against W. Y. Butler, a man she had barely heard of. Then she realized, for dramatic impact, O'Dell was probably saving Will and the other leaders for the very end of his argument. This strategy became even more apparent as O'Dell spent the next four hours, with only two fifteen-minute breaks, summarizing and detailing as best he could the evidence against each of the other forty-eight defendants. For most of these, he offered nothing more damning than their membership in the FLPA and the fact that they attended meetings where treasonous acts were discussed. But as the judge had explained, the mere fact of this attendance could constitute a conspiracy to commit treason. As the prosecutor presented his case against these lesser defendants, Bettie noticed that his histrionics diminished somewhat as the hours passed by. Even for O'Dell, it would have been impossible to keep up the level of energy and emotion with which he had summarized the case against the FLPA leadership. His presentation grew repetitive, even tedious, and the crowd seemed to grow restless and impatient.

Finally, Prosecutor O'Dell got to Risley and Powell. His summary of the evidence against each of them was lumped together because the same evidence applied to both defendants. As he told how both were statewide officers in the FLPA, his energy level began to rise. It was contagious, and the courtroom began to hum with renewed interest. O'Dell gave details as to how both Risely and Powell were involved in the drafting of the resolutions at all of the different conventions and meetings. He emphasized how they had participated in the burning of the minutes of the meetings. As anticipated, O'Dell mocked their story that the minutes were burned up because they had "too much paper around."

O'Dell said that the story concocted by Powell and Risley was the equivalent of a fairy tale. He said that they might as well have taken the witness stand and started with "Once upon a time . . . ."

After O'Dell described how Powell and Risley both played major roles in the resolutions, O'Dell reminded the jury of the testimony about the resolution which provided that Risley would become President. O'Dell told the jury that it was plain from this resolution that Risley had plans to go from town to town, take over banks, force people to join his army of revolt, dynamite bridges and other forms of communications, and finally Risley planned to install himself as President.

"President of what?" O'Dell asked the jury, his arms outstretched. "The way the resolution read, Mr. Risley seemed to have the far-fetched grandiose idea that after this revolution he was going to be President of the new country that replaced the United States. As preposterous as that seems, that is the clear language of the resolution that he presented and promoted at the Cisco convention."

Finally O'Dell directed the jurors' attention to Will Bergfeld.

Pausing for a few moments, O'Dell was totally silent. With his head almost bowed, he took three or four steps to his right and then back three or four steps to his left. He turned and faced the jury. With his hands folded across his chest he appeared almost as if he were going to pray. At the very least his new silent demeanor certainly had the jury's undivided attention. Then, in a very low and soft voice, completely different from the bombastic, theatrical posturing he had displayed in his argument against Risely and Powell, he said, "For a moment, I need to talk to you about Ned Earl Calhoun. Suffice it to say that all of us at the prosecution table were surprised and shocked to learn that his testimony was false. On behalf of the people of the United States of America, I apologize to you for presenting a witness who lied to all of us. But in a way we welcome the opportunity to ask you to totally exclude from your deliberations all of his testimony, and focus your attention on all of the other evidence presented by numerous other witnesses that proves beyond a shadow of a doubt that Will Bergfeld is guilty of all of the charges against him."

The prosecutor took a deep breath, and his manner changed again. Now, having dispensed with Calhoun, he charged on, arms flailing, his body speaking as persuasively as his voice. Bettie wondered if the jury could make such a leap, from his apology to his all-out attack, in a matter of seconds. She doubted they could.

"Mr. Bergfeld," O'Dell continued, "is asking this jury to believe a series of coincidences that I am sure defies the common sense of everyone in this courtroom. First of all, he is of German descent. Both of his parents were born in Germany. He has family still living in Germany. Early this year, the probability of war between this country and Germany was openly discussed by everyone. On February third of this year diplomatic relations between the United States and Germany were formally severed. About a week thereafter, February ninth and tenth, Mr. Bergfeld attended the state convention of the FLPA in Cisco. He presented resolutions opposing conscription to the delegates. At various times these resolutions were not only read by him to the membership, but they were written in his handwriting. War was declared with Germany during the first week of April.

"Mr. Bergfeld wants you to believe it's just a coincidence that at about that time he purchased a gun and some ammunition.

"Mr. Bergfeld wants you to believe it's just a coincidence that at about that time he purchased two kegs of dynamite, over one hundred sticks, admittedly not for his own personal use but for the use of his fellow members of the FLPA.

"Mr. Bergfeld wants you to believe it was just a coincidence that all of this was done a few weeks before the conscription law was passed by Congress.

"Mr. Bergfeld wants you to believe it was just a coincidence that within a week or so after conscription became the law he went to Henryetta and Tulsa and joined two more unions, the IWW and the Working Class Union.

"Mr. Bergfeld wants you to believe it's just a coincidence that he remained a member of these unions even after he learned they engaged in sabotage.

"Gentlemen, one of the reasons we like juries in this country is they are allowed to use their common sense. Does your common sense tell you that all of these coincidences put forth by Will Bergfeld are too much to swallow?

"Did Will Bergfeld conspire or threaten to kill President Woodrow Wilson? One thing we know for sure: Oscar Lewis told us that Will Bergfeld threatened to kill him if he ever revealed lodge secrets. If Will Bergfeld would threaten to kill Mr. Lewis, a man that he didn't really know or dislike, it is certainly easy to believe all of the witnesses who say that Will Bergfeld conspired and threatened to kill President Wilson, a man whom he hated with a passion. On this issue of Will Bergfeld threatening and conspiring to kill President Wilson, I invite you to recall the testimony of Miss Bennett. Her testimony alone constitutes sufficient evidence for you to find Will Bergfeld guilty of these charges. Now, as a practical matter, her testimony does not stand alone. It was confirmed by

Lefty Crouch, a respected leading citizen of this area. One of the founders of the town of Weinert, Texas. He heard the same things Miss Bennett heard. Another very important thing to keep in mind is that nobody, I mean nobody, has denied the testimony of Miss Bennett. Not even Will Bergfeld. Everything she said about Will's threats against President Wilson is uncontroverted. They are facts not even denied by Will Bergfeld himself."

"Gentlemen, it's just this simple. Will Bergfeld is guilty of all charges, unless you believe that Miss Bennett is a liar. In fact, let me put it this way, gentlemen. If you find Will Bergfeld not guilty, you might as well stop Miss Bennett on the street the next day, look her in the eye and tell her, 'Miss Bennett, all of us jurors think you are a liar and you should be convicted of perjury for lying under oath.'

"Now gentlemen, I don't think you feel that way about Miss Bennett. Make sure your verdict reflects your true feelings about this good woman.

"Thank you for your attention," O'Dell said before he turned and walked to his seat.

Bettie would not have been surprised if the prosecutor had taken a bow and returned for an encore blowing kisses. She was surprised that his closing argument had not been stronger. Bettie knew it would not have swayed her. But then she looked at the twelve men on the jury and she remembered how they had reacted to Anna when she had taken the stand. If not lust in their eyes, there was appreciation of her beauty or a gentlemanly awareness of her vulnerability. Bettie knew that not one of the jurors, under any circumstance, would ever approach Anna Bennett on the street and call her a liar. It would be the last thing they would say. So, as Court adjourned for the day, she concluded that O'Dell had designed a stronger argument than she had first supposed.

That night, Bill Atwell joined the Bergfeld family in the dining room of the boarding house. He explained the strategy he intended to employ for his final argument the next morning.

"First, we need to press the advantage Calhoun's lies have given us. Then, second, I plan to do something I've never done before. And that's to convince the jury that their own good judgment is more important than the Court's instructions."

"I don't follow you," Bettie King said.

"If the jury were to return a verdict today, and that verdict were based on the law as presented by Judge Jack, Will would be found guilty. And so would all of the other defendants. The judge's instructions demand a guilty verdict based on his definition of conspiracy."

"That's wrong," Bettie said.

"I know that, but that's what I have to convince the jury."

When Bill Atwell had gone and the others had returned to their rooms, Will and Virginia sat for a while on the porch, rocking, holding hands, listening to the night.

"Sometimes," Will said, "I wonder if I am all those things they say. You hear it enough, you begin to believe it."

"But it's all lies, Will."

"I mean, maybe I was wrong to be so hard against the war and the draft. Maybe I have harmed my country. Maybe in trying to do what's right, I've done wrong."

"You know better, Will."

"I don't know if I know anything anymore. I know I don't want to die or go to prison. I know that much. But if I'm found innocent, I have no idea what the rest of my life will be like. What I'll do. What we'll do."

"You can be anything you want to be. A magician. A musician. A mechanic or an inventor. Just so we're together."

A silence fell between them.

"I shouldn't have gone to Ludlow," Will said. "It was wrong. None of this would have happened if I had stayed home."

"Will you ever tell me what happened there?"

"You know what happened. It was in the newspapers."

"But I don't know what happened to you. What you saw and felt. I feel Ludlow is at the center of everything. It is at the heart of who you are. If I can't know what happened to you, there's an important piece of you I can never have."

Late into the night, as Will and Virginia lay side by side in bed, Will told her about his weeks in Ludlow. He told her about the respect he had found there among the miners and their families and how he had found a purpose for his life. He recalled how he had worked with Mother Jones to organize the miners' union. How he became close with good people doing important work. Then, near morning, Will told Virginia about the deaths of Louis the Greek and the Irishman O'Leary and the Yeskenski children who were found burned to cinders in their tent and how he vowed never again to let the poor and powerless die at the hands of the greedy. He told Virginia how he felt when he learned his friends and their children were dead. Virginia felt it was like knowing her husband for the first time.

When the trial resumed, Virginia watched and listened to Randall Morris and several other defense lawyers make brief arguments on behalf of their clients. As usual, the courtroom was packed, every bench and chair was occupied, and there was the usual crowd of spectators at the windows and on the lawn, whole families gathered as at a county fair or revival. But the usual energy and tension within the courtroom was slow to build. After all, these attorneys and defendants were merely supporting players. The stars were still waiting in the wings. Virginia felt numb and exhausted. She and Will had talked late into the night. She looked at Will now and she could feel his fear.

After a brief recess, Defense Attorney Atwell rose and approached the jury. His step was firm, yet he walked slowly, his expression one of deep thought.

"There's something I'd like to talk with you about," he began and he paused before the jurors. "Something that troubles me. And I thought maybe you could help me reason it out, think it through. It has to do with Ned Earl Calhoun, the first witness called by the prosecution. I'm sure you remember how he related in detail what he said Will Bergfeld had told him in Cisco. According to Mr.

Calhoun, Will Bergfeld admitted that he committed almost every act charged in the Indictment. As an lawyer I am always uncomfortable arguing to the jury that a certain witness lied because the jurors would hold it against me if they think the witness did not lie. But in this case, all of us in this courtroom, including Mr. O'Dell, know that Ned Earl Calhoun did not tell the truth. As much as I dislike to call a man a liar, in this case there is no other word to characterize Mr. Calhoun. He lied to you. He lied to me. And he got caught at it right before your eyes. So this is what troubles me. If the government's primary witness lied to you, and to me, to all of us, is it not possible that some of the government's other witnesses, who told virtually the same story as the known liar, also lied—but they just did not get caught at it?

"Think with me for a moment. Remember when Ned Earl Calhoun was testifying at the beginning of this trial? Everyone in this courtroom, except those of us who knew Will Bergfeld, thought Mr. Calhoun was telling the truth. He was no ordinary liar—he was good at it. If we had not learned that he was in jail in Lometa when he said he was in Cisco, most of you would still believe Mr. Calhoun's fabricated testimony against Will Bergfeld. With Ned Earl Calhoun the prosecutors came within a whisker of pulling the wool over your eyes, over my eyes, over all of our eyes. It's really a frightening thought, don't you think? Just think how close a terrible injustice came to visiting this courtroom."

Atwell paused for what seemed to Virginia like an eternity, then, facing the jury squarely, he spoke in a low, soft tone. "I am sure you see exactly what the prosecutors tried to do in this case. They tried to get you to convict Will Bergfeld of every single charge against him based on the testimony of Ned Earl Calhoun. He was supposed to be their star witness. Their first witness, who was supposed to convince you that Will Bergfeld had confessed to him all of the crimes charged in the Indictment. But when the testimony of Ned Earl Calhoun blew up in the face of the prosecutors, when it became apparent to you that he was not only a convicted felon, but a liar who should soon be facing perjury charges, what does the prosecutor do? Well, he stands before you and in a very pious, sanctimonious way, he says he is so sorry that his star witness lied to you. Mr. O'Dell is so sorry that he used a liar and a convicted felon to try to persuade you to convict Will Bergfeld of crimes that could cause him to spend his life in prison or even be put to death. The prosecution is in hopes that you will proceed with your job as jurors as though Mr. Calhoun's testimony never happened.

"But it did happen. And here is something else I wanted to talk with you about. The prosecutors and the United States government law enforcement officers had every opportunity in the world to check out the story of Ned Earl Calhoun before they brought him into this courtroom. Think about this a minute. A U.S. Marshal personally escorted him from California all the way to Abilene. Don't you know they had an opportunity to question him? To thoroughly test his credibility and believability during that trip from California to Abilene? Think about this a little more. Between the time Calhoun lied to us on the stand and the time, we, the defense, proved he had lied, he had been in Abilene for six weeks. If the prosecution really wanted to know whether or not his testimony was truthful, they had ample opportunity to find out. Don't you think with all their resources, the prosecutors could have easily dug out the truth? But they didn't. We did.

"I believe Mr. O'Dell was telling the truth when he told you he was sorry. And it is also true that he has a great deal to be sorry for. He has forced you and me to ask some profoundly serious questions. What happens in America when the prosecutors' main witness lies to the jury? Do we want to live in a country where juries find an accused person guilty even when the jury is lied to by the primary witness for the prosecution? Or do you want to send a message to all prosecutors that when your main witness lies to us, you are going to lose the case?"

Virginia was thrilled by the logic of Bill Atwell's argument. He seemed to lead the jurors along, each question he asked having only one logical or reasonable answer. As always, she was impressed by the paradox of his style. The softer, the more reasoned his presentation, the more force it seemed to have. In an even softer voice, Atwell said, "Poor Miss Bennett. I know we all feel sympathy for her. Mr. O'Dell spent a lot of time focusing on her testimony. I don't think I have to tell you that, even when reasonable people are involved, romantic relationships often result in vindictive behavior."

Then, in an uncharacteristic gesture, Atwell spread his arms like an opera singer and quoted, "Heaven has no rage like love to hatred turned, nor Hell a fury like a woman scorned."

Then returning to that soft, reasonable voice, Atwell continued his personal conversation with the jurors.

"I don't mind telling you that there is a great deal that bothers me about this case. Haven't you wondered about the heavy handedness of the arrests in the first place? The government was so overzealous in its attempt to arrest, prosecute and persecute the defendants in this case that the arresting officers totally ignored all laws that are supposed to protect us from the exact type of arrest they were conducting. For example, it is undisputed that when they burst into Mr. Bergfeld's home they did not have any warrant or document from any court authorizing such an arrest. There was no Indictment of Mr. Bergfeld. In fact, he was not indicted until approximately four weeks after his arrest. Further, the arresting officer admitted that he did not have any personal knowledge that Mr. Bergfeld was in the process of committing a crime when he was arrested. Indeed, the undisputed facts are that Mr. Bergfeld was at home playing the violin for his wife and their children. Playing the violin. I don't think that's exactly a treasonous activity, do you? Certainly not one that would justify a violent armed assault on his home and family.

"And I'm troubled by the violence of that arrest, aren't you? I'm sure you recall the testimony about how eighteen officers bashed though the windows and doors with all of their guns pointed at the entire family. When I asked the Texas Ranger by what authority he arrested Mr. Bergfeld, he said that his superior officer had instructed him to do so. Imagine being in your own home and eighteen armed intruders burst through the doors and windows in the dark of night. That may happen in other countries. But this is America. This kind of behavior cannot be tolerated here.

"So it troubles me. Don't you think this kind of arrest is exactly what the framers of our Constitution were trying to avoid? Doesn't the Constitution of this great country protect you and me and our families from such unjust abuse at the hands of the government? I mention the details of Mr. Bergfeld's arrest because they demonstrate a total lack of fairness or decency on the part of the law enforcement officers and the prosecutors. They want you to believe they arrested Mr. Bergfeld because he had guns and dynamite on the premises and that he belonged to organizations that promoted treason among its members. What we know is that when he was arrested, they did not even search the premises for guns or dynamite. Think about this a minute. The moment that Mr. Bergfeld was arrested, even before he was taken from the house, he jokingly acknowledged that he had two guns in the house, and if they didn't have enough guns they could borrow his. Do you think it reasonable if Will Bergfeld had any ideas or plans about using these guns unlawfully, or for the purpose of shooting conscription officers as the government would like you to believe, that he would have volunteered the fact that he had those guns?

"Questions. Too many questions in this case. But here's something we all know for sure. What all of us now know is that Will Bergfeld was arrested because he is of German decent. Because both of his parents were born in Germany and he has family there and he was a member of the Farmers' and Laborers' Protective Association, an organization the government wrongly believed was somehow in league with the German Empire.

"From the very moment Will Bergfeld was arrested, he has been open and honest about everything. During this trial he took the stand and answered all questions. You saw him on the witness stand. He was straightforward, he didn't hesitate, he didn't lean back and think for a while to try to make up some answer, he didn't dodge any question, he answered them all head-on."

Virginia noticed several of the jurors glance toward where Will sat among the defendants. He seemed uncharacteristically at peace. As Atwell praised his client, Will looked down at his hands.

"Will Bergfeld is not a lawyer. He is not a college-educated man. But he was not afraid that these skillful prosecutors would cross him up because he knew all he had to do was to listen to their questions and answer honestly. You and I both know that's exactly what he did. He knew he could answer all of the questions honestly because he had absolutely nothing to hide.

"Gentlemen, when a citizen of the United States is arrested, what protection does he have when the government, state and local prosecutors, and law enforcement officers of all kinds come after him? What protection do we as citizens have? The jury system, that's what. The jury system.

"In their wisdom, the framers of the Constitution made sure that all persons, such as the accused in this case, would have the right to a trial by jury. I submit that nothing is more important to the well being of our country than the right to trial by jury. When all else fails and our citizens are charged with crimes for all the wrong reasons, you gentlemen on this jury stand as the last wall of protection. The last hope for these fellow citizens to obtain justice.

"Throughout this trial you've heard about freedom of speech, freedom to own guns, freedom to own dynamite, freedom to criticize the President and freedom to oppose conscription. People have fought and died to preserve these freedoms. In fact, they are doing so now.

"Here is something I want you to know. Among those boys fighting in the trenches for Mr. Bergfeld's rights are my two sons. I haven't mentioned this before and I won't mention it again because I want you to make up your mind with clear logic and the calm intelligence God gave you, not with emotion or passion. But I know if my sons knew Will Bergfeld and the facts of this case, they would be as proud of my work to advance the cause of freedom here as I am proud of theirs over there.

"You gentlemen of the jury must act wisely and decisively to make certain that the government of the United States does not use its vast power to deny the individual freedoms of those accused in this case. If this case is about anything, it's about individual freedoms. Don't let the prosecutors tell you that these freedoms should be denied just because men belong to an organization that has unpopular beliefs, or whenever men take a position that happens to be unpopular with a lot of people. These freedoms are not defined by what the prosecutors like and don't like. They are defined and guaranteed by the Constitution of this land. Your verdict can say to the entire world that freedom is alive and well in America and we are pledged to protect that freedom on our watch. It is a pledge we make now so that our children and grandchildren can live in a land that is free. Thank you."

Virginia listened to the silence that fell on the courtroom as Atwell returned to his seat. What did it mean, this silence, this apparent lack of response? She had found herself moved by Bill Atwell's appeal and she sensed that several jurors had also been moved. Atwell had stressed that he was appealing to their logic and reason and sense of fair play, but Virginia knew better. He had been appealing to their emotions all the time. And if the tears in her own eyes were any indication, his appeal had been effective.

Judge Jack asked if O'Dell wished to present his closing rebuttal and the prosecutor was instantly on his feet, as if eager to respond to Atwell's closing statement. He moved to the jury quickly and began speaking without his characteristic pause for effect.

"Freedom!" The word rang in the air. "If Mr. Atwell wants to talk about freedom, let's talk about freedom. He mentioned the freedoms that we all love, the freedom of speech, the freedom to join organizations, freedom to criticize our government and so many of our other freedoms. Freedom! Let's talk about freedom."

Only then did he pause, his bright eyes burning, like beams of light reaching across space for the hearts and minds of the jurors. When he continued, his voice glided over the lower octaves, musically. "Gentlemen, these are not ordinary times when we can sit back and listen to intellectuals pontificate about the theories of freedom. We are at war. If we lose this war you can kiss all these freedoms good-bye.

"Right now members of our families, our friends and neighbors are spilling their blood on foreign soil to preserve our freedoms by defeating the Germans and winning this war. It's up to us back home—indeed, right here in Abilene in this courthouse—to do our part. We have to stomp out our enemies who are inside our borders and who are in our own communities. There is a battle going on right here in this courtroom.

"Our young and able fighting men will take care of business in Germany, but at the same time we have to do our duty here at home. We cannot let men and organizations undermine this country's war effort. We cannot allow individuals and their organizations to engage in sabotage and threats that weaken our country in time of war.

"Mr. Atwell says you should come back with a verdict that shows your willingness to protect all of these freedoms.

"I agree with that, but I say a verdict of 'guilty' of all defendants on all charges is the only way to strike a blow for liberty in this case. Your verdict of 'guilty' will show that we will not tolerate these men and their organizations. Your verdict will tell these men, and indeed the entire nation, that in time of war the good, law-abiding citizens of this country, who truly love this country, will not allow men like these defendants and their organizations to help our enemies by undermining the war effort.

"Gentlemen, I am confident that you will do your duty to your country and that you will do what is clearly right by returning with a verdict of 'guilty' on all charges for all defendants. If you love freedom, if you despise tyranny, if you cherish liberty, there is no other verdict that makes sense but 'guilty on all counts.'

"Thank you."

XXIV.

Abilene, Texas.
October 1917

The three women waited. It was the day after Judge Jack instructed the jury to retire to the jury room to begin their deliberations. He informed the jurors that they would be sequestered at the Grace Hotel, where sleeping quarters had been arranged and where they would take their meals. He had also sternly warned them that there would be no discussion of the case among the jurors except in the jury room and they must not talk to anyone about their deliberations, even to their own families. Judge Jack explained that a bailiff would be available to them at all times if they had any questions. Because passions about the verdict ran high, U.S. Marshals were assigned to guard the jurors at all times. Judge Jack further told the jurors that they would be sequestered until that time they could return with a unanimous verdict. And so, six weeks after the trial had begun, they had retired, twelve good men, to consider the fate of the fifty-two defendants.

For a day and a night the three women waited. Often they lingered in the courtroom. Bettie was piecing together quilt blocks from scraps of cloth she had cut from remnants. Virginia was crocheting little caps and scarves for the girls, who were staying with the Cockrells at their boarding house in Abilene. Louise was reading Upton Sinclair's new book, *King Coal*, an exposé of the mining industry. The book had been sent to Will by Mother Jones, but Will had passed it on to his sister, unread. Louise was still sick, her fever unabated, but she often joined the conversation, amusing the others with tales of her struggle to remove a drunken, barely conscious Deputy Draper from his own jail, convince him that he could be a star witness in the biggest case ever tried in Texas, and then with the help of a lovesick boy, had delivered him, sobered by the prospect of celebrity, to Atwell and the defense team. The deputy had taken the stand, sober and convincing, just in time to totally destroy O'Dell's star witness. Louise slanted the story of her adventure toward what was humorous. How she had suffered and the pain and fever she still felt were things she was trying to ignore. Humor was a way to break the almost unbearable weight of waiting.

When the jury retired, a few spectators remained in the courtroom. Others loitered around in the hallways and on the courthouse lawn. It was as if they feared missing the climax of the great drama they had been witnessing. If history was to be made, they wanted to be a part of it, to feel the terrible anxiety of the accused, to see the expressions on the faces of the condemned, to ponder what it was to walk the fresh pine stairs toward the noose. Everyone knew the deliberations would take some time. After all, there were fifty-two defendants and each would have to be discussed. But then, maybe not. Maybe the case against them was so convincing that a verdict could come at any minute. They stayed. Their arguments in the courtroom were extensions of those the lawyers had made. The spectators tried the case again, voices raised in anger, fists and arms punctuating their convictions. There was no judge's gavel to keep the peace and several times the Marshals had to quiet them. The man who had been selling miniature gallows marked with the names of the accused was inside the courthouse now, his product selling even better than those of the peanut vendor or the hot tamale man. Newspaper reporters wandered through the crowd, taking notes, gathering opinion, interviewing the families of the accused. "How do you feel now that the jury is deliberating?" they asked innocuously, their pens poised. Louise said if a reporter asked her that question, he would find a few pounds of Upton Sinclair upside his head.

And so they had waited, Bettie, Virginia and Louise. They sat quietly, talking softly, anxious as they had ever been, frightened, conscious of their heartbeats, seeking to know the thoughts of the jurors. They were incredulous to find themselves in a room where money was being exchanged by men who were placing bets on the possibility the man they loved would be hanged. Sentiment seemed to lean toward the gallows.

As the hours, then days, passed, there was endless debate in the courtroom and in Bettie's mind about how the length of the jury's deliberation would affect the verdict. Some felt the longer the jury was out, the more certain it was the jurors were leaning toward conviction. Others felt the opposite was true. When Bettie asked Atwell, he assured her that absolutely nothing could be read into the length of time the jurors deliberated. "You just can't tell," he had said. "In all my years waiting on verdicts, I've never been able to see a pattern." So the women waited, half wishing the jurors would make up their minds soon, half hoping they would stay out a little longer.

Outside, it was not as cold as it had been when Louise had brought Deputy Draper north from Lometa. But today the air was heavy and the sky was still hidden by dark, low overcast. The darkness seemed to linger overhead, as if the clouds, too, were waiting for the verdict, the violence within them suspended until the jurors returned. Often people glanced warily upward because these were the kind of skies from which tornadoes came. Groups stood restlessly on the courthouse lawn, umbrellas folded, waiting, wanting to leave, but also reluctant, afraid of missing a glimpse of the jurors on their way to the Grace Hotel, or the relatives of a defendant bearing their bitter sorrow into the courthouse and the jail.

Occasionally, during the monotonous hours of waiting, a note would be passed from the jury room to the bailiff, who would then carry the note to the judge's chambers. Each time a note was passed, the courtroom erupted into confusion. People rushed in from outside, reporters and spectators stood, some on benches and chairs, to follow the bailiff with their eyes. The risen sound was like a choir of maniacs, everyone talking at once, shouting to the bailiff, hoping from a word or his manner to know if the jurors had reached a verdict. But usually, the jurors were asking about lunch or refreshments, and soon the courthouse settled back down to a kind of disorderly tedium.

Another day went by. There was a subtle change in the character of the spectators in the courtroom. The tension turned inward. It was not a stillness exactly, but voices were not as loud as they had been, there was less conversation and no laughter. Bettie thought, *The people around me are a part of something very like a death.* Voices became hushed, almost reverent. The air inside was heavy and hard to breathe. Outside thunder rolled forth.

While waiting for a verdict, in the evenings Will had spent much of his time playing his violin and working on his watercolor portrait of Louise. Virginia thought his music now had a curious blending of celebration and sorrow, a Gypsy quality, and she remembered the strange lament he had been playing the night of his arrest. It came to her that Will might well be a Gypsy. His dark beauty, the aura of mystery that surrounded him, his gift of magic, his absolute flaunting of convention, all this made her certain that she had married a Gypsy prince, and even in the agony of waiting she had to smile. *Just look at Louise*, Virginia thought. *Never have I known anyone who looked more like a Gypsy than Louise.*

Louise was puzzled about her portrait. Now, as the empty hours stretched on, she often sat for Will as he sketched. She loved to watch him work, his head tilted slightly to one side and then the other, his eyes dancing from her face to the paper. When he looked at her, he seemed to be focused beyond the surface, into some dimension within that only he could see. But then he would sit back, study what he had done, and he would lay the drawing aside.

"Let me see, Will!" Louise would say.

"It's not right, yet." And he would begin again.

Virginia crocheted, listened to the voice of the storm and she prayed. *Dear Lord, give Will peace. Make his waiting not as hard as it must be. Please give the jurors the wisdom to do what is right. I know I should not pray for myself, and I have tried not to be selfish in my talks with you, Lord. But just this once I pray for something I need, that I would die without. Just this once, Lord, please give me Will. Let him walk from this place a free man. But if that is not in your plan, Lord, please give us the strength to face what comes.*

The rain that had threatened all week came down hard as hail. Thunder cracked, sounding to Virginia like Will's whip. Each time lightning ripped down through the ragged gloom, the people in the courthouse looked toward the ceiling, as if they could see through the roof and perceive God's intentions. From his chambers, the judge ordered that the American Flag on the courthouse flagpole be lowered and brought in from the rain. When the bailiff came back in, a spectator helped him fold Old Glory in the traditional manner. Those spectators who had been waiting outside rushed in, filling the courtroom once again to overflowing.

Now it was the fourth day. The three women waited. Bettie watched the bailiff move to the jury room door. It cracked open and someone within spoke to the bailiff and this time he was not handed a note. In that electric moment, Bettie knew that the long wait was nearly over. There was something in the bailiff's hurried step, the way he held himself as he moved toward the judge's chambers, that suggested great import. Little by little others sensed it, too. Conversations ceased in mid-sentence. Reporters grew alert, antennas out, seeking to memorize the scene so they could re-create it later in print. A hush dropped softly, accentuated by the rumble and roll of thunder outside. More people moved in from the storm, shaking the rain from their hats, folding their umbrellas, faces flushed and solemn. Now it was certain that word was going out to the lawyers, the defendants and to the families of the accused and that the end was beginning. Henry King arrived with Louise's husband, Rob Tewes.

Soon the defendants were brought back from their cells and chained to their benches. Mournful was the sound the chains made on the wood floor. Bettie thought of slave ships and was again struck by the injustice of those chains. Then the bailiff led Will and the others who had made bond to their places. Bettie's eyes followed Will, knowing that he must be feeling the same tightness in his chest that she felt, the same suspension of reality, the same hopeless yearning to wake from dreaming. Then Will stopped dead still and turned, staring at something or someone standing against the wall. Bettie followed his eyes and there he was, a tall, dark figure dressed all in black. Arthur Bergfeld made a small bow to his son and then touched his temple in salute. Will responded with a smile so slight and so brief that only those who knew him would know he smiled at all. Bettie thought Will walked a little taller as he moved to his place among the other defendants.

Judge George Jack entered, his robes flowing like black flame. At that moment, as he reached the bench, the room turned snow white with light and a sharp crack of thunder shook the courthouse, and the stone trembled and shook as the electric lights flickered and died. The jurors had been filing in and they now paused and looked around wide-eyed at the walls and at the crowd and each other, probably supposing that God was letting them know in no uncertain terms of their error.

For a long moment, those in the courtroom waited for the roof to fall or for another hammer blow of thunder. They were like soldiers in a fort besieged by cannon fire. Even Judge Jack stood unmoving at the bench, staring out the window, contemplating powers far more vast than his own. Then he turned, cleared his throat. "Has the jury reached a verdict?" Judge Jack called.

"We have, Your Honor."

"Please hand your verdict to the bailiff."

The bailiff approached the bench. He handed a sheaf of papers to the judge. The judge leafed through the documents, then looked up and removed his glasses. "I am now going to read the verdict and I will not tolerate any disturbances or outbursts." Judge Jack replaced his glasses and read the words before him.

"In the case of *The United States versus George T. Bryant,* we the jury find the defendant guilty on all counts."

A woman sobbed. The rain fell. The judge read on.

"In the case of *The United States versus Zachary L. Risley,* we the jury find the defendant guilty on all counts."

Bettie heard the rattle of chains, a whispered sigh, the wooden ticking of the courthouse clock. It was almost impossible to sit still. She had an uncontrollable urge to move, to get up, to ease the pain of not knowing. Louise silently recited the words to the Lord's Prayer. Virginia looked at Will and saw that he was looking back at her, and she mouthed the words, "I love you." The judge read on.

"In the case of Samuel J. Powell, we the jury find the defendant guilty on all counts."

Bettie felt she was sinking through the Earth, falling. Louise thought she could hear Virgin Annie singing as she rocked her brother to life. Virginia wondered if she were dying. The judge read on.

"In the case of *The United States versus William A. Bergfeld,* we the jury find the defendant. . . ." The judge paused, removed his glasses. The Earth ceased its turning. Time was a myth. There was no sound at all. Even the rain had stopped falling. And then the words came: ". . . not guilty."

Later Bettie would remember the startling fact that there had been no celebration. There was a stunned silence. Bettie was numb and her mind seemed cleansed of thought, her body exhausted. As the judge read the not-guilty verdicts of the other forty-seven defendants, Will bowed his head. Virginia merely stared at her husband, tears flowing down her cheeks. Louise comforted the little girls who had begun to fret.

Then it was over. The family gathered to embrace. Bettie said a brief prayer of thanksgiving. Arthur was there within the circle. The foreman of the jury came, embraced Will, and shook hands with the others. The family walked toward the sunlight.

Outside, the bailiff was raising Old Glory again.

"Come on, Will," Virginia said. "Let's go home to Seguin."

EPILOGUE

Louise Bergfeld Tewes never recovered from the illness she suffered during the trial. Within a month, she died of influenza and was brought by train from her home in Karnes City to Seguin, where she was buried in the Riverside Cemetery next to her mother and grandmother. For the first few nights, armed with his whip, Will stood guard over her grave. Then he returned to the King homeplace on Court Street, where he and Virginia made plans for the rest of their lives and where he was at last able to finish his sister's portrait.

AFTERWORD

- Defendants George T. Bryant, Samuel J. Powell and Zachary L. Risley were all sentenced to Leavenworth Prison and released in June 1922 by Presidential pardon. Prison records reflect that Bryant left "with a wedding ring, a writing tablet and five dollars." Powell left "with a pocket knife, a pocketbook and fifteen dollars." Risley left "with one pair of canvas gloves and three dollars and seventy-five cents."

- Many of the goals of the Farmers' and Laborers' Protective Association were ultimately achieved, including minimum wage, woman's suffrage, and favorable laws for labor unions and farmers' organizations.

- Little Virginia Bergfeld to this day has memories of the arrest of her father Will Bergfeld. For more than fifty years she has lived in Seguin in the King homeplace on Court Street. She married Wilton Woods in 1936 and is the mother of the author, Janice Woods Windle. Mrs. Woods was the primary source for this story, along with three thousand pages of transcripts of the trial.

- The main characters in this book, Will and Virginia Bergfeld, lived the rest of their lives in the Seguin area. During World War I, in July 1918, nine months after the trial, Will volunteered and served in the 2nd Cavalry of the United States

Army. During the 1920s and '30s, Will owned the Moulton Motor Company, a Ford dealership, and as a hobby he continued racing automobiles. In World War II, Will again volunteered and served as an instructor of mechanics at Camp Polk, Louisiana. After he walked out of the courthouse, Will never again spoke German nor spoke a word about the trial.

William Hawley Atwell ran an unsuccessful race for governor of Texas in 1920. Later, he had a distinguished career as a United States District Judge in Dallas, Texas. In his autobiography he wrote about this case, "In many respects, this was one of the most remarkable trials ever held in America."

Bettie and Henry King lived out their lives in the house on Court Street in Seguin. Sgt. George King, their only son, returned from World War I, married Nellie Ethel DeLany and built a home at 1117 East Court Street. They had four children. Their son George Henry King, a marine, was killed in World War II.

From 1917 to 1956, Peachtree lived in the Guadalupe River bottoms in Seguin and never missed a Fourth of July parade. Always marching behind the Fort Sam Houston Army Band, he wore a miniature flag in his hat band, carried his pet owl on a chain on his shoulder, pulled a raccoon on a leash and had a pack of barking dogs following behind.

In the years after the trial, Will and Virginia had three more children: Maxine Baenziger, William A. Bergfeld Jr. and Henry Edsel Bergfeld, all of whom reside in central Texas. Their oldest child, Mary Louise Bergfeld, married 2nd Lt. Albert I. Orr who was in the U.S. Army during the invasion of Normandy. He was decorated by General George S. Patton Jr. on the field of battle and received a Distinguished Service Cross. Maxine Bergfeld Halm was an X-ray technician at Fort

Sam Houston military hospital during World War II. Her husband, Virgil Halm, served with distinction in the Navy.

- Arthur Emil Rudeloff Bergfeld continued to operate the Bergfeld Drug Store in Seguin until his death in 1937 at age eighty. Arthur and Elisabethe Louise Bergfeld had two grandsons (in addition to Will's son) who fought in World War II. Dr. Jack Bergfeld was a physician, and Pvt. 1st Class Max Bergfeld Jr. was killed in combat.

- Antonie Bergfeld, Will's paternal grandmother, never came to the United States. She died in 1924 shortly after her son, Arthur Bergfeld, visited her in Germany.

- Maria Theresa Louise Jurcza Naumann, Will's maternal grandmother, died in 1914 in a runaway horse and buggy accident in Seguin.

- Will and Virginia's son, William A. Bergfeld Jr., was a Staff Sergeant in World War II. He fought battles in North Africa, and up the Italian Peninsula. William A. Bergfeld Jr. was awarded the Bronze Star.

ACKNOWLEDGMENTS

hank you… My husband, Wayne, is an extraordinary trial lawyer whose talents made this book possible. While we had thousands of pages of trial transcript and documents to work from, there were blank spaces in the records that needed a lawyer's expertise to fill in what had been said. Readers who know him will hear Wayne's voice and see his influence in the final arguments of Bill Atwell and Wilmot O'Dell.

With Wayne as a partner on this project, I was able to reconstruct what actually happened in the case and give the reader an accurate portrayal of the trial proceedings.

Thank you, Wayne, for everything.

As it was in the preparation of *True Women*, *True Women Cookbook*, and *Hill Country*, *Will's War* is the joyous accomplishment of my family and many friends who helped me by providing interviews, research materials, access to letters, photographs, and personal papers.

My mother, Virginia Bergfeld Woods, was the primary source for the book and a mainstay in my life.

Wilton Eugene Woods, my brother, is retired from his career as Associate Editor of *Fortune* magazine and gave mightily of his talents as an editor, as a steadfast supporter of his sister and as an advisor.

Very special thanks to Mary Kaye Fenwick, my friend of many years since we were roommates and Alpha Phis at U.T. Austin. Mary Kaye spent many hours researching in libraries, agencies and archives of Washington D.C., where she uncovered government papers that revealed the names of Will's accusers.

Deep appreciation to my friend Barbara Rust, the Archivist who went out of her way to help me find the transcript of the trial.

A big thanks to our personal friend, Jack Ratliff, Professor at The University of Texas at Austin School of Law, who set me on the track to locate records of the case.

Thank you: Donaly Brice, Archivist at Texas State Archives, the Seguin Public Library; Brenda Gunn, Librarian, State Bar of Texas; and Marlyn Robinson, Reference Librarian, Jamail Center for Legal Research, the University of Texas at Austin School of Law.

Thank you to the archivists at the National Archives and Records and Administration in College Park, Maryland: John E. Taylor, Louis Holland, Fred Romanske and Wayne DeCesar; Amanda Cartwright, Texas Tech University Southwest Collection, University of Texas at El Paso Library, and to Scott & Hulse law firm. To Dallas Public Library for the papers of Judge William Hawley Atwell and to R. S. and Betty Sanders for their book *Just Passing Through Weinert.*

Thank you to the professional advisors, authors and friends who have helped to promote my books: my agent Robert B. Barnett, my agent Mathew Snyder of Creative Artists Agency, Leann Phenix of Phenix & Phenix Literary Publicists, and Marah Stets of Simon & Schuster; to Liz Carpenter, Chris Bohjalian, Jim Lehrer, Nolan Ryan, Fannie Flagg, Anne Rivers Siddons, former Governor of Texas Ann Richards and First Lady Laura Bush.

I will always be grateful to Scott Bard, publisher of Longstreet Press; to Tysie Whitman, my editor; and to Longstreet's fine staff for the publication of this book.

Many thanks to: Anthony Atwell, William Webster Atwell, Jean Angelone, Kay Banning, Bea Bragg, Connie Quarles, Patty Dalton, Jacqueline Maitland Davies, Detective Jamie de la Garza, Dottsy and Robin Dwyer, Herbert Ewald, James Chapman, Wanda Ham, J. B. Hill Boot Company, Walter Faust Jr., Edith Firoozi Fried, Jeff and Melissa Koehler, Nelda Kubala, Paula and Stan Ledbetter, Mrs.

Alf Lechnaker, Dr. Henry Moore, Jane Moss, Vonnie Mae and Nealie McCormick, Leonard Mandell, Sherry Nefford, Paul and Jacqueline Rutledge, Dorothy Schwartz, Lynna Thomas, Patrick and Dinah Simek, Nancy Bitter Snyder, Evelyn Schuchardt, Juanita and John Taylor, Bette and Sterling Wehner, Annette Waite, Elizabeth Whitlow, Dr. Dianne Wilcox, and friends who are now deceased: Dr. Jack Bergfeld, Joyce Latchman, Bertha Naumann, Carroll and Jane Smith, Leroy Schneider, Seguin Chief of Police, and Eugene Schwartz.

To the Board of Directors and staff of El Paso Community Foundation, thank you.

Also thanks to: Mary Louise Bergfeld Orr and Albert I. Orr; Maxine Bergfeld Baenziger and Harold Baenziger, Larry Wayne Halm, Elsie and William A. Bergfeld Jr.; William A. Bergfeld III; William A. Bergfeld IV; Bo, Boon, and Bronson Bergfeld, Charles A. Bergfeld and Debbie, Lauren and Chase; Bernice and Henry Edsel Bergfeld, Susan and Henry Bergfeld, Brent, Colt, Ann and Beau, Shalon, and Trenton; Cindy and Richard Allen Bergfeld, Becky, Katy; Edna and George King Bergfeld, Tammy and Sam Pugh and Ashlyn, George King Bergfeld Jr.; Thomas Lee Bergfeld and Kari, Lauren and Bradley; Bonnie Bergfeld Cheatham and William Landon Cheatham II, Callie and Landon.

Thanks to Donald and Marilyn King, Michael and Marlene King, Marshall and McLain King, Janet King Tschirhart and Terry, Benjamin and Tyler Tschirhart; Larry W. King, Donna King; Kenneth W. King and Adrienne Kirklan W. King and Jennifer Delany and Kathryn King; Kamela King Fiedler and Kevin, Mason Fiedler; Kyle Wendell King.

In a multigenerational saga based on the Bergfeld family, it is, unfortunately, impossible to use all the family members as characters in a historical novel. Many wonderful lives of relatives I know and loved could not be told in *Will's War*. However, I do want readers to know the names of the children of the main characters.

Arthur and Elisabethe Naumann Bergfeld had six children. In addition to Will and Louise, they were Antonie Bergfeld

Rosenbush, Arthur Jr., Max and Paul. Arthur and his second wife Emma Greifenstein Bergfeld had one son, Edwin.

Thank you to the loyal readers who have taken the *True Women* and *Hill Country* book tours to homes and buildings in Seguin, Gonzales and San Marcos. The tours are offered by the Seguin Chamber of Commerce and Around South Texas Tours.

I would welcome hearing from readers at jww@jwwbooks.com.

Will Bergfeld (left) with a string of rattlers from snakes he killed while delivering mail on his motorcycle

Wedding portrait of Virginia King Bergfeld

The King homeplace, 920 East Court Street in Seguin

Bettie Moss King

Defense Attorney Bill Atwell (right) in his law office

Louise Bergfeld Tewes

Arthur and Emma Bergfeld's home
at the corner of Milam and College Streets in Seguin

Emma Greifenstein and Arthur Bergfeld
on their wedding day

Will with baby Mary and his motorcycle

Elisabethe Jurcza as a child in Germany

The Bergfeld Drug Store in Seguin

The Schulz Saloon fire

The author Janice Woods Windle
and her grandfather Will Bergfeld